CRITICAL P... ...VELS OF ...

Technical Hitch

"…warm and funny…" —*Cosmopolitan*

"A crowd pleaser." —*Booklist*

"Readers will appreciate Jane Sigaloff's satirical look at to be or not to be married."
—Harriet Klausner of *Bookreview.com*

Lost & Found

"Funny and heartwarming." —*Company*

"…witty, warm and highly enjoyable – and the sort of romance that's quite believable." —*Closer*

"We love! Five stars." —*More*

Name & Address Withheld

"Escape to a comfy chair and enjoy." —*Company*

"A hilarious first novel." —*OK!*

"Moving and cleverly written…a great present for a girlfriend in need of some love advice."
—*handbag.com*

JANE SIGALOFF

Born in London, despite brief trips into the countryside, Jane has always been a city girl at heart. After studying history at Oxford University she entered the allegedly glamorous world of television, beginning her career as tea and coffee coordinator for Nickelodeon UK.

Progressing to researcher and then to assistant producer her contracts took her to MTV and finally to the BBC where she worked for several years.

Since 2000 Jane has enjoyed a double life as a part-time PA which has given her more time to write and feel guilty about not going to the gym. She lives and writes in London. *Like Mother, Like Daughter* is her fourth novel.

Find out more at www.janesigaloff.com

Like
Mother,
Like
Daughter

JANE SIGALOFF

MIRA

All the characters in this book have no existence outside the imagination of the author, and have no relation whatsoever to anyone bearing the same name or names. They are not even distantly inspired by any individual known or unknown to the author, and all the incidents are pure invention.

*First published in Great Britain 2006
MIRA Books, Eton House, 18-24 Paradise Road,
Richmond, Surrey, TW9 1SR*

© Jane Sigaloff 2006

ISBN 0 7783 0111 7

58-0306

*Printed in Great Britain
by Clays Ltd, St Ives plc*

For my mother.

Thank you for making the unconventional the norm.

ACKNOWLEDGEMENTS

As ever, incalculable thanks to my family and friends for all their cheerleading and support.

For SoCeLoW, Charlotte Cameron. For international rescue, Kate Meikle. For answering lots of questions, Piers Garnham. For neighbourly distraction, Feras, Gill & Luke. And for everything else, Paul.

Many thanks also to my agent, Carole Blake, my editor, Margaret O'Neill Marbury and Katrina at Midas PR for being on my case and in my corner.

Chapter One

'So, why don't you let me take you out for dinner?'

'Tonight?' Alice switched her mobile phone from one ear to the other, wedging it between her neck and her shoulder as she rummaged in her bag for her house keys. Her weekend was only minutes away and no one was getting between her and her sofa this evening. Even if George Clooney had been on the line, she would have taken some persuading. As it happened, it was only Richard.

'Well, it's Friday night and I'll hazard a guess you're on your way home when you should be on your way out…'

Now he was sounding like her mother. Alice felt her hackles rise as indignation threatened to surface noisily. She certainly didn't have to justify her movements to him these days.

'…And besides, it's our anniversary. Viva Las Vegas.'

Alice visualised him feathering an imaginary quiff as he started a rendition of the same Elvis number he had sung excitedly in their limo on the way to the wedding chapel. Just the two of them. On the run. A perfect sun-baked June afternoon in Nevada. They'd been back on their sun beds within the hour, Alice in the totally impractical, white bridal bikini that Richard had bought her. The most rock 'n' roll week of her life.

'Make that Rest In Pieces.' Rock 'n' roll to rock bottom, Alice struggled to reconcile the three-year-old memory with her reality as she stepped off the bus. 'And just for the record, anniversaries no longer apply once you're divorced…'

Twenty-nine years old and she already had a Decree Absolute to her name, which made her: quirky/a failure/worldly/toxic—from now on every man she met would delete where applicable.

'You've always been so conventional.'

Alice could hear the smile in his voice and despite the fact he was a phone call away, she could see the tanned creases around his pale blue eyes.

'Damn you, Mr. Harrison. Just when I thought I'd found the one. Just Gay Enough. Only you turned out to be Not Quite Straight Enough.'

Despite herself, Alice could feel her irritation subsiding as the bus pulled away, the slipstream threatening to coat her in a hot cloud of West London dust and empty crisps packets. She gritted her teeth momentarily and exhaled fiercely, hoping to dissuade any particles of dirt from settling as she hurried along.

'…So have you bought me a huge anniversary present…?'

In her head she'd sounded coquettish. Out loud she suspected it was more like demanding. She'd never been good at "little girl lost". But she did love presents. And while money may not be a valid currency when it comes to the purchase of love, it worked perfectly for buying goodwill. Plus, she'd always really wanted a Mulberry weekend bag and three years in, traditionally it would have been their leather anniversary. In the absence of any significant others, it would appear that she was still counting.

His silence said it all and Alice scolded herself. Unbridled optimism had been another of her past-life vices. She changed tack. 'Look, don't mind me. I've spent three days incarcerated in soulless boardrooms doing in-house corporate coaching and today with private clients at the clinic. My smile is cracked, my ankles are getting on for twice their normal size and I am practically hallucinating about lying down, watching television with my eyes closed and, if I can muster enough energy to read a menu and pick up the phone, ordering a takeaway.'

'Fine.' Richard's tone made it clear that her decision was everything but.

'You really shouldn't be taking this personally. Another time, okay?'

'Well, if you'd rather spend the evening with *her*…'

'It's only been a week. She had to put up with me in her personal space for twenty-two years.'

'So what, now it's payback time?' Richard didn't sound impressed. Alice reminded herself that it didn't matter what he thought.

'She's not your mother-in-law anymore. Really, we're having fun.'

So Alice might have been a touch tidier than Suzie. And quieter. And more considerate. But she knew that overall she was very lucky, even if her mother did tend to act her shoe size rather than her age, which, depending on whether you were going with European, British or American sizing, was 38, 5 or 6.

Alice opened her gate and walked up the path to the front door she and Richard had painted dark red together in the days when Labour had been New and love had been blind. Home. Where the heart is. And the fridge is.

'Look, I've got to go, but catch up soon.'

'Promise?'

'Of course.' Alice hesitated. Richard wasn't normally the needy type. 'Is everything okay with you?'

'Everything's great. Busy but good. And I miss you…'

Despite everything, Alice was curiously flattered. At least when it came to ex-husbands she had snagged a good one.

'I miss you, too.' Alice realised her tone was almost flirtatious.

'Of course you don't. I was the one that screwed up your life, remember?'

Alice smiled. 'Vaguely…'

'Well, as long as you're not trying to avoid me. I haven't seen you in weeks.'

'Well, I look just the same. Sorry about tonight, but being upbeat all day can really take it out of a girl. Sometimes I just need to lock the door and scowl.'

'Scary. So when's *Get A Life* back on TV? At least *then* I'll get to see you at your best once a week.'

'That's Grade A emotional blackmail, Mr. Harrison.'

Alice consulted her watch for the date. 'We start taping in three weeks, new series transmits from September—not that, going on last season's ratings, more than a handful of people are watching.'

'I am…'

'I'd bloody well hope so. The programme was your idea.'

'I like watching you give people a new lease of life. Don't underestimate the power you have.'

'I just give a bit of focus to what they already know they want.'

'Hey, remember, it's a makeover show with another dimension.'

'That might be the pitch you sold, but everyone's much

more interested in the "getting a new wardrobe" section of the show.'

'A little less self-deprecation, a little more action.' Richard was singing again, this time customising Elvis's most recent remix for his own purposes. 'You're by far and away the most popular of the presenters.'

'I'm just the least pierced, bronzed, tattooed or smug.'

'Your common touch is your greatest asset.'

'What, so now I'm common?'

'People relate to you. They like you and so they listen. Do you really think, once the show is over they're going to spend hours constructing pick-up lines and feng-shuing their bedrooms? You're the one who really changes their lives. You give them attainable goals, self-confidence, a direction…'

Alice nodded silently. That was definitely the plan.

'…And I was watching the show along with nearly half a million people, who aren't all friends of friends.'

Alice shook her head. 'You'd be surprised. My mother knows a lot of people.'

Richard was the one who'd encouraged her to put herself in front of the camera. It was the perfect marriage of her new career with her old one and, frankly, as close to any marriage as she was going to venture for a long time.

'…Soon you'll be everyone's favourite life coach.'

'As long as I'm my favourite life coach, that'll do me.'

'I'd enjoy your anonymity while you can…'

'Look, the man behind the counter in the post office barely recognises me and I'm in there at least once a week.'

Ignoring her protestations, Richard continued to paint a picture of Utopia according to Alice Harrison. '…then a book deal, your dream house in the country, an orderly queue of eligible men begging for your hand in marriage…'

Alice snapped back to reality. 'It's not about that.'

'Whatever you say, dear.'

Half a million people had watched her on-screen simultaneously. Maybe one day she'd be able to fill a stadium. Of course, it might have helped if she was a singer-songwriter rather than a life coach, but hey.

Richard's optimistic enthusiasm was still incredibly contagious, despite the fact it had landed her in trouble in the past. People did learn from their mistakes, but only when it suited them, and having money regularly paid into her bank account was extremely good for the soul after the turbulence of the last few years. She didn't stand to inherit a large fortune, after all. An ever decreasingly small one, in fact, as her mother viewed spending as a sport. Which was absolutely her prerogative, but as the newspapers repeatedly raised the question of a pension crisis, Alice couldn't help fretting about being old, alone and poor every now and again. Since Richard had left she'd started worrying about the long-term grown-up stuff. Now she valued her mortgage more than her music collection. She really was twenty-nine years old.

'Anyway, less about me, how's your meteoric rise going? Haven't they given you your own channel yet?' Alice paced between her gate and her front door.

Richard feigned disappointment. 'Unfortunately not. But they are encouraging me to pitch more lifestyle programme ideas.'

'That's brilliant, love.' Alice's congratulations were genuine. Richard knew he was good at what he did, and fortunately for him, so did his employers. It was a rare case of genuine talent being rightfully rewarded. Plus she got a career guardian angel—arguably much more useful than a mere husband.

'Actually, I've got a few things I'd like to talk to you about. Hence, my offer of dinner and/or a silly number of cocktails.'

She should have known he was gay from the start. All the signs were so clear now.

'What's happened to the lovely Rob? Can't he go out drinking with you?'

'He's working his arse off at work.'

'Not literally, I hope.'

'Allie.'

'What, so now I'm not allowed to crack jokes? Rob always thinks I'm hilarious.'

'He's an architect. He spends all day poring over plans. He treasures light relief.'

'Oh.'

'Plus he thinks you're fabulous.'

'I always knew his taste was impeccable.' Alice managed a wry smile. For some reason she seemed to be far more attractive to gay men than she was to straight ones.

'Why don't you e-mail me your availability for the next couple of weeks and let's get something in the diary.'

'E-mail, of course. Why talk when you can type?' It was Alice's pet hate. The latest cancer of society and as yet, no charity had been set up to find a cure.

'We could do brunch and the papers at Troubadour, just like the good old days?'

'Great.' Millimetres from her comfort zone, Alice paused momentarily in her tracks. Richard might have turned out to be a gentleman who preferred blonds of the male variety but it was still difficult. Three years ago she'd been getting married and now she was merely getting home. Alone.

One syllable was all it took for him to sense a shift in her demeanour. '…You take care, Mrs. Just remember you will always be the only woman for me. Love you.'

'Loved you, too.' It was their standard sign-off these days

and it never failed to make Alice smile, even if today it was accompanied by a pang of melancholy. Bloody hormones. All she needed was a jacket potato or a slab of chocolate and she'd be fine.

Dropping her phone back into her bag with one hand, she placed her key in the Chubb lock with the other. It was definitely time for a drink. Especially as the front door wasn't double locked and pop music was filtering out of the keyholes and letterbox. The thud of a bass line more suited to late-night Ibiza than early-evening Hammersmith ricocheted through her house. Alice closed the door loudly behind her.

'Mum?' Provided her mother's builders got a move on, she'd have a houseguest for a mere four to six short weeks, and Alice was sure she could lay a few bathroom or kitchen tiles herself if things got desperate.

Stooping to pick up the post still scattered on the hall floor, Alice's heels clattered on the antique terracotta tiles as she walked through to the kitchen, the lack of tranquillity threatening to send her straight out again. Absently resting her palm on her forehead, she filled her lungs to capacity and, taking a step towards the stairs, shouted as loudly as she could.

'MUM. PLEASE.' She honestly didn't know where women got the patience or the strength to survive having husbands and children at the same time, she could barely cope with her mother staying for a few weeks.

The volume dipped, shortly followed by fast-moving bare footsteps on the stair carpet. Moments later Suzie swept into the kitchen in a cloud of freshly applied moisturiser and perfume, wearing what looked like Alice's new black trousers and a decidedly lacy bra. Relief flooded through Alice as she realised her people-free evening-for-one was back on track. She was currently in the presence of someone who was definitely on her way out.

'Hello, darling. So glad you're home. Now you can help me decide what to wear.'

Alice looked up from sorting through the post. 'I'd probably go for a top.'

Suzie smiled as she leaned in for a double air kiss. She definitely had moments when she couldn't believe she was old enough to have an adult daughter, and this was one of them. 'I didn't hear you come in.'

'Not surprising really.'

Suzie did her best to look apologetic despite the fact she really wasn't in the mood. 'Sorry. Just trying to clear my mind.'

'I don't know how you can hear yourself think.' Alice flinched as she listened to her tone. Her mother brought out a parental side in her that she didn't even know she owned.

'I've been concentrating all day, now I'm getting ready. And I can't bear arriving somewhere on my own if I'm not on the crest of a musical wave. Thank God for the Scissor Sisters.'

'Why can't you listen to Norah Jones or Dido like every other woman of your age who wants to own a top-40 album?'

Still nodding her head in time to the last track, Suzie shrugged as she filled a glass with white wine from a started bottle in the fridge and offered one to Alice. 'It's Friday night. I need energy, not wistful introspection.'

'I'll drink to that,' Alice muttered as she wandered over to the back door, unlocking the complex series of bolts which had been a prerequisite of the insurance company, to invite the evening in to join them. Alice felt her spirits lifting as fresher air, infused with the scent of rosemary and jasmine reached her. She feared her recent interest in gardening, albeit on a micro scale, was another—at least mercifully invisible—sign of ageing.

Suzie decided to take advantage of Alice's moment of tranquillity. 'I don't suppose I could borrow your new Orla

Kiely bag this evening, could I? I just had a quick rummage in your room but I couldn't find an alternative…'

Alice did her utmost to let the words *rummage* and *your room* wash straight over her as she took a large sip of wine and slipped off her shoes. The cool, flat, smooth tiles of the kitchen floor were straight from heaven, and as the newly liberated bones in her feet rearranged themselves, she could feel perspective approaching.

'…I almost went with the black crushed-velvet evening bag, but it just didn't work somehow. Too wintry.'

As Suzie's eye caught the object of her desire, resting on the dark granite work surface, Alice watched her mother edge ever closer. How could it be that her mother didn't pay a shred of attention to the generation gap? Why did she still shop at Gap?

Suzie turned, her eyes wide with the excitement of having the perfect outfit in her sights. 'I promise I'll look after it. The pink even matches the stitching on the top I was thinking of wearing.'

Too tired to protest, Alice emptied the assorted contents of her handbag onto the kitchen table and silently surrendered the item. 'You could, of course, just buy one yourself.'

Suzie checked her appearance in the mirror of Alice's compact before wiping her lips back to neutrality with a piece of kitchen towel and helping herself to Alice's lipstick. She looked up midapplication. 'You made me promise not to copy you without asking first.'

'Well, at least you pay attention, which is something.' Alice refused to be duped into apologising. Out loud it sounded petty but the bottom line was that, whereas wardrobe cloning might have made her mother feel young, it only made Alice feel old.

'Speaking of which, you don't mind if I borrow these trousers, do you?' Suzie didn't give her a moment to answer.

'And before I forget, Richard called. He was going to try your mobile. I've just realised, it's your anniversary, isn't it?'

Alice nodded. 'I've just spoken to him.'

'What did he want?'

'My house, my phone, my business.' Short-tempered, Alice rubbed her temples with her thumb and third finger. And she'd turned down a drink with Richard this evening because…?

Suzie ignored Alice's hostility. 'You know I'd always thought you could do much better.'

'Really, you've never said.' Alice arched an eyebrow and smiled ruefully at her mother who at least had the honesty to grin back before giving her daughter a hug. Time had proved to be an excellent healer.

Barefoot, they were almost exactly the same height, and, standing there cheek to cheek, Alice felt herself relax as she wished she could still tuck her head under her mother's chin for extra comfort. 'I just wish you'd told me how you felt about him before you told everyone else in the whole world.'

'I tried. You just weren't listening. And for the record, "the whole world" does not read my column. I wish they did.'

'I'm a child. I'm supposed to rebel.'

'But you never had, that was the point. And then you run off, get married and deny me my mother-of-the-bride moment.'

'Just admit you handled it badly. Richard was, still is, a great guy.'

'Hey, I wouldn't worry. These days you're barely an adult until you've had your first divorce. I mean, look at me.'

Alice ended the hug moment, careful not to say anything. Her mother was definitely not her role model when it came to picking life partners.

Suzie observed her pride and progeny. 'So, sweetheart, have you had a difficult day?'

'Not really.' Alice had left Mayfair in an excellent mood, yet she seemed to have misplaced it on her way home. 'Tiring, that's all.'

'You know, your father used to get those grey circles under his eyes, too.'

Alice raised her eyes to the ceiling and back again, spotting a couple of cobwebs en route and added dusting to her mental list of not-so-glamorous chores for the weekend. 'I just need the sun to shine on consecutive days so I can take the edge off my panda look. A hint of a tan would be ideal before filming starts.'

'You could always treat yourself to a couple of sun-bed sessions.'

'And skin cancer.'

'Look, way back when, in the 70s and 80s, we had a fairly irresponsible good time and most of us are still alive…'

Alice didn't look impressed.

'Besides, Richard uses a sun bed.' Suzie's tone was disparaging.

'He's much vainer than I am.'

'Well, luckily for you, I read somewhere that pale and interesting is the way forward this summer.'

'No doubt the latest fashion conspiracy invented by blondes or Nicole Kidman. Alabaster skin never works with dark hair, unless of course you are going for Goth, vampire or funeral-parlour chic. And that's never going to happen on my shift.'

'There is another way to cheat. I do.'

As Suzie proffered her arm for inspection, Alice studied her mother's perfect bottled tan and wondered why when she tried to fake her own, it appeared all too obvious.

'And those dark rings are nothing a bit of Touche Éclat and powder won't fix.'

Alice was sure that somewhere inside that sentence, there was a compliment determined to fight its way out.

'Anyway, I'll be off in a minute, so you'll have plenty of peace and quiet.'

'I hope you don't feel you have to go out.' It was a fleeting pang of guilt from Alice.

'It's Friday night. Of course I do.'

Alice always forgot that their perfect evenings were poles and postcodes apart.

'Well then, have a good time.' Alice could feel herself retreating from the conversation. She didn't need every last detail.

Suzie hesitated, momentarily awkward. 'You do know how much I appreciate you letting me stay.'

'It's a pleasure,' she replied more genuinely than her lackadaisical tone suggested.

Alice opened her fridge door and stared at the contents, waiting for inspiration to strike. Carrot baton or taramasalata and pitta bread. Thin thighs or extra-long gym visit on Sunday? Alice reached for the dip. She'd only had a salad for lunch. As for the Atkins diet, only a man—someone who had never been premenstrual—could have come up with a regimen that involved cutting out carbohydrates. Alice savoured the rich, fishy taste on her tongue, her mood immediately lifting. Why was it that fat tasted so damn good? Why was she so preoccupied with food? It was Richard's fault for mentioning filming. And Vegas.

Standing with her back to the worktop, Suzie raised herself up on to the surface next to the fridge, the movement eroding what remained of Alice's space, personal or otherwise. 'It's perfect. At last we get to spend some time together. Amazing that now you can put *me* up, don't you think?'

'Thank Daddy's life insurance, my ex-husband and my

mortgage adviser.' Alice raised her almost empty wine glass in a mock toast. 'To the three most important men in my life.' She'd go for a run in the morning.

Suzie studied the collage of photos and postcards fixed to Alice's fridge door with a random assortment of magnetic nouns and verbs—all that remained of a much-loved fridge-poetry kit. All things considered, Suzie was impressed that Alice wasn't lost for words more often. Instead, she had thrived in adversity. It was a family trait. 'You and I used to be so much closer.'

'We are close.'

'But you don't tell me anything anymore.'

'I don't tell you everything,' Alice corrected. 'Believe me, it's not that interesting.'

Suzie stretched out her legs at right angles to her body and examined her pedicure. 'Maybe we should go away for a weekend together. Two single women going it alone in an unjust world—you know, some quality time—'

'As opposed to the downright average time we usually have?' Alice couldn't help interrupting. 'Do you know, some mothers only see their daughters at Christmas and on Mother's Day.' She couldn't help thinking that some more time apart might be better for the both of them.

A travel plan on the horizon, Suzie's selective hearing was in force. '...We could get away from the humdrum, buy ridiculous outfits, get henna tattoos, have a few drinks, be very indiscreet, tell each other how much we love each other and then share a hangover the next morning....'

Alice traded the dip for a handful of sugar-snap peas and started to crunch through them. Her mother could huff and puff all she liked but this little piggy wasn't feeling the need to discuss her life in any detail.

'How about Barcelona? Or Rome? My treat.' Suzie had built a career on the back of terrier-like tenacity.

'I'd have to reschedule some clients.' Alice wasn't so sure that sharing a hotel room with her mum was going to enhance their relationship. Her three-bedroom house was feeling a little on the small side already.

'So do it. Mothers and daughters are supposed to share everything.'

'Including their wardrobes, it would seem.' It was a subtle but effective change of subject as Alice did her utmost to ignore the fact that her mother had clearly been standing on the backs of her most expensive pair of trousers, which, without heels, were an inch on the long side.

Suzie ran her hands down the front of her legs approvingly. 'Frankly I'm amazed I can still get into any of your stuff. Have you put on weight since Richard left?'

Alice dreamed of a day when she'd receive acclaim with no subtexts or strings attached.

'No.' Sighing silently, Alice walked over to the doors to the garden, determined to keep positive, and reminded herself that she was still celebrating her recent purchase of a pair of size ten jeans at French Connection. They'd probably been mislabelled at a sweatshop somewhere, but strutting along Oxford Street, clutching her paper carrier bag, she'd felt more euphoric than she had in ages.

'It wasn't a criticism. In my opinion you were too thin for ages.'

'I had a lot on my plate.'

'Well, you clearly weren't eating any of it. I've never found that divorce has affected my appetite.' Sliding off the work surface, Suzie added a splash more wine to her glass before admiring her reflection in the eye-level oven door.

'Everyone's different.' Alice focused on breathing in positivity and exhaling negativity. It was unfortunate that the only person who could wind her up in under a minute was the woman who had sacrificed her flat stomach to have her.

'I do have to exercise more now that I'm not having regular sex.'

Suzie bent over and placed her hands flat on the kitchen floor and exhaling deeply, held the pose for a moment before returning to the upright position.

'I'd even settle for some irregular sex.'

'Mum!'

'Yoga and Pilates have changed my shape completely. Not that you'll meet any straight men that way. You're probably better off going to one of those military fitness classes in the park.'

'Or at least, thinking about it. As you well know, I'm about as flexible as a water biscuit. And I'm not sure I'm in the market for a man.'

Suzie's eyes gleamed with excitement. 'You dark horse, you've met someone, haven't you?'

'Since yesterday?' Alice looked at her mother with incredulity.

'Never mind, you should always be keeping an eye out. You never know—'

Alice finished off her mother's sentence '…who you might meet. Nice men always turn up in the most unlikely places.'

It was a mantra her mother had drummed into her since her early teens but, as far as she knew, had only proved to be true on the one occasion Suzie had met someone in a traffic jam.

'So, come on, who's the man you're seeing tonight?' Alice was determined to reroute her mother's focus.

Suzie smiled enigmatically. 'Who?'

'Come on, Mum. You don't usually make this much effort unless you have a date. Don't tell me, you met someone at the Agent Provocateur account holders evening?'

Suzie's eyes lit up. 'They do store cards?'

Alice was determined to get an answer. 'Is it Andy?'

'Andy?' Puzzled, Suzie searched her mental database for a match.

How many A's could there be to go through? Alice decided to put her out of her misery. 'You know Andy. Apostrophe Andy. Your copy editor. He's always flirting with you on the phone.'

'Is he?'

'Mum, you know he is.'

'Can't say I'd really noticed…'

'Come on, he phones at least once a week and your grammar isn't that bad.'

'Well, he's pretty cute if you don't mind a man on the short side. I might just have to see if there's any future mileage in that one.'

'So if it's not Andy, it must be Geoffrey again. He's getting quite keen.'

'Geoffrey? Don't be daft.'

'He's always calling you.'

'Exactly.'

'You've been to the cinema together a couple of times.'

'Every single girl needs a man to take her to the movies.'

'I go on my own quite a bit. I enjoy it.'

'You would.'

'Well, for the record, I think he's a nice guy.'

'If you don't mind your men a little on the boring side.'

'Are you sure you've given him a proper chance?'

Suzie folded her arms in front of her. 'Look, for a start he's called "Geoffrey."'

'That's hardly his fault.' Alice racked her brains for sex symbols called Geoffrey and gave up. Geoffrey Rush was the only one she could think of and he wasn't exactly your traditional pin-up.

'Plus, he's old.'

'He's only a couple of years older than you.'

'But I don't feel old.'

'How do you know that he does?'

'You have to admit it, darling, he looks it. Plus, he's retired.'

'From the law, not from life. And so what if he hasn't got shares in La Prairie, lines give a man character.'

Suzie fidgeted. 'He owns fleece clothing in colours that should be banned in order to preserve common decency.'

'Probably only because no one has taken him shopping since his wife died. And by the way, if you'd had to wear a suit for forty years, you'd probably be wearing a fleece, too.'

'Honestly, Alice, if you like him so much, you go out with him.'

'Mum, please. It would be like going on a date with my dad.'

'Finally. That's my point.'

'Not *your* dad.' Alice sighed as she faced up to having to ask the inevitable next question. 'So, come on then, who's the mystery man?'

Suzie attempted to feign nonchalance for about three seconds before clapping her hands excitedly. 'He's brand new.'

'Blimey, you've met more men than I have in the last couple of years.' Alice's tone was laced with admiration.

Suzie frowned. 'Don't take this the wrong way, but that's hardly difficult.'

Alice's patience was starting to wear thin. 'You haven't secretly joined a dating agency, have you?'

'No, of course not. He's just a man I met on the train.'

'The train?' Alice took a breath, hoping to lose her falsetto in the process. 'There's nothing wrong with joining a book group, going to the theatre, watching television…'

'Don't begrudge me a bit of fun, darling. I've been single for my entire fifties.'

'Single, but not chaste—and, may I remind you, married twice in your forties.'

Suzie wondered how she'd notched up so many birthdays without noticing. Maybe a year had been made shorter under some new European directive and nobody had told her.

Alice's train of thought was on a diversion. 'In fact, I've only ever been a bridesmaid for you. How newfangled, dysfunctional and tragic is that?'

'I think it's rather sweet, actually. Think of it as my way of ensuring that you wear a dress at least once every fifteen years.'

'Very funny.'

'I was just showing you how it's done.'

'I quite like being on my own. Life's a lot less unpredictable.'

'Honestly, darling. Sometimes you just have to seize the moment or, if things are a bit quiet, create one.'

'You could choose to age gracefully. Learn to darn socks. Go the library instead of the Library Bar. Enrol for an evening class. Play badminton. Take up bridge.'

'What, and steal someone else's husband?' Suzie's tone was provocative as she slowly and deliberately added more fuel to Alice's fire.

Alice folded her arms and rested them under her breasts. 'But, picking up men on the train?' She shook her head disapprovingly. 'A likely story, not least because I'm sure you told me proudly the other day that you haven't set foot on a tube this millennium.'

'Look, there's no need to get so aerated, darling. And I met him on the Eurostar. Do you want to see a picture?'

'You already have a photo?' Alice's interest seemed to be declining in inverse proportion to her mother's levels of excitement. Why couldn't she have a golf-playing, cake-baking mother like Zoë's? A mother who bought flowers from M&S rather than from Moyses Stevens.

'My new phone has a built-in camera.'

'So you're stalking someone?'

'Hardly. He was attractive. We got chatting, I suggested a drink, we swapped numbers…'

'You took a photo.'

Suzie ignored her daughter. 'We exchanged a few texts. He called. That's it. So far, so good.'

'Amazing.' For twenty-nine long years Alice had actively avoided eye contact with everyone on public transport. 'Name? Occupation? Dependents?'

'What's it got to do with you?'

Alice put a hand on her hip. 'So he's either a drug baron or you don't know?'

'I believe he does something to do with wine bars.' Suzie paused uncertainly. 'Or was it restaurants?'

'Waiter? Barman? Gold digger? Ageing millionaire?'

Suzie shook her head slowly as she tried to recall their conversation. She'd definitely been under the influence of a couple of glasses of champagne at that point. 'A financier perhaps? He was travelling first-class.'

'Wedding ring?'

'Please, Alice. There's no need to use that tone of voice.'

'Just out of interest, were you wearing a sandwich board advertising your availability at the time? Or a magnet?'

While she wasn't about to admit it, Alice was genuinely

curious and more than a little impressed. Maybe all she needed to find the man of her dreams was a railcard.

Suzie was impressively unruffled. 'No ring. And a few years younger than me, I think. He had his own hair, own teeth and a touch of Harrison Ford about him. Well, before he went grey. Or maybe I mean Liam Neeson.'

Suzie squinted as she stared into the middle distance, conjuring up ageing screen idols. 'Anyway, early days yet.'

'First drink, Mum. One evening. No *days* at all, so far.'

'Look, I've only got six weeks left.'

'You're going to be sixty, not six feet under.'

'I'm going to be a senior citizen, a concession...' Suzie could barely say the terms out loud. 'And besides, I don't want to be paying a single supplement for the next thirty years of my life...'

Alice should have known her mother was planning to stick around until she was in her nineties.

'Speaking of which...I have a plan. For both of us.'

'Really?' Going on instinct, Alice didn't like the sound of this.

Suzie held Alice's gaze. 'What if I said my birthday wish was for the two of us to be dating by the time of my party?'

Alice rolled her eyes. 'What if I said my birthday wish was for world peace and longer legs?'

'I'm being serious, darling.'

'So am I. No way.' Alice took a soothing sip of her wine and, gripping the floor with her toes, prepared to stand her ground. 'Surely you'd have far more fun flirting with all the old flames on the guest list.'

'Most of them have second or third wives now.'

'Well, it's never stopped you before.'

'Alice.' Suzie's tone contained an iota of hurt.

'Well, what do you suggest, mail order? Male order...now

there's an idea. I'll pop out and pick someone up tomorrow. Fine. Anything else?'

Suzie was not amused. 'It's far from impossible, you know.'

'I'm assuming when you say dating, that you mean seeing the same person more than once?'

Suzie shook her head. 'I knew you'd be defeatist.'

'Try realistic. I haven't been on more than three consecutive dates with anyone since Richard and I split up.'

'Some might say you haven't been trying very hard.'

'Some might say you were really lucky to have somewhere to stay.'

Suzie pouted. 'Go on, it'll be fun.'

'Why can't you just want a cashmere jumper, a weekend at a health spa, a carriage clock, a…a…handbag…?'

'I've got everything I need and plenty I don't. But I would like a nice man. Every woman deserves to be complimented and complemented, to be loved and desired.'

'Have you been hanging out in the Romance section at Borders again?'

Suzie refused to rise to the bait. So what if she'd briefly dated a man she'd met in the Romance section? It could have been worse. He could have been a horror aficionado.

'Look, allow me to be a mother for a second, or at least a friend. So things didn't work out with Richard. That's not it, you know. You're only twenty-nine. You just need to start looking properly. We both do. And you have to shop around. I'd have thought that's one thing I've managed to teach you over the years.'

Alice knew her mother was right. She'd just always favoured the notion of being swept off her feet by a tall (or even a short) dark stranger method of meeting someone; lots of hope, no action and therefore no taking any responsibility whatsoever for her singleness. Actively looking seemed somehow desperate and more than a little bit tacky, not to mention terribly unromantic. 'Do you really think…' Alice did some almost mental arithmetic, the sort that involved using her fingers as a backup. '…that we can both be dating in forty-three days…?'

'Well, we've got nothing to lose except, with a bit of luck, some sleep.' Suzie's giggle was mischievous. 'And I figure, worst case scenario, there might be an article in this for me.'

'Well, going on tonight's man, how about "All Aboard the Love Train"?'

'Ooh, good one.'

As she grabbed a pen from the pot next to the phone to scribble Alice's title down, Suzie caught sight of the kitchen clock. 'Jesus, how can it possibly be seven-fifteen already? I'm supposed to be in Covent Garden in forty-five minutes.'

'You'd better get a move on then. You know what they say about second impressions.'

Suzie made no attempt to rush. 'Women are supposed to be late. And poor timekeeping is one of my not-so-hidden talents.'

'It's rude.'

'It's all part of the game.'

'I thought you told me not to play games.'

'I'm on a tight schedule. I might be changing my mind.'

'Maybe you should call or text…?' Alice observed her mother's ample cleavage with a certain degree of envy. 'Or send him a photo…'

Suzie drained her glass and, Alice's empty handbag tucked under her arm, headed back upstairs. 'He'll be there. I'm worth waiting for.'

Alice followed her up the stairs, the contents of her bag cradled in her arms. 'I think you should leave me his name and number. You know, just in case.'

Suzie laughed. 'You are sweet to worry, darling. We're meeting in a bar, not a back alley.'

Sweet? Sweet? Alice didn't want to be sweet or sensible. She wanted to be sexy, sultry and spontaneous. 'Just promise me you'll keep an eye on your drink at all times. You don't know this guy at all.'

'Well, at least I've met him face-to-face before, not like all these couples who meet on the Internet.'

Alice reached the sanctuary of her bedroom and, shrugging off her jacket, lifted open the sash window before collapsing onto her bed. Pulling her shirt out from her skirt, she stroked her stomach. Her body wasn't used to being imprisoned in a suit from eight until seven. The joy of telephone clients was that she could wear whatever she liked. A bit like phone sex, she imagined. No need for sexy lingerie or hairless legs.

Suzie shouted from the next room. 'So are you in? It'll be an adventure…'

Alice sighed. 'I'm not sure the pursuit of love should be a team or, for that matter, a timed activity.'

'You'll be shopping around for the right outfit for my party, so why not for the right man?'

Alice hated the way that her mother managed to make even the most ludicrous ideas appear to be totally logical.

'I do feel sorry for your generation sometimes.' Suzie's tone was one of pure pity.

Horizontal, Alice rolled her eyes at no one in particular. 'Don't bother. We're the most emancipated yet.' Lying on one side of her double bed, relishing the cool linen against her skin, she grabbed the edge of the duvet and rolled herself up, safe from attack.

'But with the most anxiety. Fear of infertility, fear of not living up to your potential at all times, fear of abuse, fear of terrorism, fear of complex carbohydrates…' Suzie paused for a second as she pulled a top on, over her head. 'You need to take the weight of the world off your shoulders and have a bit more fun.'

'I tried that.' Just five minutes of power napping and she'd be ready to start her evening of doing absolutely nothing.

'And if at first you don't succeed…'

Her mother really needed to stop talking now.

'Your trouble is that you're too busy helping everyone else. You might be an excellent life coach but you need to get a life.'

'I've had quite a lot more life than most, thank you.' Alice could feel a headache approaching. Maybe she could hire an escort for Suzie's party. At least that way she could guarantee that the man would stay all evening and laugh at her jokes. And apparently some of them didn't look like strippers at all. Maybe if she paid enough, the man in question could come over for Sunday lunch the week before.

'And, just for the record…'

Suzie had increased her volume but Alice had no idea why. She'd heard every syllable so far.

'…renting a man for the evening doesn't count. I think we should genuinely try to be dating. It's always good to have a deadline.'

Now completely dressed and having apparently doused herself with another bottle of perfume, her mother popped her head around Alice's bedroom door. 'So I'm off to road test a potential. What are you up to tonight?'

Alice stared out of the end of her duvet roll like a startled caterpillar. 'Zoë and I were thinking of seeing a film.' Not really a lie. They were both intending to watch the same film, if from separate sofas.

'A film? You two should be out working your way through the cocktail menu in a bar or going speed-dating…'

'And then we could write off a man every three minutes.' Alice was pleased with her perfect riposte.

'You're not going to meet a man sitting in the dark.'

'You never know.'

'If you don't mind me saying so…'

Alice braced herself. With an opener like that, she was definitely going to mind.

'…but you two seem to do a lot together on your own.'

'She's my best friend.'

'You would tell me if something was going on, wouldn't you?' Suzie's hands were clasped expectantly.

'What?'

Suzie smiled encouragingly. 'I was reading an article about Ellen DeGeneres the other day and—'

'Mum. Honestly.' Exasperated, Alice was unsure whether to be amused or insulted.

'It's just—I only ever see Zoë in jeans.'

'Oh, well, she's bound to be a lesbian then.'

'But when was the last time Zoë had a serious boyfriend?'

'I don't know. Four years ago?'

'Plus, she hardly ever wears any makeup. Maybe you could give her some tips, you know, in a professional capacity. Maybe she'd like to be part of our plan.'

Alice stared at her ceiling. 'Definitely *your* plan.'

'Don't get me wrong, Zoë's a great girl, one of a kind.'

Alice wondered how her mother could have the audacity to try and take the credit for the calibre of the best friend she had chosen all by herself at Edinburgh University—and the closest thing she had to a sibling.

'Well, you two have fun and there's no need to worry about me. I promise I'll text you if I'm not coming home tonight. Okay?'

Not at all okay but Alice nodded all the same as she

forced herself to sit up. Slipping into her dressing gown, she headed to the bathroom. Maybe if she had a shower… 'Oh and Mum…'

'Yup.'

Alice watched Suzie blotting her lipstick via the landing mirror, in awe of her mother's energy level.

'I've got a private client coming over tomorrow morning so if you could keep your clothes on and your nose out of my study…'

'Of course, darling. I wouldn't do anything to get in your way, you know that.'

'That goes for any tall dark strangers, too. I need to build my client base, not scare them off.'

'Got it.' Suzie delivered a mock salute. 'Any overnight guests will be kept on a leash and off the soft-furnishings.'

Alice raised her eyebrows as she stared past the newly cluttered shelf of beauty products, at her reflection in the bathroom mirror. How was it that her mother got to act less mature as she aged, yet still always had the last word?

There was a knock on the half-open bathroom door.

'Don't wait up. It's fun having a housemate, don't you think?'

Alice kissed her mother's cheek gently. 'You look fabulous.' She did.

'Thank you.'

Sometimes Alice felt that she and Kate Hudson would have a lot in common. Having a mother as beautiful, desirable and successful as Goldie Hawn was bound to leave a girl with a few issues.

'Don't forget, six weeks and counting…' Suzie's wink was playful as she walked down the stairs and out of the front door, slamming it behind her.

Forty-three days and forty-two nights. There was something almost biblical about the challenge and yet Alice didn't remember agreeing to anything. As she searched her bathroom cabinet for the Nurofen, her headache doubled in strength when she discovered a gleaming new box of Durex. If Suzie had been anyone else's mother Alice would probably have been filled with admiration at both her get-up-and-go and her continued awareness of STDs. But she was hers. In her face and on her case. And it was just the two of them, at least for the time being.

Chapter Two

43 days to go
Suzie 1, Alice 0

Suzie held her mobile phone at arm's length to check that predictive text was making sense of what she was trying to say and cursed her eyesight for ageing faster than the rest of her. She couldn't resist messaging Alice. It was notoriously difficult to get a late table at J Sheekey and yet, there they were, at a table for two in the wood-panelled back room. Plus, she'd cleared the first hurdle and made it to the dinner stage. So far, so very good.

'Sending an SOS?'

Damn. Tom was clearly the fastest pee-er in the West End. Concerned that he might be able to see the screen, Suzie hurriedly held down the power button and surreptitiously slipped her phone back into Alice's bag. She felt like a badly behaved teenager as Tom squeezed past her to his seat, his head shaking almost disapprovingly, his bottom, enticingly, at eye level and perfectly packaged in a pair of cream cords.

'Don't you think it's quite frightening just how addicted we've all become to instant communication? I have to confess I take great delight in being off the radar sometimes. You'd be amazed how long a day feels without e-mail or mobile interruptions.'

'I'm sure.' Suzie couldn't think of anything worse than not being contactable. 'I'll have to try it sometime.'

Probably around the same time she took up macramé. She couldn't wait to get a BlackBerry and had absolutely no intention of being parted from her phone for more than a couple of hours at a time, but tonight she was flirting and hopefully with some success. Tom was much more attractive than the pixelation on her phone had allowed her to remember. Tallish, darkish and interestingly handsome, he sat back in his seat exuding self-assurance, or maybe it was apathy, the lack of clear message perversely making him all the more appealing. Rubbing her lips together to ensure her lipstick was evenly distributed, she leaned forward slightly to indicate interest on her part. In forty years of dating, it was a technique that hadn't become any less effective.

As Tom smeared some butter on his bread, Suzie ascertained, from the almost imperceptibly angular edges of his fingernails, that he was a nail-clipper man. Raising his food parcel to his lips, he paused. 'So, are you married?'

Taking a bite, his question hung over the table as Suzie took her time, pausing for a sip of water. Two hours in, small talk was clearly over and Tom had tacitly moved them on to the information-gathering, deal-making (or -breaking) part of the evening.

Suzie returned her glass to the table. 'Divorced.'

'Rather not talk about it?' Tom's gaze was direct, his tone challenging.

'What do you want to know?' Suzie didn't skip a beat. 'I

have three ex-husbands. The first one died on me, which is a real shame because he was far and away the best yet.' She still hadn't forgiven Henry for leaving her and Alice to fend for themselves. Not really.

'I'm so sorry.'

'I was thirty-eight with an eight-year-old daughter and we thought the world had ended. But it's a long time ago, now.'

Tom leaned in closer. 'My father died from a heart attack when I was seven. From then on I was at the mercy of my mother and my sister. I didn't even have an uncle to teach me the rules of cricket.'

Suzie nodded slowly, hoping to convey empathy and sympathy without overreacting. 'My cricket wasn't too hot, either.'

Tom smiled warmly.

Encouraged and not wishing to lose momentum by allowing a reflective silence to descend, Suzie continued. 'Anyway, turns out that our world kept on going. Husband number two was having an affair and the third one just didn't cut the mustard, but my last divorce was over ten years ago and I've been fairly young, totally free and stubbornly single ever since. Having a good time, the odd fling, nothing serious, you know how it is.'

'I know all about the nothing-serious thing.'

Tom took a long sip of his wine as Suzie tried to read between the lines. He was being far too enigmatic for her journalistic likings. Her past was fast becoming an open book and yet his was still shrink-wrapped.

'Never been married?'

'Never.'

'And there hasn't been anyone, well, special?' Suzie wondered whether she might be able to call on Richard to assess Tom's potential. A favour it would definitely have been easier to ask if she'd been friendlier to her ex-son-in-law.

However hard Alice defended him, Suzie still couldn't quite forgive him for letting her only child down with such a thud. On the bright side, at least she wasn't going to be called "granny" any time soon.

'Oh, there have been women.'

Suzie's heart skipped along in relief.

'But few and far between. Mainly good-time girls…'

A euphemism for prostitutes? Suzie frowned.

'My trouble is I've been far too married to my work to meet anyone of real substance. My only dependents are my four godchildren who double as my niece and nephews. It would appear that my older sister is single-handedly determined to make me a family man.'

'Probably not entirely single-handedly.' Suzie raised an eyebrow suggestively. 'How old are they?'

'My sister is forty-eight.'

'And I'm sure she'll thank you for sharing that. I actually meant the children.'

Tom paused, his gaze apparently fixed on a light fitting. Suzie wondered why people always looked up when they were trying to recall facts. It wasn't as if there was a shelf of files up there.

'The boys are fifteen, thirteen and ten, and Natalie is five.'

'Daughters are the best. Mine practically brought herself up and tidied up after me.'

Tom smiled. 'How old is she now?'

Suzie blanched, not so much at the directness of the question as to the truthful answer. She suspected Tom was going to be a dab hand at maths.

'Twenty-five.' Suzie took a gulp of her wine, hoping to swallow her guilt. Not that four years was going to make a difference in the grand scheme of things. 'I still can't believe it. It's gone so fast. So, no children of your own?'

Tom shook his head. 'None that I know about. Unless you count a Triumph Speed Triple.'

Suzie racked her brains. 'Classic car?'

'Motorbike.' Resting his elbows on the table, he suddenly became more animated.

'Wow.' Suzie did her best to sound enthused.

'I've got a car, too.'

'You're quite a rarity then.'

'I am?' Tom knew lots of people with more than six wheels to their name.

'I mean a man without much baggage.' Suzie leaned in again, her top obligingly slipping suggestively to reveal a black lacy bra strap.

Amused by Suzie's attempt at off-the-cuff and off-the-shoulder interviewing, Tom sat back in his chair. 'Carry-on only. When you travel as much as I do, it's essential.'

Suzie stalled. She wasn't sure he was on her wavelength anymore.

Tom took the initiative. 'So tell me about your column…'

'My column?'

'Did you really think I wouldn't have Googled you before asking you out? I'm not in the habit of dating total strangers.'

'I…I honestly hadn't thought about it.' Momentarily thrown, Suzie wondered what else he'd managed to find out about her. On a more positive note, this was definitely a date.

'So, Suzie Fletcher.' Tom sat back and rested his arms on the back of his chair. 'Should I be expecting to feature in "The State I'm In" next Saturday?'

Finally, a hint of flirtation from a man who was proving as hard to read as Alice could be. The communication generation was full of mixed messages.

Suzie lowered her gaze flirtatiously. 'That all depends. Would you want to be?'

'That hinges on what you're going to say. Are we talking Love on the Orient Express, Boring Businessman or Younger Men Aren't All They're Cracked Up To Be…?' Tom smiled as Suzie blushed. 'Seriously, I'm interested.'

'57 minutes 28 seconds.' Alice checked the digital display on her phone as her oven timer bleeped a reminder. 'Zo, I'm calling you back.'

Hanging up, she redialled her best friend and reset the countdown on her oven door for another fifty-nine minutes. It was turning into one of her favourite types of evening. She'd painted her toenails plus she and Zoë had cooked, eaten and watched TV together. Nearly two hours of virtual-flatmate behaviour and so far, thanks to her phone deal, it hadn't cost them a penny. Alice still derived enormous satisfaction from getting something for nothing, even though logically, she knew she paid a healthy stipend to the phone company for hour-long free evening calls every month.

Zoë picked up halfway through the first ring. 'I love this bit.'

John Travolta and Olivia Newton-John were going through their Rydell High School years on the small screen for the umpteenth time. Sandy was just about to arrive post-makeover with her big perm and her shiny, tighter-than-tight trousers.

Alice checked to make sure her fast-drying nail polish had lived up to its promise before gingerly tucking her legs underneath her as she curled up on the sofa.

'I used to think we'd have a funfair when we graduated high school.'

'And then you woke up.'

Alice ignored Zoë. 'And don't you think "graduated high school" sounds so much more glamorous than "finishing A-levels"?'

Zoë grunted her affirmation. 'We didn't even have boys at my school.'

'Neither did we. In fact, we were known as the Virgin Megastore.'

'I think I'd rather be known for my propriety than my pimples.' Zoë took another swig of beer from the bottle in front of her, happy that she wasn't technically drinking alone. 'So where's your mum tonight?'

'She's out on a date.' Alice couldn't have sounded any less enthusiastic.

'Cool.'

'Whatever.'

'You don't mean that.'

'No, I probably don't. But if she's hoping to sleep her way to retirement age, I don't need every microscopic detail, either. And get this. Suddenly her only birthday wish is for both of us to have a date—sorry my mistake—for us to be *dating* by the time of her sixtieth birthday party.'

Zoë laughed. 'Presumably she already has someone lined up?'

'I think she's hoping to close the deal tonight. I, on the other hand, have got six weeks to find a suitable man.'

'I assume you told her what she could do with that idea?'

Alice hesitated. 'I don't think I said anything except that it was ridiculous. It wouldn't make any difference. You know she never takes no for an answer.'

'So you're going to do it?' Zoë sounded surprised.

'Of course not…I mean if I wanted to, I'm sure I could find a date.'

'I believe you said *dating*.'

Alice sighed. 'Between you and me I'm quite tempted to have a go. I mean, how hard can it be?'

'Let's see. A multimedia multimillion-pound dating industry to help you find the one, and we've been single for what, pretty much ten years between us…I'd say quite difficult.'

Alice laughed at Zoë's deadpan assessment of their situation. When it came to the quest for "the one," they'd both tried, they'd both failed and they were both in self-imposed retirement. Or at least she had been until now.

'Sometimes it's good to have a deadline.' Oh no. Alice was sure she'd stolen that line from her mother. The brainwashing had clearly already begun.

'At work maybe.' Zoë wasn't at all convinced. But then she hadn't been got at.

'It's probably good for me to at least survey the scene from time to time, don't you think?'

'I can't help feeling the view will be very similar. Besides, I like things the way they are. I love being my own boss.'

'You love being bossy.'

Zoë sighed. 'Look, I've got loads on at the moment.'

Alice knew better than to push her, especially when she had a favour waiting in the wings. 'I know, sweetie. However, I was wondering if you might have a few minutes to help me update my wardrobe or at least give me a shopping list?'

'You always look great.'

'Zo, if I am competing with my mother and her DKNY addiction, any high-street tips you can give me will be gratefully received. What did you guys buy in for the summer?'

'We're in the changeover to autumn now.'

'It's barely July.'

'Allie, most people have been buying summer clothes since April, but I've definitely got some samples you can have. Red hair only really works with certain colours.'

Alice smiled. 'Your loss is my gain.'

'As Richard's loss was my gain. Now, you're not going to get all coupley on me, are you?'

'What, me and my invisible boyfriend?'

Alone on her sofa, Zoë was struck by a bolt of imagination. 'That's it, that's who you take to the party, the emperor's new boyfriend—or should that be empress?'

'As if Mum's going to fall for that. Oh, and by the way, goes without saying that you're welcome to join me in the search.'

Zoë rubbed her chin thoughtfully. 'Of course I'll give you a hand.'

'No, I mean for a man of your own. The Next One. After all, you'll be at the party, too.'

'I think I'll pass.'

Alice sighed. She hadn't really been expecting Zoë to agree, but it had definitely been worth a shot. 'Anyway it's not like I've agreed. I haven't signed on a dotted line or anything.'

Zoë laughed. 'I don't think you're going to have much of a choice.'

Alice rubbed her temple. 'I just wish I could trade her in for a more conventional model. One who likes cooking, who considers black to be the colour of death rather than Prada and who believes that regular sex is an urban myth—or at least the preserve of the under thirties.'

'Don't be daft. She's one in a million. And if she starts giving you a hard time, just get her to call me. I think she's hilarious. But then my mum wouldn't be able to find Brazil on a world map, let alone know what a Brazilian is.'

'Speaking of which, how is all that going?'

'I chickened out, too painful.'

'No, the other thing.'

'Oh, well, I haven't done much. I've been busy and...'

'Zo...'

'Honestly, it's almost impossible to make personal calls from work. Everyone, and I count myself, is so bloody nosy. Plus, you know...maybe it's too late. I mean what's the point? I've got a mother who loves me, shouldn't that be enough?'

'I thought you'd discussed this with your mum?'

'I have. I even discussed it with Dad when he was still alive and they both claimed they understood.'

'There you go.'

'It's just I've spent so much time wondering, and now...' Zoë peeled the label off her Budweiser in one and smoothed it onto her jeans. 'I guess I'm scared. Why rock the boat? I mean I know I'd always said I would look into tracing my birth parents when I hit thirty. And I'm nearly thirty-one and not a child anymore, but...'

Silently, Alice transferred her washing from the machine to the tumble dryer. Life really could be perverse sometimes. Zoë had spent her whole life wondering about her birth mother, torturing herself with unknown details, and yet Alice knew exactly who and where hers was, and occasionally wished that she didn't.

Turning the machine on, Alice held the mute button down on the phone and sprinted away from the rumbling, back to the sitting room so as not to dispel the illusion of complete attention. 'How about you find me a date and I track down your mother?'

'Deal...'

'Seriously, Zo, you know you only have to ask if you want some help—moral support, chocolate ice cream, anything really.'

'Thanks Al. Face it, I'm never going to find a man who

is there for me quite like you are.' Zoë twirled a strand of her hair between her fingers.

'Oh, men have their uses. Sex, changing tyres, sex, you know.'

Zoë laughed.

'And not that I'm monitoring good behaviour or anything, but it's definitely my turn to be there for you.' Back on the sofa, Alice watched John Travolta and Olivia Newton-John drive off into the sky towards their happy ending. 'Now, what are we going to watch next?'

Suzie sipped her peppermint tea. She really would have preferred a double espresso but she was trying not to drink coffee after eight. Gone were the days when she'd pass out cold, however high the caffeine level in her system. Not that she was planning on going to sleep anytime soon.

She'd given up waiting for Tom to volunteer any real information about himself halfway through the main course and now had started to interview him, albeit playfully. It was an approach that seemed to be working for them both and as yet Suzie hadn't stumbled across any landmines. 'So, favourite live band?'

Tom paused for thought. 'Does Kylie count?'

Sexuality alarm bells ringing, Suzie shook her head vehemently.

'Just kidding. Queen were amazing in '86, U2 are great in a stadium but overall I'd probably have to say the Rolling Stones.'

Suzie bet he had quite an extensive black T-shirt collection. 'Hyde Park—summer of '69?' It had been an amazing day.

'Wembley Stadium '96…'

Suzie decided to gloss over the twenty-seven-year gig gap.

'…and I did see Simon & Garfunkel in Hyde Park a couple of years ago. They'd aged a little—well, probably a lot. I couldn't actually see any detail from where I was sitting.'

Bad eyesight or bad seats? Suzie didn't like to ask.

'…On the big screens it looked like Art had borrowed Jack Nicholson's eyebrow stylist and Paul Simon's hair dye was a little more red than brown under the lighting rig. Superficialities aside, it takes a lot to beat a little harmony, acoustic guitar and the sun setting over London. And their sound is still unique.'

She smiled. Revival tours definitely had their uses. 'How about the Scissor Sisters?'

Tom wrinkled his brow as he dug deep into the recesses of his mental jukebox. 'Were they 1970s?'

'No, they're right now.'

'That's it. I surrender.' Tom threw his hands in the air in mock disgust at his lack of knowledge and grinned apologetically. I've obviously been at work for twenty years too long. Although I do own a couple of Eminem albums.'

'Really?' Suzie loved it when people surprised her.

'Shocked?'

Suzie sat back. 'I'm pretty unshockable. Although I'll admit I am amazed.'

'I ran the London marathon four years ago and in my pre-iPod days it was great stuff for training to. There's nothing like a little anger to keep you going at the fifteen-mile mark.'

'You ran the marathon?'

Tom sat up proudly. 'In just over four hours. Part of my Life Begins At Forty crisis, I think.'

'Well, well, well. The real slim shady.' Suzie decided to skip past the reference to running just over twenty-six miles for fun and the fact he was fifteen years her junior.

'Who?'

'That's him, Marshall Mathers.'

Tom couldn't have looked any more confused.

'M and M, get it?' It probably wasn't his fault. He undoubtedly had to spend hours a day watching Bloomberg and reading the financial pages, whereas Suzie barely understood her mortgage or her pension. She reminded herself that differences were good and that opposites allegedly attracted.

'And to think I thought that M&M feeling was something to do with chocolate.' Tom smiled and absently stroked his small sideburn.

Suzie beamed back at him. 'So you're mid-forties?'

'What is this? Everything I say can be used in evidence against me?'

'Or for you. And don't forget, I haven't put you through an Internet search engine…yet.'

'So, what else do you want to know?' Tom couldn't remember the last time a woman had really taken an interest in him and not his bank balance or the fact he had a villa in Spain. This dating-from-scratch thing was much more honest.

'That'll do.' Now they were having fun, Suzie didn't want to push it.

Tom drained his espresso cup. 'Anyway, surely now more than ever, age is literally just a number.'

'Usually the number of a good cosmetic surgeon.'

Tom laughed. 'Do you have one?'

Suzie faked indignation. 'Of course not.' So what if she'd treated herself to Botox for her fifty-fifth birthday? It hadn't lasted very long.

'Well, you're looking pretty good to me for a fif—'

'Go on…'

Tom realised his mistake a minute too late. 'You tell me…'

'Oh come on, surely the World Wide Web supplied you with that little detail.'

'Actually—' Tom's smile was a wry one '—there was a surprising amount of variation.'

'I'm fiftysomething.' Suzie wondered whether by being nonspecific he now knew she was definitely fifty-nine.

Tom hesitated, not quite sure where to go next. Absently helping himself to a sugar lump, he started using it as a stress toy. He was on very unfamiliar territory.

'Well, you don't look it.'

At least with her clothes on. Sure, she had a few extra lines on her neck and a slightly crepey décolletage but her youthful personality more than compensated.

Silently, Suzie thanked the inventor of highlights and lowlights for his or her services to grey areas.

Tom found his feet. 'Seriously, you don't.'

Suzie marvelled at his display of perfect manners. She'd thought gentlemen had been phased out around the same time they'd removed lead from petrol. Making sure she had Tom's full attention, she decided to up the ante. 'You know toy boys are all the rage these days.'

'Says older women?' His tone was playful. His pulse, however, had definitely quickened. Excited or terrified? He wasn't sure.

'Take Demi Moore, Cameron Diaz and Joan Collins…'

No coffee left, Tom downed the last few sips left in his wine glass and catching the waiter's attention, ordered them both another one. 'I'd rather take the first two. You know, when I bought my motorbike I thought I might be revving up for a midlife crisis.'

'Quite literally I bet.'

Tom looked peeved at the interruption.

'…but that's invariably when men go for younger women, not older ones…so clearly I'm fine after all.'

'What on earth have you got to have a crisis about? I've

got retirement age to send shivers down my spine. Not that writers ever retire, we just start a new chapter.'

Suzie fiddled with her earring in what she hoped was an intriguing rather than an irritating manner, as she reminded herself that she might have been nearly sixty but she was gorgeous. Her usually cast-iron nerve was starting to falter. At least older men were grateful to have you on their horizon, plus their eyesight was likely to be worse than yours.

'Well, my work/life balance is nonexistent. I've been promising myself a gap year since before I started university. My business partner is thinking of taking some time out to spend more time with his family, only damn, I forgot to have one.'

'Do you want children?' Suzie tried to sound matter-of-fact. It was the million-dollar question in every relationship, but the most common single reason for younger men to move on from their older women. Men o pause. Men o leave.

'Not at the moment.' Tom shrugged. 'Maybe one day, but only if I meet the right person. Helen's four keep me pretty busy and it's the perfect scenario—children you can borrow for the day or the weekend but return at bedtime or when things get a bit busy.'

'Sounds perfect.'

'But the bottom line is, I think all men want to go forward and multiply at some point. On paper I'd be the perfect father.'

'Tall, handsome, modest…'

'Seriously, I'm not too old to kick a football, I've built up my own business, I'm my own boss and I earn good money…'

Suzie mentally ticked a few more boxes.

'But recently, I don't know, I've started to feel lethargic, defeatist, more tired than usual. Maybe I just need to start taking multivitamins or book a holiday.'

Suzie nodded empathetically. First date and he was already admitting he wasn't perfect, as opposed to most guys who couldn't wait to tell her how perfect they were. Plus, he didn't have a wife or a girlfriend. Although it didn't sound like he had much time for one, either.

'Sorry. I don't want to put a downer on the evening.'

Suzie faked a smile. *Where had all the good-time guys gone?* She really didn't want to spend the rest of the evening pretending to be his therapist. She clasped her hands in front of her. 'You know, maybe you should see a life coach.'

'A what?'

'A professional who'll help you focus on your goals and do their best to ensure you reach them. I happen to know an excellent one.'

Tom didn't look convinced. 'Is he your coach?'

'He's a she. And yes, sometimes. Seriously, let me give you her number.'

Suzie started rummaging for a pen, when she spotted and extracted a business card from the inside pocket of Alice's bag.

'Give her a call. If you mention me, I'm sure she'll squeeze you in as soon as she can.'

Because she's my daughter. It was the obvious time to mention it and yet Suzie remained silent. Possibly because Tom thought the child in question was merely twenty-five.

Tom swirled his wine around his glass as he thought about it. 'All sounds a bit New Age to me. What's next? Aromatherapy massages? An ashram? I probably just need to pull myself together, sleep a bit more and stop whingeing. I mean, it's summer for goodness' sake.'

'Trust me, you'll feel better for going. And she doesn't have all the answers. She'll just make you answer your own questions. You might have heard of her, actually, she's one of the resident experts on *Get A Life*.' Suzie felt a flutter of maternal pride.

'I'm afraid I don't get to watch much television.' Tom was contrite. 'Usually just the news and a bit of a sport when I get a chance. I'm rarely at home.'

'Really?' Not comfortable on his own or not enough hours in his day?

Tom glanced at the business card before filing it in his wallet. 'Isn't it a bit like paying someone to tell you what you already know deep down?' He started looking around for a waiter. 'Do you mind if we get the bill? I've got an early start tomorrow.'

Suzie wondered if she'd just been relegated to "extreme nutter" in his date journal as she felt a sense of formality return to their conversation. 'You do know it's Saturday tomorrow?'

Tom nodded. 'I'm off sailing. I have to be down in Portsmouth by eight. I really should have gone down this evening.'

'Oh, right.' Sailing. Which along with motorcycling and marathon running probably also meant skiing, hiking and never sitting still. Hence the lack of television. But no one was perfect. And on the bright side he'd never be fighting her for the remote control when she wanted to watch *Desperate Housewives*. Suzie stopped herself from getting carried away. Sometimes a fertile imagination was not a good thing. And it was probably the most fertile part of her these days.

Tom clearly had interpreted her wistful expression as one of disappointment. 'Look, I wasn't—I mean—I don't normally do this sort of thing at all.'

'Surely a man has to eat.' Suzie stopped herself, remembering that demure was far more attractive than defensive or direct in a woman. Especially, she imagined, an older one.

Tom extracted an expensive-looking pen from the inside pocket of the jacket hanging over the back of his chair and instantly and silently a waiter appeared, and handed him the bill.

'No, you know, meet someone on a train, ask them out…'

'Me neither.' In her experience, dating was all about creating a common bond and Suzie was hoping not to let Tom go just yet.

'I hope you've had a good evening?' Without checking the amount, Tom slipped his Amex into the leather sleeve.

'A lovely evening, thanks.' Damn. Suzie could sense him slipping away. She sat back and thought of her freshly waxed bikini line.

'Good. Well, I'm around next weekend, I think, and definitely the weekend after that, if, maybe, you want to do something then?'

'Why not?' Suzie fluttered her eyelashes gently. She could always change her mind if something better came along. His lack of urgency had thrown her slightly. Surely he should have wanted to inspect her choice of underwear today, not a week on Saturday. His animal instincts were proving to be more Bambi than Lion King.

'Excellent. Where did you say you were living?'

'I'm staying with a friend in Hammersmith. I've got builders in at my place. You?'

'Bachelor pad in Shad Thames and house in Oxford-shire…'

Suzie was impressed. Usually by his age, the ex-wife had ruined any chance of multiple properties.

'There's no point in having 128 break horsepower between your legs if you're just going to potter around London. You ever ridden pillion before?'

'Of course.'

Once in the late sixties, in the south of France, for about

an hour. And she hadn't owned a pair of leather trousers for over twenty years.

'Great, and I've got a spare helmet that should fit you.'

Unfortunately it looked as if she was going to have a week or two to find out. Was he playing hard to get, or was he merely out of practice? It was difficult to tell. But she'd definitely be giving him a second chance. Even if it looked like tonight she'd be ordering a cab for one.

Chapter Three

41 days to go
Suzie 2, Alice 0

Alice felt her mobile phone ringing in the breast pocket of her denim jacket as she cycled along the Embankment. Her thighs were burning but, sunglasses on and wind in her hair, she was full of the joys of being single in the summer. And for once her serve had been pretty consistent.

The tennis courts at Battersea Park had been packed with relatively attractive men and while she may not have come close to asking anyone out nor acquired any phone numbers, thanks to the sunshine, she was feeling very positive. All that remained was for her to decide whether she actually wanted to start dating again.

It was nearly a year since her last flush of activity and that had only left her anxious to return to her autonomous girl-about-town status. Mr. Mediocre had been everywhere. And she'd rather be Ms. Independent-Divorcée than Mrs. Medi-ocre any day.

Her phone stopped and then started ringing again. Pulling over, Alice groped for the handset. Forget the fact it was illegal, she'd never been nearly coordinated enough to even consider chatting on the phone whilst cycling.

'Hello?'

'Morning, darling.'

Judging by the buoyant singsong delivery of those two words, Suzie had more than likely had sex last night and probably again this morning. In the bedroom next to hers. At least, hopefully in the bedroom.

'I'll be home in ten minutes, Mum. I'm on the bike.'

'I don't suppose I could borrow your car for a minute or two?'

'Where's yours?'

'Good question.'

Alice's suspicion turned to concern. 'Oh no, Mum, you haven't had it stolen?'

Suzie laughed. 'Unfortunately not. Much more expensively for me, it was clamped and towed. Bloody London. If only the mayor had a car, things would be so different.'

'Hard luck.'

'My fault for chancing it on a double yellow. Anyway, would you mind if I just nipped down the road? I need to give Ryan a lift to the station.'

'Ryan?'

'I'll give you the lowdown later, it's just at this rate he's going to miss his rugby sevens tournament. Incredibly, it seems to be midday already.'

'It's only a ten-minute walk to Hammersmith.'

'Actually, I need to take him to Waterloo.'

Alice took a deep breath. 'Fine. Whatever.'

'You're a star. I'll pick up some food on the way back and we can have brunch together.'

'That'd be lovely. I'm starving.'

'Serves you right for being so bloody active. What are you up to later?'

'Why?'

'Maybe you could give your little housemate a lift to the pound?'

Suzie was up to her usual tricks. There was no such thing as a free brunch.

Alice looked up from the newspaper. 'So, tell me, Mum, how did you come to be saving Ryan's privates?'

Suzie had arrived back without any food and Alice had done her best to ignore the stale smell of alcohol seeping through its faltering mouthwash camouflage. But now they were eating out. And while she had a smoothie in one hand, a latte in the other and eggs Benedict on the way, heaven was indeed a place on earth. Suzie, meanwhile. was reverently sipping black coffee, having just popped a couple more ibuprofen.

'A few of us got guest passes from the paper for a new club-night at The Ministry. I just ran into Ryan at the bar.' Suzie laughed as heartily as her headache permitted. 'A media planner, I think. He can't have been much more than thirty. South African. Very fit.'

'What on earth was he thinking?'

Suzie gazed out of the window, hoping to be distracted from the thumping in her head. 'I'm not sure he was thinking very much. He was, however, very charming.'

'So you thought you'd bring him home?'

'I am allowed overnight guests, aren't I?'

'I guess so.'

'You know, the great thing about Vodka Redbull is that you just keep on going. We didn't even stumble home until fourish. The downside is you can't get to sleep for ages…'

Suzie smiled absently as Alice counted her lucky stars she was a heavy sleeper.

'…And, of course, that you're still awake when your hangover kicks in.'

Sternly, Alice looked at her mother over the Sunday paper she had been trying to read. 'Tell me you weren't even thinking about driving home.'

'Bloody London never used to be such a nightmare when it came to parking.'

'You must have been way over the limit.'

'I'd stopped drinking hours before.'

'Really? Then how is it possible that your breath still smells of booze?'

'We may have had a cheeky little nightcap when we got home.'

Alice pursed her lips in silent fury.

'Calm down. I didn't drive.'

'Only because the car wasn't there.'

Suzie shrugged. 'This blood-alcohol-limit thing is all relatively new. When I learned to drive—'

'Yes, yes, I know, you all used to drive home pissed, with one eye closed to prevent double vision. You were so bloody cool—and I'm not.'

'I didn't say that.'

Alice buried herself in the travel supplement until she had cooled down. One feature article about Scandinavian cruises and she was ready to return to civility. 'So, is Ryan going to be your date for the party?'

'Not a chance. I'd be a laughing-stock. He was just the warm-up act.'

'And what happened on Friday night?'

'Mr. Eurostar?'

Nodding, Alice noisily vacuumed the bottom of her smoothie glass with her straw.

'I don't really know.' Suzie took another sip of coffee. 'He said something about maybe doing something next week-end, but I'm not sure if he meant it, or if it was a super-polite fob-off.' She decided not to mention the business card moment. She wasn't sure how much disapproval she could take from her daughter in one morning, plus she already had a headache. 'We'll just have to wait and see. Not even a kiss, although the restaurant called me a taxi and we're a bit old to be necking in the doorway. How about you?'

'Clearly, I've slept with five men in two days and want to marry all of them.' From the sudden silence at the adjacent table, Alice wondered if perhaps she had been speaking more loudly than she had realised.

Alice felt she had to come up with something. 'Zoë and I did spot quite a few attractive men in Battersea Park this morning.'

'And?'

'And nothing.'

'All you have to do next time is hit a ball into their court and go in hot pursuit…'

Whilst that was a tactic that would inevitably have worked for Suzie in the golden age of very little cellulite and tiny tennis dresses, Alice knew it definitely wasn't going to herald any results for her.

'Of course, you might want to think about investing in a tennis skirt instead of those shorts.'

'You might want to think about minding your own business.'

As they waited for their food, Suzie and Alice immersed themselves in separate Sunday supplements. Fortunately for Suzie—and very unfortunately for Alice—there were articles on dating everywhere. Alice could almost hear her mother's mind whirring as she scanned the personals.

'So how about we advertise, darling?'

'Suzie Fletcher, columnist, and Alice Harrison, life coach,

seek decent men for fun, birthday capers and more.' Her tone was mocking. 'You must be joking.'

'Not as ourselves.'

'Right, of course.' Alice was confused already.

'Why don't we write an anonymous ad?'

'And put it in the paper?'

'In the paper, on the Internet…'

'Did you leave your sensibilities in the car last night?'

Suzie ignored her. 'Well, if you want to meet a man who knows how to use a computer… Seriously, it's all about Internet dating these days. But if you'd rather go the speed-dating route…'

'Where did that come from? And it's not a question of either-or.'

'We can do both if you insist.'

Alice exhaled slowly and calmly, reminding herself that she loved her mother, most of the time. 'Mum. You've already ruined my relaxing summer with your dying-wish approach to dating. I think you should give a girl a break, don't you?'

'Well, you know they say that the only thing you need to get a date is another date.'

'Even when it's a date you've paid for?'

Suzie nodded. 'You'd advertise for a cleaner if you needed one.'

'That's different.'

'Why?'

'Because you aren't meant to be attracted to your cleaner. Because you're advertising for someone to do a job, not to be your soul mate.' Alice paused. 'Somehow writing an advert smacks of desperation.'

'Try replacing that last word with selection. Look, we're not twenty anymore.'

'Some of us are a lot nearer twenty than others.'

'Okay then, fine. Just out of interest, when was the last time you were invited to a party where there were lots of single men?'

'A couple of wee—'

'Gay men don't count.'

Alice fell silent.

Suzie seized the moment. 'See? Aren't you even curious to see what sort of men would reply?'

Of course she was. 'You know they'll be disappointing.'

'If that's the case, then you choose not to meet up with any of them. Simple.'

Alice could feel herself being backed into a corner. 'Mum, I'm not playing.'

'Fine, then let me write an ad for you.'

'No fucking way.'

'Well then.' Suzie rummaged in her bag and handed Alice a pen and a paper napkin. 'Better get thinking.'

Back in the semiprivacy of her back garden, the sunshine and white wine acting as creative lubricant, there was nothing private or personal left about Alice's afternoon. Previous drafts had been balled up and littered the small garden like snowballs.

'Okay.' Alice put her pen down authoritatively. 'Time's got to be up. You go first.'

Suzie sat back, taking another sip of wine, and smacked her lips together. 'Okay, how about this one:

Birthday girl. Independent, attractive, intelligent, happy woman seeks fun, inspiring and energetic M, 35-55 for fun, adventure and maybe more. GSOH essential.'

'That's it?' Alice took the piece of paper from her mother and reread it.

Suzie watched, her discomfort increasing as Alice brandished her pen. 'It's already on the long side if you compare it with some of the ones in the papers.'

Alice disagreed. 'I'd be inclined to say, the more specific you are, the better.'

Suzie squirmed in her seat. 'Surely the aim is not to alienate too many people.'

'I'd say a little honesty goes a long way.'

Suzie knew what was coming next.

'Starting with your age.' Alice was firm. 'The oldest man you want is five years younger than you.'

'Everyone lies about their ages in these things. You have to play the game.'

'Plus, "fun and energetic" just sounds like you want lots of sex.'

Suzie stretched out in her chair. 'I'd say that was honest. And I did say intelligent, too.'

'Great. But you haven't said they have to be attractive.'

Suzie leaned over the table to reread the page. 'Haven't I?'

'Well, at least you're not pretending to me that looks don't matter.'

'Of course they matter. Just let me add it to the wish list.'

'I still think you need to be more honest.'

'Come on then, what would you put?'

Alice thought for a moment and then started scribbling on an adjacent piece of paper. It was much easier writing one of these for someone else. Nodding as she reviewed her handiwork, she drew a box around the ad for extra authenticity and handed the sheet to Suzie, who read it back to her.

'**Age is really just a number.** Attractive, high-energy, young-at-heart but mature fiftysomething woman, WLTM good-looking men of all ages with a sense of humour and life-experience for fun, companionship and adventures.'

'"Young at heart but mature"? Well, that makes me sound like I'm weeks away from my Zimmer frame.'

'It does not. Besides, it says you're high-energy and attractive.'

'Which I am.'

'Exactly.'

Suzie reread the copy silently. 'You don't think "companionship" sounds like I'm too old for sex?'

'Of course not.'

'I'm not so sure. Not bad—in parts—I suppose.'

Alice accepted the compliment graciously by punching the air. 'You're welcome, it's a pleasure.'

'Do you think I could stipulate own hair, own teeth? You know, OHOT.'

'I'm not sure that's a universally recognised abbreviation.'

'Well, it should be.'

'I wouldn't alienate people by adding mysterious categories. God knows who you'd get responding.'

'Come on then, let's look at yours.'

It was Alice's turn to hesitate. Clearing her throat, she started reading aloud at breakneck speed.

'West End Girl.'

Suzie interrupted her with a snort. 'Well, that's a blatant lie for a start.'

'Hammersmith is west.'

'West End says Bond Street to me. Definitely Zone 1.'

'It also happens to be the name of one of my favourite Pet Shop Boys singles.'

Suzie shook her head. 'Which the man replying may never have even heard of.'

'Then, to be frank, I don't want to hear from him anyway.'
'Now who's being picky?'
'I've always been picky. So are you going to let me finish?'
'Sure.'
Alice cleared her throat and started again.

'**West End Girl.** 29-year-old woman seeks attractive and intelligent n/s man with both a sense of humour and a serious side, for good times, evenings out and maybe more. Must know own mind and be capable of self-sufficiency. Serial monogamists need not apply.'

'Could you be any more negative?'
'That's not negative.'
'And what the hell is "n/s"?'
'Nonsmoking.'
'Oh, for goodness' sake, what if he has the occasional cigarette but is perfect in every other way?'
'If he has the occasional cigarette he's not going to be perfect for me, now, is he?'
'I'd try to be a bit less of a fascist if I was you.'
'It's my ad.'
'Clearly.'
'Well, go on then, do your worst...' It was fighting talk from someone who was only pretending she was way beyond caring.

Suzie took Alice's copy and annotated it before reading aloud.

'**Once bitten forever shy.** 29-year-old cynical divor-cée seeks attractive guy with both a sense of humour and a serious side, for good times, nights out and maybe more. Must know own mind and be capable of self-sufficiency. Serial monogamists need not apply.'

'Oh, come on, it's practically the same as mine.'

'Except in this version you have a history.'

Taking the page from her mother, Alice reread the lines, mouthing the words to herself to get a complete sense of what she was shopping for. She looked up. 'Do you have to put divorcée in there?'

'Well, you are one, aren't you?'

'You're one three times over and I didn't feel the need to point it out.'

'At my age people expect it. At your age it's a unique selling point.'

'It wasn't my fault though.'

'Where does it say that it was? Anyway, it'll be a good conversation starter.'

'I always thought it was better to start off looking forward.'

'You were the one who was championing honesty a moment ago.'

Suzie's polyphonic ring tone interrupted them. Sliding out from behind the table, she went into the kitchen to find her phone.

Alice shouted after her. 'Maybe Ryan wants you to collect him from the station, too.' Angry, she threw herself back in her chair.

Suzie consulted the call display before answering. 'Geoffrey.'

Relieved to no longer be under scrutiny, Alice moved her chair around to face the sun, and knotting her T-shirt under her breasts, closed her eyes and slouched down into a semi-comfortable sunbathing position.

Suzie sat on the back step with the phone. 'Lovely afternoon, thanks. Lavender bushes? No, she's already got one.' Suzie laughed. 'I don't think so, have you seen the size of her lawn…?'

Alice kept her eyes firmly closed, pretending she couldn't

hear a thing, determined not to interject. It was something Suzie always did when she was on the phone and it was intensely irritating.

'...Cinema tonight? What's on? Oh, I'd love to see that. Seven-thirty in Putney would suit me perfectly.' Suzie paused. 'I don't suppose you might be able to pick me up on the way? Fab. In fact...'

Alice listened as Suzie's tone became more appealing.

'...you don't fancy helping a damsel in distress, now, do you? It's just I've been having a little car trouble.'

Alice smiled to herself. Suzie was shameless. And "trouble" definitely sounded like something mechanical rather than irresponsible.

'...I take it you haven't been drinking? Excellent. Well, that makes one of us.'

Her knight in shining Honda on his way, Suzie went upstairs to change. As Alice scrunched up their handiwork and filed it in the recycling bin, she realised that when it came to men, she still had a lot to learn.

Chapter Four

36 days to go
Suzie 3, Alice 0

'Tom. Tom Taylor?' Alice stood in the overly feng-shuied reception area of the Whole Body Centre, and gingerly resting her hand on her next client's shoulder, increased her volume slightly. 'Mr. Taylor?'

Tom opened his eyes. The voice was so smooth, the walls so white, and the decor so stark that for a split second he wondered if he was in heaven.

'I see you're finding this month's *Marie Claire* riveting.' Alice took a couple of paces back, hoping to put him at his ease. She hated waking people. Plus, personally she always felt at her most vulnerable when she'd just been roused.

Colour filled Tom's cheeks as he realised he must have dozed off. One minute he'd been half reading an article about G spots, and then… Luckily, the well-thumbed magazine had fallen forward onto his stomach and his dignity was intact.

He'd always had the ability to fall deeply asleep in spare minutes. Perfect power-napping skills if you were Ellen MacArthur and had a sail to trim, distinctly less impressive if you were getting seven or eight hours of sleep a night, as well.

Alice stepped forward, determined to put him out of his misery. 'Hi. I'm Alice Harrison. We spoke on the phone on Monday. Can I get you anything? Water? Coffee? A duvet?'

'No, no. I'm fine.' Tom pretended to scratch his nose whilst exhaling into his semicupped hand to check the freshness of his breath. 'Well, maybe a glass of water. And a water butt.'

Alice stopped in her water-gathering tracks.

'You know, to immerse my head in.' Tom wondered what on earth he was talking about.

'We try not to stockpile our rain in Mayfair, but a glass of water I can definitely do.' Alice removed a bottle of mineral water from a glass-fronted fridge in the corner of the plush waiting room. 'Feel free to pour it over yourself if it helps. So sorry to have kept you.'

'On the contrary, thank you for squeezing me in. I just suspected that if I left it too long, I'd leave it all together.' Tom shifted his weight from leg to leg and willed himself to stop rambling on. It wasn't a usual trait of his.

'Well, if you'd like to come this way, we can get things moving...'

Alice managed to contain a smile as Tom followed her, clutching a motorcycle helmet, his hair sticking up in several places where, from the looks of things, he had raked it with his fingers.

Thanks to Suzie's labelling skills, Alice's kitchen calendar had effectively become a countdown to August 26th and as a result, no one was safe from her scrutiny—man in street, man in HMV, man on television, man in front of her in supermarket queue. On Saturday, she'd even decided the boiler-service man had nice shoulders, although as her hot water remained as lukewarm as ever, that had appeared to be the extent of his attraction.

Tom was certainly a physical improvement on most of her clients. Dark jeans, brown Timberland boots, a slightly creased beige V neck over a white T-shirt and a fairly new black leather biker jacket with wine-red lining, slung over his shoulder. His dark hair sported grey flecks of distinction and a musky waft of something expensive accompanied him into her consulting room.

Fully awake by the time Alice ushered him past her temporary name plaque on the door, Tom automatically turned his mobile phone off before extending his hand to greet her formally and start again. Alice shook it firmly as she watched him surveying the plain white walls and modern paintings— squares of colour carefully placed to add warmth but not to provoke any thought.

'Nice place.'

'If you like clean lines and cacti. But for one day a week it does the job. Do take a seat.'

'One day a week? I'm clearly in the wrong business.' Tom smiled disarmingly as he lowered himself onto the sofa opposite Alice's chair.

'Actually, it's more like six. But most of my individual client work is done over the phone. Clients have less and less time these days.'

'It's a twenty-first-century disease. If you're not busy, you're not important.'

She was much younger than he'd imagined and more attractive—or at least she would be if she literally let her hair down. Idly he wondered if he should have been lying down, hands clasped on his chest. He wasn't at all nervous. Just intrigued as to what she could possibly know about life that he didn't.

Alice wrote Tom's name at the top of a page and underlined it authoritatively.

'So, Mr. Taylor. First things first. Do you mind if I call you Tom?'

'If you want me to answer, I'd suggest that was an excellent plan.'

Alice smiled wanly, hoping his cocksure attitude was down to nerves rather than an ego she was going to have to wrestle.

'Right, so Tom, I'm just going to take some notes while we're chatting and if at the end of today's session you think you'd like to come back for more, I'll start a client file for you. As I mentioned on the phone, there's no charge for today, but if you want to go ahead I'll need you to commit to six months.'

Suddenly feeling a little less comfortable and a lot more under observation, Tom reminded himself that he hadn't committed to anything yet.

'So, first things first, why do you think you're here?'

'On the planet?' He was surprised at the depth of her opener.

Alice kept her tone as neutral and welcoming as possible. It had been a long week. 'I was thinking more along the lines of, in my office, this afternoon.'

He paused.

'It's okay. It's not a test.'

Tom smiled. 'I better warn you that the only coach I've had since school was a personal trainer at the gym and that didn't last very long. I'm not very good at being told what to do. You could say I'm a bit of a control freak. That said, there are aspects of my life that aren't really under control at all.' Tom stopped abruptly before he incriminated himself any further, surprised at his candour.

'This is exactly where I come in. My aim is to help you discover what it is in your life that you want to change, improve, redress, balance, whatever it may be… The idea is for us to work together as a team to create goals for you and then make sure you reach them.'

Tom nodded. 'Sounds simple enough.' This certainly had been a month of firsts. First time he'd spontaneously cancelled a meeting and left London for a breath of noncorporate air. First time he'd been chatted up on the Eurostar. First time he'd taken an older woman out on a date. First time (Rene Russo aside) he'd even fancied an older woman. First time he'd confessed to a third party that something might be missing from his ostensibly perfect life. First time he'd made an appointment to see a life coach.

Alice smiled encouragingly. 'The theory is indeed very simple. The execution is the more difficult bit. So why don't we start with you telling me a little bit about yourself. Whatever you feel comfortable with. As much or as little as you like at this stage.'

Alice sat back in her black leather swivel chair and jotted a few things down on the notepad on her lap as Tom went into his career in an unnecessary and incomprehensible level of detail, no doubt sticking to his comfort zone. Alice was only too happy to watch and listen. Finally he paused for a moment of reflection.

Alice seized her moment. 'So, why did you come to see me?'

Tom shrugged his shoulders. 'Curiosity, I guess.' He was starting to wonder if, perhaps, this was a first he could do without. But Tom Taylor wasn't a quitter. And if he'd survived a bungee jump, he was sure this would be a walk in the park.

'Right.' Alice doodled a flower on her pad, using the *o* in Tom as the centre. 'So no specific issues or problems?'

'No. None.'

Alice knew she just had to wait.

'Any areas or feelings of concern at work or in your personal life? Any changes you'd like to make?'

Tom's lower lip protruded as he shook his head emphatically and Alice smiled at her notepad. Denial was all too common in new clients, particularly male ones.

'Excellent. Although you wouldn't be failing in any way if there were one or two, however small. We've all been programmed to believe we can cope with everything. But there's a huge gulf between coping and living, and an even greater one between living and living life on your own terms. We need to know what your goals for the future are, or at least help you define and establish them.'

We? Tom was faintly amused. In fifteen minutes they had apparently become a team of two. But there was something quite comforting about the idea of having a personal cheerleader. 'I'm not sure there's anything I want to change outright. It's more, I guess, a case of improve or refocus.' Was that his final answer?

'That's an excellent start.'

Despite himself, Tom felt his chest swell at the compliment. He knew he was going to be good at this. He was good at everything he put his mind to.

'All you need to do now is give me a starting point. Anything. A feeling. A thought. An aim. Don't think too hard.'

Obediently, Tom barely paused to consider his options before replying.

'Well, I guess on paper I have more than enough and yet I've definitely started to think that something might be missing. Not that I wake up under a dark cloud or anything as dramatic as that but…' Tom wondered whether Alice had laced the air-conditioning with some sort of truth serum. 'What I tell you is confidential, isn't it?'

'Of course. Exactly as we discussed on the phone last week.'

'I'm lonely.' He was? Maybe someone had hypnotised him in the waiting room.

'And why do you feel that needs to be a secret?' Alice wrote a few things down as Tom craned his neck to try and make out some of the words.

Tom was tentative. 'I suppose I've had so much success on so many levels—well, maybe I feel that I have no right to be complaining. I've made my own choices.' He stole a look at his watch.

'Don't worry, not much longer to go, Tom.'

Damn. Apparently she had eyes in the top of her head. Typical woman. But it was definitely beer o'clock.

She looked up. 'Take as much time as you need.'

Tom stared at one of the squares of colour masquerading as a picture, and focused on trying to remember what he was supposed to be taking time over.

'You were saying that you're lonely.' Alice's prompt was timely.

'Not lonely, exactly. I'm with people most of the time. I'm busy…'

Alice nodded. Here was a client she could relate to.

'Yet I'd say that very few people really know me. I'm great at networking, at befriending clients, but it's all a load of crap really. I play golf and talk bollocks to people who don't care about me—it's just in their business interest to keep me on side.'

Alice met his gaze for a second before noting a few more words down. 'Good news, Tom—you're human.'

'Look, I don't want to waste your time.' Tom crossed his

legs and folded his arms before forcing himself to rethink his body language.

'Oh no, that's not what I meant at all.' Alice silently berated herself. 'I meant to insinuate that the human condition is a complex one. No two days are ever the same.' Much better.

Tom sat back, the jiggling of his uncrossed left knee the only remaining visible sign of tension.

'Sometimes it just feels like my life, my personal life especially, is a messy desk and I've suddenly looked up to notice there's a whole lot more out there and I want to get out of my chair. And—'

He interrupted himself.

'I'm sorry, that sounds like such a pretentious load of metaphorical wank... Jesus, I really didn't mean to swear. Bollocks. Crap. Sorry. Words aren't really my thing. Give me a loan agreement or a balance sheet and—'

'No need to apologise. Life's fucking tough sometimes.'

Tom smiled as Alice succeeded in putting him at his ease. 'Look, I'm not sure that this wouldn't be easier to solve over a few pints in the pub... That is, if I could get more of my mates to meet me after work these days. Most of them are rushing home to read bedtime stories or pretending to be having a beer with me whilst playing away from home—a pretty sorry state of affairs, really. It's not that I'm short of friends. They just have no idea that I feel like this, I guess.'

'No doubt because you haven't told them.'

'No doubt.' No shit.

'So can I take it you're quite sceptical of all this?'

'What, paying for a human sounding board?'

'Is that what you think I do?'

'Well, um...'

'Fair enough.' Alice was almost enjoying his slight discomfort. Which made her a mild megalomaniac? She suppressed her dark side and sent St. Alice to the rescue.

'I may be cynical but I'm also ignorant, your worst nightmare, really.' Tom smiled. 'I'm afraid I haven't seen you on TV, either.'

'Thank goodness. Seriously, there's no brainwashing allowed. You can stay, you can go, you can think about it for a while. All I'm here to do is try, if you'd like me to, to help you reach your potential. Tell me, honestly, why you came along today.'

'I made an appointment.'

Alice raised an eyebrow. 'Okay, there's no point being defensive. I am definitely not the enemy.' Alice retied her hair before getting up and relocating herself behind her desk. Silent, he stared at her. She prompted him. 'You're here today because…'

'You came highly recommended.'

Alice nodded, clasping her hands together to prevent herself from fiddling with her pen and hoped it didn't look like she was praying. Networking was her lifeblood. 'May I ask by whom?'

'Suzie Fletcher.' Tom stopped there. He wasn't ready to tell her everything yet.

Alice hesitated.

'She writes that column in the Saturday papers, you know, "The State I'm In," and she's a friend of mine…' Tom stopped himself as he noted Alice's expression. 'What?'

'Oh, nothing.' Alice suppressed the smile on her lips. At least Richard had given her a different surname. 'I've known her for years. Quite a character.'

Delighted to have someone in common with Alice, Tom built his part. 'Most definitely.'

Alice observed Tom carefully and wondered why, amongst

all the irrelevancies Suzie seemed determined to bore her with, her mother hadn't mentioned giving her number to this particular chap.

Tom sat forward expectantly. 'So, do you think I need you? Sorry, let me rephrase that. Do you think you can help me or do I just need to stop expecting so much?'

Alice rested her forearms on the table, shoulder width apart.

'I'd suggest a few more sessions but it's important that you find the right person at the outset, so if you'd rather see a man, or someone else, I can make some recommendations now. And as I mentioned earlier, whoever you choose will need to see you regularly for a period of at least six months.'

Getting up from her chair, she walked over to the water-cooler in the corner of the room, refilled her glass and took a couple of restorative sips before perching on the front of her desk, pleased that she was wearing her favourite suit.

Tom watched her. 'Do you think I might be having a mid-life crisis?'

'I think that's a conveniently general, umbrella term used to cover any slightly erratic male behaviour between the ages of thirty and fifty. So, no, not per se, although—' Alice nodded in the direction of his crash helmet and flashed him a grin '—off the record, clearly you already have the motorbike.'

A sheepish half smile appeared at the corner of Tom's mouth. 'Hey, even London air feels fresh at thirty miles per hour.'

'I suppose the next question is whether you have the younger trophy girlfriend to complete the set?' Alice wished she'd thought to pause for breath and vet her response.

Tom had apparently not been fazed by her amateur heckle. 'Is this confidential?'

'Of course.' How Alice wished it wasn't. Although there

would be something quite empowering about not giving Suzie the satisfaction of dissecting yet another man she had sent her way.

Tom paused. 'How would a slightly older woman fit in to the stereotype?'

Alice was encouraged to finally observe a self-deprecating note of cheekiness in his expression. 'You're all clear. Nothing midlife about that crisis.'

'But you do think it's a crisis? I mean, nothing's happened, but…"

Tom looked up at her so earnestly that Alice wanted to give him a reassuring hug. 'I doubt it very much. A crossroads perhaps, but, well, you know what they say.'

'I'm not sure that I do.'

'Variety is the spice of life.' No wonder she loved curries. In the absence of variety, she had to get her spices from somewhere.

'Before we go any further—' Tom interrupted Alice, anxious to get everything out in the open before he changed his mind '—I guess I should probably mention that I've never been good at, make that I've always been terrible at, commitment—except where work is concerned. It's almost a condition. On the personal side of things it's almost as if I've never really wanted to grow up or take responsibility for myself…'

Tom forced himself to stop talking. She hadn't even asked him a question.

Alice scribbled Peter Pan on her jotter. 'We're only talking about a few phone calls.' She hoped her tone was reassuring. 'I call you and if you want to reschedule I promise I won't take it personally. Just don't stand me up more than once or I will dump you. And believe me, it'll cost you.'

'Doesn't it always?' Tom laughed, relieved that Alice had

dissipated some of the tension. 'Trouble is, I'm not used to not being in charge of situations or meetings. When I say "not used to" I do of course mean "not terribly comfortable with".' See, he could see right through this therapist stuff.

Alice nodded. 'Thanks for the disclaimer. I suggest that you take the weekend to think about whether or not you think this is a good idea or just a load of New Age, newfangled, time-wasting, overpriced, state-the-obvious nonsense.'

Tom wondered how she'd managed to tap into his thoughts quite so accurately. 'Do you do mind reading, too?'

'Don't think you're the first sceptic I've come across. I used to work in television and I'm sure I would have thought this was all a load of claptrap in those days.'

'What changed?'

'Everything.'

Suddenly Tom wanted to know more.

'Now, if you have any questions over the next few days, feel free to give me a call on the mobile. My number is on my card.'

'I wouldn't want to disturb you.'

'If I don't want to be disturbed my phone won't be on.'

Tom smiled. He had a feeling they were going to get on just fine.

As Alice pointed Tom in the direction of the Gents, she noticed the silhouette of another man sitting in the darkened waiting room. No sign of the receptionist, either. And they were closed.

The figure stood up and, stepping into the light, turned to face her. 'Hello, Al.'

'Richard! What on earth are you doing lurking in the shadows? Something wrong with your phone?' As he approached, she noticed something unusual about his appearance. 'Oh, no, Rich, did someone die?' She honestly couldn't remember the last time she had seen him wearing a suit, and his hair was much less messy than normal, or at least a lot less fashionable.

'I had a job interview.'

'As a lawyer?'

'Yeah yeah. Go on, mock me. Chisel away at my self-esteem. I just wanted to make a good impression.'

'Sorry, you startled me. So what's the position? Director General of the BBC?'

'Not yet.' Richard may have appeared laissez-faire but underneath his usually dressed-down exterior lurked a fiercely ambitious core.

Alice cocked her head. 'You're not going to tell me what it is, are you?'

'I promise you'll be in the first round of calls if I get it.'

Alice took a breath. *First round of calls.* She used to be his first port of call.

'Come on, let's get a drink.' Richard leaned in and gave her a fleeting kiss on the lips.

At his touch, Alice could feel herself capitulating. His presence was comforting. If only his true colours hadn't turned out to be pink and purple.

'I don't know if you've been deliberately avoiding me or not, but I've missed you.'

Richard had always been genuine. His brand of introspection, intensity and slight geekiness, reminded her of Andrew McCarthy in his brat-pack heyday. And she missed him, too. He was the only man she'd ever lived with. And now she had to live without him.

'I've missed you, too.' Alice stroked his cheek affectionately.

'Hi.' Tom approached awkwardly, out of the corner of Alice's eye, and instinctively she took a step away from Richard.

'Hi.' For the first time in her life she wished that Richard was more overtly gay. Hot pants, silver T-shirt, a Freddie Mercury moustache, that sort of thing...

'Sorry to interrupt—but thanks for just now. I'll admit I arrived not expecting much and now—well, now I guess I'm keen to see what happens next.'

'That's great, Tom.'

'So...'

Alice watched him fiddle with the strap on the motorcycle helmet in his hand.

'...Where do we go from here?'

'Why don't I give you a call on Monday and we can set up another appointment. I have a few slots available...' Alice quickly silenced Richard's approaching guffaw at her accidental innuendo, with a look he knew only too well. '...And we went through the fee structure on the phone, didn't we?'

'Yup. Perfect. Well, you've certainly given me lots to think about.'

She hadn't even started yet. 'You have a good weekend.'

'And you.' Tom acknowledged Richard with a nod.

Alice snatched the opportunity to set the record straight. 'Sorry, Tom, how rude of me. Allow me to introduce Richard, my ex-husband.'

If Tom was surprised she had one of those, he didn't show it.

The men shook hands.

'A pleasure. Now I've really got to go. There are four excited, hungry children waiting for me at Planet Hollywood...'

Four children? Alice made a mental note to bring that up in their next session.

'...And Helen wouldn't believe me for one minute if I tried to tell her where I've been. Speak to you next week.'

Helen? Maybe he was being less open than he'd first appeared. And maybe she hadn't been quite as thorough as usual.

Richard followed Alice back into her office as she gathered the papers from her desk and placed them in a cardboard folder, which she then slipped into her soft brown leather briefcase. She wasn't due back at the centre for another week.

He sat down in the chair opposite her desk. 'So, what's going on there?'

'Where?'

Richard mimicked his ex-wife. '*That's great Tom. This is my ex-husband.*'

'Richard.' Alice's tone was humour free. 'He's a client.'

Richard linked his fingers behind his head. 'I'm not surprised you were flirting. He's lovely.'

'Seems to be.' Alice surprised herself with the candour of her answer. 'But totally off limits. And that wasn't flirting.'

'Of course not.' Richard maintained eye contact.

'Don't do that.'

'What?'

'Undermine me with your tone of voice.'

'I'm not.' Years of experience had taught him to back down while there was still time. 'But sometimes you really ought to live a little. *We* met through work.'

'And look how stunningly well that went.'

'We had some great times. Besides, pressure's on, Zoë's told me about your mother's idea.'

Total lack of privacy. One of the few disadvantages to Zoë having become and remained a friend of Richard's.

'Make that scheme.'

'So does that mean you are back on the open market? I'm sure I can help you with a few blind dates if this Tom thing doesn't work.'

'Tom's a potential client. He has come to me for professional help.'

'Well, maybe you could help him personally, too.' Richard loved winding her up.

'Didn't you hear him mention his four children? And he doesn't strike me as the unfaithful type.' Alice loved piecing a new client's life together.

'There you go, already defending him.'

If looks could kill or merely maim, and Richard hadn't had the skin density of a rhino, he would have been on his way to intensive care. Instead, he sat sideways in her chair, hanging his legs over the armrest, successfully taunting her.

Richard fiddled with something under his cuff. 'I think you really like this one.'

'I only met him forty minutes ago, how could I possibly know anything?'

'I think you have an inkling. And I'm happy to inform you he's got heterosexual written all over him.'

'Good. But I hardly think I need your gaydar on this one. He's just said he's got children.'

'I had a wife, don't forget.'

Alice juggled her collection of bags.

Richard leapt to his feet. 'Here, let me carry those. And just for the record, should you be interested, he likes you, too.'

'This is your final warning, Mr. Harrison. No one invited you here tonight.'

'The thing is, I need your help, too.'

'Oh, really.' Alice couldn't have sounded any more cynical.

'Firstly, I need you to find the nail scissors that you no doubt have in that capacious handbag-cum-holdall and help me remove this cotton friendship band that Rob brought back from his last business trip before someone thinks I've joined some cult or Kabbalah group.'

'As if anyone would think that, let alone notice it.'

'Actually, it was the second question I was asked in my interview. And secondly, I need you to escort me to the nearest bar.'

'Finally—' Alice linked arms with Richard, signifying a truce '—something I can help you with.'

Alice couldn't wait to have a drink or six. A night away from her strategising mother could only be a good thing. Suzie's intricate and convoluted plans to find herself a man would have made Thomas Crown look slapdash.

As Alice locked the office door behind her, the weekend officially began. Her own life had definitely been on much more of an even keel since she'd removed relationships from the equation. And now she only had five weeks to rock the boat. She was feeling seasick already.

Somewhere in the midst of the tangle of bags, her phone was ringing. Alice ignored it and moments later Richard's mobile started buzzing. He looked at the screen before handing it to Alice. 'Zoë, for you.'

Alice flicked the handset open. 'Hello, gorgeous. Happy Friday. Want to come for drinkies with me and Richard?'

'Just like the old days, eh?'

'I'm not going to let my twenties go without a fight.'

'Good for you. Although I think my thirties are better still.'

'That's what I like to hear. So, coming to meet us?'

Zoë paused. 'I can't, actually. I'm going out.'

'On a date?' Alice teased.

'Just a few drinks with a guy from work.'

Alice started paying attention. 'On a Friday night? This is me you're talking to. It's never just "some guy" and it's never "just a few".'

'The sky's blue, the sun's shining and I fancy a cold beer or three. Plus, I've known Jake long enough to know he's not an axe murderer and that he's married.'

'Controversial.'

'Happily so. She's just out of town.'

'Dangerous.'

'Not at all. I have no spare emotional energy. I just thought it'd be more fun than drinking alone and, newsflash, married men can go out for a beer without having an affair.'

'No need to justify it to me.'

'You're the one reading into it. You sound like your mother. Anyway, I predict that soon you'll be asked out for quite a few drinks yourself.'

'Don't give up your day job.'

Zoë hesitated. 'So I take it you haven't seen tonight's paper?'

'I'm only just leaving work now.'

'Make sure you check page 55.'

'Will do.' Alice started to wrap the conversation up. Now that Zoë had mentioned a cold beer, she was incredibly thirsty.

'Hang on, I bet Richard's got a copy.'

Alice checked out her ex-husband. Not only did Richard have one, but it was conveniently tucked under his arm. Attracting his attention, Alice pointed at the paper. 'Page 55. What's he looking for? Zo?'

'Take a guess.'

Richard looked up. 'Are you sure about the page number? In my edition, it's the personals.'

Alice's heart raced. And not in a good way. 'Shit, Zo. Tell me she hasn't.'

'I'm not a hundred percent sure. But from what you've told me, I'd say halfway down, second column. Women seeking men. They're yours, aren't they?'

Alice scanned the page. Both versions. All four of them. In black and white. 'But I don't understand. Where did she…'

'Just thought you'd like to know. Got to run. I'm late.'

Zoë had gone. Just like that. And well before Alice had had a chance to ask her what she was doing reading the personals anyway.

'Sorry, Richard. One more call and we're on our way.'

'Take your time.' Sitting down on the steps to the building, Richard immersed himself in the pages. 'Some of these are hilarious.'

Effusive, her mother answered after half a ring. 'Hello, darling. Guess what?'

'You're an interfering old woman?'

'Just call me Cupid.'

'How about stupid?'

'Oh, shush, darling, it's just a bit of fun.'

'I thought I threw the drafts away.'

'You put them in the bin for recycling. I recycled them.'

From now on Alice was going to shred anything important or, better still, incinerate it.

'You are the most unlikely bin lady.'

'Better than being Bin Laden.'

'What is the matter with you?'

'At least I haven't had a sense of humour bypass.'

'Why on earth run with all four of them?'

'Think of it as a social experiment.'

'You're unbelievable. You're a total crackpot.'

'You can thank me later. Oh and, just so you know, I've posted them on a dating site, too.'

'You're unbelievable, Mum.'

'I know.'

'I didn't mean in a good way.' Alice shook her head. 'Do you have any idea how embarrassing this is?'

'They're anonymous. That's the whole point.'

'What a waste of money.'

'Consider it my treat.'

'Why couldn't you just treat me to a facial or something?'

'You can have one of those before your first date if you're good.'

Alice was furious. 'Why stop with the Internet? How about a billboard?'

'Listen, when you calm down and you get a chance, check out *www.cupidcantypetoo.com*. It's the site everyone's talking about at the moment. I have to say, we look great.'

'There are photos?' Alice's voice was becoming squeakier with each sentence.

'Only small ones.'

She closed her eyes and opened them again in the hope this was all a dream. Now she knew how Jack Bauer must feel. This wasn't even one hour of revelations out of a potential twenty-four and she was already losing her grip.

'Which you took while I was asleep/looking the other way/in the shower?'

'There's no need to get hysterical, darling, I just scanned a couple of good ones.'

'Scanned? At your age you're barely supposed to understand the concept of e-mails.'

'Look, if you want your log-in details, let me know. I've got to go.'

Alice hung up and collapsed onto the step next to Richard. 'I need a drink now. Vodka on the rocks, next to the rocks and under the rocks. Make it a double.'

As he arched an eyebrow, Alice could tell he thought she was overreacting. 'I thought this dating thing was just supposed to be a bit of fun.'

'That was her initial pitch.'

Richard put his arm around her and felt Alice relax slightly. 'Look, it can only be as serious as you allow it to be.'

'Who's the coach?'

'You are. But you forget, I'm really quite good at this analysis stuff.'

'Ah, but you forget, I remember perfectly.'

'So, are you really looking for The One this time?' Richard linked his arm in Alice's and leaning on each other, they stood up together.

Alice shook her head. 'I don't think so. Just a Half-Decent One.'

'For one night only?'

'Not necessarily. But her birthday is one party I can't go to alone.'

'Is that the Fletcher competitive gene kicking in?'

Alice frowned. 'Unfortunately, I think it probably is. That woman knows me far too well.'

Chapter Five

24 days remaining
Suzie 4, Alice 0

Alice's fists punched the air in turn as she increased her pace for the home straight. The music from her iPod Shuffle obliterated the sound of her panting as, against all the odds, her legs kept going. She hadn't grown to love jogging any more over the years, but being outdoors, especially by water, was definitely more life-affirming than going to the gym and watching news channels whilst undertaking a "forest walk" on a cross-trainer machine that had never even been exposed to fresh air.

It was a beautiful June morning, and just after nine the sun was already warm on her skin, the solar power putting an extra spring in her step as she watched a few rowing crews sharing her pain on the river. Fortunately for everyone in the vicinity, she didn't have enough spare breath to sing along as her playlist offered up another of her favourite exercise anthems and her heart did its best to keep up with the musical beats per minute.

Wishing there was a way to dance and run at the same time, Alice left the path at the River Café and wove her way between the parked cars and into the maze of near-identical residential streets of the Edwardian Crabtree Estate.

Slowing to a walk, she breathed deeply and reached the end of her road in a state of near euphoria as endorphins flooded her system. Having her mother to stay was certainly doing wonders for her exercise regime. A running-along-the-river-before-work habit: the perfect way to avoid endless dating analysis over morning coffee by simply ensuring their paths crossed less often than normal.

Alice raced into her kitchen and downed a pint of cold water in one, enjoying the slightly salty flavour coming from her top lip as a stream of sweat ran down her back.

As she drained the last few drops, Alice caught her mother's eye through the base of her glass. Apparently perfectly at home, Suzie was sitting at *her* kitchen table, in one of *her* dressing gowns, *her* as-yet-unread copy of the *Times* open beside her. It was like a scene from *The Hand That Rocks the Cradle*, only in this case it was the mother who was stealing her daughter's life. No nanny required. Regardless of the distortion, Suzie's expression was an unflattering combination of shock and disgust. Alice returned to the tap and prepared herself another pint of Thames Water's finest.

Suzie broke her stunned silence. 'Look at the state of you. I know we haven't got long but I didn't mean we literally had to chase men. And before you start following the sporty types along the towpath, you might want to pop in to Niketown or check out the new line of workout gear that Stella McCartney's been designing for Adidas. You've had that T-shirt since university.'

Alice was still on her post-exercise high. Nothing could touch her. Not even the thought of her first date that evening, nor the fact that she no longer had even a centimetre of personal space.

'I bet you haven't even thought about what you're going to wear tonight.'

'Aren't you running hideously late, Mum? I thought you had a ten o'clock editorial meeting in town?'

'Postponed. I'm a bit behind schedule, plus I've managed to book myself a last-minute bikini wax at that place round the corner, you know, the Ugly Stick.'

Alice smiled despite herself. 'You mean the Beauty Branch.'

'Whatever. And I can't afford to get stuck late at the office.' Suzie's smile was far from enigmatic. 'I have to leave enough time to get ready for my date tonight and you know I'm not a quick slick of lip gloss and a wave of the hairbrush sort of a girl.'

If Suzie was still a girl, Alice was still an embryo.

'But you had a date yesterday.'

'So?' The glint in Suzie's eye was audacious. 'I also have another one lined up for tomorrow.'

Three dates in three days. Alice did her best to mask her admiration with disapproval. In the presence of Superdater, she felt like a dating tortoise.

'How about you? Any more in the pipeline?'

Avoiding eye contact by burying her face in the hand towel, Alice dried herself before throwing it into the washing machine. Time to change the subject.

'Do you know, I never used to sweat this much. Do you think it's hormonal?'

It was probably nerves. Alice couldn't believe she was meeting a man for a drink later who had contacted her over the Internet. She couldn't help feeling she was a dead woman walking. But at least now she knew that she could be sprinting if he looked truly awful.

'Doubt it. You just never used to run so much…' Bemused Suzie watched Alice over the rim of her unofficial glasses. Magnifying x 3, and available over the counter, she had justified their purchase to minimalise the proliferation of lines in her eye area whilst maintaining her vision was still perfect. '…I remember the days when getting you to run anywhere was impossible. You used to ask me to write you a note every week to get you out of gymnastics.'

'That was only because they used to make us do forward rolls on the wooden floor.'

'Ingrown toenail, I don't think so. More like ingrown attitude.'

'I could have been crippled. Plus, who ever looked good in a leotard? I mean, really good?' Alice sighed. 'I'm never going to have any secrets while you're still alive, am I?' Slowly she started to stretch her calves and quads. She didn't want to be limping to the restaurant later.

'Parents have a duty to embarrass their children, and as you only have one parent left…'

Alice shuddered. The thought of having two parents around was almost inconceivable, although maybe her Dad would have been on her side.

'Anyway, look how well you've turned out.'

Alice felt a ripple of pride. As old as she got and as reluctant as she was to admit it, she still wanted her mother to be proud of her.

'All this exercise clearly suits you. I'd try to join you one morning but there's only so much I can expect of my knee joints and my cod liver oil supplements…'

Suzie took a sip of strong black coffee. Enough caffeine, Alice noted, to undoubtedly reverse the positive effects of the green tea she liked to be seen drinking in public.

'…Anyway, what is this, a half day?'

Alice composed herself. From the moment she had squeezed past Suzie's cervix nearly thirty years ago, she had, apparently, been supposed to be able to take as much criticism—loosely rebranded as advice—as Suzie felt like giving her.

'It's not even ten. I haven't got a client call for another half hour.'

Tom Taylor. His third phone session in ten days.

'And filming for *Get A Life* starts when?'

'Monday.' Alice drained her pint glass for a second time.

'And what are you going to do with your hair this series?'

Alice subconsciously retied her scrunchie, now damp with sweat. 'Wash it?'

'Seriously, darling, that stylist didn't do you any favours…'

Alice forced herself to take a deep breath, grateful that UK citizens didn't have a right to bear arms.

'…I'm just saying that maybe you should think about a slightly newer look. Why don't you see if Leo can squeeze you in before Monday. He'd be only too happy to help.'

'Mum, the last time I let Leo anywhere near me, I left the salon with a few red highlights. And while that might work for Sharon Osborne, it definitely doesn't do it for me. Especially when the nearest I've ever got to heavy metal is my Le Creuset casserole dish.' Alice stopped herself mid-rant and headed to the hall. 'I'm going to grab a shower.'

Suzie shouted after her, 'It's only because you don't flirt with him.'

'I don't even like him.'

'What's wrong with paying the man a few compliments?' Suzie looked up at the kitchen clock. 'Are you sure you've got time for a shower?'

Counting to ten silently, Alice jogged upstairs and straight into the bathroom out of harm's way.

★ ★ ★

Still-wet hair dripping down the back of her neck, Alice reached her study with a couple of minutes to spare. Her much-loved and much-faded old jeans were soft on her clean and freshly moisturised skin and her favourite working-from-home, once-black-now-grey T-shirt smelled comfortingly of fabric conditioner. Her feet were relishing their nakedness on the carpet after the sweaty confines of her trainers.

Seated at her desk, she looked out proudly over her handkerchief-size garden and those of the neighbours and wondered how Richard had ever managed to convince her that sunbathing topless had been an option. Thanks to him, there must have been at least six households that had seen her breasts—and only a few more men.

Extracting Tom's file from her brushed-steel filing cabinet, she flicked through the notes she'd made during their last few phone sessions before dialling his number.

'Hey, Coach.' Tom was sounding very relaxed as he picked up. 'You'll never believe where I am right now…'

Alice's imagination raced through her fantasy destinations and headed home none the wiser. 'Enlighten me.'

'Lounging on the riverbank in Walton on Thames with a bacon sandwich in my hand…'

If Alice had been a dog she would have been drooling. Exercise didn't seem to suppress her appetite. In fact, she really ought to have been making the most of her new, improved, metabolic rate. She wondered if it was too late for breakfast.

'…It was such a beautiful morning and I really wanted to see sunlight on water.'

'Right.'

The feeling of cool air on his scalp was a welcome relief from the sweltering protection of his helmet, and after the absolute concentration of riding, Tom could feel his mind starting to wander again.

'Is it time to have me committed yet?'

Alice smiled. 'I doubt it. Only insane people would choose to be in an office today. I was down by the river myself earlier.'

'Really?'

Alice stopped herself. This conversation was not about her. Her life was not under the microscope. 'But what are you doing in Surrey? I thought you could see the river from your flat?'

Tom was impressed. 'Good recall.'

Alice tapped her pencil on the page. 'It's all here in front of me. As far as I'm concerned, your life is an open book.'

'Well, I'd better watch my step then. But you really can't beat a motorbike on a day like today.'

'I bet you can.' Alice had meant to think it.

Tom's mouth was full of a new bite of his sandwich. He chewed and half-swallowed. 'We don't all have beards, fringes on our jackets or smoke roll-ups, you know.'

'Listen, I adore my skin and I cherish my limbs. Besides, most drivers in London appear to be far too busy to be checking their wing mirrors. Instead, they're wondering whether or not to risk answering their ringing mobiles, surreptitiously typing out text messages from their laps or retuning the radio in an attempt to find out if there is a reason for the traffic to be as bad as it is.'

'Meanwhile, I'm making steady progress on two wheels and having a lot more fun.' Mouth finally empty, Tom laughed. 'Life coach and surrogate mother. Buy one, get one free. I should have read the small print when I signed up.'

Alice froze. It was all Richard's fault. She was supposed to be a carefree twentysomething, not a risk-averse one.

'Now, a convertible on the other hand…' See, she could do young and flirty. Not that she was supposed to be doing that on a business call.

'So, I was thinking about what you said on Monday…'

Alice was grateful that one of them was keeping their conversation on track. 'Go on.'

Tom sat back on his elbows, his denim-clad legs stretched out in front of him. He flexed his feet. 'You know, about whether I take the time to really enjoy moments. About my strengths and my priorities, and I think I'm starting to come up with some answers.'

'That's great. But remember, there's no rush. This isn't a timed challenge.'

'Just making an hour for myself every day has been a real eye-opener. It's amazing how rarely I used to stop to think.'

Alice sighed. 'That'd be modern life.. We're bombarded with information and stimuli all day every day. If you want to press pause you have to do it manually.'

'Which is, I guess, what you help me to do. Although if I'm honest I'm still not quite sure what I'm paying you for.'

Alice felt her heart sink. 'Are you not starting to feel the benefits?'

Alice hoped this wasn't about to get difficult. She'd already spent his sign-up money about three times over.

'I feel great.' Tom wasn't sure what he'd been expecting. 'It's just that I don't normally have friends on a salary.'

'I'm not your friend, Tom, I'm your coach.' Although having managed three phone sessions in ten days, Alice could empathise with his mistake.

There was a pause.

'Tom?'

Tom let his head fall back onto the grass and stared at the

sky above him so hard that he thought he could almost see the individual particles that made up the blueness.

'Are you still there?' Alice eyeballed her handset. The green light was still on.

'I didn't know the two had to be mutually exclusive.' Tom's reply lingered long after he'd finished speaking.

Alice felt her pulse quicken. There he went again, pushing the boundaries, playing with her. And despite her best intentions, he wrong-footed her every time.

Confident he had her attention, Tom continued. 'Which reminds me, I have an idea.'

Alice paused. 'Go on.'

'How about we go out?'

'I don't think that's a very—'

'I didn't mean—well, not like that.' Tom stopped himself and rerouted his sentence. 'I meant how about we take this life-coaching thing into the field? The sun's shining. Let's spend a few hours living my life instead of talking about it.'

'Most of my clients find it easier to be honest with themselves if they don't have to look me in the eye.' Alice congratulated herself on coming up with a sensible response.

'Well, maybe I'm not your average client.'

Once again he'd derailed her. There was nothing average about Tom at all.

'Just lunch, then. Go on. You need to eat. And you started all this. All those questions about life balance, about happiness, about motives…'

Alice closed her eyes and tried to think of a legitimate reason why not. It wasn't the most unconventional request she had received in her career to date. She dared herself to say yes.

'Well, I guess, in theory, we could do a working lunch. In practice, there is, of course, the question of timing.'

Perfect. Alice congratulated herself on the good old-fashioned "I'd love to see you but don't have the time" ploy.

'I have filming commitments next week. And juggling that with everything else, I'm not sure I'm going to be able to find a few consecutive hours to meet you.'

Despite her mother's machinations she was still self-protectively on an indefinite sabbatical from men. And yet, if she were honest, she *was* curious.

'I don't suppose you're free this afternoon?'

'I don't suppose I am.'

'How about Friday?'

'As in, the day after tomorrow?' Alice shook her head firmly, her wet hair spraying drips of water across her desk. 'I'm afraid that's my day at the clinic.' She looked at the calendar adjacent to her desk. There were only a few lines to go until August 26th.

'I'm sure you have a lunch hour.'

'Sometimes.' Alice wasn't sure whether his persistence was complimentary or irritating. It wasn't her job to drop everything when he needed her. Well, actually, in some ways it was.

'We can do it another time if you're fully booked.'

Now he was happy to leave it, the idea of lunch with Tom seemed very appealing indeed. She could surf the Internet whilst eating a sandwich any day of the week.

'Thank you.' But Alice wasn't even relieved. More like disappointed. Oh, sod it. 'Look, Friday could work. But it'll have to be a quickie.'

Alice wished she had chosen a different word.

'That's great, really great.' Tom's enthusiasm was flattering. 'Let me book somewhere central and get back to you.'

'Cool.' Despite her recent shower, not something she was feeling right now.

'I'm really looking forward to it.'

'Me, too.' Part formality, part true and judging by the fact she had just doodled a tick in the margin of his notes, Alice suspected more of the latter than the former. Which was probably not a good thing.

Chapter Six

23 days to go
Suzie 5, Alice 1

'Well, doesn't this feel familiar?'

Alice still wasn't sure what she was doing opposite Richard at a table for two in the Gallery at Sketch. Little bubbles burst in front of her as the waiter poured their champagne. Glasses charged, she took a sip and surreptitiously scanned the room around her for famous faces.

'May I just say, Ms. Harrison, that you're looking fabulous this evening.'

Alice felt the start of a blush. 'Thank you.' He wasn't looking at all bad himself. His pale blue shirt almost matched his eyes perfectly and she knew that wouldn't be a coincidence. He was a very good-looking man. She had great wedding photos.

Richard studied her face. He cocked his head quizzically. 'Something's different.'

Self-consciously Alice pawed at her black boots, killer

trousers and sleeveless top, a delicate silver necklace hopefully drawing attention to her freshly exfoliated chest.

Richard clicked his fingers and pointed straight at her. 'I know what it is. You're having sex.'

Alice tried not to laugh too incredulously. 'Not a chance. Guess again.'

Richard hesitated, his tone suddenly unsure. 'You've finally got a personal trainer?'

'No.' Alice's denial was emphatic. 'But I did have a dinner date yesterday.'

'God I'm good. And?'

'Not bad at all.' Alice did her best to keep her smile neutral.

'Really? That's great. Name? Vital statistics?'

'Actually.' Alice smiled sheepishly at her lap. 'It was dreadful…'

She'd never been able to lie to Richard and it's not as if she was trying to make him jealous.

'…He didn't eat meat, he only had one glass of wine, he doesn't own a television and he asked me if I believed in positive-energy chakras over coffee—decaf, of course. He wasn't any of the things I'd asked for in my ad.'

Richard grimaced. 'I don't suppose you kept the receipt?'

Alice laughed. 'I don't think I'm entitled to my money back.'

Richard frowned. 'Maybe you could get him under the Trade Descriptions Act. Please tell me you at least let him pay.'

'We split it.'

Richard rolled his eyes. 'Alice.'

'What? I didn't want him thinking he was entitled to a kiss good-night.'

'You're a cruel, heartless woman.'

'Yuh. That's me.' Alice sighed. 'And then of course he called today.'

'And?'

'Maturely, I didn't answer my phone. Why is it the least interested you are, the more interested they get, based, may I just add, on no encouragement from me whatsoever?'

'Men love a challenge.'

'Well, he can challenge all he likes.' Alice smiled and visibly relaxed. 'Hey, I know what's different about me.'

Richard dipped down in his chair and pretended to refocus. 'Should I be seeing energy fields?'

Alice shook her head, allowing her hair to flick from side to side.

'What's this? Have I stumbled into a shampoo commercial?'

'I had my hair cut this morning.'

'That's it.' Richard clapped his hands together and everyone else in the restaurant pretended not to have just jumped at the sudden and unexpected crack of noise. 'Thought you'd cut that man right out of your hair, eh? Don't worry, last night's veggie won't recognise you now.'

'Rest assured I'll have to dry it myself tomorrow and it'll be back to normal.'

'I like it straight. And it's a great length for your face.'

Alice held her hand up. 'Hey, steady with the compliments.' She looked around at their surroundings. 'So, Mr. Harrison, what do you want? If this is a lavish attempt at you trying to secure entrance to my mother's sixtieth birthday party, fine, you win, you can come with me.'

'Now that would be a birthday surprise for her.' Richard's eyes twinkled. 'No, the party is your problem, not mine and, by the way—' he raised his glass of champagne '—I got the job.'

She blew him a kiss across the table. 'And now are you going to tell me what it is?'

'Controller of Channel 6.'

'Bloody hell.' Alice took a large sip. 'You're unbelievable. That's fantastic.'

Richard looked into his lap as, modestly, he fiddled with his napkin. 'I know.'

'What, that you're unbelievable?'

Richard gave her a wry smile. 'How lucky I am.'

Alice stopped teasing him. 'Congratulations. You must be thrilled. And you're still so young.'

'I'm thirty-five this year.'

'I repeat—still so young. Plus, you're not even distantly related to the Murdoch family.' She was genuinely impressed. 'There really is no stopping you. I'm so proud. Rob must be delighted.'

Richard swilled the champagne in his glass. 'It's difficult for him. He's a little bit older, a little bit fed up with his job, and I suspect, a little bit bored of me and my buoyancy.'

'Surely not?'

Richard shrugged. 'He hasn't said anything yet, but he will. Watch this space.'

'Since when have you even been able to spell defeatist? Well, if—and I hope it's only a hypothetical—but should you need somewhere to stay, you can always move home.'

'That's your place now, Al. It's time I bought somewhere new whether or not I end up living in it. I'd be lying if I said the enormous salary hike wasn't going to come in useful.'

Alice nodded pensively. 'You know, I like Rob.'

'I love the bastard.'

'Then make sure he knows how you feel.'

'I do.' Richard reconsidered his answer. 'I will.'

'He's probably feeling inadequate and decidedly unglamorous. Whisk him away for a weekend.'

Richard interrupted. 'I didn't bring you here for advice. I have a proposition for you.'

'Oh, God. It doesn't involve white bikinis, casinos and marriage licences, does it?'

'Alice.'

Richard's tone was serious. She paid attention.

'I want to offer you a job.'

'Another one?'

'A better one. I need someone to work with Dermot on the breakfast show.'

'Dermot Douglas?' Alice's voice had become uncharacteristically shrill. But Dermot was a household name and whatever Richard said, she wasn't. 'What's happening to Janie?'

Richard looked around him to check for media gossips. There were too many to count but fortunately there was also enough ambient noise to make eavesdropping impossible. He leaned in imperceptibly. 'She'll be off shortly.'

'I take it from your body language that she doesn't know that yet.'

'Right. And I don't need to tell you, that it's highly—'

'Got it. But why? Dermot and Janie go together like bacon and eggs, at least where breakfast is concerned.'

'Not anymore. She needs to go and dry out somewhere.'

'Really?'

Richard nodded gravely. 'Her orange juice on set has vodka in it.'

'No way.'

'Plus, ratings are dropping—she's made some mistakes, she's started looking like shit and it's only a matter of time before she gets caught out and falls on her face. She needs a break and then maybe we'll give her a low-pressure afternoon slot. Something less high profile for the channel but that'll keep her fans happy and watching 6. We need new talent.'

'But me?' Alice's heart pounded in her chest.

'You always see the same people on TV. I want Channel 6 to become known for championing and grooming new talent.'

'Don't you think you'd be better starting with someone you haven't slept with? Won't they accuse you of packing the place with your cronies?' Alice willed him to disagree but she wanted to get her worst fears out into the open before she allowed herself to get any more excited.

Richard shook his head firmly. 'Not if you're the right person. And, if I may be so bold, I also think you should change your name back to Fletcher.'

Alice felt tears welling up and silently instructed herself to be a grown-up. He wasn't dumping her; they were divorced. And he was offering her the opportunity of a lifetime.

'I just think it's probably better if you're not so obviously related to the boss. I'm not ashamed of my past, you know that. But you also know what media people are like.'

'We *are* media people.'

'Exactly, and that grapevine can get red hot.'

Alice surveyed their fellow diners. 'Maybe we should have had this conversation at home.'

'I'm not saying we have to keep our relationship a total secret. And, of course, you'll have to screen-test like everyone else, but you'll walk it.'

'And what about all my clients?'

'That's something you need to think about. You'd definitely have to scale things down dramatically.'

Alice wondered if maybe she'd be able to hang on to a few favourites. 'And *Get A Life*?'

'Finish this series and if there is a third I'm sure they'll be only too happy to coordinate with your new schedule.'

'Blimey, Richard, you've thought of everything.'

'You can't be too careful with your career.'

'Maybe it's time to rebrand it "our career". I thought I already had one.'

'Actually, you have two. I just happen to think you should focus on this one. It pays better, for a start.'

'But I've never done any live presenting before. What if I'm a one-show wonder? I'll be left with nothing.'

'Talk yourself out of it if you like.'

'I didn't say—'

'Listen, you spend your life helping other people. They move on and up and you get left behind. I just think it's time you did something for yourself and I happen to know you'll be great at this.'

'But my clients need me.'

'You need them, too.'

Alice nodded. He had a point.

'Sometimes I think you care too much. You get too involved. You need to think less and do more. Put yourself first. And Dermot's quite keen to get you on board.'

'So he knows about Janie?'

'He was the one who told us we had a problem. And, for the record, he knew exactly who you were.'

'He did?' Alice felt a flutter of pride as she felt life as she knew it accelerating away from her, Richard in the driver's seat. 'But I've only just started building up my client list. I have a good reputation. What, one day I'm life coach and the next—'

Richard rescued Alice from herself. 'I'm not expecting you to make a decision before dessert. Think about it for a few days. Take your time. Tie yourself in knots. Do whatever it is you have to do. I'd say it was pretty low risk but then again, I'm biased.'

Alice did her best to take all the information on board. 'So now I've got a few days to decide on a new career and twenty-three days to find a man I want to date more than once.'

'I guess if you insist on quantifying everything, both statements are true.'

His mission accomplished and seeds of change firmly sown, Richard seized the chance to shift the focus of their evening. 'So how's the man thing going overall? I mean, not counting last night, of course.'

'Well, it's Thursday and I'm out having dinner with you. How do you think it's going? From the minute I sat down with Nigel yesterday I wanted to leave.'

'Mr. Chakra was called Nigel?'

'It's not his fault.' Alice had no idea why she was defending him.

'It's why he's still single.'

'He could have been a great guy. His surname was Goodfellow.'

'I think that's called clutching at straws.'

Alice sighed. 'Okay, he wasn't even an average fellow but at least he wasn't physically intimidating.'

'On no. Weedy, too?'

Alice smiled. 'Well, put it this way—if I'd hidden his glasses I doubt he'd have been able to find me on the opposite side of the table.'

'Oh dear.' Richard was doing his best not to snigger. Clearly his best was nowhere near good enough.

'He could write a good e-mail though.'

'Love at first byte?'

'And his telephone voice was quite sexy. It was just the

rest of him.' Alice's despondency was flagrant. 'I mean, if I didn't have to ever see him or touch him…'

'He'd be fictitious. Al, everyone has bad dates. If you didn't, how would you know when you were having a good one?'

It was a valid point, well made. For that second Alice felt nothing but affection for her ex-husband.

'So…' His proposition out in the open, Richard sat back, truly relaxed for the first time that evening. 'How's your mum doing?'

'Much better than me, of course. She's really in demand.'

'All set for the party?'

Alice shook her head. 'I think she's having far too much fun compiling a shortlist.'

Chapter Seven

22 days to go
Suzie 6, Alice 1

'A weekend away sounds very promising.'

Holding her phone to her ear, Alice did her best to sound enthusiastic as she consulted the printout of her map, rotating it until it matched exactly the way she was facing. Looking around for distinctive landmarks, or at least a road name, she did her best to keep calm. Why was it that, rather like single men, street signs were difficult to find, never in sensible places and always totally absent when you actually needed them?

It didn't help that Tom had booked a table at a place she'd never heard of and she'd pretended to know exactly where it was. Alice took a few steps in what she hoped was the right direction.

'You think?'

Suzie clearly operated in a super league of expectation. In the courting phase of a new relationship, Alice had always been happy with dinner invitations, delighted with prebooked theatre or cinema tickets and ecstatic if the film selection didn't feature Vin Diesel or a submarine in the starring role. Mr. Eurostar, on the other hand, had suggested a weekend away and now her mother was fretting.

'I mean, he wouldn't have asked you if he didn't like you, would he?'

'No.' Suzie paused for thought in the cosmetics hall in Selfridges and was immediately approached by three salesgirls brandishing the latest scents. Avoiding eye contact with all of them, she walked on. 'But, I just don't get it. We've been seeing each other on and off for three weeks now and we still haven't got past first base. In fact, we've barely even been there. Maybe I should make it three strikes and out.'

Suzie tried to sound as unbothered as she could but it wasn't working. Her usually impenetrable veneer of confidence had been chipped. And he hadn't even seen her cellulite yet. Subconsciously she clenched and unclenched her buttocks, hoping for some last-minute muscle tone and praying wherever he was taking her had sympathetic lighting. At least by Sunday she would know what the real deal was.

'I didn't know there was a such a rush.'

'What are you talking about? We've only got three weeks left.'

'Well, maybe he's a thinker. Maybe he's impotent. Maybe he still wants you to respect him in the morning. Or maybe this is why he's still single.' Finally confident that she was now heading in the right direction, Alice increased her pace and turned off the Brompton Road.

'It doesn't make sense though. When we're together we have such fun.' Suzie took a second to recall whether he had seemed to be having as good a time as she was.

'If I were you, I'd enjoy the moment and stop worrying about the big picture.'

'So you think I should go?' Suzie made her way through the Art Deco revolving doors and into the bright sunshine on Oxford Street.

'Definitely.' Alice wondered if she should be telling her mother to be more cautious. 'I mean if you want to, of course. And I'm kind of assuming that as tomorrow is Saturday, you've already said yes?'

Suzie was pensive. 'Well, I didn't have any other men scheduled in. Geoffrey's usually around but...'

'Never let it be said that you are not a romantic.' Alice looked at her watch as she checked her map again. The roads in The Boltons were a maze. So much for a shortcut.

'Well, it would appear that most men prefer their first date midweek. Less pressure I guess.'

Alice interrupted her. 'Well then, you've decided. And you've got nothing to lose. Plus, much better to know you are away for the night than leaving for a day trip or a dinner date without being able to take an overnight bag and having to go through the nightmare of having to stash enough toiletries and a spare pair of knickers into your handbag, just in case.'

Suzie laughed. 'Sometimes you are way too wise for your years.'

'I am nearly thirty, not thirteen.' Selfishly, Alice was looking forward to a mother-free weekend. *Get A Life* started filming again on Monday and she desperately needed some good old-fashioned downtime and maybe an unsupervised moment to catch up with her online suitors. Importantly, albeit solely for reasons of an egotistical nature, she'd received plenty of replies, even if there were far fewer that she wanted to take further. But she wasn't counting herself out of this competition just yet.

'Okay, I'm going. I've only got a few more things to do in town. Just one more thing though. The next problem—at least from a packing perspective—is that I don't know where he's taking me.'

On the verge of losing her patience, Alice reminded herself that she loved her mother very much, albeit more when they weren't living together. 'Has he told you to take a passport?'

'No.'

'Well, then you're staying in the U.K. And it's early August. So you'll need to take everything except a fleece and wellies. In fact, to be safe, you should pack those, too.'

'Oh.' Suzie's image of herself at a luxury poolside evaporated.

'But U.K. is definitely better than abroad.'

'It is?' Suzie wasn't convinced.

'Definitely. This way, if it's dreadful and all he wants to do is play Scrabble or whatever it is that people your age do for foreplay, you can just get a train home, or a cab, or call me to come and rescue you. Dial *D* for daughter, that sort of thing.' Alice noticed that she had a definite spring in her own step that had nothing to do with her new shoes and everything to do with the fact that she was about to do something a little reckless—at least by her standards.

'Just for the record I have never played any sort of board game before sex, or indeed after it, for that matter. Although I did know one chap who had a Twister duvet cover. And he was definitely old enough to have known better. I was terrified he was going to put his back out.' Suzie giggled.

'Mum, I know you find this hard to understand but I am in a vague hurry.'

'Tell me about it. I'm supposed to be in the office and instead I'm outside Selfridges. So, seriously, you don't think it's weird to be going away for a night before we've even had sex?' Suzie glared at a couple of tourists who were loitering outside the store and clearly eavesdropping on her personal life. One rule for her, another rule for everyone else.

'I guess maybe it puts a bit more pressure on you both. But I sort of think it's quite sweet that he wants to go away for you to have a special moment together.'

'You always were a bit soppy, darling.'

'Come on, it's not like either of you are going to be virgins at this stage in your lives.'

Suzie ignored Alice's deliberate prod at her vintage. 'And what if he's dreadful in bed?'

'You'll come home well rested.'

Indignation forgotten, Suzie laughed. 'So wry, darling, so wry. You definitely got your quick wit from your father.'

Finally reaching the Fulham Road, Alice checked her appearance in a shop window and wished she'd inherited her cheekbones from her mother instead. 'Well, if he's a real gent he'll probably have booked you a separate room.'

'And here I was wondering whether I should go for a full wax.' Suzie's irritation wasn't even thinly disguised.

'I'm not saying he'll be expecting you to sleep in it.'

'Oh, I see.' Her mood returned to the ascendant.

'Mum, I've really got to go now. I've got a lunch meeting.'

Suzie clearly wasn't receiving incoming information. 'So do I pack saucy underwear or walking boots, or both? I was hoping to get away with a small bag.'

'Perish the thought he should know the truth.'

'I'm not high maintenance.' Suzie's indignation was genuine.

'No, of course not.' Anything for a quiet life.

'It sounds like you're just saying that.' Suzie paused for a second.

'Mum, I need to go.' Alice was rapidly becoming a disinterested party.

'Then of course there is the question of whether I'm going to need anything really smart, because that will mean another pair of shoes. Oh, I don't know. Sometimes I don't think this is worth all the bother. And then I sit down and try and find something to watch on TV and I know it is. It's about time that ex-husband of yours started making things I want to watch…'

Alice blushed as she realised she hadn't really given herself a minute to think about Richard's offer.

'…Damn, is that really the time? Listen, I've got to go. The eyebrow threader is a bit of a punctuality Nazi. I'll see you at home later.'

Alice resisted the urge to kick something. Her mother had just hung up and yet she had been trying to excuse herself ever since the call had started.

Barely touching the button, Tom silenced his iPod, pausing Maroon 5 midbeat and imagined them all frozen in time; drumsticks midair, guitar mid-riff, lyrics mid-verse, just waiting for him to unleash them later. Slipping it into the inside pocket of his tailor-made suit jacket for safekeeping, he tried to clear his mind of the catchy refrain, but seconds later he was tapping his fingers against his thigh. He couldn't remember the last time he'd bought five albums at the same time and now in possession of a few recent releases, he was feeling surprisingly youthful. He was looking forward to the weekend almost as much as he was looking forward to his lunch.

Resisting the urge to play air drums, he pushed aside the glass-and-chrome door of the Oasis and made his way to his favourite table in the garden. Maybe it wasn't too late to join a band? Yeah, and maybe the Broccoli family would want him to be the next James Bond. Hanging his jacket on the back of his chair, he rolled up his sleeves and delighted in the feeling of the sun on his forearms. Saving the world or saving himself? He had to start somewhere.

'Zo…'

Alice spotted the door of the restaurant and walked straight past it, turning into a mews until she had finished her call. Looking down her three-quarter-length khaki trousers, she studied her ankles. They were definitely looking slimmer than they had in the mirror this morning. Optimism or an optical illusion? She wasn't sure. And if they weren't tanned, they were at least smooth, thanks to some last-minute depilation. The summer months were such hard work.

'…It's me, just wanted to say good luck with the social worker. Are you nervous?'

'No.'

Zoë's monosyllabic response was a sure sign she was lying.

'Good for you. So how are you feeling?'

'Oh you know, guilty, excited, apprehensive, wondering whether or not to invent another commitment and cancel. I've been chain drinking Diet Coke all morning. I'm wearing a bloody suit, for goodness' sake.'

'You don't have to dress up for this.'

'I know, I know. But somehow it just felt wrong to not have made an effort. I mean, I'm going to meet my mother.'

'Not today you're not.'

Zoë sighed. 'I know. It's pathetic. But I suppose I didn't want anyone to think I wasn't taking this seriously. And then I started thinking, since when have I done anything seriously. To be brutally honest, my resolve is deserting me.'

'Want me to cancel lunch and come with you?' Alice willed Zoë to remain the independent woman she knew and loved.

'No, I'm fine. I think I need to do this alone.'

Alice could have kissed her. 'You know you don't have to do anything you don't want to.'

'Ah, of course. The old reverse-psychology trick. You professional coach you.'

'I'm just saying it's your choice. And you have to feel ready.'

'Will you please stop with the mind games.'

Alice was indignant. 'I'm not playing with you. This could be the most exciting thing you ever do, or the most disappointing. Either way, you won't regret it. No doubt they'll go over everything with you again.'

'I think we covered every conceivable angle last night.'

'Or at least every conceivable cocktail.' All things considered, Alice's hangover had been minor. Her liver handled spirits a lot better than beer these days. Not that that was necessarily a good thing.

Zoë giggled. 'You get extra points for making me laugh today.'

'Believe me, the world is quite serious enough without losing your ability to see the funny side.'

'Maybe my real mother is a billionaire.'

'Excellent to see you're approaching this with the right combination of maturity and reality.'

'It's too a big a deal to take seriously.'

'I'm sure. Well, let me know how it goes.'

'Of course.'

'Love you, Zo.'

'I know.'

'No…' Alice's tone was playful. 'That's when you're supposed to say "love you, too".'

'I'm at work. And you know I do.'

'Listen, I'll be off the radar for the next hour or two but call me as soon as you're done.'

Alice switched her phone off and applied a fresh coat of gloss to her lips before walking back to the main door of the restaurant. She was a perfect five minutes late and, rather marvellously, had managed to get to her lunch destination without having to explain herself to anyone. Having a self-obsessed mother, a best friend in search of her birth parents and a reputation for being all work and no play recently, had generally guaranteed her movements went unchecked. Of course, she could have mentioned it. Could have, but had decided not to, which meant what? Nothing. Alice stopped herself. She'd already been thinking about this far too much.

Tom pushed his sunglasses back onto his head, a few strands of shorter hair falling forward. 'Thanks for coming to meet me.'

As Alice made herself comfortable, Tom knew this had been one of his better ideas.

'I think I find this self-analysis stuff easier face-to-face.'

The sun on her back, Alice congratulated herself for allowing herself to bend the rules. She hadn't really done spontaneity since Richard had persuaded her to elope. And if she was going to retrain herself to be the old, fun Alice, Tom was the first person she had come across in a long while who she felt certain could help.

'Plus, I guess I'd rather see your gut reaction to what I'm saying instead of wondering whether you're pulling faces at the other end of the phone.'

It was only the second time they'd actually met and studying Alice's face, Tom noted that her radiance was something that many women failed to achieve. Unlike most of her peers in London who made a huge effort even if they were only going out to post a letter, there was a total absence of the heavy-handed make-up so common in the corporate world where women seemed to invest almost as much in their appearances as they did in their careers. Her light brown eyes were gleaming.

Alice did her utmost to suppress a blush. She had been known, very occasionally, to hang out washing, make a sandwich or even cut her nails during some of her clients' longer anecdotes. But she was a woman and therefore genetically predisposed to being able to do two things at the same time.

Tom thought he'd test her straight away. 'In fact, just before you arrived I was wondering whether I was too old to play in a band.'

Alice kept her expression as neutral as possible. Laughing at clients was taboo. Laughing with them, however, was to be positively encouraged.

'Really?'

Tom peered from one of her ears to the other.

Alice wiped her face self-consciously. 'What is it?'

'Just wondered where you were hiding a patronising smile…'

Alice held firm. 'Do you play an instrument? No, wait, I guess you might see yourself as the lead singer.'

'Why do you say that?'

'Well, you're going to want to run the show…aren't you?'

Sitting back in his chair, Tom accepted his fate. 'Problem is, I'm not the best singer. But I've played a fair bit of air guitar, or maybe I should go for drums? I've got pretty good rhythm. So I'm told.'

Alice smiled at her napkin as she laid it out on her lap. 'You know, life coaching isn't about impressing the coach. It's about discovering what's best for you.'

'Can't I do both?'

'And by the way, no one ever fancies the drummer.' Alice looked around the small garden, delighted to be sitting outdoors after the dimly lit, stale, smoky bar area she'd just walked through—probably fine when it was midnight at the Oasis, less appealing at lunchtime. 'For the record, bass guitarists are supposed to be the nice guys.'

'I'll bear that in mind.' Tom smiled. 'So—' he slid his shades back on as the sun came out from behind a cloud '—still not convinced by the working-lunch idea?'

'I'm just not entirely sure what you think this is going to achieve.'

He was paying for the privilege of talking to her. It was a win-win situation from where she was sitting.

Tom shrugged. 'I've been giving myself more time to think and now I guess I want feedback.'

'And to feed me.' Alice smiled cheekily.

Tom felt the atmosphere thaw as she set the tone. 'That, too. And I suppose I do want your approval that I'm doing the right thing. Pathetic for a man of my age, I know.'

'Hey, the client is always right.'

'Always?'

'Definitely when he's buying lunch.' Alice could feel herself relaxing. Not that she thought she'd been particularly tense before. Taking in her surroundings, she noticed a small pond. Overgrown and green with algae, it was clearly supposed to be the centrepiece around which the tables were arranged. Instead, she feared it might have been a drop-in centre for homeless mosquitoes. 'So what is this place?'

'Just one of my regular haunts. Do you like it?' From her question, Tom suspected otherwise.

Alice shrugged. 'Good location but it could do with a bit of work.'

He hung his head comically. 'You hate it.'

'I didn't say that. And I haven't eaten anything yet.' Alice was circumspect. 'Being able to sit outside is always lovely and this certainly beats my minuscule garden but—' Alice looked at the overgrown flower beds '—I guess it could do with some love, and the inside seems to be more of a smoky cave than an oasis.'

'Tips for the management?'

Alice paused. 'Open the windows. Get an interior designer and a landscape gardener.'

'Three out of ten. Must try harder.' His fingers grasping an imaginary pen, Tom pretended to make notes on his napkin.

'Anyway, the menu looks fine.'

Tom grimaced. 'Fine? That's hardly going to win us rave reviews or awards.'

'Us? Oh God, I should have guessed. It's your place, isn't it?' Alice wished she could erase the last couple of minutes.

'Not mine, per se, but it is one of the Taylor-Made group's most recent acquisitions. I don't suppose you want to oversee the refurbishment in your copious free time, do you?'

From his tone she had no idea whether he was being serious or not. Alice took a large gulp of her mineral water and wished it was something stronger. She looked around the garden.

'Well, having a walled garden is fantastic and it must be great being able to eat outside in the evenings—British weather permitting, of course. You could always construct some sort of cover for some of the tables using old sails or something.' Alice was desperately trying to make amends.

Tom surveyed the area. 'Good idea. And thanks for your gut reaction. Honesty is a rare trait in this day and age.'

'Yeah, right.' Silently, Alice reprimanded her big mouth.

'Seriously.' Tom was emphatic. 'Most people are only too

happy to tell people what they think they want to hear if it's going to benefit them in the long run, but genuine, unedited, unadulterated honesty is an endangered quality.'

'Not in my world, I'm afraid.'

'Which is why, no doubt, you are fantastic at what you do.'

'At stating the obvious and being a sounding board?' Alice didn't know what was the matter with her. At this rate her honesty was going to be the death of her career. Maybe it was just as well she had another one in the pipeline.

Upbeat, Tom laughed. 'I admit I needed converting at first.'

Alice needed to claw her way back into the driver's seat. Tom's boyish enthusiasm was dangerous and, as Alice reminded herself, probably not as genuine as even he thought at the moment. He was undoubtedly confusing his feelings of gratitude and positivity at his progress with something else. She was helping him, he was grateful. End of moment.

Tom rested his elbows on the arms of his chrome chair. 'Please don't take this the wrong way but you're really not what I was expecting.' Their phone conversations had been the highlight of his week, which made him a loser…or interested.

'Really? In what way?'

Alice was sure a few of her clients would rather she had been older but it wasn't just an age thing, it was a perspective thing, and an experience thing. And she'd had to pick herself up several times in her life already.

'If I'm honest I was worried you were going to be evangelical about self-improvement. You know the sort—a guru who'd been brainwashed, a woman with a smile as all-encompassing as her positive attitude, who was caked in lipstick and power dressed in suits. A woman who'd had her colours done. You know…?' Tom adopted his best effeminate voice. 'Oh, no, I just couldn't do blue, it's not in my palette. I'm more of an autumn myself.'

Alice laughed. 'Believe me, when I started doing this, I was worrying about all that, too.'

Tom gave her a quick look up and down. 'It's not difficult to understand why you are doing so well for yourself.'

'Thank you.' As she readjusted her sunglasses on her head and tucked a stray lock of hair behind her ear, Alice reminded herself that he was complimenting her professional skills.

'I've decided that after lunch I'm going to show you my perfect afternoon. You know, so you can understand me, and therefore advise me better.'

Alice smiled nervously. 'I'm sure that would be lovely but I do have to be back at the centre in an hour and a half.'

'Oh, but you don't.'

'You're not my only client.' Alice stopped herself as irritation at his sudden show of arrogance started to surface and she felt their meeting judder to a halt.

'I am today.' As Tom sat back, his chair shifted in the gravel. 'Have you not checked your appointments for this afternoon?'

Frowning, Alice rummaged in her bag for her BlackBerry and switching it on, stared at the screen and waited for it to synch up with her Outlook.

She scrolled through the menus. 'My next appointment is at two-thirty.'

'Your two-thirty is with me.' Tom folded his hands behind his head.

'Then I have one at three-thirty, one at four…' The triumphant tone in her voice faded.

'As are your three-thirty, four-thirty and five-thirty.'

'You can't just rent me by the hour.' Alice bristled.

Tom leaned in. 'What happened to the "customer is always right"?'

Alice's mood was in the midst of a U-turn.

'Come on, relax, it's Friday.'

Alice hated people telling her to relax almost as much as she hated it when total strangers told her to "cheer up, love" in the street. It wasn't her fault her default expression involved pursed lips instead of an inane smile.

'You're the one who told me to take the time to enjoy moments. Besides, this is business.'

Alice was wondering what could possibly have gone so wrong before they'd even ordered.

'Hey—' Tom could sense her unease '—I just wanted, I thought, I presumed…I'm sorry. Look, if nothing else, I'm sure I can provide you with a fun Friday afternoon.'

Alice winced.

'Go on, accept my apology. Let me introduce you to Tom Taylor's Friday afternoon off.'

'So now you think you're Ferris Bueller, do you?'

'Trust me on this one.'

'Why should I?' Why shouldn't she.

Tom sighed. 'Your secretary at the centre didn't really think this was a good idea, either. But you do coaching for companies all day, so why can't I have your company all day.'

Alice folded her arms. 'Have you been rehearsing that line?'

'Of course not.'

'But it was a line?'

'It was a sentence, a statement. It definitely wasn't a line.' He hadn't thought it was that bad.

'Good, because it was terrible and if it wasn't overstepping the professional mark, I'd say it's not surprising that you don't have a w—'

'Whoa. You're approaching the mark rapidly.' Tom smiled.

Alice sighed in defeat. If she had no other clients to see,

there was no point in going back to the office. 'So what did you have planned?'

'Well, first, we're going to order a nice glass of white wine.'

Zoë stared out of the window of Starbucks wishing she could lose herself in the crowds outside. As her mobile rang she swallowed a sip of boiling-hot coffee, the searing latte river cauterizing her oesophagus. She should have waited for it to cool more, but she needed the caffeine urgently and this place didn't sell Diet Coke or Red Bull. She looked at the screen on her phone. It was Suzie.

Right family, wrong person. Zoë really wanted to speak to Alice. She felt like a child bluffing in a world of adults. Exactly the same way she had felt the first time Jean, her adoptive mother, had let her take their black Labrador, Pepper, out on the lead for the first time. Intrepid, independent, brave, responsible and terrified something bad might happen and it would all be her fault.

She flipped open her phone, concerned. 'Suzie? Is everything okay?'

'Fine.'

'Where's Alice?'

'At work, I presume.'

'I wish she was.' Zoë had left a message for Alice at the clinic but that had been hours ago now.

'Well, she's not answering her phone. Ignoring her mother, the usual sort of thing. I was hoping she might have been with you.'

'No.' Zoë stared into the middle distance and told herself not to panic. Alice was most probably with a client or in a meeting.

'You okay?'

'Not really.' The deafeningly high-pitched grating of

china on china temporarily put their conversation on hold as a barista filled a tray with empty mugs. 'I'm hiding in a cup of coffee. Traumatic day.'

'Work trouble? Man trouble?'

'Mother trouble.'

Suzie sucked air in between her teeth. 'The worst. Need some advice from an expert?'

'Not sure you'll be able to help on this one.'

'Try me.'

Zoë barely paused. She needed to talk to someone. 'I don't know if Alice has mentioned that I'm in the process of trying to trace my birth mother?'

'Of course.' Suzie lied flawlessly. To her chagrin, Alice hadn't said a word to her. 'And?'

'Well, I had my first meeting with the social worker today and it was harder than I'd been expecting. A lot more difficult in fact…'

'Presumably because you hadn't been expecting it to be tricky at all.'

'That may have been part of the problem. Only now I've started the process, I'm not sure I want to finish.'

Zoë watched a smart young mother leaning over to coo at her child as she pushed her along in a buggy. A few metres behind her, a washed out young woman, grey with exhaustion, literally dragged her toddler along behind her.

'There's no need to rush these things.'

Grateful for Suzie's perspective, Zoë laughed. 'Hey, you're right. After all, it only took thirty-one years for me to make the first move. At this rate I'll be sixty before I pick up the phone.'

'Sixty being incredibly young, of course.'

'Of course…'

Zoë raised her mug to her lips and felt the steam condense

on her top lip. The roof of her mouth already felt rubbery where she'd just burned it.

'…It's just that one moment I feel that this is the biggest deal in the world, and ten minutes later the world is just the same and I'll wonder what all the fuss was about…'

Zoë took a gentle sip.

'…So please, save me from myself. What can I help you with?'

Suzie basked in the cooperation coming from the other end of the phone. Zoë always went out of her way to help her at times when Alice was, frankly, difficult. Daughters were always greener on the other side of the fence and at the other end of the phone.

'I need some counsel.'

Zoë was flattered. 'Man-related?'

'I guess it is.'

Zoë almost rubbed her palms together with glee, relieved by the distraction. 'Go ahead. Alice has told me all about this younger man you've been seeing.'

'She has? She's barely asked me a thing about him.'

'Well, you know how it is with mothers and daughters. Best friends, firm rivals and often just a wee bit too close for comfort. And I exaggerated. All I know is he's younger and that you met him on the Eurostar.'

'He's also far too enigmatic when it comes to his emotions.'

'Surely that just makes him a real man.'

'He's harder to read than most.'

'You should realise that I can't claim to be on the front line when it comes to male psychology. The last time I was in a proper relationship, the Spice Girls were still together.'

Suzie laughed. 'Here goes. Your starter question—I've been invited away for the weekend. Do I pack something to sleep in?'

Zoë only paused for a second. 'My gut reaction is yes, so the right answer has got to be, definitely not.'

'You think? I'm not talking about a winceyette nightie. I was thinking more girl-next-door, you know strappy vest top and Nick & Nora pyjama bottoms. Then again I guess I could just take a top half, "forget" the bottoms and hope he'll lend me a pair of boxer shorts, unless of course he wears briefs, in which case we really shouldn't be going away together in the first place.'

Alice looked at her watch for no particular reason. Her day was no longer about a timetable. But at 6.30 p.m. the air in Brighton was still blissfully warm as the sun beat down on the pebbles surrounding her deck chair. Stretching, she arched her back contentedly before springing back into her sun-kissed slouch. Listening to the waves crash only a few feet away, she didn't hear the crunch of footsteps behind her as Tom appeared, clutching a parcel of chips and a Mr. Whippy ice cream. Clearly his ideal afternoon involved having a heart attack.

'Here you go. Which do you fancy first?'

'First?'

'Share and share alike.'

Alice eyed the chip paper, translucent with vinegar and fat, and was sure she could feel her arteries flinch. 'I'll go sweet.'

'Excellent choice. If only because I prefer my savoury and sweet in the right order.'

Tom sat down in the adjacent deck chair, his suit out of place on the rough stripy nylon, his brogues dusty and salty from the shingle. He lowered his Oakley sunglasses over his eyes and leaned back in his chair, almost making it a hammock, his bottom only millimetres above the ground. Yet, sat side by side on the first ridge of pebbles on the beach, it was as if they'd booked front-row seats in the stalls. Today's show: life.

Alice licked the ice-cream river running down the cone as Tom rustled his chip paper. He sounded like a boar snuffling for a truffle.

Two hours ago they'd been on the South Bank admiring the capital from the Millennium Eye, then a dash by cab to Victoria Station and now Alice was sitting on the kerb of her continent, looking out to sea. And all in an afternoon's work.

He had been upbeat all day. Secretly, Alice was starting to wonder if she had more issues that needed resolving than her client did. Once she'd got over being stitched up, it had been the best few hours she'd had in far too long. She couldn't remember the last time she hadn't been in charge of her day.

Tom licked his fingers noisily. 'I'm not sure if there's more salt in the air, in my nose or on my chips.'

Alice smiled.

'As for this crap imitation ketchup, it's just red vinegar. Where is Mr. Heinz when you need him. Hang on.' He wiped his fingers on a paper napkin. 'Almost forgot.'

Tom proffered a still semi-chilled can of Diet Coke from the pocket of his suit jacket and took a full fat one out of the other side for himself.

Alice cocked an eyebrow lazily. 'What are you saying?'

'Nothing. I just bet you prefer it.'

'Might do.' Alice relieved him of the can.

Tom smiled. 'Typical female. An ice cream and a diet drink.'

'Ah…' Alice waggled her finger authoritatively. 'But what you don't know is that I actually prefer the taste.'

'That's your official line. You've just trained yourself to think that.'

'No, really, I do.'

'So nothing to do with the teaspoons of sugar you know are lurking within the red cans?'

'Not really.'

Tom returned to his chips in almost reverential silence before leaning across and swapping them for the remains of the ice cream. 'So, a fairly tolerable afternoon so far?'

'Not bad.' Alice relished the mixture of sweet and savoury on her palate. It triggered some distant memory of junior-school birthday parties when crisps and chocolate had been natural plate mates.

'And only enhanced by the fact that we should both be at work, don't you think?'

'I *am* at work.' Alice grinned at Tom.

'Still? Surely now it's time for an after-work drink?'

'Don't you think we should be heading back to London?' Alice wondered what her rush was. It's not as if she had plans.

'Already? Surely I can tempt you to a couple of sea breezes?'

'I'm afraid I'm off cocktails after last night.'

'Appletiser? A Virgin Mary?'

She challenged herself to lighten up. 'I'm sure I'll manage a beer or two.'

'A beer?'

'Hey, mister, it's the twenty-first century. Men can bring up babies and women drink what they like.'

'As long as you won't be insulted if I stick to white-wine spritzers?'

'It's a free country.'

'I sense disapproval. Rest assured I'm a real man.'

'Whatever that means.'

'And we definitely can't leave yet. We haven't been to the pier.'

'The pier?' Alice eyed the funfair on stilts protruding over the sea with suspicion.

She had never really understood the attraction of playing computer games that cost around a pound a minute and were designed to be so difficult that you never got very far. But then, not having had a dad after the age of eight or a brother to play with, she didn't understand lots of things, like carburettors or rugby, Clive Cussler novels, nuclear submarines or the difference between a Chinook and a Cessna.

'Let's just soak up the sun for a little bit longer.' Alice wondered how different her life would be if she lived in a sunnier country. "Don't worry, be happy" was not a mentality that went hand in hand with blustery wet weekends.

She let her hand drop into the sticky damp shingle and absently sifted small, salty stones through her fingers. A small, dark grey, exceptionally smooth pebble stuck to her palm. Closing her hand around it, Alice brought it up to eye level and examined it. Now warm from her hand, Alice touched it against her cheek.

'May I?' Tom extended his arm and Alice handed her pebble over. It was the size of a small new potato. He turned it over in his fingers. 'It's almost as if it's been polished. Just goes to show.'

'What, that life's a beach?'

Tom shook his head. 'That you get thrown around for years and yet come out more beautiful on the other side.' Tom slipped it into his suit pocket.

Alice rolled her eyes. 'There you go again making a metaphor out of nothing.'

Tom sighed and leaned back in his chair—'I've often thought I could live down here.'

'So why don't you?'

'And commute to London every day?'

'Plenty of people do. Or maybe it's time to give that music career a go.'

Tom watched as wisps of a cirrus cloud dispersed in the sky above his head. He turned to Alice. 'Do you have any idea how successful the Taylor-Made group are?'

'I can guess. But at least then you could afford to take some time out. There's got to be more to life than work. It's important to have some balance.'

Where was hers? As a child she had dreamed of being an astronaut, a surgeon, a newsreader, a mother. So many lives, so little time.

'There you go again, sounding like a life coach.'

'Which is funny, because…'

Tom's focus was absolute. 'Trouble is, I have a lifestyle and a salary that I am very used to and it's difficult enough to make a big change when you know what you're aiming for.'

Alice listened. His sentiments were only too germane at the moment. She needed to give Richard an answer before he retracted his offer. Whoever said luck was a lady, hadn't been looking properly; he was clearly a man in drag.

She nodded. 'But I'm not saying become a gardener. Just take stock and if you want a change, make it happen sooner rather than later. Otherwise, in thirty years' time you'll be a grumpy old man complaining about the things you haven't done. You never find yourself complaining about the ridiculous or daring changes you did manage. In fact, I find I am often proudest of those.'

Alice watched a wave race onto the shingle, raking through, desperate to cling on as it was forced to retreat. She was going to have to say yes. Goodbye late nights, hello early mornings.

'So,' Tom turned to face her and leaned on the edge of

his deck chair, his sudden invasion of her personal space both unnerving and exciting.

Alice forced herself to concentrate on what he was saying as opposed to how she and Tom must have looked to the other people on the beach, most of whom were in shorts and T-shirts. They, on the other hand, were clearly on day release from London. She wondered if people thought they were having an illicit affair. She wondered if she hoped they were having an illicit affair.

'…What happened with your marriage?'

'My marriage?' Alice didn't know why she was stalling for time. She'd heard him perfectly the first time.

'That guy you introduced me to after our first session seemed nice enough.'

Alice nodded proudly. 'Richard's a great guy.'

'So?'

'What is this, Twenty Questions?'

'I was hoping it was more of a conversation.'

Alice paused. 'He's gay.'

'Really? Bummer.' Tom stopped himself.

'Very poor choice of expression.' Alice smiled as Tom reddened.

'So, did he need a British passport or something?'

Alice shook her head. 'Obviously I didn't know he preferred men until later.'

'Oh my God. That's terrible.' Tom's shock was genuine.

Alice still got a slight thrill from people's initial reaction to the whole thing. For the girl who had never managed an adolescent rebellion, it was good to have a revelation in her armoury. Plus, she got all the kudos without any of the blame.

'That's life.'

'You'd think you'd have noticed.' Tom closed his mouth before he detonated an emotional land mine.

'More importantly, you'd think *he'd* have noticed. But he didn't have every ABBA album, he wasn't super tidy, he didn't spend lots of time at the gym. Okay, he read *Hello!* magazine, he enjoyed cooking and he loved shopping, but I couldn't believe my luck. I thought he was metrosexual.'

'Metrosexual—what's that? Likes having sex on tube trains?'

'Promise me you'll never risk everything to go into stand-up comedy.'

Tom feigned surprise at her reaction. 'I thought that was quite a good one.'

Alice frowned.

'Oh well, I'm very sorry to hear…very bad luck, for you I mean.'

Alice sighed, more out of habit than distress. 'There's always a bloody catch. He liked me, he loved me. We had a great friendship, we still do. And the sex was fantastic.' Alice felt her ears redden, shortly followed by her neck. She didn't know why she'd thrown that little detail in. What had she been hoping for, congratulations? Plus, now he probably thought she'd probably had anal sex, which she hadn't. 'I wasn't the only one taken in. None of us noticed. Not me, not my best friend, or my mother—but she didn't really like him anyway.'

'You see, mothers always know best.'

'I'm not so sure.'

'Mine did. Not that I would ever have let her know that she was right about anything while she was alive.'

Tom watched a couple coming out of the sea and felt their pain as they tried to find a route through the pebbles suitable for their soft, unusually naked, feet. They should have followed the lead of the majority of the other swimmers and left flip-flops at the water's edge.

Idly, Alice wondered whether she should run her career options past Suzie. She was sure she'd approve, but she'd be annoyed if she hadn't been amongst the first to know.

Tom interrupted her silent debate. 'I guess it shouldn't be a surprise that our mothers understand us the most. I mean they're the ones that spent years watching our every move, worrying that we weren't sleeping, eating, passing wind, passing enough exams.'

'Well, mine still thinks I'm exactly the same person that I was when I left home.'

Tom turned to face her. 'Aren't you?'

'Are you? When I left home I was a slightly overweight, self-conscious twenty-two-year-old with a penchant for baggy jumpers, fresh out of university where I had survived on a diet of pasta, pesto and toast. And somehow in her company I almost revert to that persona.' Alice reminded herself to take note and do something proactive about it.

'And is she the same?'

'Not really. If anything, she is getting less mature and more irresponsible every day.'

'Good for her…'

'I don't know. I mean, she's nearly sixty.'

'You see, you're expecting her not to have changed, either.'

Alice watched a small gang of seagulls screeching, almost laughing, as they swooped towards the pier on their way out for the evening.

Following her gaze, Tom observed them making their approach to land as nonchalantly as possible.

'So what has today told you about me?'

Relieved that the focus of the conversation had reverted to Tom, Alice jumped straight in.

'That you can take a day off when you feel like it without running the risk of being fired, that you find it hard to do nothing, that you like spontaneity, being in the driver's seat, being outdoors, eating and that you like to travel.'

Tom nodded. 'Although I do always seem to want to be in the one place I'm not. And I always miss London when I'm not there.'

'You should be trying harder to enjoy the here and now.'

Tom turned to face her. 'Which I am.'

Alice broke eye contact. 'I meant in general. Wherever you are…'

Looking away, she licked the sticky remains of ice cream, salt and vinegar from her fingers.

'…And I still haven't quite worked out whether you love travel because it makes you appreciate coming home, whether it really is about exploring new things or just straightforward escapism—you know, old-fashioned running away.'

'I suspect it depends. Fancy getting some dinner soon?'

Alice wriggled round in her deck chair so she could make full eye contact with Tom. 'I've also learned that if you stopped exercising, you would be the size of a house. I don't think I've consumed so many calories in one afternoon since—'

'University?' Tom patted his stomach affectionately. 'I suspect my Body Mass Index at college was higher than some of my results. Forget all these health scares, I think we're all getting better with age. I definitely weigh less now than I did in my early twenties.'

Alice really was enjoying his company. She hoped this wasn't some sort of father-figure thing. But fifteen years wasn't really a big enough gap. Realistically, any attraction she was feeling was far more likely to be a time-pressure thing.

Tom studied Alice's face. 'But what about you?'

'Me?' Surely he wasn't expecting her to tell him how much she weighed? She hadn't had bathroom scales since she'd left home.

'Yes, you. How did you get into all this?'

'Someone suggested we go to the seaside for tea...' Alice pulled her thin, pale pink cardigan up over her shoulders.

'Seriously, I'm interested. I hadn't even heard of life coaching before.'

'It's been very fashionable for a few years now.'

'Not in my circles. And when we first met, you said that you used to work in television. Although I guess with this *It's My Life* thing you still do.'

'Get A Life.'

'Apologies, but I'm afraid I've never seen it.'

Alice smiled. 'I think I might be more concerned if you had.'

'But I am interested to know how you got into all this.'

'How long have you got?'

Tom didn't skip a beat. 'All evening.'

All evening? Alice hesitated.

Tom looked concerned. 'Was that the wrong thing to say?'

Alice thought for a second and shook her head. Actually, it wasn't a bad response at all. She brought her knees up to her chest, her heels resting on the edge of her deck chair. 'Okay, I'll answer your questions, on one condition.'

'Name it.'

'From now on, I'm officially off duty.' Alice didn't know exactly what she was doing but she was having fun. And that was something she hadn't had in straight male company for far too long.

Pack light.
Going on the bike.
Tom

Suzie reread the text message again before emptying everything out of her large leather weekend bag for the third time. She rummaged through the pile of clothes on the duvet, careful not to smudge any of the rejuvenating, rehydrating face mask that she was currently sporting on to anything. Plus, she had already changed the bed linen—just in case.

Sighing, she dragged a pristine backpack out from under the bed and started the reduction process again. Swimsuit or bikini or both? Then again, they only occupied as much space as a pair of socks. But this wasn't a spa weekend, and with a bit of luck she'd be getting all the exercise she needed in the room.

Suzie paced between her chest of drawers and the bed. If she'd been going to the Caribbean she could have made do with a capsule wardrobe or just a sarong and a pair of linen trousers. Dress up, dress down…maybe a dress…but on a motorbike? Suzie opened her wardrobe again and extracted a thin fleece. Blue lips and purple nail beds were never a good look.

Suzie caught a glimpse of her alarm clock. Nearly 9:00 p.m. and still no sign of Alice. She couldn't remember her mentioning she'd be out for the evening, but then she couldn't remember much at the moment. From now on she was going to be a better mother. Fuck it, Alice hadn't really needed one of those since her teens. She was going to be a better friend.

Alice was only dimly aware of the noise of the train as, replete with red wine and steak, her body dragged her down towards sleep. Her clothes were comfortingly imbued with the smell of caramelised peanuts roasting and candy floss from the pier. She was definitely going for a run, or liposuction, tomorrow.

Slightly chilly, she snuggled down in her seat and leaned to her left, resting her forehead against the window. As the vibrations of the train juddered through her, repeatedly bumping her head against the glass, semiconsciously she jerked back to the centre of her headrest. Then leaning to the right, finally she found a comfortable position before realising whose shoulder was so accommodating and shock absorbing. Startling herself awake, she found herself in the very formally upright position.

'Good nap?'

Tom's face was far too close to hers and now he was putting his arm around her. Totally inappropriate behaviour and yet, it felt perfectly normal.

He sighed contentedly. 'I love trains. I feel free—which I know is ridiculous since I'm actually trapped and someone else is driving. And, I hope, paying close attention to red lights, bricks on lines and signal boxes. But there's something blissfully liberating about not having any control or having to make a decision. About knowing where I'm going to end up and being able to switch off for the ride.'

'A bit like being on a plane?' Alice was sleepy.

'I guess. But without having to know where my life jacket is.'

Alice could feel Tom's breath on her hair as he spoke. Tom Taylor. He could have been a film star, an artist or a rock god. In fact, with a name like that he could have been the sixth member of Duran Duran. Fleetingly, she wondered if the forcefulness of his name was purely due to the alliteration. "Alice Harrison" could sound a little hissy. "Alice Fletcher" sounded much stronger. And she needed to start putting Richard behind her, or at least to one side.

'So, when do you think we need another session?'

She kept her eyes closed. 'You're probably best taking a few weeks off. Let it settle. Think about some of the big stuff. You've had quite an intensive time of it so far.'

'I'd say.' Tom stroked her hair back off her face.

She didn't need to have her eyes open to see what was going to happen next. As Tom leaned down and kissed her, she looked up to capture the moment and then pulled away. First of all, she'd had garlic prawns as a starter and second of all this was almost as bad an idea as Michael Jackson allowing Martin Bashir to make a documentary about him. Sitting as far back as she could and turning in her seat until her back was against the window, she surveyed the scene. He was smiling.

'No. Tom. No.'

'No? Right. Of course.' His expression told a different story.

'Definitely no.'

Tom nodded dreamily. 'Got it.'

As he leaned forward and kissed her again, Alice was only brought back to reality when seconds later, the driver announced over the intercom that they were only minutes from Victoria Station.

Alice shook her head. 'I can't do this.'

Tom cocked his head. 'Can't or shouldn't?'

'Both. Either.'

'Personally or professionally?'

'This is bound to end in disaster.'

'Whatever happened to the power of positive thinking?'

Alice fiddled with her hair nervously, finally tying it back with the hair tie that had been doubling as a bracelet all day, and instantly feeling more sensible. 'So, did you have this all planned?'

Tom was sheepish. 'Not at all. This is pretty complicated for me, too.'

'Wife? Girlfriend? HIV positive?'

'Are you always this optimistic?'

'Thanks to Richard, always.' Alice was firm.

As the train slowed past the four chimneys of Battersea Power Station, she wrestled herself free. Quite a feat, bearing in mind that she had Tom on one side of her, a window on the other and a table in front of them. Mercifully, the two facing seats were unoccupied. She was no Houdini.

'I'm sorry.' Tom's attempt at remorse was only betrayed by his poorly disguised grin.

Alice wondered how she had let this happen. He was an attractive man, but first and foremost, he was a client. And then another Tom fact elbowed its way to the front of her subconscious.

'Hang on, I'm sure I remember that you mentioned you were seeing someone a few weeks back?'

Tom's trace of a smile vanished instantly. Alice's wasn't far behind.

'I was. I guess I still am. But, well, I don't know exactly what's happening there. I'll sort it out, I promise.'

Alice made sure she had eye contact. 'Okay.'

'Not okay. But it will be. So, might I be able to see you again?'

Professionally, Alice knew what the answer had to be. 'I can recommend you someone else and pass over your notes.'

'I think I might be cured.'

Alice smiled despite herself. The trouble was, so did she. Sometimes her mother deserved praise for her outlandish ideas.

Tom took a chance. 'And how about seeing you personally…?'

At that moment the train finally came to a halt and despite the lateness of the hour, everyone rushed to disembark. After the rest of their carriage had pushed past, Tom rescued the oversize toy dolphin from the luggage rack and jumped down off the train onto the platform ahead of Alice. Taking her hand, he did his best to emulate the perfect gentleman. In Victorian times there would have been steam, leather luggage, heeled boots and capacious underskirts. Now it looked much less romantic as Alice stepped down the six inches to the platform in three-quarter length trousers and backless loafers. She shivered. The temperature had dropped significantly.

Tom held on to her hand. 'So, what now?'

Prize dolphin tucked under his arm, Tom stood next to her at the empty taxi rank at the front of the station as Alice searched the horizon for an orange light.

'So how about we make a social appointment?'

'That would be nice.' Secretly, Alice was delighted by his determination.

'Nice?'

'Great.' Alice conceded her emotional hand.

'Excellent.'

'Except.'

'Except what?' Tom didn't like the sound of this.

'Except what was that other thing?'

'What other thing?'

'The "it's complicated" thing.'

'I promise I'll sort that out.'

Alice pursed her lips.

'So now you think I'm a liar?'

'Right now, I have no idea what I think.' Alice paused. 'Stop looking at me like that. I'm getting in a cab, on my own.'

'Of course.'

'Is it Helen?' Alice could have sworn she'd just closed that conversation.

'Helen?'

She'd started, so she'd have to finish. 'You mentioned a Helen a few weeks ago. Planet Hollywood, remember?'

Relieved, Tom smiled. 'That's quite a memory you've got there.'

'It's my job to remember everything you tell me.'

'Well, remember this—she's my sister. The children are hers. As I've told you before, I have no wife and no children.'

'Just double-checking.'

'Still want your own cab?'

Alice nodded. 'They always turn up eventually, like…'

'Buses?'

'I was going to say "men".'

Tom smiled. 'So how about I give you a moment to let all this sink in and I call you next week?'

'Do.'

'Or maybe I shouldn't give you time to think at all.' Tom stopped himself. What did he think he was doing?

Alice smiled as a taxi pulled up. Getting in, she lowered the window. 'I'll leave the ball in your court.'

Tom kissed her lightly on the lips. 'Sometimes I wish I was a woman.'

Alice fixed her gaze on his. 'Now you're sounding dangerously like my ex-husband.'

Tom laughed. 'Thanks for today. Hopefully you'll let me see you soon.' He proffered the large sea mammal from under his arm. 'Are you sure I can't persuade you to take Flipper home?'

'He's your prize.'

'I thought dolphins were a girl's best friend.'

'That's diamonds and normally I'm a sucker for a present, but on this occasion I'm going to have to say no on grounds of taste and decency.'

'Charming. Well, your loss is Natalie's gain.'

'Natalie?'

'Relax. Niece. And now your friend for life.'

As her taxi pulled away from the kerb Alice resisted the urge to turn around and wave at an ever-decreasing Tom from the rear window. Dancing with danger or flirting with disaster? But everyone knows that dancing is good for the soul.

Chapter Eight

21 days to go
Suzie 6, Alice 2

Wide awake, Alice lay in bed beaming at her lampshade. Sleeping was so last weekend. This one was all about morning-after-the-night-before analysis.

She'd finally made it home just after midnight, fizzing with adrenaline, and it had been the one evening in recent memory that Suzie had already been asleep. She hadn't even stirred when Alice had noisily gone in to turn her bedside light off and remove the open book from her duvet.

Still buzzing, Alice stretched out beneath her Egyptian-cotton sheet and ran her hands over her naked torso. Magically, despite the previous day's calorie and carbohydrate abuse, her stomach had returned to its normal size, and as she rolled over onto her front she could feel her muscles aching. Laughter clearly was the best medicine. Maybe she could smile her way to a six-pack?

Reaching on to her bedside table for her home-phone

handset, she consulted the display on her alarm clock. A mere 9:27 a.m. Way too early to call Zoë. Saturday mornings were sacred, barring emergencies. Besides, chances were, in two and a half hours' time she'd need her even more. Euphoria never lasted very long these days.

'Shit.' Alice sat up abruptly at the sudden guilty realisation that she hadn't spoken to Zoë since her meeting. The memory of her perfect day already tarnishing, she rummaged in her bag on the floor for her mobile phone.

The screen was blank. Battery dead or still turned off from lunchtime? Power restored, there was nothing in the message department. And then a flourish of beeps piggybacked each other, each and every one a prick to Alice's guilty conscience.

Two text messages and eight missed calls. Six from her mother, and two from Zoë. Alice let her head fall back onto the pillows. A friend in need is a friend at the seaside. These things happened all the time. She was sure they did. But maybe she should pitch up with coffee and pastries at noon and beg forgiveness.

The perfect potential of the day already in tatters and nothing she could do to remedy the situation for a couple of hours, Alice decided to get up.

The house was quiet, although a faint aroma of fresh coffee was detectable. With an overnight date in the offing, her mother was undoubtedly up, packing and repacking, and for once Alice was looking forward to the distraction. Poking her head around her bedroom door, she checked to make sure the landing was clear before tiptoe sprinting to the bathroom with a hand over her breasts to minimise any jiggling.

As she dried her freshly washed face, Alice couldn't help but laugh at the wildness of her hair. Pure scarecrow. Wind

+ sea breeze + wine + dream-filled sleep = Edward Scissor-hands school of hairstyling. Taking her white bathrobe from the back of the bathroom door, she belted herself in to the thick toweling and knocked lightly on Suzie's door. Opening it gingerly, to her surprise the bed was empty and neatly made. Closing it behind her, Alice descended the stairs, following the caffeine trail as eagerly as The Bisto Kid.

For the first time in as long as she could remember, the kitchen door was closed. In fact, if you'd asked Alice whether she even had a kitchen door she would've been hard pressed to answer. Two motorcycle helmets rested, cheek to cheek, on the hall table. Had her mother discovered a Hammersmith chapter of Hells Angels? In Suzie's world, everything was possible.

'Knock knock.' Alice padded into her kitchen, a definite lightness to her tone and her mood. But as two heads turned to greet her, her day hit self-destruct. Subconsciously she rubbed an eye, just on the off chance it was an optical illusion. Disappointingly, all that happened was that suddenly there were two of everything.

'Morning, darling. So glad you made it down here before we set off…'

Suzie was wearing tight jeans and what looked like a new black long-sleeved T-shirt decorated with a no-doubt designer bejewelled skull and crossbones. A barely worn leather jacket hung over the back of her chair.

'I was hoping you two would meet…'

Alice's eyes were suddenly as dry as her throat. The man of her moment was in her house and yet this was no time for celebration. A flume of acid rose from her stomach and she swallowed hard.

Suzie beamed at her date and then her daughter. 'Allie, this is Mr. Eurostar himself. Tom, this is Alice.'

Alice felt her stomach twist. Her fingertips tingled. Twenty-nine years of life and three years of life coaching had not prepared her for this moment.

Forty-four years of life and three weeks of life coaching had clearly not prepared Tom, either, as bewildered, he stared at Alice. He stood up, he sat down, he stood up again.

Alice remained motionless.

'Alice is the friend you're staying with?' Tom addressed Suzie slowly, confusion permeating his tone.

Nodding, Suzie blushed, but despite Alice's somewhat eccentric appearance was overcome with a moment of maternal pride. 'And my daughter.'

Alice thought Tom's knees were going to buckle. Thankfully for him, his leather trousers and armoured biker boots were keeping him upright. Unfortunately for Alice, her bathrobe offered no such support. She tightened the towelling belt firmly, almost winding herself in the process. Thank God she'd at least washed her face. It wasn't much to hold on to, but it was all she had at the moment.

On automatic pilot, in self-preservation mode and imbued with good old-fashioned British manners, Alice proffered her hand. She had the rest of the weekend to nosedive towards a nervous breakdown. 'Pleased to meet you.'

Puzzled, Tom returned the formality with the same hand that had stroked her hair less than twelve hours earlier. His tone hardened, along with his grip. 'Well, this is all very cosy, isn't it?'

Alice reclaimed her hand.

Oblivious, Suzie looked on proudly. 'We're friends, too. It works perfectly.' She winked at her daughter.

'I'm sure it does.' Only the evening he had been chatted up by a transsexual on his now-brother-in-law's stag weekend was going to top this. On second thought, this won, hands down. And worse still, he was stone-cold hungover.

Suzie looked from Alice to Tom and back again. Her concern about getting on the back of a motorbike was suddenly dwarfed by something she sensed was going to be a much bigger deal.

Tom was officially floored. Like most men, he had harboured the occasional alcohol-induced fantasy of dating sisters, of a threesome, but he'd never expected to be faced with the multigenerational reality. His throat closing, he could only mutter. No whole words were emerging.

'Tom's a client of mine.' Alice barely recognised her own voice.

'Oh good, so you two have met?' Suzie appeared to relax as she thought the mystery was solved. She turned to Tom. 'After your response at the restaurant, I didn't think you'd call her.'

Alice raised an eyebrow incredulously at her mother. 'This was your idea?'

Suzie nodded as Tom interrupted her.

'Believe me, right now I'm wishing that I hadn't listened to a word she'd said. I was doing fine. Three weeks of "help," my arse.' Disgusted with himself, Tom glanced at Suzie before returning his focus to Alice. 'And I told you she recommended you.'

'You didn't say you were sleeping with her.'

Suzie interrupted. 'I'm not.'

Tom folded his arms. 'You didn't ask.'

The triangle of confusion far from over, Alice was suddenly dizzy. 'You said she was a friend.'

Suzie butted in again. 'So you knew I'd sent him.'

Alice wheeled. 'Why didn't you say something, Mum? He's not the first client you've recommended to me.'

'Why on earth didn't *you* tell *me*?'

'My clients expect confidentiality.'

'Or maybe it just didn't suit you.'

Tom needed a faster processor. His operating system was in danger of crashing. 'What is this, some sort of twisted social experiment, a conspiracy?'

'Have you lost your mind?' Alice was incandescent. 'You're the one who should be apologising. You should have put two and two together. I'm not in the habit of sharing men with anyone, and certainly not with my mother.'

Suzie approached Tom and prodded him in the chest with a perfectly manicured finger, the skull and crossbones on her chest glinting in the sunlight coming through the window. 'And to think I thought you were a gentleman.'

Wisely, he took a step backwards. 'How the hell was I supposed to know? You don't even look the same.' Tom glanced from one woman to the other to convince himself this wasn't his fault. 'You don't have the same surname, the same mannerisms…'

Alice folded her arms. 'So we're not clones.' She dug her hands into the pockets of her bathrobe and gripped the fabric until her hands hurt. 'You're not supposed to be seeing two people at the same time.'

'It's a long time since I've seen one woman.'

'You should have said something last night. You should have told me you were sleeping with someone—with her.'

'But I'm not.'

'Well, whatever you two get up to.'

'It was complicated.'

'And now it's impossible.'

Tom shook his head. 'Well, this is just fucking great. I hope you two will be very happy together.' He gritted his teeth. 'Feel free to have a laugh at my expense and—' as he turned to address Suzie, his eyes narrowed '—you can leave this out of next week's column.'

Pushing past Alice, and taking the helmets from the hall table, he slammed the front door behind him, leaving two stunned women in his wake.

Suzie turned to face her daughter. 'Well done, Alice.' Her tone was cold. 'Thanks.'

Alice's emotional pendulum swung from anger to hurt and back again. 'What on earth…?'

'Well, he *was* here, and now, thanks to you and your big mouth, he's not.'

'I'm sorry? Surely you weren't expecting me to take that all in my stride.'

'Maybe the situation was salvageable.'

'Look, all I was doing was trying to get a cup of coffee in my own kitchen.' Alice slumped into a kitchen chair, suddenly faint.

Suzie thumped the table with her fist out of sheer frustration. 'He could have been my last chance at happiness.'

'Along with Ryan, Geoffrey…' Alice spat her words out. 'You spend so much time boring me with irrelevant trivia and yet you fail to mention that you've sent one of your boyfriends to see me.'

'He's not a boyfriend. You've certainly seen to that.'

'He's hardly a pen pal. You were about to go on a dirty weekend. You'd even bought a bloody leather jacket.' Alice swallowed hard. 'I didn't even know you were seeing a "Tom".' She was determined to clear her name and her conscience.

Suzie was pacing backward and forward, her thumbs in her belt loops. A few twirls and a bit of fancy footwork and she would have been line dancing. 'I only suggested life coaching to him once, it was late, we were flirting and he'd never mentioned it again.'

Alice wasn't listening. 'He told me he was a friend of yours. "Friend" doesn't mean shagging. Or does it? Maybe I'm just out of date.'

'No, I'm the one out of a date. And we haven't even slept together.'

'Whatever you say.'

'You'd already know that if you actually listened to me from time to time.' Suzie's demeanour was hostile. 'Besides, you'd never even asked me for Mr. Eurostar's name.'

'To be fair, you don't normally wait for me to ask.'

'I didn't want to jinx anything. To say nothing of what clearly has been going on at your end. What happened to your professional code of conduct?'

'Nothing has been going on.'

'Men don't run for the hills at ten o'clock on a Saturday morning for no particular reason.'

'Nothing's been going on. It went on. Once. And all because I followed your advice and went with the moment.'

'Fucking great timing, darling.'

'I should've just stuck to my way.' At this precise moment Alice would have pledged eternal celibacy in exchange for an even keel.

Taking the stairs two at a time, using as much downward force as possible, Suzie stomped to her room and slammed the door behind her.

Blinking back tears, Alice shouted after her teenage mother. 'I thought you said we should share everything?'

One minute she was sitting at the kitchen table, the next moment she was sobbing. Headache approaching, she stopped herself and sniffed hard. Today was going to be hard enough without a migraine. Leaning forward, she rested her forehead on the oak, wishing that the rush of blood to her brain would speed up her understanding of the situation. She was flushed and yet she was shivering. Forcing herself to her feet, she flicked the switch on her electric kettle. Blitz mentality. Everything always felt better after a nice cup of tea.

Walking to the front door, Alice peered out of the window and down the street. Predictably, there was no sign of man or motorbike, only the postman, currently next door and approaching rapidly. Exchanging platitudes as he handed her a selection of envelopes, she left her mail on the hall table and headed for the spare room. One of them had to be grown-up about this. Plus, she didn't have the energy to be at war.

'Mum?' Alice knocked and then leaned against the closed door of her spare room. 'Mum?'

'Go away.'

'I'm not going anywhere. This is my house.'

'Then I'll go to a hotel.'

'Please, Mum. This isn't my fault.' Alice gritted her teeth. 'It isn't yours, either.' She wondered if she could nominate herself for the lesser known Nobel-Keeping-the-Peace Prize. 'It's Tom's.'

'I'd packed a bag, I'd had my legs waxed, we were going away for the weekend.' Suzie was whining.

Alice was still trying to come to terms with the last half hour. 'The man is clearly a fantasist. He was whispering sweet nothings to me last night.'

'I just don't get it.'

'This isn't all about you. For once I thought I'd met someone special.' Heavy-hearted, Alice stared at the doorjamb and idly wondered if it needed repainting.

'Join the club.'

Alice turned her back on the door frame and slid down until she was sitting on the floor. From beyond the door, Alice could hear her mother padding across the carpet inside her room. She focused on a small patch of the wall opposite and pretended not to notice as Suzie opened her bedroom door a fraction. If there was one thing her mother couldn't resist, it was a conversation.

Sighing, Suzie sat down next to Alice. 'Well, at least this explains why you weren't answering your phone last night. Zoë and I were almost worried. It's not like you to go AWOL.'

'You spoke to Zoë?'

'You didn't tell me she was tracing her birth mother.'

'Sorry.' Alice was sheepish. 'I forgot.'

'Of course you did.'

'Well, you forgot to tell me you were sending Tom to see me as a client.'

Suzie knew when she was beaten.

Alice turned to face her mother. 'So how was Zo?'

'Wanting her best friend.'

Alice sighed. 'As if I needed reminding that I was in the wrong place at the wrong time…'

At this precise moment, she was caught between wanting to laugh the whole thing off, wanting to punch something really hard, wanting to punch her mother fairly hard and wanting to go to sleep for a hundred years, hopefully being woken with a new identity at the end of it.

'…Fancy sending a guy you are seeing, to see me professionally and not mentioning it.'

'I didn't think for one minute he'd take up my suggestion.' Suzie oozed nonchalance. 'Anyway, I thought it might compromise your position.'

'I'll give you a bloody compromising position. And I'm not talking about sitting at my breakfast table.'

'I thought you'd tell me he was too young.'

'Glad to see you think so highly of me.'

'I thought you'd be disapproving. I mean, you usually are. Look at you now.'

'For God's sake, Mum, I'm upset.' Alice felt her voice crack and did her best to recover. 'For the record, I would have said he was highly suitable.' For herself.

'Well, if we're talking about being economical with the truth, I didn't even know you were seeing anybody.'

'Neither did I.'

'Oh really.' Suzie's tone was acidic.

'And now I'm definitely not. Why didn't you tell him I was your daughter?'

Suzie snorted with ridicule.

'I didn't realise I was such an embarrassment.'

'This is not the time to start tugging at my heartstrings.'

'I'm just trying to find out the truth.'

'I don't lie to you.'

'But if I'd known… Why would you keep me a secret?'

Suzie pushed the sleeves of her T-shirt up. 'Because I'm old enough without having to point out that a beautiful young woman like you is my daughter. Call it self-preservation, call it vanity, call it—'

'Idiotic…' Alice hadn't even spotted the earlier compliment.

'Actually, that wasn't on my shortlist.'

'Since when have you even been able to spell *insecure*? You've always looked fantastic for your age. As for poaching from my peer group…' Alice buried her face in her hands. 'I should have known there'd be a catch. It was all going far too well.' Her shoulders slumped.

'He's hardly your peer group. He's fifteen years older than you.' Suzie put her arm across Alice's back, surprised at her overriding concern for Alice over herself. 'And for the record, most decent men my age want women your age, which leaves me in a bit of a dating vacuum.'

'I should never have let him kiss me.' Alice buttoned her lip a second too late.

'You kissed?' Suzie retracted her arm.

Alice nodded. 'Last night on the train back from Brighton.'

For a split second she was back in her seat in the carriage and cursed the fact that moments, by definition, were short-lived.

'He's a great kisser.' Suzie's expression was wistful.

'Mum, you're freaking me out.' Alice scrabbled to her feet and going into the bathroom, splashed her face, her hot tears disguised by the cold water. She wondered how deep cleansing her face wash really was.

Curious, Suzie appeared at her side. 'So you weren't at work yesterday? Sometimes you surprise me. You can't just go gallivanting around. You have responsibilities.'

Alice felt her fuse ignite. 'I was at work. I'm the responsible one, remember…?'

Suzie bristled.

'…And thanks to you, Tom was my business. He'd booked me for the whole afternoon.' Alice sighed. 'This is why I don't do men.' Still standing at the basin, instinctively she started brushing her teeth. Maybe she should just go back to bed and start today again.

'I just don't get it.' Her mood darkening, Suzie retreated and closed her door dramatically. 'I really don't.'

Spitting and rinsing, Alice heard the springs of the mattress as her mother fell onto her bed and, walking into the next-door room, dived onto her own.

If only she hadn't gone downstairs they might both have had a better weekend. Alice reached for the phone. The situation had just been upgraded to a crisis.

Alice counted as Zoë's phone rang eight times before the answering machine cut in. Hanging up, Alice pressed redial, repeating the process several times. Finally the voice she wanted to hear picked up groggily.

'Alice?' Zoë's voice was thick with sleep. 'Thank God, you're alive. Where were you? Are you okay? Where are you?'

'At home.'

If she had been a fraction more awake, Zoë would have remembered that she'd just recognised the incoming number. 'So you're just ignoring me then? For the record, that's much worse.'

'I'm not ig—'Alice changed her approach from defensive to apologetic. 'I'm so, so sorry. I turned my phone off at lunch, forgot all about it and didn't get back until late. You should have left a message here.'

'I left one at the clinic and with your mother. I thought that would probably suffice.' Zoë yawned herself awake.

'You should have left one on my mobile.'

'If it was switched off, there clearly wouldn't have been much point.'

'But you didn't know that.'

Zoë sat herself up. 'No, by then I probably thought you were in an ambulance while your phone was being rechipped and sold on by a gang of muggers. So where the hell were you anyway?'

'With a client.' Alice felt terrible.

'For five hours?'

'For twelve.'

Zoë sighed. 'Well, I trust that in that amount of time you were creating a whole new life for her.'

'Him, and actually, I think I may have inadvertently ruined it. So how did yesterday go?'

'Fine. Enlightening, terrifying, routine. You name it, I've felt it. I am now the proud owner of my adoption file and I've never wanted to be an adult less in my life. I went to bed at ten-thirty last night craving Angel Delight. I am officially regressing.'

'You have a file already? I had no idea they would… I'm so sorry I wasn't here.'

'Me, too. Never mind, no doubt you have a brilliant excuse for this uncharacteristic behaviour?'

'If you'd asked me half an hour ago you'd have got one version. Now, on the other hand…'

Suzie appeared in Alice's doorway clutching her towel. She had obviously decided to drown her sorrows or at least wash as many of them away as possible. And judging by the state of her mascara, she was clearly more upset than she had been ten minutes ago. She pointed her crusty loofah at Alice.

'Just say—well, what if he was *the* man?'

Alice held the phone to her chest. 'Mum, there's no need to be quite so dramatic. There isn't an Oscar for best unsupporting mother.'

'Well, he could have been my date for the party at the very least.'

'I'm talking to Zoë. Let's discuss it in a minute.' Her distress in remission, Alice needed time. She was a lot crosser than she had realised.

'You have no idea how excited I was about this weekend. I thought he might be the one.'

'You mean the next one. It's not like I meet men with potential every day or even every year.'

Suzie shifted her weight from one leg to the other. 'You slept with him, didn't you?'

'Mum.' Alice wondered if she sounded as exasperated as she felt.

'It's okay, you can tell me. I want to know.'

'For goodness' sake. Enough with the self-flagellation.'

'I knew it.'

'I barely kissed him. I certainly did not sleep with him. I did, however, doze off with my head on his shoulder, so I guess I may have slept *on* him. That's it.'

'Oh.'

'Now you almost seem disappointed.'

'But you would sleep with him?'

'Would have? Possibly. Maybe.' Alice paused. 'I'm not sure either of us will get the chance now.'

'This isn't a joke.'

'I'm upset, too, but you've got to see the funny side. Girl meets boy. Girl's daughter meets boy. Boy is the same. Besides, he was wrong for you in so many ways.'

'I don't agree.'

'You wouldn't. But I think his unsuitability is pretty well demonstrated by the fact he was simultaneously pursuing your daughter. He was far too young for you.' Alice felt the edge of her headache start to recede. Getting everything off her chest was certainly cathartic.

'How can he be too young for me and not too old for you? Besides, it makes perfect demographic sense. If there are more women than men out there and women are living longer, I'm obviously going to have to cast the net that bit wider to land a catch.'

'If you weren't staying here, we'd have been none the wiser. You'd be whizzing down the motorway and I'd be waiting for him to call.'

'Which would be better?' Suzie was confused.

'Face the facts, there aren't enough heterosexual men out there, single or otherwise.'

Suzie sighed as she down sat on the edge of Alice's bed. 'Sometimes I wish I was a man. It's just so damn disappointing. I was really looking forward to seeing what happened next.'

For once Alice was in total agreement with her mother as they shared a reflective moment.

'Mum.'

'What now?'

'Enough with the attitude. There's no point in us falling out. The prize at stake is missing in action and I'll bet Tom is currently riding into the sunset as fast as he can.'

Mood plummeting as she realised she was spending the weekend at home, Suzie stood up. 'Sadly, I don't think he'll be back in a hurry.'

Both women paused for a moment to indulge themselves in their own personal fantasy as to whom he would return for and how.

Suzie sighed. 'You know, I really hoped we might have had something.'

'Now you always will have. A history.'

'I'm glad you think this is all fucking hilarious.'

'I don't. And by the way, you haven't even asked me how I am.'

'How are you?'

'Shit, thanks. I just tend not to get hysterical about things.'

'Well, aren't you little Miss Perfectly Controlled. So what now?'

'What now? How about a round of tea and toast? I haven't even had breakfast yet.'

'I mean what do we *do* now?'

'You can start by changing out of those Miss Sixty jeans. They're not for people of your age, despite their name. And what is that T-shirt?'

'Vivienne Westwood. Hey…' As Suzie's features lit up, Alice felt her stomach muscles contract. 'Why don't we toss a coin for the right to see him again? Alternatively, if you'd just like to put your mother's happiness before your own…you could consider my right to pursue as a birthday gift.'

Alice's silence said it all.

'I suppose you think we should just leave it and move on?'

Alice nodded. 'First of all, there is our pride to consider and secondly, did you not see his face?'

Suzie shook her head.

'Maybe you should have had your glasses on.'

'I was having trouble focusing on anything. He was obviously in shock. We all were. He'll get over it…'

Suzie willed herself to believe what she was saying.

'As for you, sleeping with a client, it doesn't look good.'

'For the last time, we didn't have sex.'

Alice realised she was shouting at the same moment she remembered she was still clutching the phone. 'I'm really sorry, Zo, just give me a minute and I'll call you back.'

'Allie, don't you dare hang up on me now.'

Too late. She was gone.

When seconds later the phone rang, Alice was instantly and irrationally a bundle of nerves.

'You can't wake me up, feed me nine-tenths of a soap opera and then hang up. I couldn't be more awake now, so do you want to come over here, or am I coming to you?' Zoë wasn't ready to let her get away two days running.

'I'll come to you.'

'On one condition.'

'On one condition?' Alice was surprised.

'Ten minutes more of this and then we are moving on to me. I am traditionally the irresponsible, emotionally overwrought, flighty one in our relationship. And whether you and your mother are sleeping with the same man or not, I am trying to find mine, to ever prevent that from happening. Got that?'

Alice smiled. 'Loud and clear.' Never before had she been so grateful for somebody else's crisis.

Chapter Nine

Still 21 days to go
Suzie 6, Alice 2. Overlaps 1

Zoë's green eyes were wide as she watched Alice from over the rim of her fresh mug of tea.

'I'm not sure what I find more appalling. That Tom turned out to be a fraction of the man I thought he was, or the fact that my mother and I fell for the same guy.'

Alice was finding her confession very therapeutic. Everything was always easier once Zoë was in the loop.

'Well, you know what they say?'

'All men are bastards?'

'Like mother, like daughter…'

Alice forced a wry smile. 'But we couldn't be any more different.'

Zoë decided it was probably best for her life expectancy if she kept silent at this point.

'Speaking of which…' Zoë produced a manila A4 document wallet from under the coffee table.

Alice slid down from the sofa onto the floor and sat down cross-legged next to Zoë. The move was partly out of support and partly out of necessity. An estate agent might have described Zoë's flat as cosy but as far as Alice was concerned, it was cluttered. Years of working in the fashion business had taken their toll and piles of thumbed magazines, along with clothes and shoes—some in use, others samples—had been abandoned everywhere, blurring the boundaries between rooms. Indeed, one corner of the sitting room and one half of the sofa resembled a brightly coloured jumble sale.

Zoë slid the folder across the table towards her.

'Oh my God, Zo, this is it.' Alice took Zoë's life in her hands. 'I'm so proud of you.'

'That's good, because I'm not sure I'm so proud of me.'

'You must be so excited.'

'Curious—yes. Nauseous—yes. Scared—yes. Excited— definitely. Although I have spoken to Mum more times this week than any time I can remember, I do feel a bit guilty. Like she might feel she hasn't been enough, and she's been outstanding.'

Alice smiled. 'I'm sure that's only natural.'

Zoë nodded. 'The social worker told me it was.'

'What else did she say?'

'Everything that you would expect—that this could be a difficult process, that some women weren't over the moon about being contacted, that they may well have families of their own, that I may have half siblings, that I might be a dark secret; basically not to expect some hearts-and-flowers fairy-tale reunion.'

Alice put her arm around Zoë supportively as she tried and failed miserably to really empathise with what her friend was going through. Zoë was in search of a stranger. A stranger who had given birth to her, so not really a stranger at all. And here Alice was risking falling out with her ever-present and generally nurturing mother over a man she'd only known for a few weeks. Thank goodness she hadn't gone back to his place.

Perspective returning, Alice was beginning to wish she'd given her mother a hug before she'd left the house, or had at least said goodbye. In the cold light of lunchtime, she knew it wasn't Suzie's fault. Yet in Tom's absence, she'd had to be cross with someone.

Zoë stared at the file. 'There's a letter in there assessing her state of mind and health at the time of the adoption and outlining why she gave me away.'

Alice could barely bring herself to give away old pairs of trainers and coats and yet all over the world, for all sorts of reasons, women gave away brand-new babies.

'And?'

'And I haven't been able to read it.'

'Oh come on, you can't even buy *Hello!* magazine without flicking through it in the queue to pay.'

Zoë shook her head. 'I wouldn't believe me, either. The social worker went through the contents page by page and I barely took anything in. Then I said thank you very much, grabbed the folder, found the nearest Starbucks and called you.'

Alice examined a cuticle guiltily. 'And called me and called me.'

'Well, something like that. Then I gave up and went to bed.'

Alice felt terrible. 'It's official. I'm a very bad friend.'

'Ninety-nine percent of the time you're fantastic.'

'And then when it really matters… God, Zo, I'm so sorry. Stereotypical rotten female behaviour. One afternoon in the company of an attractive male and I forget the rest of the world exists.'

'Well, you're here now.'

'A mere twenty-two hours late and until a moment ago, talking about myself. So come on then, a summary. You must have at least had a peek.'

Zoë's voice wobbled along with her resolve. 'I thought this was everything I wanted and now—now I'm terrified.' Colour rose in her cheeks as she battled with her emotions. 'I don't really want anything to change and I don't want to hurt anyone.'

'You don't want to hurt yourself.'

Zoë nodded. 'That, too. But what if I really can't deal with this?'

'Think about all those times you've told me that you couldn't feel complete until you knew who your birth parents were, whatever the outcome.'

'I was young and feisty.'

Alice frowned. 'Past tense?'

'Just tense.'

Humour under fire, she was going to be just fine.

Alice took her hand. 'So what's changed?'

Zoë shrugged.

'Did your mum ever meet your birth mother?'

'Never. I checked. It was all done through an agency.'

'And have you told Jean you've got the file here?'

Zoë's body language was apologetic. 'I should think Mum's probably guessed by now. I mean, she's pretty astute and I've been calling her about everything but this. Knowing her, she'll be trying not to interfere.'

Alice smiled to herself. All mothers were not the same.

'Well, I'll bet you'll feel better once you've come clean. On top of everything else, you're just feeling guilty. Try and deal with one emotion at a time.'

Zoë sighed. 'I've already got a mother. Why do I need two?

What if the real one's dreadful? What am I talking about? The real one is in York and perfectly lovely.'

Alice nodded sagely. Jean Hudson was a practical, down-to-earth, no-fuss-no-frills, no-nonsense sort of woman and Zoë was her only child. Her most treasured possession.

'Come on, Zo, you've wanted to do this ever since I met you.'

Zoë blinked, lips tightly squeezed together. She sighed. 'But now it's like Pandora's box.'

'Or Pandora's file.'

Despite herself, Zoë smiled. 'Anyway, I was thinking, why don't *you* take a look at it first.'

'Don't be daft. I'll sit here while you read it, but this is your life.' Alice decided against the obvious big red book joke.

'Okay.' Zoë breathed deeply.

'Okay what?'

'Okay. I'll be okay.' She put the file back on the coffee table and just stared at the cover. 'Thank you. I don't know what I'd do without you.'

'It's not something you need to worry about. Now don't be cross, but can I give you some soul-sisterly advice?'

Zoë pawed at her green and purple T-shirt. 'This doesn't suit me?'

'You're doing it again. Focus.'

Zoë nodded earnestly.

'Excellent. Now, just do it.'

'Á la Nike?'

'Exactly. You're making it into a bigger deal than it is.'

Zoë's tone was steely. 'I don't think you get much bigger a deal than this.'

Alice stood her ground. 'I'm just saying, if you're waiting for an appointed hour, a drumroll, a glass of champagne, whatever, you're just adding to the pressure.'

'I know. Listen, do you think you can give me a few hours and then come back?'

Alice hesitated. 'Do you really want to me to leave? I could just sit outside in the car? I could take a nap? That way I can be here in seconds, if you change your mind.'

'No. Go.'

Alice grabbed her bag and car keys, wondering where she was heading next. Home wasn't an option yet. She gave Zoë a hug. 'Love you.'

Zoë squeezed her hard. 'Love you, too. And promise me you'll sort things out with your mum?'

Alice fiddled with her car keys. 'I'll talk to her later.'

'How about sooner?'

Alice turned as she reached the front door. 'Hey, tell you what, if you don't like what you read in the file, you can have my mum.'

Zoë looked up from staring at her name, typed on the cover.

Alice softened her tone. 'It'll be okay, Zo. Whoever this woman is, she has no idea just how much she has been missing.'

Alice opened Zoë's front door.

'Allie.'

'Yup.'

'Forget about the Tom thing. Just think of him as a cat-alyst. The One Who Got You in the Mood. You'll find a better one.'

Alice smiled bravely. 'I know.' If only Zoë knew how much she wanted that to be true.

'So run that by me again.' Richard stopped laughing to wipe a tear from his eye. 'Poor guy.'

'Poor guy?' Alice hurled a light grey suede cushion at him from her prone position on the sofa opposite his.

Suede cushions were so impractical. But then, so was being gay. And the soft furnishings were totally in keeping with Rob's new Manhattan approach to living in London. Almost everything was white, brick or glass.

Dodging the incoming interior-designed missile, Richard hid his smile in his next sip of coffee.

Alice's expression was stern. 'This isn't funny, you know.'

Richard did his best to think solemn thoughts, hoping that gravitas and maturity would start to seep from every pore.

Suddenly Alice sat up. 'Oh my God, it is, isn't it?'

Relieved, Richard grinned heartily. 'Although I can't even begin to imagine how humiliating it must have felt.' Involuntarily, he shuddered at the thought.

At last, someone who understood. And that was why she had married him.

'Oh, Allie, it could only happen to you…and just for the record, in case you were wondering, I never found your mother even remotely attractive.'

'Watch it, my sense of perspective is fully stretched at the moment.'

'You have to hold on to your sense of humour.'

'I fear it may be in critical condition.'

'Totally understandable. He was a good-looking guy.'

'There was more to him than a nice smile.'

Richard clapped his hands. 'You see, I knew there was something going on.'

'Easy there, oh smug one, there wasn't when you met him.'

'And when I saw you on Thursday?'

Alice shook her head. 'Nada. It all happened on Friday. It was like a twenty-four-hour bug.'

'Only it would appear you're not cured yet.'

Alice counted on her fingers. 'It's a mere fourteen hours

since we kissed… Which entitles me to ten more hours in recovery.'

'Who are you fooling?'

Alice was pragmatic. 'It's the way it has to be.'

'Says who? You know they say the course of true love never did run smooth.'

'Who's "they," because I'd like to have a word?'

'Um.' Richard hesitated. 'You know—people, papers, grannies.'

'And even if that is the case, this isn't a few potholes, it's more like all terrain.'

'Be honest with me, Allie. How long before you kissed had you been hoping that something might happen?'

'Okay, here's the thing. I really didn't see it coming.'

Richard slapped his forehead with the palm of his hand. 'I love that about you.'

'What?'

'That even after everything you've been through personally and after all your training, you've retained some innocence.'

'I'm desperately trying to see that as a compliment.'

'You should. And now?'

'Now?'

'When you woke up this morning what was your gut reaction without beer goggles on?'

Alice barely hesitated. Her tone was resigned. 'That he was great.'

'I knew it. You can't just let him get away.'

'Let him get away? He was gone before I could do anything about it.'

'That's just geography. This is so exciting.'

'Richard, he's history.'

'Call him.'

'Are you out of your mind?'

'Well, he's not going to call you.'

Alice paused. Discreetly she'd been checking her mobile for messages and missed calls several times an hour. Zoë was the perfect excuse.

'Well, for a start, your mother might answer the phone.' Richard giggled.

Alice rolled her eyes. 'I'd been assuming that he'd call my mobile.'

'Ah, but you had been assuming he would call?'

Alice avoided eye contact. 'I might have hoped. Once or twice.'

'You see.'

'I was only hoping for an apology.'

'However you want to justify it. I say call him.'

'And how on earth would I explain that to Mum?'

'For all you know she's on the phone to him herself right now.'

Alice shook her head. 'She wouldn't do that. I told her how I felt.'

'You told her you didn't like Jonathan and she still went ahead and married him.'

'That was totally different. And by the way, it turned out I was right.'

Richard was silent. Alice could almost hear him thinking.

'Well, whatever happened this morning, Tom is still your client, right?'

Alice paused. 'I guess so.'

'And whatever you were hoping might develop, yesterday was just a kiss.' Richard was gathering momentum.

Alice willed him to get to the point.

'And who better to talk to in a crisis than your life coach?'

Alice wasn't convinced. 'I'm not sure in these circum-stances…'

Richard crossed his legs tightly. 'It's such a great story. I can't wait for the speeches at your wedding.'

Alice hurled another cushion across the divide. 'That's quite enough from you. Besides, Mum and I have to stick together. It's just the two of us. And we're living in the same house.'

'Just think though, if you didn't, you'd be sitting here telling me you'd met a lovely guy.'

Alice blushed and drained her glass.

Richard watched as she went to the kitchen for a refill. Standing at the tap waiting for the water to run cold, she shouted over her shoulder.

'Do you know what's the most galling about the whole Tom Taylor thing?'

Chief sounding board, Richard shook his head gently.

'Yesterday was supposed to be strictly business and yet, when I agreed to meet him for lunch, I knew it wasn't.' Alice made her way back to the sofa.

'And yet you still said yes. You went with the moment. I'm so proud of you.'

'It was a mistake.'

'I'm afraid I would have to disagree.'

'Since when did you become my relationship guru?'

'Well, did Zoë know you were going to spend the afternoon with Tom yesterday?'

'Erm, no…'

'Your mother?'

'Please, I'm twenty-nine years old.'

'And did you tell me? I can answer that one. Of course not, and yet we had dinner on Thursday evening.'

'Hold your fire. I didn't even know I was spending the afternoon with Tom on Friday until lunchtime the same day.'

'But you did already know you were going to have lunch with him.'

'I was just meeting a client. No big deal. It was a business lunch.'

'If that's the case, why not mention it? May I boldly suggest that you didn't mention Tom to either me, Zoë or your mother because you knew you were playing a dangerous game?'

Alice shrugged guiltily.

'So there you go.'

'I'm sorry.' Alice wasn't sure. 'Where do I go?'

'After Tom.'

'That's so not my style.'

'Well, maybe it's time for a new look. Shake things up for once. Do something different. Make a change.'

Alice could see exactly what he was doing. Advice for her life, love and career all rolled into one. Richard was a grand master of manipulation. 'Rest assured, I'm seriously thinking about your offer.'

'Good. You should be. You'd be perfect, and ten out of ten for almost deftly changing the subject, but back to the man in question, tell me you really, hand on heart, don't like Tom.'

'Have you not been listening to a word I've said?'

'It's not what you've said, it's what you haven't.'

'Look, can we swap sofas?'

Richard looked at her, surprised by her request.

'It's just I've run out of cushions to throw at you from this one.'

Silently Alice and Zoë read and reread the photocopied pages of correspondence between Zoë's mother and the administrators responsible for finalising the adoption, as Alice refilled Zoë's glass with red wine and her own with elderflower cordial.

Zoë raised her glass. 'To finding Margaret Riddick. Finally

my birth mother has a name. To Margaret, Maggie, Madge, whoever she is. Can you believe she wanted to call me Daisy? She must have been on drugs.'

'Maybe you were conceived in a meadow?'

'You're supposed to be helping.'

'Sounds like you were a very healthy baby.' Alice read from the pages in her hand. 'No complications, average weight, no cause for concern. And here it is in black and white. Margaret was very reluctant to give you away.'

Alice scanned the next few paragraphs. 'She was twenty-three, in her first job, not ready for children, nowhere near a steady relationship, no money to support you with.'

'Probably a bit of a slapper.'

'There's no evidence for that. Maybe she was desperately in love but not ready for children, maybe her parents didn't approve of him—that counted for a lot more in those days—maybe, well, there are hundreds of maybes.'

'Thanks, Al.'

'Well, we can't even begin to imagine what she must have gone through after carrying you for nine months, giving birth and then walking away.'

Zoë's imagination was working overtime. 'Maybe she was married to someone else. Maybe he was married to someone else.'

'Right, no more alcohol for you until you promise to make a concerted effort to at least try to be positive. And whatever her reasons, Jean and David collected you when you were three days old. Can you imagine their excitement?'

Zoë couldn't suppress a smile.

'That's it. Much better. Now, does it not say anything about your father in the correspondence?'

Zoë found a sentence on the next page. 'A fleeting relationship with no long-term potential.'

'Is that it?'

Zoë nodded. 'But I've requested a copy of my original birth certificate from the General Register office. That should at least have his name on it.'

'Imagine…' Alice paused, focusing on a light switch. 'Well, maybe he doesn't even know he's got a daughter. And yet I'll bet there isn't a day that goes by that your mother doesn't wonder where you are, who you are, who you're with, what you're doing. So what do we do next? Google?'

'I'm not Googling my mother.'

'Why on earth not? Or you could try Friends Reunited?'

Alice ignored Zoë's range of dismissive expressions.

'Our mother's generation did go to school, you know. My mum's got in touch with a few old friends that way.'

Zoë raised an eyebrow. 'Friends or old flames?'

Alice laughed. 'What do you think? But they were friends, too.'

'So you're asking me to assume that Margaret is computer literate and a U.K. resident?'

'I can come up with plenty of excuses, too, if you want me to. I'm not saying she's just a few mouse clicks away. But it won't take a second to look and I was just suggesting we start somewhere.'

'We?'

'Surely you don't think I'm going to let you do this alone.'

Chapter Ten

In a much more conciliatory mood, Alice brought two glasses of wine over to the sofa and sat herself next to Suzie.

'Can you believe there were over two million Riddick-related entries on Google and nothing on Friends Reunited...'

Suzie was only half paying attention, as Saturday-night light-entertainment television burbled away. Since Alice had arrived home she'd been waiting for the right moment to say something. She knew she had to confess sooner rather than later.

'...So she's decided to drive up to see Jean first thing tomorrow. She's hoping her mother might have been given some documentation at the time that might help to narrow the search down.'

'Interesting.' Barely listening, Suzie seized her moment as casually as she could. 'Would you mind if I wrote an article or two about this?'

'About Zoë?' Alice slipped her flip-flops off and crossed her legs underneath her. Good old British summer. Her feet were freezing.

'Zoë?' Suzie wondered if she'd missed an important point.

'Mum. You haven't been paying attention to a word I've said.'

Suzie transferred her attention from the small screen to her daughter and ventured the humorous approach. 'The odd word.'

Annoyed, Alice reached for the remote control. She needed something all-consuming and compulsive to inject a little excitement into yet another Saturday night on the couch, and to drown out her housemate.

Alice surfed the channels, skipping past popular archaeology, a children's film, a western and a home-makeover series revealing yet more people trying to fix their lives by changing their wallpaper and their soft furnishings. As Suzie became instantly gripped by some DIY paint-spattering-on-canvas idea for pictures, Alice felt old. These days she only seemed to be visited by the zeitgeist of Christmas Past.

'So, Mum…' Alice pressed mute to ensure she had Suzie's attention. While the last few weeks had been far from dull, Alice didn't want Suzie giving her builders any more projects. 'Any idea how your wet room and kitchen are coming along?'

'Actually, I popped home this afternoon to pick up some post and they're looking pretty good. It's going to be fabulous.'

At this rate not only was Suzie's house going to be unrecognisable by the time they were finished, but Alice's life was going to have gone the same way. She wondered if maybe she could suggest Suzie move back, order takeaway and shower at the gym to encourage them to get a move on.

'They assure me I'll be back at home soon.'

Soon. One of the great non-time specific answers designed to cover a whole host of scenarios from it'll be getting dark *soon*, to the planet will have run out of oil *soon*.

'That's great.' Alice did her best to put her faith in the builders finishing while there were still fossil fuels, as she moved on to the next channel. *Who Wants To Be A Millionaire.* Perfect—entertainment with a hint of education. She turned the volume up and prepared to check out of her day.

It was a special family edition. Two generations battling with each other, as well as the questions, and currently deliberating over the capital of Peru. One of them thought it was Lyon. Alice shouted "Lima" impatiently at the screen.

Uncharacteristically silent, Suzie watched the next round dividing her attention between her daughter and the screen as Alice berated the contestants for taking longer than she deemed necessary to make their decision.

'We'd be good at this, darling.'

'What, at blaming each other for losing lots of cash?'

Suzie laughed softly. 'That, too. You know, maybe they should come up with a dating show with a similar format.'

'What, a mother and daughter pick the same man and then try and seduce him to see which one he prefers? Matricide and filicide figures would go through the roof.'

Suzie cocked her head. 'I was thinking more along the lines of mother picks date for daughter and vice versa.'

'Just as long as I can phone a friend.'

'It's funny, I've never thought of you as a "glass half-empty person" before.'

Alice took what she hoped would be a mood-enhancing sip of wine. 'So I'm having a bad day.'

'Still?'

Alice couldn't hide her disbelief. 'It takes some people more than a few hours to get over a man.' Since she'd got back from Zoë's she'd been thinking of little else.

Suzie smiled wryly. 'I guess I've had more experience.'

Alice had had enough of being brave. 'I really thought he had potential, Mum.'

'I know.'

Not "I know and why don't you call him," just I know. Damn.

Alice remembered interrupting her mother earlier. 'So what were you thinking about writing an article about?'

Suzie wondered if perhaps she had got the timing of asking all wrong. Too late now. Barely taking her eyes off the television, she played it down. 'Oh, you know, this finding-the-same-guy-attractive thing.'

'Mum.' Alice wielded the remote control threateningly wishing she could turn her off.

'Just wait a second. I bet it's much more common than you think.'

'I doubt it.'

'Are you telling me that Demi Moore's daughters don't fancy Ashton Kutcher?'

'Frankly, I'm not really that interested in speculating.'

'Well, you're not being much fun then, are you?'

'I guess not.'

'Anyway, it's not like I'm going to identify Tom or mention that the man in question was a client of yours or anything like that.'

Alice forced her mother to make direct eye contact with her. 'You've already written it, haven't you?'

Suzie's expression was semi-apologetic. 'Only a first draft. And they may not run with it next Saturday anyway.'

'You really have no shame, do you? Maybe I should write something about controlling mothers. An article, a book, a survival guide… I mean just hypothetically of course. Don't worry, I wouldn't identify you by name but—'

'It's my form of therapy. You talk to Zoë and Richard…'

'You talk to me.'

'…And then I write it down. It's cathartic.'

'I thought your brief was to reflect life all around you, not all around me?'

'I can't help it if that's a bit of a grey area at the moment.'

'And what if Tom sees it?'

'So what if he does? It's not just about him.'

'It makes you look petty.'

'It makes me look like I'm a columnist.'

'Is everything in your life research?'

Suzie hesitated.

'Fine, do what you like. Write the screenplay, too, for all I care. But I think I should warn him—out of courtesy.' Alice sat up a little straighter. Who said she couldn't turn a negative into a positive.

Suzie brightened. She couldn't believe that hadn't occurred to her. 'What a great idea. I'll give him a call.'

Alice held her hand out in the internationally recognised sign for "stop". 'He's my client. And I should contact him anyway over the next day or so, you know, professionally.' Alice did her best to sound as matter-of-fact as possible.

'I see.' Suzie did her best to be practical. 'And I don't suppose we could call him together?'

'I don't suppose we could.'

Suzie and Alice stopped and stared as right on cue the house phone started ringing. Suzie got to the handset first.

Alice could have growled with frustration. When it came to her land line, surely she should have had mortgage payer's priority, or something.

Suzie answered the phone in as casual a manner as she could manage while Alice pretended to watch television as she eavesdropped. She had to admit that in some respects they were both as bad as each other.

Alice listened. It was definitely Richard. Suzie was even pitching her dating-by-committee programme idea. When Alice was finally given a chance to speak to her ex-husband, she wandered off with the handset in search of a moment of privacy.

'So how were Mum's big television proposals?' Alice's tone was mocking.

'She might just have something there, although I'm not convinced that people wouldn't just pick the men they wanted for themselves. Anyway, that's not why I called. I haven't really got time to chat—Rob is about to be wined and dined to within an inch of his waistband.'

Alice dropped her voice to a whisper. 'You didn't say anything to her about Tom, did you?' Alice practically hissed his name.

'Of course not.'

'Good.' Now in the kitchen, which still felt very much like the scene of the crime, Alice started looking through the pile of post she'd ignored earlier.

'I was only calling to check you were watching your finest televisual moments.'

'My what?' A handwritten envelope caught her attention. The script was very familiar, although she couldn't quite place it.

'They're trailing the new series of *Get A Life* with a compilation of all the best bits and you are featuring very heavily at the moment. It's ridiculous. We no longer live together and yet you're still making me late.'

'They're trailing the new series?' Alice was so impressed, she forgot to be annoyed with Richard's jibe at her timekeeping, which was really rather good these days.

'Of course.'

'Well, thanks for the heads up. Although I'm hardly going

to sit here and watch myself, am I? I mean, what is this, the ego has landed?'

Too late. Her mother's batlike hearing and advanced sleuthing had clearly deciphered the contents of the call and there she was, in two places at the same time. Only, as far as she was concerned, she was actually in a third place altogether.

Chapter Eleven

Helen put her G&T on the coffee table and sat down in her favourite armchair to watch her brother at play. Uncle Tom was certainly much more of an attraction than Mummy Helen. And she wasn't complaining one bit.

'So, lovely as it is to see you—and by the way I do wish you'd come down in the car occasionally, how are we ever going to persuade Alex that getting a motorbike is out of the question when his uncle rides around on one all the time? Anyway, are you going to tell me what is going on or am I going to have to prise it out of you with multiple glasses of red wine after supper?'

On all fours, his five-year-old niece putting him through his best dressage paces, Tom turned his head to address his sister.

'Can't a younger brother just wake up one morning and decide to visit his beloved sister, nephews and niece without a reason?'

'Uh-uh.' Helen shook her head. 'Not when he's got a diary

as busy as yours and definitely not when he refers to us as "beloved." What's going on?'

'My plans changed at the last minute and I had some time on my hands.' Tom tried to come up with plausible reasons for his surprise arrival. 'You don't mind me popping down here, do you?'

'Mind? Are you mad. We love seeing you. You managed to get the boys to communicate in whole sentences and turn their PlayStation off for two hours earlier and Natalie gets her best-loved uncle and own pony for most of the afternoon.' Helen smiled as she watched her youngest digging her heels into her little brother's sides.

'Her *only* uncle.'

'Same difference. So who is she?'

'Who?'

'The woman who let you down.' Helen had never understood why Tom didn't have an orderly queue of nice girls following him around. It's not that she was unduly biased. She'd wanted to kill him for most of her teens but then again he was her brother. And he'd turned out pretty well in the end. Something for which she felt she could take quite a bit of credit.

Tom conceded defeat. He'd never been able to get anything past Helen. 'Try *women*. And actually, this time I think I may have let myself down.'

'Enigmatic as ever.'

Tom indicated the innocence of his niece with a flick of his head. 'I'll tell you later.'

'Right you are.' Suddenly speculative, Helen took a long and thoughtful sip of her drink before easing herself out of the armchair. 'Time to feed the masses.'

'I'll do it. Why don't you put your feet up, watch TV or something.' Tom couldn't keep himself busy enough.

'Is it Sister's Day? Blimey, Tom, you haven't killed anyone or done anything stupid like that, have you?'

'Of course not. Now, how about I rustle up some omelettes for the kids and we get a takeaway curry later when James gets back from the nineteenth hole?'

'How about you come and live with us forever?' Helen sank back into the cushions and flicked the television on, grateful for the break.

As the screen buzzed into life, Tom wondered if he was seeing things. He sat up, unseating Natalie mid-ride. She slithered to the ground as he turned to Helen.

'What's this?'

'Oh, some highly brainless, totally addictive personal-makeover programme. Actually, it's one of the better ones.'

Natalie clambered aboard her new stuffed dolphin and continued playing.

'That guy in the faded jeans—' Helen pointed out a good-looking guy, probably in his twenties '—wants a makeover.'

'He could do with a new pair of trousers.'

'They *are* brand new.'

'You could have fooled me.'

'Look, he's already had his wardrobe redone but it's not just about his clothes. There's more. He used to be a solicitor but…hang on, I saw this one a few months ago, it must be a repeat.'

The programme cut to Alice sitting next to the same guy in a trendy restaurant. He was telling her why he wanted to change his life around and talking nineteen to the dozen about his love of food.

Tom sat back on his heels and watched a few seconds. '*Get A Life.*'

'Look, when you've got four children under fourteen and

a husband who is away on business most of the time, you don't get out much.'

'No.' Tom shook his head slowly, so as not to miss a frame of the action. 'That's what this show is called.'

Now Alice was sitting in the guy's kitchen while he cooked her supper. He was chopping vegetables like a professional chef. Now they were driving along in a pale blue convertible. From the look of the signage, they were in the States.

Surprised, Helen double-checked the listings. 'And to think I thought you were up to your eyeballs in big deals. Oh no, Tom. You haven't gone bust, have you?'

Tom stared at Alice, now full screen, back in the studio on a very orange sofa. The programme cut between her and the wannabe chef as she dispensed yet more eminently sensible advice in her uniquely natural and nonjudgemental fashion. Her dark eyes were warm and genuine. And then suddenly she disappeared. The TV clicked off.

'Helen.' Irritated, Tom turned to his sister as she slyly observed his behaviour, the remote control in her hand—she had the power.

'I thought you thought we all watched far too much television.' Her glance was sidelong. Tom knew he'd been rumbled.

'You do. We all do.'

Helen wasn't buying any of his sweeping statements. 'You don't.'

'I've had some time recently.'

'I've been your sister for longer than you can remember. I think you need to tell me exactly what is going on.'

Tom sighed as he recalled his morning. 'I wish I knew.'

'Tom.' Helen's tone was not to be messed with.

Defeated, Tom held his hands up in surrender.

'Four people to feed and then I'm all yours.'

Chapter Twelve

> **Come & celebrate the last 60 years**
> **Suzie Fletcher invites you to drink and dance**
> **the years away**
> **On: Saturday 26th August**
> **At: Bar 19/21 Soho House, London W1**
> **From: 7:30 p.m. until way past your bedtime**
> **Dress: The last sixty years**
> **RSVP**

Alice still had the envelope in her hand. The owner of the familiar handwriting had been there all along and was, apparently, determined to ruin her summer.

'You can't make it fancy dress.'

Suzie wasn't budging. 'I can do what I like.'

'You're not Elton John. Nobody will come.'

'Nonsense. Everybody loves a theme.'

'That's crap and you know it.'

'Okay, I admit I saw the perfect dress and built my party around it. Happy? But it's not like I've asked everyone to come as a clown or a movie star. People can make as much or as little of an effort as they like.'

Alice shook her head. 'Why couldn't you just have made it black tie?'

'I wanted to be different.'

'You *are* different, you don't have to try. And I can't believe you posted me a formal invite. We decided on the date together nearly a year ago.'

'But it's nice to get post, isn't it? And it's a special occasion.'

'One minute you can't bear to say you're sixty, now you're throwing the party of the season. This must be costing you a fortune.'

'If you're going to do something you might as well do it properly. And the fact is, by the time I'm seventy, depressingly, no one will be able to dance properly anymore—all the more reason for us to have someone decent to dance with.' Suzie proffered Alice her laptop again. 'Go on, register. It's one little evening and, just think, twenty-five new men.'

Alice waved it away.

Suzie closed and returned her laptop to the coffee table. 'Well, at least promise me that you'll think about it.'

Alice couldn't believe her misfortune. Suzie was indefatigable. Far from down and out on her challenge, she seemed determined to bounce back higher than ever and to drag Alice along with her, every step of the way.

'Look, we're already on the Net, we've been in the papers. You've met up with a few no-hopers, I've met up with one and didn't even stay for dessert.'

'But speed dating isn't like going on a blind date with one person or joining a dating agency… I think you should capitalise on your renewed interest in men.'

'One man.'

'Who had enough potential to make you realise there may

be others out there. I'm not saying you're going to find true love, but you might at least get a shag out of it.'

'Marvellous. Maybe a free STD, too, if I'm lucky, or an unwanted child.'

'I still can't believe you didn't tell me about Zoë.'

'You weren't listening when I gave you all the details earlier.'

'I mean before then.'

'I just wasn't sure she'd want everyone to know.'

'I'm not everyone.'

'Well, now she's told you herself and if you could try not to write about it I think she'd probably appreciate it.'

'Some people actually think I'm quite nice.'

'Sorry. You just caught me by surprise on this costume thing.'

Suzie raised an eyebrow. 'You're the one making it into a costume drama. It's my birthday. Besides, Zoë could probably do with a distraction of a sartorial nature. She'll love dressing up.'

'I'm sorry to be such a disappointment.'

'Oh, shush, darling. Stop making this all about you.'

'Look who's talking. Anyway, I'm glad you know about Zoë. It's been a pretty grown-up thing to have to deal with in isolation.'

'Well, luckily you're a pretty grown-up.'

'Thanks.' Alice received the compliment shyly.

'Hang on a minute.' Suzie reverted to her mission. 'Would it be easier if I came speed dating, too?'

'Yuh, good one, let's pick from the same pool of men. That's worked a treat so far.'

Exasperated, Suzie sighed. 'Obviously they run different groups for different ages.'

'What were you thinking, thirty- to forty-year-olds?'

'Actually, it's not quite so specific. They only have over forties and under forties.'

'Promise me you'll be going to the former?'

Suzie nodded. 'I just think we should make the most of our hormonal renaissance and get back out there. I mean, obviously Tom has to be off limits. Agreed?'

Alice sighed. 'Agreed.'

'Good.'

'Although I am going to call him on Monday—professionally I can't just vanish into thin air. If he wants to, that's up to him, but in theory I have to hand him over to someone else. We made an agreement for a minimum of six months.'

To Suzie's frustration she knew she couldn't object. 'Fair enough. But no funny business.' Suzie paused. 'I do think it's fascinating that he found us both attractive.'

'It shows that he clearly doesn't have a type.' Alice still couldn't believe it.

Suzie shook her head. 'We're more similar than you think, you know.'

Alice didn't know, or she didn't want to know. 'Damn it, he really got to me. I so need to get an upgrade for my emotional firewall…a client, too. Bad Alice.'

'Hey, he was the one behaving badly. Come on, let's sign up for speed dating, we can put our names down right now… Isn't the Internet amazing?' Suzie knew she had to make the most of Alice's moment of self-doubt.

'…Go on, for me, darling. It'll be good for you to let go and stop being so uptight.'

'I am not uptight.'

'Look at this place. All the videotapes are labelled with what is actually on them, you have five types of tea bag in different jars, you never run out of anything, your kitchen cupboards are immaculate when everyone knows the whole point is that you can hide loads of stuff in them so people can't see the chaos.'

'Why can't you be normal?'

Suzie scoffed. 'What's normal these days?'

'Why can't you want a sixtieth birthday present from Tiffany, a pet unicorn—anything would be easier than this… challenge.'

'Fine, I'll go speed dating without you. I'll win. At least my generation know how to have fun.'

'So do mine.'

'If you think working hard, banning smoking in public places and only drinking fourteen units of alcohol is being wild. Look, I don't care if you want to carry on sulking and blaming everything but your own apathy.'

'I'm not sulk—' Alice clamped her lips firmly together as her tone betrayed her. Damn Suzie for knowing her so well. Competitive streak piqued, Alice opened her mother's laptop to register while there was still enough wine in her system.

Chapter Thirteen

Helen scraped the last of the chicken tikka masala from the foil takeaway carton onto her plate. 'Rewind a minute. You have a life coach? You clearly have too much money.'

Tom shovelled another forkful of sag aloo into his mouth. 'Tell me something I don't know.'

'It's rude to speak with your mouth full?'

Tom mumbled an apology through his now-closed mouth.

'Seriously, you should just ring me more often. I'd charge you a lot less.'

Tom swallowed. 'I know you like to think you give me good advice.'

'I don't think, I know…'

'Don't take this personally.'

'If it's going to be a criticism, how else would you suggest I take it? Generally? Publicly?'

'Like most women, you talk but you don't listen.'

'And to think I wonder why you're still single.'

'I said *most* women. Listening is something Alice does very well. In fact, she's pretty good at lots of things.'

'Clearly.'

Effortlessly, Tom ignored his sister's interruption. It was a skill he'd perfected in their teens when their bickering had reached an all-time high.

'...I wasn't expecting much at first but, well, it's been pretty painless and I was starting to relax for the first time in years. In fact, I was feeling much better about everything.' Tom played with the piece of chapati in his hand.

Helen eyed the surplus of sauce on her plate and battled with her inner dietician. She won in seconds. 'Are you going to eat that or just play with it?'

'Blimey, Hel, when you become a mother do they issue you with a book of stock phrases to use?'

'Very funny. Seriously, I'll eat it if you won't.'

Tom looked surprised. 'You're not pregnant again, are you?'

'Don't be ridiculous. Three is already a crowd in the back of the car. And you can't get pregnant when you're not having sex.'

'Is everything okay with you two?'

'We're fine.'

'Does James not normally feed you at the weekend?'

'It's such a treat not to have to cook. When, like tonight, James decides to eat at the golf club I usually have a bowl of cereal and leftovers, or at least I used to. The boys eat everything these days.'

Tom handed over his bread and a cold onion bhaji. He really wasn't that hungry.

Helen mopped up his food greedily. 'So you were saying, you're feeling better about everything?'

'That I was. And now I'm not.'

'You see?'

'Not really.'

'It's all about codependency. It's a scam. These therapist

people make you think you need them when you were fine beforehand. The whole thing's a con.'

'That's what I thought at first. Hey, it's what she thought at first.'

'Alice?' Helen was doing her best to keep up.

'Yup. Alice. The one who was on TV earlier.'

'Right. So if she's not the right shrink for you...'

'Life coach.'

'Whatever. Surely you just get a new one, or take up another dangerous sport or whatever it is you do for kicks these days.'

'It's not that easy.'

'Of course it is. Buy a bigger bike, have a bloody guitar lesson. I don't know, just do what you want.'

Tom rubbed his neck pensively. 'I could sell my stake in the company and release some capital.' He waited for his sister to explode.

'I don't think guitar lessons are that expensive unless you were hoping Eric Clapton might want to teach you.' Helen wiped her plate clear of the last traces of sauce.

'I mean, I could take some time off.'

'Really?' Helen stopped chewing. 'Sell up?'

'I could travel.'

'Do me a favour and don't change everything at once just because a girl turned you down.'

'That's not why this has come up.'

'Of course not.'

'Don't wind me up.'

'Just listen to what you're saying.'

'But what have I got to show for my life?'

'Where would you like me to start?'

'I mean outside of my work. I need to be proactive not reactive.'

'Did she tell you that?'

'I'm not getting any younger, Helen. I've got enough money to last me a while. If I sell my stake, well…'

'You're not going to go riding around the world on that bloody bike or anything stupid like that?'

'Ooh, now *that* sounds like a great idea.'

'Ever since university you've always wanted to take off and do something like that.'

'But I never have.'

'You can find yourself in the U.K., you know.'

'Who said I was lost?' Tom changed tack. 'Anyway I haven't really thought it all through yet.' He wasn't in the mood for one of Helen's full-blown lectures.

'Exactly my point. Say you sell up in a fit of peak, in a month you'll have had some sleep, got through this bad patch and then suddenly you'll have all the time in the world and no impetus—probably not ideal when contemplating a whole new career, especially when you've got a fantastic one already. More time mulling things over on your own is not what you need. Take a break, by all means, goodness knows you deserve it. But take someone with you. Alternatively, start a new company, advise other people. But you're not good in a vacuum…'

'I'm not good with a Hoover, either.'

'I know I'm your older sister and therefore you're genetically programmed to disagree with everything I suggest, but for once I'm being serious.'

'So am I. And what you're saying isn't true. I'm always on my own.'

'With lots of people close to hand. Look at you, something goes wrong and you turn up here rather than spend the weekend alone at your place.'

'We don't see each other nearly enough.'

'Agreed. But that's not why you're here. Be honest with yourself.'

Tom went to get another beer from the fridge. Opening it, he downed a long sip, relishing the numbing properties of the cold and the alcohol. 'But who would want to go with me?'

'Why not take the girl of your dreams?'

'It would help if I'd met her.'

'It sounds like you already have.'

'Helen, please. You don't know the half of it.'

'Invite Alice. Right, now that's sorted. My invoice will be in the post.'

'I don't know.'

'It's the obvious solution.'

'It's the fantasy option. And seriously, her mother wouldn't like it.'

'Since when has any mother liked her daughter going off with a biker. You're no-good sorts.'

'And I'm not sure this daughter is going to be interested anymore, either.'

'Fine, accept defeat. But this isn't like you.'

'It's more complicated than you can imagine.'

'Try me.'

'I was seeing them both.'

'The mother is a life coach, too?'

Tom shook his head. 'No. *Seeing* them both.'

Helen picked her jaw up from the table.

'I told you.' Tom rested his forehead in his hand.

Helen tried to scroll through the information she'd been given so far. 'How does that work?'

'It doesn't. I met the mother first. She seemed nice enough, quite a laugh, young for her age, and then I met Alice. I didn't know they had anything to do with each other until this morning.'

'This morning? That doesn't sound good. But it does finally explain what you're doing here.'

'It was terrible. I'm so embarrassed. It's not how I would normally behave.' Tom shook his head. 'I really don't want Alice to think I'm…'

'And what about the other one? Erm…' Helen did her best to keep up.

'Suzie?'

'The mother?'

Tom bowed his head in admission. 'Obviously I don't want her to think badly of me, either, but Alice is different. She's special. Oh, crap. But she's, well, more vulnerable somehow, if that makes sense.'

'I can honestly tell you that nothing you've told me so far makes sense.'

Tom nodded. 'Welcome to my world. This isn't what I wanted.'

'What did you want?'

Tom shrugged. 'I never thought I'd get to my mid-forties so fast.'

'Okay, rephrase that, what do you want now?'

'Alice… To get away… To start today again.'

'Which one?'

'What's with the inquisition?'

'I'm trying to help. And you have to understand that, since I left London, nothing exciting ever happens. People's children change schools, families get dogs, get new cars, get divorced, get done for drink driving, get caught sleeping with the au pair, but that's about it. And I promise, I only want what's best for you.'

'Well, I think you might be too late.'

'And whose fault is that?'

'Mine.' Tom hated to admit it but it was true. 'Unless there really is a male menopause and I can blame my hormones.'

'You can blame whoever you like if it makes you feel better.'

'Thanks.' Tom drained his beer bottle and went to get himself a fresh one. He wasn't feeling better yet. But with a bit of luck, his sorrows were soluble in Stella Artois.

Chapter Fourteen

19 days to go
Suzie 6, Alice 2

'Okay everybody, that's great.'

Alice checked her watch as Sean, the young floor manager, walked on to the podium of the predominantly orange *Get A Life* studio set, his headphones around his neck, his black T-shirt half tucked in to the hipster waistband of his carefully distressed jeans. He was wearing trainers that Alice had worn at school when they'd been at the cutting edge of shoe technology as opposed to part of the Nike retro collection. It was official. She was getting old.

Sean fiddled with his spanking-new wedding ring. 'Okay, team, we're going to break for half an hour and then we'll come back for the final interviews. If any of the panel would like to see the VT packages again let me know, otherwise we'll see you back here in thirty. If you want some privacy, leave your microphones in make-up or turn them off—you have been warned. If you need sustenance, one of the runners will be only too happy to help.'

Raising a hand in farewell to the other "experts" Alice got up, relieved at the tight schedule of her studio day, and walked towards the exit. One of the few disadvantages to working from home was the ability to find far too much time to check e-mail in an average twelve-hour period.

She'd left a voicemail for Tom first thing but when she'd keenly checked her messages at lunchtime she'd only been rewarded with an e-mail from his secretary cancelling the rest of his sessions and promising a cheque for the rest of the contracted period. Alice had almost replied to say that wouldn't be necessary. Almost replied.

In a world of her own, and mentally drafting a variety of responses, she strode towards her dressing room.

'Alice…'

A lanky, red-cheeked youth caught up with her almost apologetically, even though he was panting at the effort of having tracked her down.

'Alice Harrison?'

She wheeled. 'Can I help you?'

'Sorry, I'm Joel, production runner.'

He proffered a sweaty palm. He looked about fourteen. The carefully shaved fine goatee could well have been stuck on to his otherwise smooth face.

'I'd love a cup of coffee, thank you. White, no sugar.'

Alice unlocked the door to her dressing room and let it slam behind her. She only had a moment of peace before someone knocked.

No longer on camera and the disappointment of the day starting to get to her, she opened the door irritably. 'Yes?'

He was still standing there.

'Is there a problem with coffee, Joe?'

'It's Joel, and of course I'll get you a beverage…'

Who on earth said beverage? Alice folded her arms. He was feistier than his stature suggested would be wise.

'…but I actually came to let you know there's a courier to see you in reception.'

'A courier?'

'You know, a man with a package for—'

'I know what a courier is. Can't you pick it up for me?'

Alice didn't normally snap. But she didn't normally have school leavers standing in her personal space stating the obvious when she was trying to cram a bad mood into a thirty-minute break.

Joel seemed unflustered. 'Sorry. Heightened security measures. All packages have to be signed for in person.'

'Right.' Alice exhaled, determined to keep her cool. 'Is there any way you could get a pass and bring him here? I've just got some calls to make and as I'm sure you know, we've only got half an hour before we have to be back on set.'

Alice didn't think Joel could have looked more bewildered by her request if she'd asked him to strip naked and roast a chicken right there in the corridor. Clearly, initiative classes started next week, although she suspected he had graduated in the top few percent at red tape and rule-following.

Alice waved him away. 'Don't worry, I'll go myself.'

Relieved, his energy returned. 'Great. I'll get your coffee.'

'Thanks.' Alice made sure she had her key and walked to main reception.

A gaggle of motorcycle couriers loitered on the smoking side of the automatic glass doors, triggering their constant indecision. Timing her exit carefully so as not to be caught between the two plates of glass, Alice walked outside and into their midst. The group fell silent.

Alice surveyed their bandanas, battered jackets and improbably thin roll-up cigarettes. 'Package for Alice Harrison?'

After much shuffling, shrugging and shaking of heads, it was clear there was no package.

As Alice turned on her heel, she wondered what she was going to say to Joel. Realistically, probably nothing, but in her fantasy mean-girl incarnation there'd have been a barrage of four-letter words and maybe a smidgen of physical violence, a touch of kick-boxing perhaps. Fortunately for him, her annoyance was only ever fleeting.

Walking back into the throng in reception, a familiar motorcycle helmet caught her eye. Next to it a familiar face was watching the bank of television screens, apparently mesmerised by some athletics coverage. As she watched him watching, Tom looked up.

'Alice. At last.'

She walked over to where he was sitting. 'A Taylor-Made courier, eh? Bit of a comedown from the boardroom.'

Tom looked sheepish as he debated whether to get up or stay seated. 'I wasn't sure you'd want to see me if I said who I was.'

Alice remained silent. She certainly wasn't stupid enough to be hoodwinked into answering loaded questions. 'So have you come to bring me a cheque?'

'Right, um, no. I was going to post… Sorry. I haven't carried a cheque book for about ten years.' He stood up.

'No rush.' Alice berated herself for being so businesslike. He was here, in her foyer, and she was trying to spoil it all.

'I'm actually here in a personal capacity.'

Alice nodded. If she didn't say anything she couldn't ruin anything. She checked her watch.

Tom noticed. 'Sorry, this shouldn't take long.'

'I wasn't hurrying you.' Alice was quick to set the

record straight. 'I have to be back in the studio in twenty minutes but only for another hour or so. We could meet later?'

'I don't need long.'

Now Alice was disappointed. She couldn't keep up with her emotions anymore.

Tom remained calm. 'I just wanted to say sorry. In person. Properly. It wasn't, I mean I never expected. No, that's wrong.'

Tom took a breath and started again.

'I was wrong. I just wanted to say that I really enjoyed Friday and I'd love to do it again sometime.'

Secretly delighted at aspects of his apology and wishing she had a photographic memory, Alice folded her arms. 'And are you going to ask my mother, too?'

Tom's head shake was vehement. 'Look, this was all a terrible coincidence. I'm not that sort of guy. I don't meet women I want to date very often.'

'And then two in the same family.' Her tone was sour. Finally a chance to get across how she'd been feeling, although aloof would have been preferable.

'Alice, please, don't. I'm just asking you to give me another chance.'

Alice had to confess, if only to herself, that it was tempting. She couldn't afford to let herself consider his request. 'I can't.'

Tom looked down at his boots resignedly. 'I had a feeling you'd say that. But I wanted to check in person. E-mails are woefully inadequate sometimes.'

Her overactive imagination presenting her with a variety of scenarios, Alice stuck to her guns. 'I really can't.'

Tom tried to read her body language. Couldn't, shouldn't or wouldn't? 'What if I suggested we went somewhere else?'

'I'm due back in the studio in fifteen minutes.'

Tom was frustrated by his inarticulacy. Deal closing was his thing.

'Not now. In a week or two. I was thinking the South of France, maybe Italy.'

Alice sighed. 'Running away, your personal speciality.'

The warmth of Tom's smile would have melted an ice cap and yet Alice remained frosty.

Tom shrugged. 'I thought I'd take some time out. See something new. Make time for me.'

'Well, at least the sessions have been of some benefit.'

He perched on the back of a bank of armchairs, bringing himself down to her eye level. 'You've helped me more than you know. Come on. Come on an adventure with me. Because you want to.'

Alice looked away. 'And what about work, mortgages— you know, the sort of mundane stuff that most of us have to deal with?'

'Everything is surmountable. You told me that.'

'Well, yes it is. And it isn't. I've got some big work commitments at the moment plus it's Mum's sixtieth at the end of August, and as we are a family of two these days I have to be there.'

'Your mum is going to be sixty?'

She dared to look at him again. 'I thought you knew that.'

Tom smiled. 'What's a few years between friends. Just for the record, she told me you were twenty-five, although now I know better.'

Alice shook her head, a smile involuntarily creeping onto her face. If things got tough she was sure she could sell her story. This was her Jerry Springer moment.

'I guess I should give her a call. Clear the air, you know. I can't emphasise enough how sorry I am.'

'I could pass on a message?' Alice was hopeful.

'No, I'm going to call her myself. It's only fair.'

Fair schmair. Alice didn't want to be a grown-up right now and she didn't want him to go. Then again, she hadn't given him any reason to want to stay.

'I'm a big boy. I need to face the music.'

'And dance?'

Not even a flicker of a smile. He was a man on a mission, doing one thing at a time. 'Seriously, Alice, whatever I've done wrong, whatever does or doesn't happen next, I want to say thank you. I know this hasn't exactly worked out well, but you've really helped me.'

Alice didn't know what to do with his compliment and so she sidestepped it.

'You have, more than you know.' Tom took one last shot. 'How about we go somewhere in September?'

Tempting, very tempting. Alice shook her head. 'I have filming commitments.' Until she'd had a screen test and she'd signed a contract, she knew she couldn't say a word about her new career direction. 'You'll just have to ask a student or a retired person.'

'Someone, say, around the age of sixty?' Tom wondered if it was too soon for their lives to be a joking matter, but to his relief Alice laughed, and as other people turned nosily to see what was happening, he savoured their moment of intimacy. 'Not that I can blame you. I've hardly made myself a sensible or an attractive option. Maybe it's better if I go alone. I just really feel that I need to get away for a few weeks.'

'As your coach, I think that's a good idea.'

'As my coach?'

'As your coach.'

Tom hesitated as his moment came and went. 'I guess I thought, well…' He lost his nerve. 'I was getting the impression that maybe you are a bit of a lost soul, too.'

'Lost soul?' Alice could feel her defences prickling. Then again, she was speed dating on Wednesday. How lost could you get? Now, to top it all, here was Joel with her bloody coffee. Alice reminded herself that none of this was Joel's fault. The poor guy hadn't met her on her best day.

Joel handed her the thick paper cup with a proud flourish of efficiency. 'Just to let you know, seven minutes to go.'

'Thanks, Joel. I'll see you in there.'

Beaming at the fact she had remembered his name and managed a basic level of civility, he scampered off—hopefully to tell everyone she was much nicer than he had first thought.

Tom shifted his weight from foot to foot. 'So, can I be in touch when I get back?'

'Probably best not.' Alice wished she didn't have a conscience. After all, promises were made to be broken. Or was that rules?

'Right.' Picking himself up from the foot of another virtual brick wall, Tom had run out of impetus. At least for today.

'Right.' Wrong. Very wrong.

'Well, I'd better let you go then.' Defeated, Tom prepared to put his helmet on.

Alice couldn't think of anything she wanted less.

'Have a great trip.' She proffered a hand.

Tom kissed her lightly on the cheek. 'I'll send you a postcard.'

'Do.' Reluctantly, Alice turned to leave.

'See you later.' Tom turned towards the doors.

Alice took a sip of her coffee as, rapidly composing herself, she headed back to the studio. She hated that expression. Later in the day? Later in the week? Later, as in the afterlife?

The analysis could wait. It was time to advise another punter on how to make the best of his life, even if at this precise moment she didn't feel like such an expert.

Chapter Fifteen

Clinically measuring out all the ingredients, Alice mixed a couple of Cosmopolitans while Zoë speed flicked through *Vogue*, a large holdall at her feet.

Zoë closed the magazine and reached for the bag. 'So, I've brought a few things round that I thought might be useful for Wednesday evening. I still can't quite believe you're going to do this.'

Alice tilted her head in the general direction of the stairs and Suzie's room even though she wasn't at home. 'You honestly have no idea how manipulative she can be.'

'I hope I have as much zest for life when I get to her age. I think it's great.'

'That's because you don't have to play this game.'

'You never know, the men might be really fun guys.'

'Or just really, really desperate.'

Alice took a medicinal taster sip straight from the cocktail shaker before pouring their drinks and, a glass in each hand, led Zoë out into the garden. 'I refuse to spend valuable time beforehand worrying. Three minutes is nothing.

Worse-case scenario, I'll spend the time pretending to hunt for my lip balm in my bag.'

Zoë shook her head. 'I don't know, three minutes is longer than you think.'

'Whose side are you on?'

'Well, you know they say first impressions are made in a few seconds.'

'Then I definitely won't even need three minutes, will I?' Alice handed Zoë her drink. 'Don't try and tell me the men are going to spend any time thinking about what they are going to wear until Wednesday morning at the earliest.'

'That doesn't mean they're not expecting the women to have made an effort.'

'That's double standards.'

'Yuh.' Zoë refused to be wound up. 'That's life. Anyway, as far as you're concerned, I wasn't thinking of anything radical, I was just going to suggest that you didn't wear a black V-necked sweater.'

Alice frowned. 'But that's my look.'

'It's not *your* look, it's a look.'

'It's a classic look.'

'I just think you might feel better if you've made more of an effort.'

'Or I might feel a bit keen. I thought it would be best if I went as myself. I mean, I might wear some bigger earrings and I've got quite a funky bracelet from Accessorize…'

Zoë recognised Alice's stubborn tone. It was one she knew only too well herself. 'Well, that's a start.'

'But I'm not going to reinvent myself for one evening.'

'All I'm saying is, it's August and the shops are full of colour. I wasn't thinking miniskirt or boob tube, but I did happen to bring a great little top with me. Think Native American. Blues, oranges, browns…a few beads.'

'Pocahontas?'

'More like Poke-A-Hopeful…'

Alice reminded herself that Zoë was her so-called best friend.'I still think black works for me. It matches my mood.'

Zoë laughed. 'Okay, let's continue this conversation in a couple more drinks' time.'

'Maybe we will and maybe we—'

'For the record, I think it's incredible that Tom came to see you.' Zoë deftly changed the subject.

Alice shrugged.'He can do what he likes. He's his own boss.'

'It's even more amazing that you sent him away. Good for you. It should make it much easier to move on now.'

'I know.' Alice was familiar with the theory. She had been going through it all afternoon.'Trouble was, he was so bloody apologetic and polite that it was almost impossible to be angry with him.'

'But you're still cross with him?'

Alice sighed wearily. 'I honestly think he thought going travelling together might be mutually beneficial.'

'I'll say.'

'Not like that. All "lost souls" together on some sort of road trip.'

'Well, at least if he's off to find himself he's not going to be walking around London at the same time as you are, cluttering up your personal space.'

'It's not as if he was a genuine bastard.'

'I think he was shaping up pretty well.'

'The whole thing was an accident, Zo. A stupid mistake.'

Zoë cocked an eyebrow. 'Sounds like the apology worked then.'

'It'd be easier if he was still furious, or if he really hated me.'

Zoë shook her head. 'Oh no, you still really like him, don't you?'

Alice took a tactical sip of her drink. 'So, way too much about me. Any sign of your birth certificate yet?'

Zoë shook her head. 'Nope, I'm still waiting to be reborn.'

'You'd think in this day and age they could just e-mail it to you.'

'Oh, you know what these government departments are like. The photocopier has probably jammed or run out of toner.'

'And in the meantime?'

'I guess I have to be patient. I could start bothering the Riddicks of the world but I thought I should wait just in case there's anything more concrete to go on. I've been drafting and redrafting a letter to send to the address in the file, but realistically the chances of anyone remembering Margaret over thirty years later have got to be minuscule. No one stays in the same place for that long these days. No such thing as a job for life or a man for life, let alone a home for life.'

'Want me to take a look at the letter?'

Zoë nodded. 'Yes, please, in a few more drafts' time.'

'I'm sure it's perfect. Presumably you're just trying to locate Margaret at this point?'

'As opposed to?'

'Telling her why you need her.'

'Of course. One frustratingly small baby step at a time.'

'Cool. So...' Satisfied that Zoë was in good shape and her defences softened by vodka and triple sec, Alice knew she couldn't keep her secret any longer. 'I've got something else to tell you.' Stalling, she bent down and studied her huge terracotta pot full of lavender. Close up it looked like a speed-dating venue for bumblebees as they all dropped by the crowded bush for a few minutes at a time before moving on. She bet life was much easier in their world. Wake up, fly to work, get pollen, make honey. One queen and hundreds of boys to make sure she got exactly what she needed.

Zoë put her glass on the table. 'What next from the girl who claims she never has any news? You're one news flash after another at the moment.'

'There must be a full moon or something. I'm sure this will be it for the year now.'

'Out with it.'

'A job opportunity has come up. Quite a big job, in fact. Presenting the breakfast show on Channel 6.'

Zoë clapped her hands together with delight and disbelief. 'With Dermot Douglas?'

Alice grinned at her best friend, buoyed by her reaction. 'The one and only.'

'He's gorgeous.'

'Traditionally I've always preferred men with more hair.'

Zoë was almost hyperventilating. 'No, no. It's all about those eyes and that smile. Just send him my way.'

'Hang on, don't tell me I've inadvertently stumbled across a man you actually desire.'

'Possibly.'

Alice saw mischief in her eyes.

'But—' Zoë frowned '—I didn't know Janie was leaving.'

'I don't think she knows yet, either. You mustn't say a word to anyone.'

Zoë crossed her heart as passionately as any eight-year-old, forgetting that moments earlier she had been trying to play it cool. 'So how did you hear about it?'

'How do you think?'

'Richard?'

Alice nodded.

'Wow. Now *that's* what I call an ex-husband.'

'I still have to audition, but he seems to think it's a done deal.'

'Well, cheers to you.' Zoë raised her glass. 'You'll be day-time-television royalty. You'll be opening supermarkets and making a workout video before you know it.'

'Shut up.' Alice looked around for something to throw at her best friend but everything to hand was either too large (terracotta flowerpot) or too precious (cocktail).

'Well, you can forget speed dating, there's about to be an orderly queue.'

'So you think I should definitely go for it?'

Zoë's expression was incredulous. 'Hello? Don't you?'

Alice frowned pensively, burying her excitement for a little longer. 'It will mean a big change again.'

Zoë wasn't convinced. 'Not really. I mean, you're doing some presenting now.'

'But just when I got a balance…'

'That'd be the all-work-no-play balance?'

'That's rich coming from you, and well, you know, I've just got into my groove…'

'Or rut.'

'Is that what you think?'

'I just want you to see both sides.'

'Zo, it's taken three years to build up my client list. What if I can't stick at anything for longer than a few years? TV production, marriage, life coaching?'

'Life always moves in cycles.'

'Next you'll be telling me there are plenty more fish in the sea and good things come to those who wait.'

'Life's all about progression. You told me that. One thing leads to another. And it's not like Richard's suggesting you give it all up.'

'I might be able to squeeze in some private client work but realistically if I get the job, it'll be pretty full-time, what with the supermarkets, the aerobics DVD and everything…'

Alice smiled impishly. She thought about all the decisions she had agonised over when she'd been growing up. Sindy versus Barbie, Tom Cruise versus Matt Dillon. In certain areas of her life she'd known exactly what she wanted, Dunlop Green Flash then Reebok hi-tops, Nike Air Max, her dad back. Exam choices had been much more difficult. She could remember deliberating for weeks over which subjects to pick, and yet she couldn't recall ever really deciding on her career. She'd fallen into television based on very little except that she liked watching it and she wouldn't have to wear a suit. Life coaching had only found her after Richard left. Alice allowed herself to get excited. 'Do you know what, hand on heart, I think I'd love it.'

Grateful that she wasn't going to have to talk her into it, Zoë relaxed. 'Honestly, your life at the moment… You haven't started growing four-leaf clovers or anything I should know about?'

Grinning, Alice shook her head, her brow suddenly furrowing. 'Hang on, what if Richard's offering me the job because of who I am rather than because I'm the best person to do it?'

Zoë tried to follow Alice's logic. 'Because he still feels guilty…?'

'Exactly.'

'Do you honestly believe Richard would risk ballsing up his new job just to make you feel better? He wants you because he knows you'll be a star and then he'll get all the credit for finding new talent for Channel 6. And if you have to put life coaching on the back burner for a while… well, you can always come back to it. But this could catapult you into a whole different world altogether. Hey, are you going to have a stylist?'

Alice scoffed. 'I doubt it.'

'No offence, but I hope they give you a wardrobe assistant at the very least. You don't seriously think that TV presenters are actually allowed to choose their own suits, shirts, ties and blouses?'

'For the record, I won't be wearing a bloody suit or a blouse… If I'd wanted all that, I'd have become a lawyer.'

'Oh really, so what were you thinking, black V neck…?' Zoë tilted her head to one side provocatively before resting her hand on Alice's arm. 'Let me talk to Richard.'

'But you're not even supposed to know anything at this stage.'

'Come on, he'll be expecting you to talk to me.'

'Zo…' Alice's tone was a warning one.

'Well then, as soon as it's official. Seriously, I could help.'

'I don't think there's much call for ripped denim and crop tops on breakfast TV.'

'You're not the only one whose career needs developing and I don't intend to die a teenage fashion buyer and freelance stylist. Believe me, there isn't a big difference between the ages in fashion these days. I mean, your mother wears cargo pants and trainers.'

'Don't remind me.'

'You own a twinset. Fashion is much more fluid now. But if you'd rather have some total stranger taking you shopping, someone who thinks you look simply fabulous in lime and peach…'

Alice's eyes widened with fear. 'Of course not.'

'So just keep me in mind.'

'Will do.'

'Because you won't be able to leap out of bed at 4:00 a.m. and throw something on.'

'Message received loud and clear.'

'And if you don't want me, maybe Dermot does. He is a man who knows how to dress.'

'In which case why would he need you?'

'It's not about need, I'd just like to get my hands on him.'

'Now I'm feeling intimidated.'

'Don't be. You're just not used to rehearsing outfits… I'll bet you anything your mum has already spent a bit of time planning what she's going to wear on Wednesday evening.'

'I'm sure.' Alice hesitated. 'Zo, don't take this the wrong way, but why don't you come along on Wednesday, too?'

Zoë's head shake was emphatic. 'I think I'll save speed dating for a rainy day.'

'Go on. I'll pay.'

'Bribery won't get you everywhere.'

'It's more a question of safety in numbers.'

'No thanks. I've got quite enough on my emotional plate at the moment.' Zoë drained her cocktail glass, her mouth suddenly rubbery as she had a hit of fresh lime juice. 'So, have you sorted out your questions yet?'

'My questions?'

'Well, you've only got three minutes to find potential or the deal breaker, so you've got to be clever. I'd go quickfire. Coke or Pepsi? Dogs or cats? *Star Wars* or *Star Trek*? New York or Los Angeles?'

Alice wished she could borrow Zoë's enthusiasm, as well as her top. 'See, you'd be great at it.'

'From a psychological standpoint, I think it's fascinating.'

'Go in my place and I promise I'll spend twenty-four hours cold-calling Riddicks all over the world.' Alice didn't realise but she was clutching her hands together as if in prayer.

Zoë laughed. 'No deal. How bad can it be?'

'How bad can what be?' Suzie stood in the doorway to

the garden laden with high-end shopping bags. She spotted the empty martini glasses on the table. 'Oh no, I hope I'm not too late for happy hour? Zo, thank goodness you're here. I almost called you earlier. I need outfit advice. Date tomorrow and multiple dates on Wednesday. By the way I did some maths earlier. Twenty-five men in one evening, total cost twenty pounds, that's only eighty pence per man. Bargain, eh?'

Zoë laughed heartily. Alice faked a smile.

'And guess what?' Suzie was barely silent for a second. Energy radiated from her every pore as Alice felt it drain from hers. 'Tom called me an hour ago.'

Alice feigned surprise as Zoë frowned at her. 'And?'

'And, well, nothing really. He just wanted to clear the air. So I told him I hoped we could keep in touch.'

Alice roared into action. 'You did what?'

'Calm down, I didn't really mean it.'

'So why say it?'

Suzie tried to be as low-key as possible. 'It seemed the polite thing to do.'

'I thought we agreed he was off limits.'

'Don't worry, darling, I have no intention of going down that path again. Anyway, he said to send his best to you.' Suzie's amusement at Alice's poorly concealed upset was not at all helpful.

'Did he really?' Alice's tone was septic and sceptical.

'Well, something like that. I'm just pleased he called. All very satisfying, don't you think? Unfortunately, I can't remember his exact words.'

'I can.'

Suzie hesitated, her exclusive ruined. 'You spoke to him, too?'

'He popped in to see me at the studio.'

'You *saw* him?'

Alice knew it was childish but in this relationship at least, she was the child and currently the victor. 'Yup, I did.'

'And?'

'And nothing.'

'You know we have a deal?'

Alice nodded, a paragon of innocence. 'Of course.'

'So, no hard feelings all round?'

Alice gritted her teeth. 'Don't push it. I'm doing my best.'

'Good girl…'

Alice tried to ignore the fact that her mother was addressing her in the tone usually reserved for a puppy.

'…Mistakes happen and the bottom line is we're all adults—even me.'

'I know.'

Suzie disappeared into the kitchen momentarily and returned with the vodka bottle, cranberry juice and a third glass.

Sitting down at the table, she poured herself a drink and passed the bottle around, the fruit juice following as an afterthought. 'Well, seeing as we're being honest, actually he didn't send his best to either of us.'

Alice halted midpour, vodka splashing onto her teak table. 'What do you mean?'

'I think it might have been something to do with our dating challenge. He didn't seem that impressed.'

Alice hoped she'd got the wrong end of the stick on this one. 'Our what?' She slammed the bottle back on the table.

'You know, the having to find a man before August 26 thing.'

'How on earth did that come up?' Alice shook her head.

'Well, you know…' Suzie skirted around, hoping for an easy escape.

'Actually, I don't know.' Alice's tone was cold.

Suzie tried to make amends. 'It's just, I jokingly told him he was leaving me in the lurch a little, you know, that thanks to him I might not make my deadline—I was flirting, teasing, competing, something, who knows. Anyway, he got all shirty about it.'

Out of sight, in her lap, Alice felt her left hand form a fist. 'Why did you have to say anything?'

'I couldn't have him thinking he had the upper hand. He was very much in the wrong.'

'But you know he doesn't date lightly.'

'Well, that makes two of you. Anyway, it's all academic now. Zo, has she talked you into coming with us on Wednesday yet? You really should think about it. When was the last time you got to meet twenty-five men in one evening?'

Zoë declined with a shake of her head. 'I don't think I've met twenty-five single men since I left university.'

'Well then.'

Zoë reached for the vodka. 'Maybe next time.'

Chapter Sixteen

17 days to go

His motorbike locked up three floors beneath his feet, Tom leaned over the rail at the back of the ferry and watched the English coast recede into the distance.

The sea frothed in the wake of the boat and Tom stared into the blue-green depths. On the whole, he found water strangely soothing, yet this swirling mire definitely matched his mood: tidal and difficult to fathom. Not to mention opaque. He could remember the days when his life had been as transparent as a bottle of mineral water. The universal truth was that life was supposed to get easier with age and yet he was finding it increasingly complex.

Well, not anymore, or, more specifically, not for the next few weeks. He was going back to basics. Or at least basics and a big bike.

Filling his lungs with a combination of sea air and diesel fumes, Tom savoured the feeling of being alone, free of responsibility and accountable to nobody but himself. The business world ground to a semi-halt in August as Europe took a summer holiday, and now, a few calls later, the office was closed for three weeks and the rest of the month was his. *Vive La France.* There was no time like the present.

Present. Damn. Tom checked the date on his watch. It was Natalie's birthday next Monday and he'd completely forgotten to do anything about it. Worse still, six-year-olds simply didn't understand that their birthdays weren't the most important day in the calendar after Christmas or that their godfathers hadn't been appointed primarily to spoil them. Reaching for his mobile, he grudgingly turned it on and dialled Helen. So much for his splendid isolation.

'Tom? Don't tell me, you're on your way.'

'Well, in some ways that's true. Only this time I'm on my way to France.'

'Business or pleasure?'

'Pleasure. I've taken your advice.'

'Blimey, you move fast. What did you do, sweep her up into your arms and into the car?'

'Actually, it didn't go exactly according to plan. Alice said no.'

'Why?'

'Too many work commitments, apparently.'

'Hang on, that's fair enough, isn't it? I mean, maybe if you'd given her more than thirty-six hours' notice…?'

'She also said that she didn't think it was a good idea that we stayed in touch.'

'Oh. I'm sorry… Well, at least you tried.'

'Anyway, I'd already decided to take a few weeks off and sooner rather than later, so we're having a few weeks in France.'

'We?'

'Me and the bike.'

'So now you're a couple. Jesus, Tom, why couldn't you have taken the car? You can't exactly bring a couple of cases of wine home on the back of a bike.'

'I'm not on a shopping trip.'

Helen was quick to correct him. 'Life is a shopping trip.'

'Well, I can always send stuff home.'

'You will be careful, won't you?'

'Of course.'

'How about you text me every night before you go to bed?'

'How about you get off my case?'

'I've only got one brother.'

'He's forty-four and he's only going to France. Now then, real reason for phoning—Natalie's birthday.'

'Would I be correct in presuming your holiday planning didn't include present purchasing?'

'What holiday planning would that be?'

Helen smiled. 'Don't worry, I'll get something small and forge your signature as usual.'

'Thanks, and the usual amount will be transferred into her savings account as normal.'

'I do wish you'd set one of those up for me, too.'

Tom laughed. 'You have James, and a pension scheme.'

'But what if I want to buy a bike or a car on my eighteenth birthday?'

'I'm afraid you're closer to your eightieth these days.'

'I hate you.'

'I hate you, too.' He smiled.

'So, I expect you want me to keep an eye on the flat?'

'From Gloucestershire?'

'I do go up to London every now and again. Besides, I'm sure my wardrobe could do with an injection of a few urban essentials.'

'I'll try not to take it personally that you'd rather visit

when I'm not there. But if you're determined to exercise your credit cards, you're passing and fancy watering some plants or need a bed for the night, do pop in. Otherwise I'm sure the cleaner will do fine. If not, I'll buy new plants. I'm only away for a few weeks.'

'How about the boys? It's the school holidays and they're getting a bit bored down here. I could just pop them on the train. You've got a PlayStation and satellite television, haven't you?'

'Aren't they a bit young to be coming up to London on their own? Alex is only fifteen.' Tom tried to disguise the edge of panic in his voice. His Bang & Olufsen sound system was state-of-the-art. The keys to his old Porsche were in the kitchen drawer.

'But you're their successful uncle and current idol.' Helen was enjoying his momentary discomfort. 'Hey, I'm just kidding.'

'Oh, right.' Clearly more relieved than he'd realised, Tom exhaled fully for the first time in minutes.

'So, do you know where you're heading?'

'St. Malo.'

'And then?'

'The open road. South of France, Italy maybe. I'll be back early September.'

'Well, bon voyage, I guess. And for God's sake, be careful.'

'Thanks. I will be.'

Hanging up, Tom walked to the front of the boat and stared out over the sea ahead of him. Rule number one for this trip: there was to be no looking back.

Chapter Seventeen

17 days to go
Suzie 7, Alice 2

Alice hurriedly applied a fresh coat of mascara as her black cab stopped at yet another set of traffic lights on Piccadilly. An hour and a half ago she'd been running late on location in Reading and now, with barely a minute for second thoughts, she was ready. New shoes, new attitude and just enough time to meet Zoë for a quick drink before the games commenced.

Thanks to the remnants of adrenaline from her day in front of the camera, Alice was feeling positively herself. She wasn't desperate, nor was she itching to have sex with relative strangers, but she wasn't prepared to surrender to her mother yet, either. And how difficult could it be to secure a non-axe murdering, semi-decent chap for a couple of dates? So what if, until now, flings hadn't really been her style? Wedge sandals hadn't been either, and now she had two pairs.

As the taxi pulled into Old Compton Street, Alice

consulted her watch—forty spare minutes and she intended to spend every last one of them with her very best friend.

Zoë shook her head as Alice approached. 'Black V neck.'

Alice removed her fitted denim jacket with a flourish. 'Black sleeveless V-necked top thingy with a twist, actually.' Alice gave Zoë a twirl to reveal a plunging neckline both front and back. 'And check out this belt. You are in the presence of none other than the Rhinestone Cowgirl.'

Alice lifted her top a fraction to expose a light tan leather belt, with a chunky turquoise and silver buckle, and Zoë was forced to murmur her reluctant approval. 'Hey, that's not at all bad.'

'And wait for it…' Alice held her hair back to reveal earrings made from turquoise feathers. 'Now come on, you don't get much more Navaho than that. Alice-dating-very-quickly-and-hopefully-with-no-wolves at your service.'

'Jesus, did you mug a budgie on the way here?'

'No good?' Alice cocked her head inquiringly.

'Not baaad but…' Zoë hesitated as she debated the merits of truth over tact so close to a dating scenario. 'Nope, I'd lose them.'

'Really?'

'Yup.'

Alice removed the earrings. 'Hey, they were only an experiment and pretty damn cheap.'

'I know.'

'Maybe that should have been cheep cheep.'

Zoë smiled. 'I'm sorry.'

'Don't be. And to think I'd always wanted siblings. You win.'

'And so, it would appear, do I.' Zoë proffered a standard office-issue brown envelope.

Excitedly, Alice extracted her best friend's birth certificate. Her eyes scanned every line, seeing but apparently not reading. Geared up for an evening of superficiality, adrenaline had apparently ruined her ability to absorb anything but alcohol. Her brain processed nothing. She needed to reboot, and fast.

She looked up. 'So anything new? Any more clues?'

'Well, not really. We're still looking for a Margaret Riddick.'

Alice ran her finger along the relevant line to double-check and smiled. 'Okay there, Daisy.'

Zoë ignored her. 'And we finally know that my father was a Mr. P. Fletcher. Unfortunately there are no occupations or addresses listed for either of them, so the only address we have to go on is still the one we have for my mother on the letter assessing her mental and physical health at the time she handed me over.'

'That's fantastic.'

'It is?' Zoë wondered if she had missed something. 'It doesn't exactly narrow anything down.'

Alice was on an entirely different wavelength. 'Don't you see, it means you're not only my sister of soul, but also my sister by surname.'

Zoë shook her head, bewildered. 'I guess.'

Alice reminded herself that in Zoë's position she probably wouldn't be particularly excited about that revelation, either. Just because she had whipped herself into a frenzy of positivity in the taxi, didn't mean that Zoë was going to be feeling anything other than midweek and, in light of her morning's post, quite adult.

'So how about we spend Saturday hitting the phones and trawling the Net? Let's see what we can find.'

Zoë looked apologetic. 'Would you mind?'

'Of course not, I absolutely insist.'

'Thank you. Really, I mean it. And, don't shoot, but I think we should start early.'

'Just name your time and I'll be there.'

'You could even come over for supper on Friday and just stay over.'

Alice hesitated. She'd never really seen the point of staying at a friend's place when she owned a house in the same town, a shortish drive or cab ride away, but Zoë rarely asked for help. 'Only if you promise we can go to sleep at a reasonable hour.' Alice interrupted herself. 'I'm sorry, did I say that out loud?'

'You did and it's fine. We're hardly going to be having a midnight feast or watching scary movies.'

'But we might suddenly decide to watch all six series of *Sex and the City* on DVD.'

Zoë grinned. 'Now that's not a bad idea. Seriously though, I might start looking for numbers tonight.'

Alice winced.

'What?'

'Promise me you won't call anyone.'

'Of course I won't.'

'That includes not dialling anyone and then hanging up just to check the number is working.'

Embarrassed, Zoë giggled. 'I can't believe you remember that. It was years ago. And only because I was convinced that guy had given me a fake number.'

'Justify, justify. But it's getting late and you don't want to be doing this after a few drinks.'

'Roger that.' Zoë beamed at Alice. 'I love the fact you know me so well.'

'I'm only thinking about what I'd be doing in your position.'

'Hello, girls.'

Alice wondered whether her mother had secretly had her chipped and was monitoring her location via a GPS. It's not as if there was a shortage of bars in Soho and Alice was sure they'd arranged to meet at the speed-dating venue in, she consulted her watch, half an hour.

'Hi, Suzie.' Zoë moved along, making more room on her banquette.

Suzie eyed the seat. 'I think I'll start at the bar. Need refills?'

Nodding, Zoë watched Suzie as she effortlessly carved her way through the clusters of people, straight to a barman who was actually ignoring other customers and waiting to serve her.

Zoë played with the plastic stirrer from her previous drink. 'Sorry, Al, hope you don't mind. She called me earlier and it seemed rude not to mention we were seeing each other.'

'I think she loves you more than me, anyway. I mean, you're much nicer to her than I am sometimes.'

'That's because she's not my mother.'

Alice watched her mother ordering their drinks at the bar. 'She looks great tonight, doesn't she?'

Zoë nodded. 'That red really suits her. And the burnt-orange leather bracelet on her wrist looks great. She does dress down very well.'

'She does everything very well.' It was meant to sound like admiration; instead, Alice felt it sounded a bit bitter. 'It looks like she's even made time to have a blow-dry on the way.' Alice was impressed, especially as Suzie was walking back to the table with a cute waiter in tow, their drinks on his tray, a started champagne bottle in an ice bucket in his other hand.

Zoë put her hand on Alice's arm. 'Just look at tonight as a bit of fun. And try not to be too dismissive at first sight.'

'Sound advice from the woman who does dismissive better than anyone I know.'

Zoë smiled. 'If he's not the right guy, you never know, he might have a fantastic flatmate.'

'When has that ever happened? And oh so easy to give the pep talk when you don't have to find a date yourself.'

'That's not the point.'

'Oh, I think it is.'

'To us all.' As Suzie raised her glass and took a large sip, Zoë was relieved to be off the hook.

Alice paused with the glass at her lips. 'What's the occasion, Mum?'

'Life. And don't worry, this is all tax deductible.'

Alice was wide-eyed. 'We're here on business?'

'It just so happens, my editor loves my proposal for a series of articles on a mother and daughter in search of a decent man.'

Zoë smiled as Alice did her best not to shout.

Suzie leaned in. 'And between us, my agent thinks it may even have legs as a drama project. I'm thinking about collaborating on a script for television.'

'Really?' Zoë's eyes were bright with excitement. Alice's were glazed with disbelief.

Suzie nodded. 'I know. How cool is that?'

Momentarily stunned, Alice sat back, watching her mother. 'I thought we had rules about this sort of thing.'

'What rules?'

'That I'm entitled to my privacy.'

'No one needs to know it's about you.'

'And exactly how many other daughters do you have?'

Suzie dismissed Alice's negativity. 'It could be huge. Do you think Adrian Mole minded, do you think Bridget Jones minded?'

Alice sighed. 'They're fictional.'

'Well, you don't know that many people, neither do I. And this could be fictional, too.'

'But it's not.'

'Oh, relax. At least until you've read some of it. Your profile is only going to be raised. It's a good thing.'

Alice wondered just how much profile a girl with relatively small breasts could have.

'See what I mean,' Alice whispered to Zoë.

'She's excited. She's sold a great idea.' Zoë was speaking out of the side of her mouth. She hoped Alice was listening. 'Besides, you might well be all over buses and breakfast tables in your own right soon anyway.'

'Shh,' Alice hissed. 'I haven't told her yet.'

'Why on earth not?'

Suzie sat up a little straighter. 'What are you two muttering about?'

Zoë took the conversation by the reins. 'You're not the only one with good news.'

'Excellent.' Suzie looked from one girl to the other expectantly. She was ready.

Alice, on the other hand, was not. She pre-empted her best friend. 'Zoë received a copy of her original birth certificate this morning.'

Suzie half raised her glass. 'Can we drink to that?'

'Of course.' Zoë drained her glass as Alice mouthed her an apology.

'And what was that other thing, about buses and breakfast tables?'

Either Suzie was one of the world's leading lip readers, her hearing was supersensitive or Zoë's whispering skills needed refining.

Alice shrugged. 'Oh, nothing, just a job I'm going for.'

'Really? What sort of job?'

'It's all under wraps at the moment.'

'I'm your mother. And Zoë clearly knows.'

'I really can't risk a rumour getting out. Not even a rumour of a rumour.'

Suzie folded her arms. 'It won't.'

Alice paused.

'Come on, darling. I promise.'

Alice lowered her voice and checked around her before proceeding. 'Well, it's by no means definite yet but there's a possibility, all things going well, that I might be co-presenting the breakfast show on Channel 6.'

'Wow, darling, that would be fantastic.' Suzie's excitement was tangible and at once Alice felt guilty at having not mentioned it to her sooner.

'I know.'

'Come on, another toast. To the future…'

As all three women tipped their heads back, Alice realised she was starting to feel warmed up enough to consider the main event.

'So.' Suzie had a couple of questions. 'When will you know? Did they approach you?'

'I guess you could put it that way.'

Bursting with no longer one hundred percent secret information, Zoë couldn't contain herself anymore. 'Richard's their new controller.'

Suzie looked impressed. 'Well then—' she raised her glass once more '—here's to Richard.'

'That's a first, Mum.'

'Nonsense. He just better not go and let you—'

'It's by no means definite yet.'

'I know. Mum's the word.' Suzie winked at Zoë and Alice.

Alice returned her glass to the table. 'Isn't it always?'

* * *

Relieved to hear the whistle blow for time, Alice put a cross in the box even before "Tom Hanks" had sidled off and "P Diddy" had replaced him at her table—this contender's nickname for the evening made all the more bizarre by the fact that this three-minute man was as pale and blond as they came—and currently silent.

'Hi.' Alice wondered how blatantly he could stare at her chest until she realised he was probably just trying to decipher her name label. She moved it to shoulder height. 'It's Minnie.' Maybe he couldn't read.

Suzie was being Julia Roberts in the room next door and she was Minnie Mouse. Alice supposed it could have been worse. She could have picked Nellie the Elephant out of the pile.

P Diddy leaned forward in his chair. 'So, Minnie, do you know what size the processor is in your computer?'

Alice reached for the emergency bowl of peanuts. Four down, twenty-one to go. It was going to be a long evening.

'So it was only when my wife left me that I woke up to what a special person she was. I'd do anything to get a second chance at our relationship, but she's living with someone else now and I guess I owe it to her not to just sit around at home. I mean, that's not going to make me attractive to her, is it? Trouble is…'

Suzie drained her glass dramatically as "Clint Eastwood" continued talking about himself and focused on attracting the attentions of the waiter. She was still waiting for her evening to take off and if Clint's experience was matching hers at this precise moment, he'd be off to grovel and beg his wife for a second chance as soon as the final whistle blew.

After a series of head bobs and eyebrow raises, none of

which seemed to faze Clint, the waiter arrived at their table. 'Can I get you something to drink?'

Suzie had a new best friend. 'Do you do vodka by the litre?'

'Sorry, madam, we only do Smirnoff.'

Humour was obviously extra. 'Vodka tonic would be great. Better make it a double.'

'Our standard measures are a double.'

'I'm not surprised.'

'I'm sorry, I didn't catch that.'

'Don't worry. A vodka tonic would be magnificent.'

'So would you like a double or a double double?'

'A single double.' Suzie was tiring of her order. 'Just a double.' She wished she'd brought a hip flask.

Clint paused his monologue. 'And I'll have another beer.'

'That'll be £10.50.'

Suzie hesitated, hoping Clint might go ahead and make her day, or at least her round.

Instead, he shrugged apologetically. 'Sorry, I don't have any cash with me.'

Rummaging in her bag for her wallet, Suzie wondered how these three minutes had managed to last so long.

Alice doodled on her master sheet as she waited for her next man. Halfway through, all things considered, she was quite enjoying herself—if only from a people-watching perspective. The last guy had been an almost-tick. And from now on, or at least for the rest of the evening, she was not going to judge a book by its cover, or a man by his sports jacket.

"Ben Affleck" took a seat in front of her and smiled in an interestingly non-cheesy way. Plus, he wasn't at all unattractive.

Alice leaned back. 'Sorry to hear things didn't work out about between you and J. Lo.'

"Ben" laughed. He had a sense of humour. One out of one in the points department so far.

He peered at her name label. 'So how's Mickey?'

And no points for originality regardless of the fact she had gone for the obvious a moment earlier. Rules were rules, and she was making hers up as she went along.

'I left him. His voice was incredibly irritating and he always wore the same pair of shorts. A mouse deserves more in her man.'

Alice relaxed as Ben smiled warmly and made himself comfortable in his chair. Maybe, just maybe, she was going to find one person she might want to give another three minutes to. She sat back and though of Zoë. 'So, Coke or Pepsi?'

'Personally, I've always preferred harder drugs.'

Was it her imagination or had he just rubbed his nose?

'Okay, um, whisky or vodka?'

'Vodka.' Ben took his cue and the reins. 'I get it now. Let's see. Your place or mine? Spit or swallow. From behind or on top?'

Alice's expression glazed over as she put a cross in his box. Two minutes remaining. She wished she had a whistle of her own. Next.

Suzie cast an eye down her sheet. Five ticks and five more men to go. Several drinks down the line she was quite tipsy and dying for a pee. Plus, she suspected the incoming suitor was wearing a chunky necklace under his turtleneck. Maybe "Brad Pitt" wouldn't mind if she went to the loo for his three minutes.

★ ★ ★

'So if you could change one thing in your life what would it be?'

"Keifer Sutherland" was proving to be more probing than most. Under pressure to come up with a sensible answer for the first time since she'd arrived at the venue, Alice was sure their three minutes must have been up ages ago.

'Well, I like my job, I even like my ex-husband…'

Keifer looked at her sympathetically, willing her to have a big regret.

Alice carried on thinking out loud. 'Maybe I would have trained to be a doctor. I do sometimes feel I should be giving more back to society. The world does seem to be becoming increasingly superficial and selfish.' Alice stopped herself. What was this, speed therapy?

Apparently having lost interest in her answer a while back, Kiefer stared long and hard. 'I've seen you on the telly, haven't I?'

Alice blushed. 'Possibly.'

'So is this part of that programme?'

Alice's response was emphatic. 'No.'

The last thing she needed was for this to get out.

'So, you're doing this for yourself?'

Kiefer sounded flatteringly surprised.

'Actually…' Could this guy be a journalist? First rule of thumb when dealing with the press, never give away anything personal that could be misconstrued. In other words, never tell them anything. 'I'm doing this for my mum.' It wasn't even a lie.

'So you're telling me there are no hidden cameras here.' Kiefer ran his fingers through his hair and started smiling at the peanut bowl, at the adjacent pillar, even, to Alice's amusement, at her almost nonexistent cleavage—hidden cameras were small, but not that small.

'None.' Alice was bemused at Kiefer's clear enthusiasm to be on television. He was definitely a prime candidate for a bit of "hello mum" waving.

As if to confirm her assessment, suddenly reduced to TV tart, Kiefer winked at her. 'You know I've always thought I could do with one of those life makeovers.'

Alice noted his black three-quarter-length leather jacket. An item probably purchased after he'd seen *Lock, Stock and Two Smoking Barrels*, and hung on to. 'Most people could.'

'I don't suppose you could give me some tips. You can have all of the next ninety seconds.'

The first, and the last, minute and a half of their relationship.

Idly, Alice wondered if her mother was making all her men sign a release form. She was sure that some of them were going to find aspects of themselves in print at the weekend. At this rate she was going to be able to make some choice contributions herself.

'Seriously, I think I'd be good on camera.' Kiefer turned his head from one side to the other so she could see both profiles. 'People often tell me they think I look a bit like Tom Cruise.'

'Really?' Alice didn't even look up as she keyed: *Help! Dating hell* into her phone and texted Zoë from under the table, but Kiefer was far too busy talking about himself to notice. And that suited Alice just fine.

Exhausted, Alice finally allowed herself to collapse in the back of the cab. Head lolling, she propped herself up against the side window, relishing the silence. One out of twenty-five. And "Pete Sampras" had only got a reprieve when she'd decided it would be too negative to reject them all. She'd also debated a couple of mercy ticks before deciding that defeated the whole object of the evening. Tired, she watched Suzie as she scanned her carbon copy of her tick list.

'So you and "Pistol Pete", eh?' Suzie giggled. 'At least he's a champion. My personal favourite was "Richard Gere".'

'Hang on, you were "Julia Roberts". That's perfect. He's your sticker destiny.'

'Excellent. I hadn't even thought of that.'

'Of course, "Mickey Mouse" had dreadful halitosis.'

'Probably all that cheese.' Suzie laughed at her own joke, which was fortunate as Alice couldn't find the energy. She'd been faking it all evening.

'So, do you think "Ricardo" ticked you?'

Suzie chuckled. 'I'm sure he did. And I'll find out for sure tomorrow. Along with the others. What about "Pete"?'

'Who knows? He's not really even my type—bit trendy for me, but he'd certainly be fun for an evening. If he seems interested and interesting, maybe I'll invite him to your party.'

'It's Invitation Only.'

'Oh come on, it's always good to have a couple of extra single men.'

'Just give me his details if he makes it past a follow-up. I do need to keep an eye on numbers.'

'Panic ye not. He'll probably fall at the next hurdle. As usual, most of the women were of a far higher calibre than the men.'

'I think a few of my guys had potential.' Suzie stopped as she heard herself. 'Am I slurring? I think I must have had more to drink than I'd realised.'

'Well, call me fussy but that roomful of men is why I'm happy being single…'

Suzie stopped trying to calculate the number of units of alcohol she had drunk. She kept losing count at around seven.

Alice was still picking at her evening. 'The concept is sound. You get to meet twenty-five men in one evening and then walk away without hurting any of their feelings, but most of those men were very average. Too many of them worked in IT, too many of them weren't nearly discerning enough. It just confirms what Zoë and I know already.'

Suzie shook her head. This hadn't been the plan at all.

'I know you think I aim too high, Mum, but actually, all I'm after is a man with kind eyes, a favourite hobby that isn't themselves, a good sense of humour and interests that don't solely involve a keyboard and a mouse.'

Suzie sighed as she scanned the rest of Alice's sheet. 'Didn't you tick anyone else?'

'I decided to go for quality—well, as far as I could. And I'd be happy to spend three more minutes with Pete, maybe even an hour or two.'

'Steady on, darling, I don't want you rushing into anything.'

Alice stared out of the window. 'I might just get a dog instead.'

Concerned, Suzie sat herself up in a more upright position for extra gravitas and perspective. 'Name me one man that wants to meet a woman with a dependent?'

'I'm suggesting a pet, not a baby.'

'You'll no longer be able to jet off on the spur of the moment without getting a dog sitter.'

'When was the last time I spontaneously took off for the weekend?'

'You did when you went to Vegas.'

'Oh my God.' Alice slapped her palm on her forehead. 'Maybe if I'd invested in a dog years ago I wouldn't be a divorcée.'

Suzie laughed at Alice's am-dram realisation of her analogy.

'Anyway, in an emergency I could always leave the dog with you.'

'I'm not really a doggy person, darling. Too much hair and life's too short to put shit in a bag.'

'It won't be any old dog, it'd be mine. Just think, a grand-dog. Practice.'

Suzie looked far from amused.

'Rest assured you're not in any immediate danger of getting a grandchild. But you never know, one day…'

Suzie ignored Alice's goading and looked over the driver's shoulder, through the windscreen and on to the Old Brompton Road as they headed home. Once upon a time she'd been thirty. And now she was going to be sixty. Was Richard Gere going to be the answer? She'd almost forgotten what the question was.

Chapter Eighteen

16 days to go
Suzie 32★, Alice 27★
including all three-minute dates
Subtract 25 from current total for more accurate
numbers.

With only sixteen days to go and still no sign of the perfect match, Alice had decided to put the rest of her life on hold, at least for one afternoon. While the world thought she was working, she had in fact been to market. Benefits of working from home #153: No one really knows what you are doing.

She and Suzie had woken up with matching hangovers and taken matching doses of ibuprofen, but while her mum had headed off to the newspaper offices for the day, Alice had taken the executive decision to exercise what was her divine self-scheduling right. When her only client booked for the afternoon postponed, she had given herself the day off.

Now, still unwashed at 3:00 p.m., she was sitting cross-legged on the floor of her study dressed in old surf shorts and a gym T-shirt. She was feeling much better since she'd had a glass of wine, careful to ensure that not a drop of alcohol had been consumed before midday, satisfying herself that she was definitely not, not even nearly, an alcoholic in any shape or form.

She'd had better days. Having checked in with cupid and scanned all the responses in her account for even a glimmer of suitability, she'd gone proactive and registered on a couple of other sites. But as yet nobody had floated her boat, rocked her world, tooted her horn or rung her bell.

Just after lunch she'd discovered that not only had "Pete Sampras" put a tick in her box, but he was in her inbox. Yet, in the very bright light of day, she was less impressed. For a start he'd made three spelling mistakes in three sentences. And, Alice realised, he could have ticked every girl in the room. He hadn't been dragged to her recycle bin yet, but she hadn't hit reply, either. Plus, despite the fact that she had handed over cash to meet him, she didn't want to seem too keen. Playing hard to get, or playing silly buggers? She hadn't decided.

Tom was still a problem. She'd been staring at the back of motorcyclists since Monday evening, watching each and every one of them as they snaked past her in traffic. And while she knew that it was probably a very bad idea, she wanted to clear the air, or at least her mental in-tray, before it was too late.

She'd started drafting him an e-mail and then a text message—but there was no way she could get what she wanted to say across in 147 characters and a handful of emoticons. She'd tried to call him at work on Tuesday lunchtime but he hadn't answered the phone and while she could have left him a message, writing a letter had suddenly seemed like the obvious, if potentially cowardly, solution.

What could be better than an uninterrupted commitment of her thoughts to paper? No U-turns, no awkward silence, no changing tack midconversation, plus he couldn't just delete it before even opening the envelope. Well, unless of course he physically threw the letter away—but how would he know who it was from until he'd opened it, at which point, however bad an idea he thought reading it might be, curiosity would probably get the better of him.

She wasn't going to become obsessed with the reliability of the post and hand-deliver it. Nor would she set up camp under the letterbox awaiting a reply. A few simple words on paper and then she could finally move on and tick Tom off her to-do list. All she had to do now was stop procrastinating and write the damn thing.

Sitting at her desk, Alice eyeballed the blank page in front of her. She couldn't remember the last time she had written anyone a letter and the acute silence in the house was only adding to the pressure. Powering up her iPod station, she left her choice of soundtrack for the afternoon to the Gods of shuffle. Madonna's "Love Makes The World Go Round" started playing. She was off to a good start.

Hi Tom

Easy. Alice let her pen roll through her fingers.

On reflection, maybe "Dear Tom" would have been better. She stared at the two words on the page for a moment before ripping the sheet in half and then in half again and filing the bits in her wastepaper basket. She placed a fresh sheet of paper in front of her. Letter writing, take two.

Dear Tom

Alice chewed the end of her pen and stared out of the window waiting for inspiration to strike. Trying to order her thoughts sufficiently to write a few paragraphs without the benefits of being able to cut, paste and edit electronically was proving harder than she'd thought it would be. And she'd been thinking about little else since she'd woken up this morning.

I just wanted to clear the air,

Alice screwed up the paper and started again. At this rate she'd run out of paper, the world would run out of rainforests and she'd allow herself to send an e-mail after all. Finally she stopped thinking and started writing, and as she removed the analytical part of her brain from the process, the words came easily.

Dear Tom,
Before you ride off into the sunset I just wanted to thank you. Yes, thank you—I don't think we, or at least I, could claim to have planned anything in my life less. But I think, I know, the last few weeks have been good for us both.
   I hope that your trip gives you the perspective you need and a much-needed break from all that has become routine. Some time to sit back, kick up your heels and think about what it is that you want. Thanks also for your offer of a break from the norm. If things weren't so busy here I would probably seriously consider it, but I have some changes of my own in the offing that mean I need to be in London, at least for the next few months.

Hunched over her desk, Alice reread the paragraphs, careful not to smudge her handiwork. Then holding the page up at arm's length, she was relieved to see she'd managed to keep the lines fairly equidistant and level. Years of schooling hadn't been totally undone by years of computer use and abuse.

Returning her focus to the matter in hand, or at least in her hand, she started humming along to Bruce Hornsby's "The Way It Is" as her iPod apparently endorsed her sentiments.

Please feel free to get in touch on your return, should you want to. Should you want to…I guess that's not really very helpful, is it? What I suppose I'm saying is that I think I would like you to.

Flushed with honesty, Alice looked up for a moment of respite. Her mother's party invitation, propped up against the bottom of her flat-screen monitor, caught her attention. Alone in her study, she shrugged her shoulders. Chewing the end of her pen, she dared herself. She had nothing more to lose. She returned to her missive.

Also, should you be in London on August 26 and if it doesn't seem too weird, do please feel free to pop in to a certain columnist's sixtieth birthday drinks. Despite my mother's determination to get me dating before her upcoming birthday, I have taken a very laid-back (albeit undeclared) approach to her harebrained scheming and am now officially hanging up my summer jacket and putting my wedge espadrilles back into their box. I can assure you that everything that developed between the two of us was entirely organic. Indeed, there is only one person I would consider taking as a date, only now I find that, frustratingly, he is off limits.

Anyway, do let me know if you fancy coming along and joining us for a celebratory drink or three. The party

starts at seven-thirty and no doubt will still be going hours later. Of course you are welcome to bring a guest.

Alice paused. Lots of Love, Love, Yours sincerely, Best— best what? Best wishes? Love and kisses? Just a few more kisses?

All the best,
Alice

As she sealed the envelope, Celine Dion started belting "Think Twice" into the study. Disbelieving, Alice stared at her iPod in disgust. The last thing her conscience needed was a psychic playlist or any messages, hidden or otherwise. Plus, she didn't know she'd ever owned any Celine Dion. Where were "Independent Woman", "Respect" and all her other feel-good, upbeat, finger-waggling anthems when she needed them?

Alice silenced her designer jukebox just in time. Either she had burglars or… There were definitely heavy footsteps coming up the stairs. Instinctively and irrationally she slid her letter under a pile of papers.

To call out or not to call out, that was the question. Quickly looking around her study, she wondered what she could possibly defend herself with. She wasn't sure a roll of last year's Christmas wrapping paper or a thirty-centimetre *shatterproof* ruler was going to stun anyone, unless it was with their inadequacy. Plus, if she was going to be found unconscious in her home, she'd rather she'd been dressed in something a little less downmarket and at least been wearing underwear, matching or otherwise.

The footsteps continued to approach. Just at the point Alice was about to start hyperventilating Suzie popped her head around the study door, removing a headphone from her ear as she did so.

'That's it. I'm bushed. Day officially over. Just to warn you, hangovers do not get easier with age. Fancy getting a DVD and having a doze on the sofa with your mother? Hang on, have you not even bothered to get dressed yet?'

Alice held her arms up in surrender. 'Welcome to sluts anonymous. I am trailer trash without the trailer.'

Suzie laughed as she removed her other headphone and dropped it into her bag. 'In your dreams.'

'All part of the joys of working from home.'

'Lucky you.'

'Excuse me, you write for a living, you don't get much luckier than that.'

'But I feel dreadful.' Moving a pile of papers, Suzie made room for herself on the sofa and spied Alice's wine glass. 'Hair of the dog?'

Alice nodded. 'Only problem is you have to keep on sipping or it all goes pear shaped again. Want me to run you a bath or something?'

Suzie kicked off her shoes dramatically.

'That would be blissful. I'm very impressed to find you in here, actually. I'd be dribbling into a cushion on the sofa if I were you. So what have you been working on?' Suzie's hawk eye surveyed Alice's now unusually empty desk.

'Oh, just getting on top of some paperwork and—' Alice proffered her laptop—fortunately still logged on to a dating Web site '—trying to find me a date.'

Suzie perked up immediately. 'Any joy?'

'Not as yet, although Pistol Pete does want to meet me for a drink.'

'That's fantastic, darling.'

'Did you hear from any of yours?'

Suzie yawned wearily. 'Seven.'

'You ticked seven men?'

'More to the point, they all ticked me, which, let me tell you, is excellent for the ego.'

'Doesn't it just make you think that maybe the men are a bit less discerning when it comes to ticking than the women?'

'Please don't ruin my moment. Who cares?'

'Well, at this rate, you're going to run out of date nights.'

'Or I'm going to have fun trying to fit them all in…'

Alice raised her eyes to the ceiling and back again.

'Don't forget, darling, I grew up in the sixties. We were much more relaxed about trying guys for size.'

'You mean "about quantity over quality".'

'How can you possibly know what you like if you don't sample a variety?'

'You mean sleep around?'

'I'm just talking drinks and dinner this time around. Times have changed and I'm not the woman that I used to be.'

Glancing at her desk to make sure the incriminating envelope was totally buried under a pile of bills, Alice set off to the bathroom to start assuaging her ever-increasing guilt complex. As she stared into the swirling, foaming waters, her mother arrived, proffering her mobile phone. 'It's Richard, for you.'

Alice hadn't even heard it ring. 'Richard, hi.'

'Al? Where are you, Niagara Falls? Because that wouldn't be very convenient…'

Alice walked into her bedroom and closed the door behind her.

'…That's better.'

'Sorry, just running a bath.'

'At four on a Thursday?'

'Are there bathing bylaws I don't know about? Anyway it's not for me. It's for the phone-answering one. I really wish she'd butt out sometimes.'

'Actually, on this occasion I'm glad she picked up for you. I don't suppose you're free for the rest of the afternoon?'

Alice looked at herself in the mirror. She wasn't anywhere near fit for her public, not even for Richard.

'Dermot just stopped by the office. He's got a few quick meetings to go to but wondered if you might be able to make it over here for an informal interview and maybe even a quick screen test.'

'Now?' Alice laughed nervously. 'Today really isn't the right—'

'I can give you an hour, hour and half, tops. He's away for a few days next week and we need to get this done as soon as possible. I can send a car for you, if that helps.'

'But I'm not even dress—'

'That's hardly an irreversible condition. You need to be here.'

Adrenaline starting to course through her veins, Alice sat down on her bed wondering where on earth to start. 'I don't suppose you could send a stylist, too?'

'Just wear some trousers and a brightly coloured top. It might not be a bad idea to bring a tailored jacket, too. Just throw a few alternatives into a bag, or I'm sure wardrobe will be able to rustle something up.'

'Can you give me two hours?' Alice wondered where Zoë was right now.

Richard hesitated. 'Not really.'

'Listen to you, Mr. Man-With-New-Power-and-Authority. You can't just do this. You know I'm not good at surprises or being unprepared.'

Richard was unrelenting. 'I'm not going to lie, the sooner you can get here the better.'

'Right you are, boss.' She could do this. Alice forced a smile as, walking over to her mirror, she stared at herself. Her hair was still smoky from last night—a bundle of strange Medusa-like curls beyond the help of any styling products. Her eyebrows needed plucking. Staring up close, she appeared to be hosting a blackhead convention on her nose. She needed to get off the phone. She was going to need both hands and a lot of products.

'The car will be with you in an hour. And probably best not to mention, you know, us.'

'That we were married?'

'I'm sure most people know or have put two and two together by now but still probably best not to go on about it.'

'Right. No kissing with tongues. Got it.'

'Good, and remember, from this day forward you're Alice Fletcher.'

'Of course, all three of my fans from *Get A Life* will be very confused at my name change…'

'They'll just think you've got married or something.'

'Great. The final nail in my dating coffin.'

'I know I'm probably being paranoid. Just humour me.'

'Again?'

Richard smiled. 'Yes, again.'

Safe within the four walls of her bedroom, Alice stood tall. 'Either I'm the right person for the job or I'm not.'

'You definitely are.'

'Then what's the point of complicating everything?'

'Let's just play it by ear. See you very soon.'

The "very" ringing in her ears, Alice hung up.

'Shit. Shit, shit, shit.' Peeling off her clothes where she was standing, she grabbed yesterday's towel from the radiator and headed to the bathroom. The door was closed.

'Bugger it. Mum?'

'Yes, darling.' Suzie sounded very relaxed and very semi-submerged. 'This was such a good idea of yours.'

'I need to shower.'

'I won't be long, sweetie.'

'I need to shower *now*.'

'Now?'

Alice rested her forehead against the door. 'I'm sorry. I've just discovered I have a meeting and possible screen test in an hour and a half.'

'Well, come in. It's not locked.'

Alice opened the door and did her best to keep her eyes to herself as, disgruntled, Suzie sat up, fresh bubble bath clinging to her.

'You really need to get a second bathroom put into this place.'

'Like this happens every week and actually, it's your fault for answering my phone.'

'It was a pleasure.'

'Thank you.'

'That's better.'

Squeezing past her mother, who was now dripping on to the laminate floor, Alice reached around the shower screen and turned the mixer tap on.

Suzie wrapped herself in a white towel. 'Want me to help pick something for you to wear?'

Alice nodded gratefully as she stepped into the bath. She could only just cope with the concept of washing at the moment. 'And maybe call Zoë?'

'There's no time, we can do this on our own. And I've got

a great hot-pink top that will look fabulous on you under a black jacket.'

Alice let the water soak her hair, wondering why Suzie was still standing there.

'Mum. Please.' Alice started to think Autocues and cameras and mentally started speaking slowly. 'This girl needs to shower alone.'

'This girl needs to start washing a bit faster. Hurry up. You'll definitely need to blow-dry your hair for this. Want me to come along with you?'

Alice shook her head, spraying a mist of John Frieda Brilliant Brunette over her white tiles.

'I could just give you a lift.'

'They're sending a car.'

'Are they now? Very nice, too. Go on. I promise I won't get in the way. I happen to think that Dermot chap is rather attractive.'

'Which is exactly why you're going to stay here. Besides, I don't think bringing your mother to introductory meetings really creates the right impression.'

Alice started speed-washing, her mother's bathwater still draining around her ankles. Turning one hundred and eighty degrees until she was facing the wall, she tipped her head up towards the jets and let her mouth fill with water before spitting it out through her teeth. Everything had to be clean. If the meeting went well, she'd be on course for the job of her life. If not, maybe she could run off and join the circus. Or Tom. Or Pete Sampras.

Chapter Nineteen

'My name is Alice Fletcher and you're watching Channel 6.' Alice gave the camera a smile and silently praised herself for remembering which surname she was meant to be using. There'd been a hairy moment when she'd been called in to meet Jez, the director, and for a split second hadn't responded to her new, make that old, identity.

'Great.' The floor manager gave her a thumbs-up from his squatting position next to the main camera as the lights came up and Alice strained to listen to the people chatting in the gallery through her earpiece. Her expression, however, gave nothing away, even when she could hear Richard's voice—albeit frustratingly not what he was saying.

'Thank you, Alice. Same again, please.' Jez's voice was loud in her ear.

As the lighting in the studio reverted to the opening titles, Alice did her best to make herself look comfortable on the sofa. Remembering to sit up straight enough to appear alert but without looking like she had a broom handle stapled to her spine, she was ready and very possibly a tiny bit drunk. Suzie had insisted on helping her to another glass of Pinot Grigio while she'd been getting ready. Allegedly to calm her nerves and remove any possibility of a hangover returning at a crucial moment, it had definitely done the trick, although she was starting to lose count of the number of pieces to camera she'd done.

Alice waited for the red light on the camera to come on.

'Actually, change of plan.'

Alice moved her head a fraction, imperceptibly to the untrained eye, just so that Jez could see that she'd heard him.

'We're sending someone in for an interview.'

Alice peered between the cameras just in time to see two very familiar figures approaching. Dermot Douglas was much taller than he appeared on-screen, his cheekbones were more pronounced and his green eyes were, as Zoë had enthused, mesmerising. Accompanied on to the set by her ex-husband, Dermot strode over and proffered a hand for shaking as the lights came up.

'Finally we meet. Hi, you must be Alice.' His lilting Irish accent was barely discernible but his smile was disarming. 'Thanks for making it here so fast. I'm on a bit of a tight schedule today.'

'No problem at all.' Alice kept it professional whilst wondering if his schedule could possibly be as tight as his T-shirt.

'Only I gather from our controller...'

Alice looked up and smiled vaguely in Richard's direction.

'...that you were right in the middle of something else when he rang.' Dermot's smile was mischievous.

'Nothing that couldn't wait until later.' Alice resisted glaring at Richard, instead crossing her legs and praying this was a test she was going to pass. She suspected Dermot knew exactly just how well she knew the man standing next to him but she couldn't be sure.

'So, what do you think you know about me?' Dermot held her in his gaze for a moment too long and cocked his head cheekily.

'Hang on…' Alice stole a glance at the camera just to her left, addressing the director and the rest of the gallery. 'I thought I was supposed to be doing the interviewing.'

Dermot stood there confidently. 'It doesn't really matter.'

'Well—' she turned to look at him '—in that case, I know that you present one of the most popular breakfast shows on British television, that you started out in kids TV in Ireland, that you first shaved your head for charity but now you do it to look like Bruce Willis.'

Dermot laughed. 'I wish.' He ran his hand over his scalp. 'There just isn't a great deal of it left these days.'

'Well, I think it's always better to give in and go grade one all over than go for the Friar Tuck look.'

'Of course.'

Alice could feel herself surrendering to Dermot's charm. Eager to please, she continued, almost showing off.

'You love your dogs—Labradors. You're close to your mum—she still lives back home in Ireland despite your offers to buy her something over here. You're pretty good at snowboarding…'

Thanks to Zoë and a couple of wasted hours on the Internet last weekend, Alice actually knew more about Dermot than was probably cool. She pretended to be thinking on her feet, throwing the occasional fake hesitation in between facts. 'You're somewhere between twenty-nine and thirty-five, the gay community would love to call you their own but you claim to be straight, if single, rather a lot of the time… Famous alleged liaisons include…supermodels, actresses and, bizarrely, a celebrity chef—forgive me for saying so, but that was bound to be a recipe for disaster.'

Dermot grinned at Alice and then at Richard. 'She looks good *and* she has a brain. Very impressive.'

A little too self-loving for her tastes, Alice fell out of love with Dermot.

Their banter off to a flying start, however, Alice was enjoying herself. 'Guess what, I can cook, too… Now, what do you think you know about me?'

Dermot shook his head. 'A lady's business is her own.'

'Unless she works in television, in which case it apparently becomes everybody's business. I know you know more about me than that.'

He smiled. 'Well, if you insist.'

Alice lowered her gaze, encouraging him to continue. 'At least give me a chance to see if you've got your facts straight.'

'Okay, here goes. You're a life coach with a life of your own and a great series under your belt. You're a Londoner. You're divorced.'

'All true.'

Dermot looked from Richard to Alice. 'I gather your husband left you for a blonde.'

Alice nodded. 'You gather correctly.'

'What was he, blind?'

'Gay.'

Dermot smiled slowly and looked over to his new boss.

Alice suddenly felt light-headed with panic as she realised what she might have done. Silently, Richard turned and left the studio and Alice thought she heard a laugh in the gallery. Underneath her makeup, Alice blushed. Playing it by the ear was so not her forte. She was much better at playing it by the book.

'So…' Dermot took a seat on the sofa next to her.

Alice admired his perfect manicure, slowly folding her

own short and unloved nails out of view. There was only so much basic pampering you could do in an hour.

'Here's the way this place works—call time is 5:00 a.m. We're on air from six until nine. From nine until nine-fifteen we record trailers for the following day's show, then there's a production meeting—always good for us to bring ideas to those—followed by any prerecords that need doing or location inserts.'

Alice nodded enthusiastically but she was only half listening. The other half was wondering where Richard was.

'We do soft news, interviews and features. The newsreaders, Serena and Tunde, have the serious stuff covered. Full bulletins on the hour, summaries on the half. Any questions?'

'When do I start?' Making it clear that she was at least half joking, Alice sounded a lot more confident than she felt.

Dermot rested his chin in hand, it was one of his trademark interviewing positions. 'So tell me why you think you'd be good at this job.'

'Well…'

Alice detested the "blow your own trumpet but not too hard" interview question.

'…I'm good with people, I'm good at listening. I know my way around a television studio, I have a very reliable alarm clock and no one who is going to try and persuade me to stay in bed for five more minutes when it rings…'

A couple of the cameramen laughed. Not quite her target audience, but never mind.

Dermot got to his feet. 'Thanks again, Alice. I really appreciate you making it at such short notice. It's great to finally meet you.'

Confused, Alice was left marooned on the sofa as she watched Dermot leave the studio. Maybe she'd been too relaxed? But surely jokes were allowed. This was an audition

for a breakfast magazine show not a serious news programme. And she was good on TV. Confidence receding,
she flicked through the sample script they'd given her, and
waited for more instructions. Dermot she could live without, but not Richard.

Again Alice could hear traces of Richard in her ear and
again he wasn't talking to her. Concentrating on the output
from her earpiece, she desperately tried to pick his voice and
his tone out of the chatter in the gallery.

Almost cross-eyed with concentration, Alice flinched as
suddenly Jez was back in her ear at full volume.

'Could you come through, please?'

Led by the floor manager, Alice was taken through a
maze of corridors and into the studio gallery, which was
strangely empty. Alice studied the bank of monitors cover-
ing every angle of the studio. From the freeze frames dis-
played on each screen, they also seemed to have captured
her every profile.

'You know you've got the perfect face for television.'

Alice hadn't heard Dermot enter the room and he definitely hadn't been there a moment ago. She shook her head.
That's all she needed, a stealth co-presenter.

Alice turned. 'I don't know. I think that's a double chin
you can see on Camera 6.'

'That's a shadow.'

Optimistically, Alice peered a little closer.

The door to the gallery banged open and Jez filed in with
a few other members of the production team. To Alice's relief, Richard lurked at the rear of the party and he wasn't
looking stern at all.

Dermot and Jez exchanged a cursory nod.

'So—' Dermot rested his arm across Alice's shoulder
'—what are you doing next weekend?'

Enlisting the cooperation of every capillary in her body, Alice managed not to blush visibly.

'What did you have in mind?' Her outer confidence masked an inner bag of nerves.

'Oh, I don't know. I thought maybe you and I should do some publicity shots.' He turned to her. 'Congratulations.'

'That's it?' Alice's eyes shone with excitement. 'You're offering me the job?'

Dermot rubbed his chin. 'Well, of course if you'd like a few more challenges, an assault course, a pre-record of an item with live animals… It can all be arranged.'

'I wouldn't want to put you to any trouble.' Alice beamed. 'Can I just say that I'm really looking forward to joining the team? Fabulous. Thank you.'

Jez rolled his eyes sardonically. 'Give it six months when the bags under your eyes are the size of check-in luggage, then tell me how much you love it.'

Dermot interrupted his director.

'Jeremy, what do you think you are doing?'

'Believe me, this one can take it.' Jez raised a smile for Alice, who returned the compliment at once. He had a reputation for being brilliant but moody and she didn't want to get off on the wrong foot with him.

Alice stepped forward and proffered her hand to Jez for shaking, her legs threatening to betray her cool. 'Let's just say I'm sure that breakfast time for me will never be the same again.'

Jez patted her on the back. 'There will, no doubt, be a few things to iron out contractually with your agent but all being well we hope to see you back here next week for photos, in two for rehearsals and in three for the real thing.'

Alice gathered herself together emotionally and insides cartwheeling, thanked everyone as she numbly walked back to the reception area. As she reached the car waiting to take her home, she heard footsteps quickening behind her and turned just as Richard caught up with her. He slipped an arm around her waist and kissed the top of her head before disappearing through a different set of double doors back into the building as quickly as he'd arrived.

Finally able to relax, Alice sat back in the executive car and grinned at West London, which suddenly seemed much more picturesque. Turning her mobile back on a few moments later, a text message from Richard appeared.

They love you more than me already. xx

Seconds later, a follow-up appeared.

Champagne at Met Bar at 8. Inner circle only. Rx

Alice hadn't felt this excited since…she couldn't remember. Thursday night was suddenly her favourite night for a party.

Chapter Twenty

14 days to go
Suzie 8, Alice 2

Alice swivelled round in Zoë's chair as she added another phone number to their ever-increasing list of her potential mothers.

'This is getting Riddickulous.' She giggled. Despite the fact that she was still hungover from Thursday evening, even at a conservative estimate she was likely to remain overexcited for a couple of weeks.

Zoë rolled her eyes 'That's it, you're no longer my friend.'

'Just think of the tortured years you would have had in the playground, Daisy Riddick. Hurrah for Jean and David Hudson.'

'Careful, Allie, this is my life you're mocking.'

'Sorry. I just think we need to try and keep this as relaxed as we can.'

'Imagine, I could have been an entirely different person.'

Alice couldn't really see it. Zoë was such a strong person-

ality. Alice was sure nature had as much to do with personality as nurture.

'Come on, time to get calling. We must have a hundred
phone numbers and so far we've only dialled one and got
through to an answering machine.' Luckily for Zoë, even if
she didn't know it yet, today Alice had more than enough
energy for the two of them.

Zoë hesitated. 'I just want to make sure we've covered all
possibilities before we wade in there.'

'Maybe you could ask your mother to check her local
phone books?'

'For once, I'm one step ahead of you.' Zoë rummaged in
a file and handed Alice the printout of an e-mail from Jean
with a few Riddicks listed. All were marked with a cross.

'X marks the spot?'

Zoë shook her head. 'Tried and failed. She called for me.'

'That's amazing. This must be hard for her, too.'

'She genuinely seems to want to help. She thinks they
probably try to have children adopted in different towns
than their birth parents'. It would make sense.'

'Time to try and find out.'

Fourteen answering machine messages and ten straight
no's later, Zoë and Alice were feeling a little less positive.
Alice had taken an executive decision to make tea whilst Zoë
carried on with a few more calls.

Three dead ends later, Zoë lay on her sitting-room floor
and willed the tension in her back and shoulders to dissi-
pate. 'That's it, I'm done.'

'You're so not done. No one said it was going to be easy.
It's only two o'clock.'

'People are so negative and so bloody rude. So they're not
the right person, they don't have to be so arsey about it. I'm

not trying to sell them anything and I've only wasted two minutes of their time.' Zoë yawned. Extreme stress always made her sleepy. 'I'm tired.'

'Of course it's difficult. People spend years looking for their birth parents. So far you've spent…'

'Three weeks?'

'More like three hours.'

'Al, that's not fair. Just because everything is super sunny in your world, we're not all having a perfect-life moment.'

Alice did her best to look appropriately serious. 'It's not all perfect.'

'Do me a favour—you're about to start your dream job with your dream man.'

'I think you'll find he's your dream man.'

'Details, details. He sent you flowers, for God's sake.'

'He probably has an assistant who sends everyone flowers. Dermot strikes me as a man who lives and breathes his own PR.'

'Oh, it's just "Dermot" now, is it? Anyway, you might be divorced but I've never even been close to marriage and my real mother didn't want me. Try living with that.'

'Zo, it's not a competition. I know this is incredibly hard for you.'

'It's not hard. Maths is hard. This is impossible. I'm cold-calling total strangers from the bloody phone book. Each call could be answered by a relative of mine who may or may not know I even exist and possibly does know but probably couldn't care less. I couldn't be any more on edge if, if—'

'Okay.' Alice stood up. 'Let's have some lunch. In fact, why don't you get some air, pick up a paper, some food—whatever you fancy—and let me carry on here for a bit. Go shopping or something. Take your mind off all of this for a couple of hours.'

Zoë's eyes were wet. 'You see, you don't want me here, either.'

'Hey.' Alice gave her best friend the biggest hug she could and hoped that Zoë was feeling the love. 'Not only do I want you as a friend, I am considering you as a stylist and even assessing my future co-host as a possible life partner for you.'

Visibly relaxing, Zoë sniffed into her shoulder. 'Don't worry, I'm not crying.'

'Crying is good sometimes.' Alice held Zoë close.

'Well, I'm not.' Zoë wiped her nose as she pulled back. 'I don't think I can take a couple of hours off. This was all my idea. It's just so bloody frustrating. I'm looking and looking and maybe I shouldn't be. She didn't want me. Maybe I should just leave it at that. Like I've got time for this.'

'Of course you've got time. And people change.'

Zoë didn't look convinced. 'I was thinking that finding my mother was going to alter everything, but in reality nothing is going to change, is it?'

Alice stood firm. Today she was Captain Rational. Emotional wavering was not an option. 'How can you possibly know that now?'

'Well, say I do find her, we might have dinner, we might chat on the phone, she might introduce me to her friends or maybe I'll just get another birthday card every year, or not.'

'But you'll be able to place her. You'll have a face, you already have a name and then maybe you'll get a chance to get to know her.'

Already calmer, Zoë looked encouraged. 'You're right. Worst-case scenario, she doesn't want to know me and I'm just back where I started. Ego a little more bruised but at least I'm not afraid to know who I am. I'm not a coward.'

Alice nodded. 'That's more like it. Come on, we've still got all day. And by the way, before you start thinking my life is perfect, have I mentioned that I need to be at the studio at 5:00 a.m. every morning?'

'Only about twice so far today, but I guess it's still relatively early and you're still relatively overexcited.'

'Oh God, I've become a prima donna in a mere thirty-six hours.'

'Al, please don't apologise. Your newfound energy is infectious. And right now I need as much of it as I can lay my hands on. Besides, you've always been good in the mornings.'

'I'm much better at 1:00 a.m. than at 5:00 a.m. I really will be waking up with Dermot every morning. Hopefully before we're actually on air.'

'As long as you're not expecting any sympathy?'

'Not a shred.'

'That's fine then. We can still be friends.'

Alice punched Zoë gently in the arm. 'Watch it.'

Zoë handed Alice her list of names and numbers. 'Right, I'm off to run errands and clear my head.' Relieved to temporarily be ridding herself of responsibility, Zoë slipped her trainers on and fastened the Velcro straps, the pressure already lifting from her shoulders. She really needed a break.

Tom was distracted from the menu by the panoramic view from his table overlooking the sun-drenched broad grin of the bay of Positano. The colours were almost 1950s Technicolor in their richness. The sea was unfeasibly blue, the sun umbrellas a uniformly glamorous orange and green. He couldn't wait to get into the water and release the tension that had built up in his muscles on the journey.

He'd ridden south for three days straight and now he'd made it to the Amalfi Coast he was going to take a few days out of the saddle and soak up the sun. He'd checked into the luxurious Le Sirenuse and swapped his leathers for a linen shirt, shorts and flip-flops. This looked to be the perfect spot to recharge his emotional batteries and take the edge off his London pallor.

A very pretty waitress arrived at his side. Tom rested his arm on the adjacent chair and smiled languidly. *'Ciao.'* It was almost the extent of his Italian.

'Can I 'elp you.'

Clearly he wasn't blending into the local scenery at all. Maybe he'd buy some leather loafers later.

His nationality now well and truly out in the open, having ordered his lunch in English, Tom picked up an English paper that had been abandoned on a neighbouring table.

Only his fourth day away and yet, as he flicked through the pages, he already felt an affection for his home city that only time away from it could bring. He'd stopped thinking about Alice just outside Paris, started thinking about her again at the Italian border and managed to finally move on just outside Rome. Now he was determined to continue the rest of his trip without her. There was no shortage of beautiful women in Italy and he was on vacation a couple of thousand miles from home where anything was possible. He was a playboy, even if he still felt a little played.

A glass of chilled white wine in his hand, Tom's karma threatened to do a U-turn when he reached page eighteen. As Suzie beamed at him from the top of her column, he closed the paper assertively. From now on his holiday reading was going to consist of trashy action-adventure novels and maybe the occasional American newspaper. Self-preservation was the name of the game. However, two minutes of staring out to sea later, the paper was open again and he was back where he'd started.

SUZIE FLETCHER
The State I'm In

Four weeks ago I set myself a deadline. Or should I say, a ManDate. I had six weeks to find a suitable man. Now, five dinners, too many drinks, eight real dates, twenty-five speed dates, two adverts in the traditional newspaper personals, two more in the e-personals, several new outfits and sleepless nights later, I am on the verge of throwing in the towel and admitting defeat. Not that it hasn't been fun trying.

In the last month I've seen more plays than can be healthy. I've attended singles' nights everywhere from the library to the supermarket. I've even tried my hand at speed dating. My trouble is, I'm not used to failing at anything. When my first husband died I went out and found another one, and when he turned out to be sleeping with someone else I replaced him with a new model—okay, so he wasn't even nearly a model, but you get my point. Husband number three lasted a few years, basically until he decided he preferred tending his garden to tending to me.

This time around I'd like a man who knows what an iPod is but who can also just about remember the Rolling Stones from the first time around. Someone who wears jeans and trainers out, rather than just for gardening and playing tennis. Someone who knows that Ford is a fashion designer as well as a make of car.

My daughter says I have raised the bar too high, that my shopping list is simply impossible to satisfy in one store. And she'd definitely rather I aimed high in terms of age if not criteria. My *single* daughter I hasten to add. Encouraged (more like brow-beaten) by me, she, too, has been dating to a deadline, and between ourselves I'm sure she won't (okay, she definitely will) mind me telling you that she hasn't found a man, either.

We both came close. I met a man with potential on the Eurostar. She met a guy through work. Imagine our dismay when he turned out to be the same chap.

However, I refuse to believe that the odds are stacked against us. If the dating game is all about statistics—vital and otherwise—about putting yourself out there and sheer numbers of dates, I should be streets ahead and yet we are both failing. She claims to have retired from the competition but I know if her interest was piqued I could still lose.

So this week, the state I'm in is one of confusion. What does a fiftysomething girl about town have to do to meet a decent man these days?

Doing her best to keep her cool, Alice put the paper down. Today was not all about her.

'Zo, please have my mother. Consider her a gift.'

'What?'

'Look at this.' Alice waved page eighteen of the newspaper at her best friend. 'What does she think she's doing? I'll tell you what she's doing. She's cheating. She's bloody well using her column to advertise for a man. Plus, she's broken every rule in the book and mentioned me.'

Zoë didn't leap to Alice's defence. 'You only have two

weeks to go. You can't blame her for trying.' If only she hadn't bought the damn paper on her trip out for supplies.

'And look at the photo she's using at the top of her column. It must be almost ten years old.'

Zoë peered up close and then held the paper at arm's length. 'She still looks like that.'

'Only in black and white.' Drumming her fingers on the table, Alice dialled her mother's mobile.

'Hi darling, any joy finding Zoë's mother?'

'Not yet. We've found an eleven-year-old Maggie Riddick but that's it so far.'

'I still think you'd be better off getting a professional in to help track this Riddick woman down. I know you two think you can do everything, but...'

'We'll see. We haven't reached the end of our road yet. Anyway, don't change the subject. I'm calling you for a reason.'

'Oh no, this doesn't sound good.'

'What do you think you're up to now?'

Suzie remained calm. Innocent until proven guilty, she never apologised if she could help it. 'I'm just having a bite of lunch.'

'Don't be facetious. I'm talking about your column. You're exploiting your position, using your day job to your advantage...'

'And to think I thought you didn't care.' Suzie could barely mask the delight in her voice. 'I did mention it to you last week.'

'You never know, desperate men might write in and volunteer their services.'

'Indeed, I was hoping some nice literate men would. It would be better if they e-mailed actually, two weeks today we'll be getting ready for the party...'

Damn. Alice still didn't have an outfit. But one good turn deserved another and luckily, Zoë was about to owe her one.

'…There's no need to get so aerated. Look, can we continue this conversation later? It's just I'm getting the distinct impression that I'm in one of those places where I'm not supposed to use my phone. If they make many more rules, it won't be long before people stop eating out all together. Let's speak later.'

'You're out?'

'It's Saturday lunchtime. Of course I'm out. You remember Andy, don't you?'

'You're having lunch with Andy?' Alice's tone was a knowing one. 'Well, well.'

'Well, well, what?'

'I thought you said you had to go.'

'There's no need to be like that, darling.'

'Well, I think he'd quite like to be more than your copy editor.'

Alice had spoken to the man in question several times on the phone since Suzie had moved in. With combined ages of nearly a hundred years, mentally they shared an almost identical teenage maturity.

'Nonsense. But it turns out he's a bit of a dab hand at writing for film and television.'

'Really?'

'It would appear that almost everyone at the paper has another creative career they'd rather be pursuing, if only it paid enough money.'

'Just promise me I will never be seeing a poster for *Suzie Fletcher: The Musical*.'

Suzie laughed. 'Don't worry. You know I can't sing for toffee. We're just putting a pitch together for a mother-daughter comedy drama.'

'As long as I don't recognise myself.'

'You can always speak to Andy about it if you're concerned.'

Alice guessed that Suzie was under the influence of a couple of glasses of wine and as a result more suggestive than usual.

'In fact, do you want to speak to him now?'

Alice detected a flicker of mischievous excitement from Suzie's inflection.

'…Or maybe I should I set up a meeting for you two?'

'Mum, for goodness' sake. And please, be tactful, he's right there. Look, he's perfectly nice on the phone, but not like that.' Alice moved their conversation on. 'You're not putting Richard in this drama, are you? You're going to have to be very careful about not upsetting people.'

'Trust me. We'll be getting permissions or changing names.'

'Good. And make sure you do it properly, because I owe Richard for the rest of my life.'

'I'd have put that the other way around.'

'I don't want you stitching him up. Look, I've got to go now and so do you—unless you want to be lynched by the maître d'.'

'Love to Zoë and good luck. That's the mother of all jobs, you know.'

'Save the one-liners for your comedy drama.'

Zoë was rewriting a to-do list when Alice got off the phone.

Alice stood over her. 'Zo, next you'll be drawing up a timetable. Too much planning is not a good thing. You're wasting time.'

'I need to be prepared for every eventuality. I want my approach to be personal.'

'Then you have to keep calling.'

'But I also don't want to get off on the wrong foot.'

'Ten more calls each and then we'll call it a day and think about letters.'

'Five more.'

'You're only cheating yourself.'

'Jesus, Al.'

'You're only feeling guilty because you know I'm right.'

Zoë got to her feet. 'Okay then. Deal.'

A joyless half hour later, Zoë dialled her penultimate number of the day.

'Hello? Am I speaking to Mrs. Riddick by any chance?'

'You are.'

'I'm sorry to trouble you and I don't know if you'll be able to help me but I'm trying to get in touch with a Margaret Riddick.'

'I'm afraid no one of that name lives here.'

'I see.' Zoë wondered why she couldn't just hang up now but Alice was watching her like a hawk—or at least like a hawk on a mobile phone—and she knew she had to do this properly and thoroughly.

'I hope you don't mind me asking, but do you have anyone in your family with that name? A sister, sister-in-law perhaps?'

Zoë stopped tidying her desk. There was definite hesitation at the other end of the line. She continued gently.

'Rest assured I'm not trying to sell her anything and I'm not from the tax office…'

Alice watched Zoë effect the same little laugh she had been forcing all afternoon. She had her spontaneity down to a fine art.

Amazed not to have been interrupted by now, Zoë continued cautiously.

'…I guess she'd be in her mid to late fifties now.'

The woman at the end of the phone cleared her throat. 'Right. Well…'

'Do you know a Margaret?'

More hesitation. 'Not exactly.'

'Not exactly?' Zoë did her best to sound pressure free and encouraging.

As Alice's call ended she moved across the room and started listening for scraps of information.

'Well, you see, my husband has a sister called Margaret, but they're, well, they're not really in touch these days.'

'Right. Good. I mean not good, but…' Zoë had never felt less articulate. 'Do you think, I mean please forgive me if this sounds a little forward, but might there be any way you have her address, or could you get a letter to her if I sent it via you?'

'Erm, it's a bit difficult, actually. Can I ask what this is regarding?'

'Of course.' Zoë's nerve faltered. 'Um, I don't suppose Mr. Riddick is there, is he?'

'No, Clive is out for the afternoon. I'm afraid you've just got me.'

'That's great. Really, you've been more than helpful.'

'Why don't I get Clive to give you a call back.'

'That would be great. Fantastic. And you said Margaret was his sister?'

'Yes.'

'Super.'

Zoë smiled as she realised that they were both as relieved as each other to be postponing this conversation.

'Can I take your name and number, please?'

Zoë dictated her name and land-line number several times over. 'Would you like my mobile number, too, just in case?'

'No need. One number is fine, thank you.'

'Thank you, Mrs. Riddick.' Zoë savoured every syllable of her birth surname.

'Just call me Barbara.'

By now Alice was practically seated on Zoë's lap.

Zoë hung up and punched the air. 'I think we might have found her brother.'

'Okay, please don't think me negative, but you know you have to brace yourself for the fact that while you only have one birth mother, there may well be more than one Margaret Riddick in the world.'

Zoë nodded. 'I know.'

'And that we've only been phoning around for a day, so statistically…'

Zoë interrupted. 'Got it.'

'So, where's this Clive based?'

Zoë checked her list again. 'I found him on Google. Surrey somewhere. Membership secretary of some golf club or other…'

Alice shuddered.

'What?'

'I bet he has an acrylic V neck.'

'Shut up.'

'I'm only teasing.'

'I'm not sure I'm up to teasing. So what do we do now?'

Alice checked her watch. It was just before five. 'We sit here and we wait.'

'Zo, listen to me, it's ten o'clock on a Saturday night, there's no way he's going to phone now. Let's call it a day.' Alice wished she'd never suggested waiting. She'd forgotten how patient Zoë could be.

Alice felt her pelvis click as she stretched out in the armchair where she'd been sitting for the last few hours. As the credits started running on yet another medical drama, the television continued to distract them just enough to let time pass. Every time a phone had rung on TV—and in A&E they ring all the time—Zoë had gone through the same routine: quick on the draw with the remote control. Mute. Clearing of throat and then, reaching for her ever-silent home-phone handset, occasionally to answer to the dialling tone.

Zoë got up from the sofa and paced the not-considerable length of her sitting room. 'Do you not think we should phone again?'

Alice rubbed her almost square eyes. 'Let's leave it until the morning.'

'The morning?'

'No point alienating our only possible lead.' Alice could hear Zoë counting the hours. 'Come on, let's get some air. I haven't been outside all day and it's not going to be much of a family reunion if you get deep vein thrombosis, is it?

'Actually I'm sure the phone handset still works down at the front door.'

'How about in the pub? I have to warn you that I am de-termined to leave the building.'

'I thought we were going for fresh air.'

'Fresh and not so fresh. I think we need a drink in the pres-ence of other people. We should raise a glass to our progress before grabbing a celebratory Chinese takeaway or a Thai. I don't care where we go, Zo, but we have to get out of here for an hour or two.'

For the second morning running and just at the point in her career when she should have been stockpiling as much quality sleep as possible, Alice woke up in a strange bed. In fact, it was less of a bed and more of an air mattress, and cur-rently on the floor in the centre of Zoë's sitting room, wedged between the sofa and the coffee table. Alice eyeballed the rug and wondered why on earth she was already awake. She didn't have to wait long for an answer.

Either she had started hallucinating in her sleep-deprived state or this time the phone really was ringing. Literally bouncing out of bed, she scrambled to the base unit where the handset had been left to recharge in anticipation of an important call and got there just in time to save the caller from the robotic tones of the answering machine.

'Hello?'

'Hello?'

Managing to focus on her wrist, Alice ascertained it was nine-fifteen. On a Sunday morning.

'Zoë Hudson?' The voice was male, clear and clipped.

'Hang on just a second and I'll get her. Can I ask who's calling?' Alice didn't want to scare Clive by assuming it was him.

'Clive Riddick.'

As Alice eased open the door to Zoë's bedroom, she wondered why it was deemed antisocial to call people after ten at night but not before ten on a Sunday. Plus, Clive sounded as if he'd been awake for hours. She wasn't sure there was any way he could even be distantly related to a girl who could sleep until midday, if undisturbed.

'Just one moment, please.'

Wondering whether she should explain who she was in case Clive was getting any funny ideas about Zoë's living arrangements, Alice decided against it. This really was none of her business. And she was quite content with her role as Zoë's PA.

Zoë was still dead to the world; the emotion of the last twenty-four hours coupled with a few drinks and a large takeaway had clearly taken their collective toll. But this was one rare occasion when there was no way Zoë would want Alice to take a message for her.

Alice found the mute button on the phone and held it in.

'Zo. ZOË.' She shook her best friend as hard as she could with one hand.

Zoë mumbled into her pillow. 'Fuck off, it's still dark.'

Alice opened the slats of the wooden Venetian blinds, flooding the room with stripes of sunshine. 'And now it's light. You really want to be awake for this. Wide awake, I'm giving you ten seconds. I have Clive Riddick on the phone for you. Ten, nine, eight, seven, six and a half….'

Confused, Zoë sat bolt upright, her red hair sticking out in every possible direction. It must have been a hectic dream. 'Clive's here? Shit. Look at me.' Zoë pawed at her vest top and pyjamas.

Alice waved the handset. 'He's on the phone. But he won't wait forever. Want me to take a message?'

'Don't be stupid.'

Zoë closed her eyes for a few seconds and then reopened them, restarting her day. She beckoned Alice and the phone over. Getting up, she grabbed a T-shirt, threw it on and started pacing.

'Good morning. Clive? So sorry to have kept you waiting.'

Alice was impressed. There was no hint of sleep in Zoë's voice.

Zoë was running on adrenaline. This wasn't how she'd envisaged the call. For a start, she'd have been showered and dressed. She hadn't even brushed her teeth.

'I gather from my wife that you are looking for Margaret Riddick?' It was a statement of fact and there was no warmth in his tone, just formality. Zoë wondered if she could ask to speak to Barbara again—she had seemed a lot less scary.

'I'm sorry to contact you out of the blue. I don't even know if your sister is the Margaret Riddick I am trying to locate, but if I could possibly take her address then I can just send a letter directly to her or, if you'd rather, I'll send it to you, if you could then be so kind as to forward it to her on my behalf. I really don't want to put you to any trouble.' Speeding up as she got to the end of her patter, suddenly Zoë couldn't wait to get off the phone.

'May I ask what this is concerning?'

'It's private, well, it's personal.' How much did brothers know about sisters?

'In which case I'm afraid this Margaret won't be able to help you. My sister died nearly a year ago.'

'Died?' Zoë swallowed hard. 'Do you mind me asking how old she was?'

'Fifty-six.'

Zoë shook her head. She should have started this process years ago. 'I'm so sorry. So very sorry.' Hope drained away.

Clive's tone softened at Zoë's clearly audible shock. 'It came as a terrible blow to us all. We're a close family.'

Zoë hesitated. Was Clive telling her that he knew something?

'Is there anything I might be able to help you with?'

'I, I don't know.' Zoë stammered her way back on course. 'I don't even know whether your sister was the Margaret I'm looking for. Forgive me if what I'm about to say comes as a shock to you. I really don't want to make any trouble for you or your family but…' Zoë had a moment of clarity. 'In fact, I don't suppose you happen to know if your sister lived in North London in the early seventies?'

Clive paused. 'Zoë, I do hope you'll forgive my direct approach, but are you her daughter?'

Prepared as Zoë had thought she was, Clive had rendered her speechless. Her eyes filled with tears.

'I think I might be.'

'Then I'm the one who is sorry. I'm so sorry, love.' Clive's voice was gentler. 'She only started talking to me about you when they told her the cancer was going to be terminal. I think she knew you might try and find her at some point. Mags was quite a determined woman and I think she suspected, or hoped, that you might have inherited her tenacity.'

Zoë hadn't heard anything after "terminal". 'She died of cancer?'

'Ovarian. But by the time they caught it, it was everywhere.' Clive had reverted to being matter of fact. He may as well have been reading a list of directions.

'Did she have more children?'

'Two. And she had a lovely husband. He's still alive.'

'Good. Great.' Zoë was speaking without thinking as she tried to take everything in.

Clive paused awkwardly, doing his best to be considerate. 'I'm not sure he knows about you. He moved down to Devon with the children after she died. He wanted to go back to his roots.'

'Right.' Zoë tried to be matter-of-fact. Her mother had been dying and still hadn't tried to find her. Zoë tried and failed to come up with an excuse.

Clive kept the conversation going. 'You know, she didn't have long after they diagnosed her. I think she had intended to write you a letter or something but then, well, everything was crazy and suddenly, it was over.'

Zoë burst into tears. Silently Alice handed her a tissue box and watched as quite remarkably and deliberately, only seconds later, Zoë pulled herself together.

'Apologies, Mr. Riddick. This is proving harder than I had thought.'

'Please, Zoë.' His voice cracked. 'Call me Clive.'

Zoë blew her nose. 'I don't suppose you could possibly

send me a photo of her, could you? A colour photocopy would do.'

'I'm sure I can do better than that.' Clive hesitated. 'Why don't you come over and see us sometime. I mean, if you feel it would be appropriate and you fancy it.'

'Are you sure? That's incredibly kind of you. I really wouldn't want to put you to any trouble.'

'Mags would have wanted it. She was like that. She'll be very very sorry to have missed you…'

Clive made it sound as if she'd just popped to the shops for a bit.

'…But I'm sure I don't need to tell you that sometimes things just don't go according to plan though, do they?'

Chapter Twenty-One

13 days to go
Suzie 9, Alice 2

It was only 7:00 p.m. but Alice was physically and emotion-ally exhausted. Carrier bags laden with food in each hand, she negotiated her front door carefully and dropped her keys onto the hall table. Having been camped out at Zoë's since Friday night, she was delighted to be back at home. Coach Fletcher had self-prescribed a light supper for mother and daughter, washed down with a bottle of wine, some quality time and then an embarrassingly early night.

As she stood in her hallway, Alice had a sense of unease. The house was unnervingly quiet. Yet Suzie always reserved Sunday evenings for catching up on all the television pro-grammes she'd recorded during the week.

'Mum?' Alice's voice echoed around her. Putting her shopping down, she reached for the phone and without even looking at the keypad dialled Suzie's mobile. As it clicked on to voice mail Alice did her best to be as laid-back as a daugh-

ter who really wanted a hug and whose mother was missing
in action could be. She started to leave a message. 'Mum, it's
Alice. Just wondering where you are. Um, give me—'

Alice's mobile started ringing. As "Mum Mob" flashed up
on the screen she abandoned her incomplete and now ob-
solete message midsentence.

'I was just leaving you a message.'

'Sorry, never can find my bloody phone fast enough.'

'Maybe you should change your ring tone to one that you
recognise.'

'Yup, I'm sure that would help, too.'

'So, where are you?' Alice's concern seemed to have inadvertently transformed itself into an accusation.

'At home, sweetie.'

'You're not…' Alice's voice cracked. 'I've just got back
with food to cook us some dinner.' Thanks to Zoë she had
been reduced to an emotional preteen.

'No, my home.'

'Oh, I see.' Inordinately relieved, Alice realised that this
weekend had clearly taken a greater toll on her than she'd
appreciated. 'How's it coming along?'

Suzie sounded puzzled. 'It looks great. It's all done. Didn't
you get my note?'

Finally Alice walked into the kitchen. Her table was
dwarfed by a huge bunch of cellophane-wrapped, hand-tied
flowers.

'Wow, a proper bouquet. They're gorgeous. Thank you.'
Alice opened the accompanying card.

At home darling. I'm officially out of your hair. There's
a bottle of champagne for you in the fridge. Thank you
so much for putting up with me. Love you. Mxx

Tears pricked the back of her eyes. 'Weren't you going to tell me yourself?'

'It was meant to be a surprise.'

'It certainly is.' Alice could feel herself choking back tears. 'I was going to cook. For us.' She didn't have the energy to be strong all the time.

'Well, I'm sure you can eat my half tomorrow. As I know you know, there's no place like your own home.'

'Of course.'

Suzie was finding it difficult to keep up with this conversation. 'Is everything all right?'

'Not really.' Alice sat down at the table in her empty kitchen.

'What is it?'

Suzie's voice was soothing.

'Zoë found her birth mum today.'

'Riiight…' Suzie advanced with caution as she tried to read between the lines of the information she'd been given so far. 'But that's great—isn't it?'

Alice sighed. 'She died last year.'

'Oh no, I am so sorry.' Finally she understood.

Alice sniffed. 'I'm sorry I give you a hard time sometimes.'

Suzie laughed. 'Don't worry, sweetheart, I'm tougher than you think. I'm sure I deserve it most of the time. Besides, someone has to keep me on my toes.'

'Maybe. But you know I don't mean most of it.'

'Of course. Now, for goodness' sake, you're not going to get all weepy on me, are you? I'm not sure I'll know what to do with you.'

'I love you, Mum.'

'And I love you. Tell you what, why don't you get back in your car and bring your shopping over here. I'd come to you but I'm a couple of glasses of wine over the limit. But that way at least we can eat in front of the television together and I can bore you senseless about something of little to no importance and remind you why you're actually pleased that I've left. Frankly, it sounds like you need the sort of mundane evening that only a mother can provide.'

Suzie appeared in silhouette behind the frosted-glass panels on her front door before Alice had even finished parking the car.

Standing in the hall with a glass of Alice's favourite red wine in hand, Suzie had to relinquish it temporarily as Alice was intent on hugging her firmly. At some point in the last forty-eight hours, her daughter had apparently become a limpet.

A few moments later, Suzie pulled back, their belt-buckle-to-belt-buckle embrace causing her momentary discomfort. 'It's okay, darling, I'm not going anywhere.'

'Margaret died at fifty-six.'

Suzie nodded. 'Which is why nobody can afford to sit around waiting for life to happen to them.'

Taking a step back, she studied Alice who, for once, was a child in adult's clothing, her jeans no longer the only distressed thing about her.

'Zoë's a pretty strong character. Once she gets over the shock and the disappointment she'll be fine, you'll see.'

Alice was grateful that for once her mother was behaving like one.

'I hope so. She's going to meet her uncle next weekend. Her mother's brother has been terrific.'

'Well, that's something then, isn't it? Every cloud has a silver lining…well, some of them are more grey than silver but…'

'And I guess she's always regarded Jean as her real mum anyway.'

'That's more like it. And you know Jean is going to live forever. She's just one of those women.'

Alice almost laughed before she remembered Zoë's reaction. 'You should have seen her. First she had no hope, then all the hope in the world and now, really, that's it. Plus, clearly she's now worrying about the fact she's going to keel over in twenty-five years' time.'

'Honestly, you really are Generation Worry. And you should have brought her along with you. No doubt she's at home steeping in her own upset.'

'She insisted she wanted to be on her own tonight.'

'Well, you've been with her all weekend. You couldn't have done any more.'

'And now I can't do anything.'

Suzie took the shopping bag from her daughter and peered inside. 'So, can I help with the cooking? Well, if it's not too complicated.'

'I daresay you might be able to manage to shave a bit of Parmesan.'

'What are we having?'

'Hot chicken Caesar salad.' Alice followed her mother into her new kitchen. 'Blimey, Mum, this is fantastic. It's stunning.'

'I know.' Suzie's tone was almost apologetic. 'I really ought to learn to cook now. I don't think the teak-topped island was designed solely for me to pierce microwave lids on.'

'You can cook.'

'But I don't. I wouldn't know how to make a Caesar salad unless it involved opening a bag of leaves, sprinkling the croutons and cheese on and squeezing the sauce out of the sachet.'

'No wonder you haven't got yourself a man. You know you have to flirt with their stomachs as well as their hearts.'

Suzie was indignant. 'Look, I do restaurants. I even pay the bill occasionally. It's just, well, cooking just isn't much fun for one. It's much more entertaining being taken out for supper.'

'Well, that's where you and I differ. Just so you know, I'm officially throwing in the towel on the dating thing. I can't do it. I've tried and I'm tired.'

'But you've only been on two dates.'

'It'll be three, after I've met Pete Sampras for a drink to-morrow night.'

'Three dates.' Suzie sounded bitterly disappointed at Alice's paltry tally.

'That's three more than I would have been on if you hadn't insisted. I don't know, I just can't seem to find the right one.'

'I know the feeling. So—' Suzie clasped her hands opti-mistically '—how about one last try? I will if you will.'

'Look, Mum, I know it was your birthday wish and ev-erything, but wishes don't always come true. We've tried everything.'

'Not quite.'

'What now—tribal love dances, boiled artichoke hearts, the poached left ventricle of an eighteenth-century maiden?'

'Actually, I was thinking, you know how you think I pick the wrong men…'

'I don't think, I know.'

'Well, don't shoot but sometimes I think you do the same.' Suzie waited for the explosion.

Instead, Alice's tone was resigned. 'You're probably right.' She was too tired to protest.

'So I was thinking, what if we look at the replies we've had to all the ads and you pick a man for me to go on a date with?'

'You must have been on twenty-five dates already.'

'Three-minute men aside, I think it's nearer ten but most of those were just drinks or dinner. Plus, I could have sent the majority home before we'd even ordered the starter.'

'And you've got more who are interested?'

'Loads, darling. In fact, I'll let you in on a little secret. You're about to spend the evening with *Cupid Can Type Too*'s Over 40s Date of the Week.'

Alice didn't know whether to be impressed or appalled. 'So run this past me again, you pick a man for me and I do the same for you.'

Suzie nodded. 'One dinner. No strings.'

'And if it doesn't work?' Alice didn't know why she didn't just replace "if" with "when".

'We'll go to the party with each other.'

'Really?' The end in sight, Alice finally perked up.

'Of course. There'd be nothing worse than us turning up with someone who's only average. Especially as all my best friends in the world will be there. And you never know, maybe one of them will bring someone of interest.'

'You never quit, do you?'

'Quitting is for smokers. So what do you say?'

Alice knew when she had been steamrollered. 'Let's get it over with.'

Chapter Twenty-Two

6 days to go
Suzie 12, Alice 3

Zoë sat at Clive's pristinely polished mahogany dining-room table and knew why she had been so determined to go on this particular adventure alone. For once she had a family thing.

Light lunch over, she was on her third cup and saucer of slightly weak, tepid tea, three of Barbara's homemade shortbread biscuits sitting at the bottom of her stomach waiting for her enzymes to break through and break down their defences. Their indigestibility might have gone some way to explain her hosts' above-average waistlines but what Barbara lacked in baking skills, she had more than compensated for in the warmth of her welcome.

Zoë took another look around. The room was very normal. Some might even say characterless. The walls were cream, the woodwork dark. The windows were crisscrossed with lead lights, an attempt to compensate for the spectacular lack of architectural features in a house that had probably only been built in the 1930s. Ornaments adorned the windowsills and a cabinet of china figurines dominated one corner. Disappointingly, Zoë had never felt less at home anywhere in her life.

Zoë forced another sip of tea down, careful not to drink too quickly in case there was yet more in the pot. 'Thanks so much for all your hospitality and for talking me through all those photos.'

Clive watched her studying her surroundings. 'It's been a pleasure to meet you. Mags would have been so proud. And you certainly have her hair. Her "flair" she used to call it.'

Subconsciously Zoë checked that the selection of photos she'd been given were still in her bag. The one of Margaret at twenty-four, proof that she had still been a child when she'd had her first one. 'I don't suppose you happen to know anything about my father?'

Clive frowned. 'Not really. Only that he wasn't available to help.'

'Married?'

Barbara butted in. 'I think she said he was engaged at the time.'

Zoë tried to mask her disappointment as her father fantasies evaporated. 'Nice guy, then?'

Clive came to her rescue. 'If Mags hadn't adored him, she wouldn't have been with him. She usually had impeccable taste. But you know, sometimes the timing of these things can be a little off. Plus, she really was very young. I have a feeling they worked in the same office but I doubt she was thinking long term at that stage. You know how invincible you feel in your early twenties.'

Barbara nodded, reinforcing Clive's counsel. 'And when he went ahead and married as intended, she left the firm.'

Zoë's hopes were rising and falling faster than Barbara's ample bosom.

Clive looked at his wife with surprise. 'I didn't know that.'

Barbara put her arm on her husband's. 'Women talk.'

Zoë went over the details again in her head, determined to commit every element of her history to memory. 'So she left the company?'

Barbara nodded slowly. 'She could hardly have gone through with the pregnancy there. He would have known it was his. Plus, you know what office gossips are like. She didn't want any trouble. She knew she was wrong to have become involved with him in the first place.'

'Did he even know she was pregnant? Did he know about me?'

Clive was circumspect. 'It's funny. Maggie was one of those people who was the centre of every conversation, yet very discreet about her personal life. She always had a secretive streak. We didn't know she had cancer until she told us that she wasn't going to be able to beat it. And we didn't know about you until after that and I'm her brother.'

Clive produced a navy handkerchief from his pocket and blew heartily.

'I don't suppose she mentioned a name? Do you know if they were still in touch?' Zoë had stopped worrying about sounding laid-back. She knew she'd never forgive herself if she let the moment pass.

Clive was hesitant. 'I can't recall.' He paused for thought. 'Isn't his name on the birth certificate?'

'P. Fletcher. That's all I have to go on. It might as well be John Smith.'

Zoë studied Clive's eyes, hoping for a glimmer of something, praying that his memory would be jogged.

'Fletcher. Actually, now you mention it, that sounds familiar.' Clive beamed, proud of himself for remembering something useful at the actual time it was required, instead of a week later. 'I'm pretty sure he was a barrister. But P...?' He shook his head. 'That doesn't ring any bells. Hang on. I remember it was a king's name.'

'Philip?' Had there been an English King Philip. 'PGeorge? PCharles?' Zoë racked her brains, wishing she'd paid more attention at school.

'I really don't think it started with a P... And I used to have such a good memory. Of course, I can remember lots of things about when I was at school and not what I was told a year ago.'

Zoë did her best to look sympathetic when actually she wanted to give him a little shake to try and focus his mind.

'Henry. That's it. I'm certain. Well, I'm pretty sure. Oh, who knows...?'

Zoë paled. How many barristers called Fletcher could there have been in the early 1970s, let alone Henrys? 'I don't suppose you can remember where the chambers were?'

'I think she worked somewhere near Holborn. I forget now. I was never as enamoured with London as she was and Mags left Hampstead after you were born. I was living up north at the time. I guess that's how she managed to hide it from me. I think she said she'd read somewhere later on that he had died.'

Zoë gripped her left arm with her right hand.

'I'm sorry. You okay, love?'

Zoë's mind started racing. Less of a family tree, more of a family bush and hopefully not a poisonous creeper.

Clive fidgeted awkwardly. 'I don't suppose you'd like another cup of tea, or maybe something stronger?'

Zoë forced herself to focus on her distorted reflection in the polished table top. 'I'm fine. Really I am. Thanks. I'm sorry.' She placed her palms face down on the table and pushed her chair back. 'If you'll excuse me, I'm actually going to head home.'

Home: London, York, Hammersmith or Hampstead? It appeared her roots, now exposed, were tangled. None of the background reading she had done, nothing any of the social workers had said, none of the hypothetical scenarios she had concocted, had prepared her for this possibility.

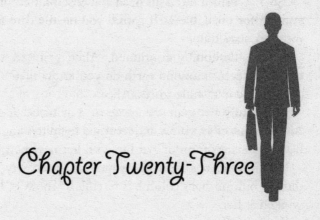

Chapter Twenty-Three

6 days to go
Suzie 12, Alice 3

Alice changed her outfit for what she hoped was going to be the last time and returned to join Dermot for the last round of publicity photos. She'd been styled to within an inch of her sanity and smiled, flirted, posed and pouted for the cameras. She'd done earnest, she'd done approachable, she'd looked at Dermot, into the lens, past the lens and she was almost past caring, although the posters were going to be up in the next few days and then she knew she'd care a whole lot more.

As they threw back their heads and laughed, simulating a long-standing working friendship with a hint of a sexual frisson, the photographers did their best to capture the whole picture for the sake of the channel, their future viewers and all their paycheques. Alice had to admit that whilst Dermot was being downright flirty, it wasn't at all unpleasant, just a little unnerving and, she reminded herself, all part of the new day job.

'So…' Dermot tilted his head and raised his eyebrow just enough for the cameras. 'I gather you need a date for your mother's sixtieth.'

As the flashbulbs continued, Alice grinned through clenched teeth. 'How on earth do you know that?'

'If you could smile for us, Alice.'

Apparently her grin was more of a grimace. A grinace. Alice unknitted her brow and returned to pretending she was having the afternoon of her life with her new best friend.

'My mother read it in the paper last week. My mother thinks your mother's column is terrific, by the way.' Dermot winked at her.

'If this is all part of some elaborate "my mate fancies your mate" build-up, feel free to ask her out yourself.'

Dermot smiled. 'Viewer research has revealed that I am rather popular with women of a certain age.'

'Dare you to say that in front of the eternally youthfully Suzie Fletcher. I swear she must have a portrait hidden away in her attic.'

'Seriously.' He took her arm and the camera shutters started again. 'How about I escort you to the party?'

'Me?'

'Well, if you don't already have a date?'

'Hey, the week is still young.' But "Pete Sampras" hadn't exactly been a love match. He hadn't even made it to the third round.

'So, what do you say?'

'Well, it'll certainly get the gossip columnists rushing back to their papers.'

Dermot put his hand on hers. 'My thoughts exactly. And a bit of sexual tension is always a ratings winner.'

Alice shook her head. 'You media boys are all the same.'

'Savvy?'

'I was thinking more along the lines of manipulative.'

'So playful yet so in control, no wonder Richard fell for you. I think I may be heading the same way.'

Alice laughed, genuinely laughed, for the first time that afternoon. This overstyled, orthodontically enhanced, breakfast favourite was declaring his alleged feelings for her. Yeah, right.

'Not so fast, Douglas.' A familiar voice interrupted them, and squinting in a lull between flashes, Alice spotted Richard standing at the back of the studio. Immediately self-conscious, she wondered how long he'd been there. 'I'm afraid you'll have to join the queue. Miss Fletcher has quite a record when it comes to romantic casualties.'

Alice was grateful for his embellishment of the truth.

'Just one final setup, you two, and you'll be free to go.'

Alice sat in makeup and wiped the matte foundation off her face with a damp flannel. Holding her mobile phone far enough away from her ear to avoid staining the keys, but close enough to be able to hear, she tried Zoë again. As her mobile's voice mail cut in, Alice left another message before dialling Zoë's flat and going through the same process. She'd been due to meet Clive five hours ago.

Zoë left the motorway. She couldn't wait for a mug of her mother's unfeasibly strong Yorkshire tea and practical advice.

Blinking hard, she concentrated on the road. She hadn't allowed her mind to wander even one step since she'd left Surrey, but four hours later it seemed determined to stray. Turning the air-conditioning dial to the far left, she gave herself a punitive blast of arctic breeze. In half an hour she'd be at home and then she could despair as much as she liked.

★ ★ ★

To Alice's surprise and delight, Richard accompanied her out of the building.

'I thought you wanted me to keep a low profile around you?'

Richard shrugged. 'Turns out I'm less uptight than you thought and really rather proud of you. Anyway, it's Sunday evening, it's pretty quiet here.'

'So how would you like me to refer to you in public? Mr. Harrison, Richie Baby, Fat Controller?'

'Fat?'

'Wait until all you have to do is sit around in boardrooms eating biscuits.'

'Don't you mean bored rooms? I think I'm really going to miss the hands-on stuff.'

'I'm sure you'll mould the role to suit you.'

'So, can I offer you a lift home? Or, your contract entitles you to a car.'

Alice took a breath of fresh air. 'I think I'll just get the tube.'

'I've never understood that side of you.'

'I don't see what all the fuss is about. I like trains. You can sit, you can read, you can think and the people watching is fantastic.'

'You can be delayed, you can inadvertently pick a seat next to someone who apparently bathes in urine… Ten pounds says you won't be using it by Christmas.'

'I'm not going to change. I'm not going to start wearing pastels and having manicures. And thanks for your offer, but I'm heading in the other direction. I thought I might pop in and see Zo.'

'Did you finally get through?'

Alice shook her head. 'I'm getting quite concerned now.'

'Maybe she's just too upset.'

'Exactly. I don't think either of us can imagine how harrowing all of this is.'

'She'll call you if she needs you.'

'Maybe she doesn't know she needs me at this precise moment. Besides, I've been tied up all day with this shoot and tomorrow isn't going to be any less busy. This is the only quality time I have to give her.'

Richard looked at his watch. 'Well, it's only seven. Why don't we pop over there together now. The car could do with some exercise.'

Alice took his arm gratefully. 'Thanks.'

Alice leaned on the bell for the third time in as many minutes and pressed her ear up against the main front door.

Peering up at the second floor, Richard turned and started down the path. 'All the windows are closed. She's not here.'

Alice didn't move. 'I'm going in.'

Richard wheeled. 'If she was up there she'd be answering her phone or her doorbell, if not both.'

'Look, we're here now. It won't take a second to check.'

'I'm not going to break in.' Richard was firm. 'And I'd rather my latest signing didn't get herself arrested, either.'

'Surely, it would all be publicity for the show?' Alice's smile was mischievous. 'If I'm going to be on the sides of buses, what's wrong with a few front pages?'

'Allie, I'm not in the mood.'

'Suit yourself. I didn't ask you to come with me. Anyway, much less newsworthy, but I have a key.' Alice produced a veritable jailer's bunch from her bag and as she let herself in, Richard was only a few steps behind her.

The flat was Zoë-free. She clearly hadn't been back since lunchtime. Alice tried her mobile again. Straight to voice mail. 'I just don't understand this.'

'Maybe she's gone for a walk. Maybe she wanted some peace and quiet. Maybe her phone ran out of power. Maybe wherever this Clive guy lives there are no mobile-phone masts.'

'She sent me a text when she arrived there this morning.' Alice walked around Zoë's living room distractedly. 'I knew I should have gone with her.'

Richard stepped out in front of her, stopping her in her tracks. He took both her hands in his. 'She wanted to go alone.'

'So, I wanted to be a backing singer. People don't always know what's best for them.'

'Al, Zoë's an adult who knows her own mind and she's hardly the weak and feeble variety, either. What are you panicking about? This isn't like you.'

Alice wrestled herself free and put her hands on her hips. 'She went to meet a man no one knows anything about.'

'She went to meet her uncle.'

'He could be a serial killer for all we know.'

Richard looked at his watch again. 'Look, give it until 9:00 p.m.'

'Then what?'

'I don't know. Have you got Clive's number?'

Alice kissed Richard's cheek. 'Logic under fire. Good work, Harrison. Thank you.'

Having located Clive's telephone number, copied it onto a Post-it note and double-checked the digits, Richard finally persuaded her to leave the flat. Alice followed him down the stairs, her mobile in hand, just in case.

Richard led the way. 'Promise me you won't call yet. You don't want her family thinking she has some clingy, overcautious…'

'I prefer concerned.'

'…nutter of a best friend.'

'I promise.'

'And remember, she's not officially a missing person for twenty-four hours.'

'As far as I'm concerned she is a missing person right now.'

'If I were you, I'd be way more concerned about how you're going to break the news to your mother that Dermot is your date for her party.'

'Oh, come on, he was just fooling around.'

'He looked pretty definite to me. Admittedly that man can sniff out a PR opportunity at twenty paces, but…'

'That's all it is.'

'But, don't you see, it means you've won…' Richard smiled encouragingly as he held the front door of the building open for her.

Alice shook her head. 'It may…'

Richard corrected her. 'Will…'

Alice stood firm '…*may* mean I have a date, but we're not dating.'

'Suzie doesn't know that.'

'But I do.'

'So, pretend.'

Alice got into Richard's Audi TT. 'I'm not a good actress.'

Turning the key in the ignition, Richard revved the engine into life. 'You're a better actress than you think.'

Zoë sat at the battered pine kitchen table of her youth and blew her nose on another piece of kitchen towel as her mother fussed around her. The kitchen was immaculate. Jean would have given Mr. Muscle a run for his money.

Jean stood next to the kettle waiting for it to boil again and used her surplus nervous energy to straighten the spice jars in the rack. 'You knew there was a risk when you started all this that it wouldn't end happily ever after.'

'I know, Mum, but I wasn't expecting…I don't know what I was expecting. I guess I hadn't factored in that I might be an orphan.'

'Your mother died last year. That doesn't make you an orphan, just an adult.'

The ever-practical Jean was right as usual, although Zoë hadn't quite found the nerve to tell her about the rest of it yet. 'But somehow I feel cheated. I mean, I suppose it doesn't really matter, but…'

'Of course it matters. But you've still got me, love.' Jean's tone softened. Her eyes were uncharacteristically watery.

'I know, Mum. Thank goodness for you. But, well, there's more.'

'More?'

'My father.'

'Oh good, so you managed to find out a little something about his side, too?'

Zoë hesitated. 'Just a little.'

Jean pushed her palms together expectantly, almost in prayer. 'How very fortunate that you found Clive.'

Zoë wasn't sure yet. 'Apparently my father had other children.'

Jean barely blinked as her brain took the information on board and filed it away calmly. 'So did your mother. Have I missed something? I don't see what the difference is?' Without even noticing, Jean aligned the tea towels on the rail on the front of her Aga.

'I don't know her other children.'

Jean looked puzzled. 'Sorry, Zoë dear, I don't understand.'

'Well, according to Clive and Barbara, who I'm inclined to believe, especially as I have nothing else to go on, I was the product of a fling with a barrister.'

'That would definitely explain your stubborn and argumentative streaks.' Jean giggled at her rare attempt at a joke. She wished David was alive. He was always good with Zoë at these moments.

'I'm not argumentative.'

'Of course not.'

'Nor am I stubborn. I might be determined but I view that as a good thing.'

'As indeed you should, we brought you up not to apologise for yourself.'

'But, back to the point, Mum, it would seem to be the case that my father, the professional arguer, was none other than Henry Fletcher.'

Zoë watched her mother's brow furrow.

'Is he famous? Oh no, he's not that MP they found wearing fishnets, is he?'

Zoë shook her head as she felt another wave of disbelief break over her.

'I guess there could be two Henry Fletchers. I'd hoped. But both in London? Both working as barristers? It seems highly unlikely to me.'

'I still don't see. Who is this Henry?'

'Sorry, Mum. I'm not being very clear. Probably because I'm not sure I want to see, but I think we're talking about Alice's father as well as mine.'

Jean's eyes widened before her innate practicality took over. 'Nonsense.'

'I know it sounds highly unlikely, but facts are facts.'

'I'd make sure you do your research properly before you go inventing yourself fanciful conclusions. Maybe Clive is confused or mistaken. The birth certificate you photocopied for me says P. Fletcher, I'm certain of it.'

'It does. And of course I'll check everything.'

'Make sure you do.'

'I suppose it could even be a typo but it's not like I can just give him a call or write him a letter.'

'You've got this far, you can't give up now.'

'Alice's father died when she was a child.'

'Oh, my dear. So you mean maybe they're both dead.'

Zoë's eyes filled with tears and her nose started to run. 'You see, I'm all alone.'

Jean sat down next to her daughter, clutching a cake tin. 'That's one thing you're not.'

The rare display of emotion passed through her voice and out the other side.

'Why not have a homemade scone, you must be exhausted after that drive and that fresh pot of tea will be ready in a couple of minutes.'

Zoë studied the grain of the pine on the table. 'I don't think Alice would ever forgive me for this. She thinks her father was perfect.'

'Zoë love, you know I can't abide amateur dramatics.'

'I'm not being bloody dramatic, Mum. This *is* a full-blown drama.'

'There's no need for that sort of language. First of all, it's not definite, secondly you haven't done anything wrong and thirdly, you don't have to tell her.'

'She's my best friend.'

'I'd maybe just let it lie for a few weeks, make some enquiries. Feel around a bit.'

'But that's dishonest and you know how bad I am at keeping secrets from the people I love.'

'Well, you two are like sisters anyway. Practically, what difference will it make? I'd just probably do a wee bit of double-checking before you bowl in with these allegations.'

'Like sisters, not actual sisters. I've been thinking about that all the way here.'

'But what does it matter whose genes are whose? I might not be your actual mother, yet we've done okay, haven't we?'

'We've done much better than that.'

'Well then.' Jean looked out of the window as she debated whether to go and scrub the draining board. 'Who'd have thought it? Maybe you were drawn to each other for that reason. I'm sure I read an article in the *Daily Mail* once that said—'

Zoë's mobile phone rang and she glanced at the screen guiltily before silencing it.

Jean raised an enquiring eyebrow.

'Alice has been calling me all day. It's as if she has a sixth sense.'

'She probably just wants to check that you're okay. Go on, speak to her.'

Zoë watched the small screen on her phone, still flashing with Alice's number, and turned her phone off. 'I can't. Not yet. There has to be more than one Henry Fletcher, Q.C.'

No reply. Alice paced the length of her kitchen again and dialled Richard.

'See, I told you she'd turn up.'

'Actually I was just wondering whether I should be calling the hospitals.'

'If it'll make you feel better.'

'I just don't understand where she could be.' Alice felt sick.

'Why don't you give Clive a call and find out if she's still there or at least, what time she left.' As usual Richard was the voice of reason.

'Okay.'

'Now, can I please finish giving Rob a blow—'

'Richard! That's way too much information.'

'Blow-by-blow account of your shoot. I can only imagine where your smutty mind was going with that one.'

Alice sat on her bottom stair, her socked feet polishing the tiles as she slid her feet backwards and forwards nervously.

'She left Clive's at two. It's just gone nine, there's no sign of her and she hasn't been admitted to any hospitals between here and Guildford.'

Stretching out on her sofa, a couple of miles away, Suzie removed her glasses and put the book she was skimming to one side in order to give Alice her full attention. 'I'm sure there'll be a logical explanation.'

'Well, Clive *says* she left then.'

'What are you suggesting?'

'Nothing. Oh, I don't know, Mum. Sometimes I wish I didn't have an imagination. Newspapers give you way too much information these days. What if she's been abducted?'

'Statistically it's highly unlikely. People get waylaid. Things come up. Do you think you're always home on time?'

'I'm never seven hours late.'

'Unless you're on a beach in Brighton….' Suzie's tone was mischievous.

'That was different.'

Suzie sucked thoughtfully on the titanium arm of her spectacles. 'Why don't you give Jean a call? See if she's heard anything.'

'And if she hasn't? I don't want her to worry.'

'Don't you think her mother might like to know if there's a problem.'

Alice's breathing was shallow. 'So you think there might be?'

'I doubt it. These things always turn out to be something very simple, but better to be safe than sorry. I'll call if you prefer.'

'I'll do it. If you call she'll think something dreadful has happened to us both.'

'Exactly.'

Despite her offer, Suzie was relieved to be off the hook. Jean scared her slightly.

'Anyway, it's still light out there. She's had a tough day. Maybe she wanted to sit and think.'

Alice wasn't convinced. 'How long for?'

'How would we know?'

Zoë lifted her mother's cat onto her lap as Jean disappeared to answer the old-fashioned tinkle of her phone.

She knew she couldn't hide forever. She did want to speak to Alice, but she was sure it'd be easier face-to-face and when she'd decided what to tell her.

There was a chance, however slim, that if it was the same man, Alice might be pleased. Then again she knew how much Alice had adored her father. No living man had been able to come close since, despite the fact that, putting her rose-tinted, Daddy's-girl glasses to one side, he had clearly been a selfish workaholic at least some of the time. And now Zoë could sympathise more strongly than she'd ever thought possible.

'Hello, Alice dear.' Alice stopped. Jean didn't sound at all surprised to be hearing from her and they hadn't spoken in months.

'I'm sorry to bother you so late.'

'I know you kids live your lives on a different timetable these days. How are things in London?'

'Oh, fine, well…' Alice felt an edge of desperation creep into her voice and swallowed hard as she remembered this wasn't a social call. 'I don't quite know how to say this, but I don't suppose you've heard from Zoë today?'

Jean smiled, moved by Alice's audible concern. 'Not in the last five minutes, dear, she's going through one of her thoughtful phases again.'

'She's with you?' Alice's sigh of relief was swiftly followed by a wave of anger.

'She arrived about an hour ago.'

'So she's okay?'

'Physically she's as fit as the proverbial fiddle.'

'And the rest of her? How did it go?'

'I think she'd probably rather tell you herself.'

'Do you think I could talk to her?'

'Certainly. Hang on a second.'

Now Alice felt ashamed for intruding, but if only Zoë had sent her a text or something to let her know she was okay…

Alice reminded herself not to be cross with her as she listened to the fading click of Jean's shoes on the floorboards.

In a world of her own, Zoë carried on stroking her feline comforter.

'It's Alice for you.'

Zoë froze. 'I can't speak to her. Not yet.'

'You can and you will. The poor girl is worried sick and you can't blame her after your disappearing act. Hudsons face facts. I didn't bring you up to be some southern softie.' Jean stood firm. 'These things don't just fix themselves. You of all people should know that. And I think you need your family and friends right now.'

Returning a slightly perturbed fur ball to the immaculate kitchen lino, Zoë took a deep breath and walked slowly towards the old-fashioned telephone handset lying on its side on the hall table.

'Alice, hi…'

'Zo? You okay? You didn't reply to any of my messages.'

Now that she knew Zoë was alive and well, Alice couldn't decide if she was relieved, concerned or downright angry.

'I just needed to check out of the real world for a few hours. I was thinking, and then I was driving. I wasn't ready to chat.'

'I see.' Alice was trying to be charitable but failing miserably.

'I wanted to come up here and help Mum to understand what I've just been through. And help me understand, too.'

What about me? Alice resisted the urge to verbalise her thoughts on the subject. 'I'm sorry I've been chasing around after you but I was worried. Very worried.'

'I'm sorry I didn't pick up, but I knew you were there for me and that was enough. I just wasn't ready to deal with anything.'

'So, how was Clive?' Concern overriding anger, Alice felt normality return. She should have listened to Richard and her mother.

'Very formal at first, but he soon warmed up. I think he finds the whole thing quite painful.'

'I'm sure that makes two of you.'

'Anyway, I can now tell you that it sounds like my mother was sleeping with a guy from the office who was engaged. When he went ahead with the marriage, she left the firm, left London and started again by giving me away.'

'Blimey.'

'Not really ideal, is it?'

'But now you know why. At least you have some answers. That's what you wanted.'

'I guess so.'

'You always said it was the not knowing that was the hardest bit. At least now, you can move on.'

'That certainly was the theory.'

'So what did your mother do? I mean, what sort of office was she in?'

'She was some sort of legal secretary.'

'Right.'

'Well, junior to my father at least. And based in town.'

'So, you're a Londoner after all.'

'Yup, I guess so.' Zoë was hesitant, her tone controlled.

'What is it? There's something else. You're holding back. I know you.'

For a moment, Zoë wished Alice didn't know her quite so well.

'Come on, spit it out, what is it?'

'Nothing.'

'Have I done something wrong?'

'Of course not.'

'Well then, is it something to do with your mum?'

'Not my mum…' Zoë sighed. She really wanted to say something, if only to clear her conscience and also because unless Alice knew, it was almost as if it hadn't happened. But she couldn't be sure.

Alice was tentative. 'Your dad?'

Zoë nodded silently. At Alice's end of the phone there was nothing.

'Zo? Come on, you know you can tell me anything.'

The moment had arrived and she wasn't at all ready.

'My mother worked for a barrister. Clive thinks his chambers were in Holborn.'

'No. What a coincidence.'

Zoë was stalling for time. 'What do you mean?'

'That's the same area where my dad worked. Hey, maybe they knew each other. Not that we can ask either of them now, shame.'

Zoë took a breath. 'I'm afraid there's more.' She looked up

at the ceiling, closed her eyes in silent prayer and prepared to rattle off the next sentence. 'My father's surname was Fletcher, too.'

Opening one eye hesitantly and then the other, Zoë waited for Alice to respond, suddenly grateful that she couldn't see her.

'Fletcher. P. Fletcher. We knew that.' Alice sounded excited. 'Maybe, spookily, he was related to my father.'

Zoë was almost in tears. 'I thought your father was an only child.'

Alice was downbeat. 'Good point. He was. But he had uncles and cousins.'

'Are you sure his first name was Henry?'

'Of course.' Alice slowed down as the information started to percolate.

Zoë wished she could be a good liar. But she didn't have a poker face or voice, whether it was secrets or surprises she was trying to keep.

'It's just…I haven't had time to check the details out, and I don't really believe in coincidence either, but…'

Alice was quiet. And then her voice was barely audible. 'Thinking about it, I think I remember some envelopes on the worktop at home when I was a child. I think he was actually P. H. Fletcher.'

There was silence as both women took stock.

Zoë was the first to come back. Everything out in the open, her strength was gathering. 'I need to check some more things out. I mean it's not one hundred percent definite.' Suddenly she was counselling Alice. 'Fletcher isn't an uncommon name but I just wanted to give you the heads up that, well, frankly I'm terrified that it might just be that we are closer than you think.'

'Terrified, eh?' Alice smiled through her confusion.

'Concerned, shocked, take your pick.'

'How can we be any closer than we already are? I see us as full sisters already.'

Zoë felt strangely emotional. 'That's very kind of you.'

'It's fact, not charity. Hey, maybe on a subconscious level we were drawn together for a reason.'

'Or maybe we were just in the same psychology lecture.'

Alice was surprisingly sanguine. 'It's an unbelievable possibility. Do you mind if I talk to Mum about this?'

'Do I mind? Do *you* mind? Are you sure you want to broach this with her? From what you've always said, Henry was pretty close to perfect. And, well, if it was him…'

Alice hesitated. She sighed. 'I don't know. I always thought he was fab but then, the older I get…I don't know. I was a child. He was a good dad. A great dad. But I have no idea about any of the other stuff.'

'No offence, but, well, if he did have an affair while he was engaged, that's pretty low…'

'Thanks for that.'

'Maybe your mother doesn't need to know.'

'It's certainly not ideal.' Alice felt herself getting defensive about her father. 'But Richard was unfaithful once. And he loved me.'

'But only once. And with a man.'

'Hey, we're talking about something that my father may or may not have done. And this would all have taken place before their marriage had even begun.' Alice paused. 'You are a year older than me.' Alice sat down on her kitchen floor. She had lost all sense of where she was. And who she was.

Zoë berated herself for being so self-obsessed. 'Look, this could all be a mistake, or a coincidence. As I said, Fletcher isn't that uncommon a name…'

Alice wasn't listening. 'But if it is him… Poor Mum.'

'Are you sure you want to tell her?'

'I don't think I have a choice.'

'I'll go and see her if you like.'

'No, leave it to me.'

'And what about you?'

Alice focused. 'Me? I'm still not sure. I just can't believe this.'

'Just think how I'm feeling.'

'Look, nothing's definite and nothing's insurmountable. But, back to basics, you should have called me earlier. I was really worried.'

'I'm so sorry. I just couldn't.'

'Fine.' Alice knew she sounded tetchy. She couldn't help it. All this, and still the thing that irked her the most was the fact that Zoë hadn't called her.

'Alice? Are we okay?'

Alice sighed. 'Of course we are. Now, could you please come home? You're of no use to me in York.'

Zoë's heart flooded with relief. 'I'll be back tomorrow afternoon. Sorry for being a coward.'

'A coward? You? I don't think so.'

'I ran away.'

'You ran home. Remember that. That's what children do in a crisis.'

Zoë smiled.

'Just make sure you drive back carefully. I'll be fine. I just need a little more time. And I need to talk to Mum.'

Zoë was cautious. 'Don't do anything you don't want to. We can discuss it together when I'm back and we've done a bit more research. In the meantime, take care of yourself.'

'You, too.'

Chapter Twenty-Four

5 days to go
Suzie 12, Alice 3

Suzie refilled both their glasses with white wine as she watched Alice push her salmon steak around her plate. Normally not one to drink much on a work night, Alice sipped at her third glass greedily. Suzie was circumspect. 'So, how many more days of filming do you have this week?'

'Just tomorrow to get through.' Alice abandoned her fish and started prodding the new potatoes on her plate, eating a couple of the smaller ones. She'd done her research and now she was delaying the inevitable. 'So, what was Daddy really like?'

'What's brought this on? It's not his birthday or anything.'

'We were talking about father–daughter relationships over lunch today. I guess I'm just curious.' Alice chastised her inner coward. She was sure it would be better to be direct. Maybe over coffee.

Suzie gave her only daughter a sidelong glance. 'You ask

me over for dinner, you don't eat, you don't finish your questions and you haven't asked about him in years.'

'Well, you know, with what Zoë's going through and this whole looking-for-a-man thing, I guess I've been thinking.'

'That sounds dangerous, darling.'

'I'm being serious, Mum.'

Suzie sat back and conjured up her favourite picture of Henry. 'He was a great guy. Witty, intelligent, attractive…all the women wanted him, and he wanted me.'

Alice felt her heart sink a little.

'Allegedly he was destined to be an eternal bachelor but I knew we were going to get married from the day we first met. I think it took him a little longer to come around to the idea but…'

It was an anecdote Alice had heard many times but this was clearly the first time she had actually been listening. 'What do you mean by that?'

'He was terrified of marriage. Thought it was bound to fail. Couldn't see how two people could be enough for each other.'

'And what changed his mind?'

'I did. If I'm honest, I was scared, too. But I told him we just had to try. That we'd simply do our best, no pressure. And we did so well,' Suzie murmured as she recalled their glory days. 'It's why I've always stayed a Fletcher. Amazing to think I nearly called the wedding off anyway.'

'You did?'

Suzie nodded.

'You've never mentioned that before.'

'It hasn't come up and before you ask, yes, it was one of the happiest days of my life.'

'One of the…'

'Only pipped at the post by the one day you turned up.'

'But why the hesitation, I mean, if you adored him so much?'

'Nerves, the usual, plus, well, I thought he was having an affair.'

Alice's blood ran cold.

'You did?'

'Okay, since you're asking so nicely, I didn't think, I knew.'

'And you still married him?' Alice's speaking voice climbed an octave.

'He ended it a few months before. Confessed all, begged me to forgive him. He promised me it was fear of committing, and assured me that he loved me more than anything. We called it his final fling. I think it was more like a couple of months though.'

'And that was okay?'

'Well, it's not quite the fairy tale. But then, what is?'

'How did you know you'd be able to trust him after that?'

'I just did. When you know, you know. I really think he just panicked at the thought of marriage—it happens.'

'Cold feet is one thing, but seeking refuge in someone else's bed?'

'I never had any reason to doubt him after that and at least he was honest with me. Most men would have denied everything. Your father wasn't like that. He was a good man.'

'But you confronted him?'

'Oh, I can't remember all the details now, it was a difficult time.'

'You don't say. You must have been devastated.'

'Of course. But we talked it through. We drank a few bottles of wine. I shouted and cried and shouted again. But honestly, deep down, I knew we'd be fine. We loved each other more than anything.'

'Why haven't you told me before?'

'It wasn't relevant and it's not how I want you to remember your father.'

'Then why are you telling me now?'

'I don't know. Because you asked? Because I want you to understand that people have flaws? You always thought he was perfect. And you expect everyone else to be, too. He loved you so much. I used to catch him just staring at you while you were sleeping.'

'I can't believe you managed to put it behind you.'

'After that we were stronger than ever before. And, well, I wasn't exactly behaving like a saint at the time, either.'

Alice was wide-eyed. The maxim was true. The only normal people were the ones you didn't know very well. She shook her head slowly. 'I thought you two had the perfect marriage.'

'We did. Ten happy years together and not really a bad day to speak of. Okay, the engagement period was a little dicier, but I think he shocked himself into behaving from then on in.'

'You know or you think?'

'I think I know. You can't monitor someone's every move, nor can you martial their mind. He would have liked to have had hundreds more children but I wasn't ready.'

Alice did her best to take the revised version of her family history on board. Selfishly, she preferred the U-suitable-for-all rated version. But then she was hardly one to talk. Any children she had were bound to find out there was more to gay Uncle Richard than first met the eye.

Suzie sighed. 'Now I wish I'd been less selfish. I found it difficult to adjust to being a mother. I suppose we perceive the final stage in becoming a bona fide adult as having children and that scared me. Then the responsibilities dawn on you and the unconditional love of your child, that total dependency, is something I was so unprepared for. Not that I would trade you in for anything. I was just worried that I was bluffing. That you would grow up realising that I had no special training or qualifications. Then when he died so suddenly, I wished we'd had more children. Then at least you wouldn't have been on your own.'

Alice shook her head. 'I've not been on my own. And you were, you are, a great mother.'

Suzie gripped her daughter's hand firmly. 'I've done my best.'

Alice stroked the back of her mother's hand. Despite an increasing number of liver spots, the skin was still very soft. She made a mental note to moisturise her own hands more often.

'Mum, I don't know how to say this.' Beads of sweat gathered in her hairline.

Suzie straightened. 'How to say what?'

Alice ignored the interruption, determined to see this moment through.

'So I'm going to come straight out with it.'

Suzie felt a cold front of panic blowing in.

'I think Daddy may have had another child.'

Suzie paused for a moment as she considered Alice's hypothesis calmly and carefully. 'No, I don't think so. He definitely would have told me. We both came with baggage and we were very honest about it.'

'But what if there was a child he didn't know about?'

Suzie hesitated. 'Well, I guess if you're a man that's always possible.'

Alice placed her mother's hands between her own in an attempt to protect her from what she was about to say. 'It's Zoë.'

Unsettled by Alice's seriousness, Suzie wrestled her hands free. 'What about her?'

'I think Dad fathered Zoë, too.'

Suzie was silent. A pulse started to flicker in her eyelid. 'I don't think so. Are you sure? I thought you said her mother was dead.'

Suzie's breathing was shallower than normal. Alice wondered why she was doing this.

'Her mother confessed everything to her brother before she died. He told Zoë, and...'

Suzie stood up. She walked over to the sink and ran the cold tap before filling a pint glass with water. Staring at the tiles, she shook her head slowly.

'I don't believe it.'

'Well, unless there was another P. H. Fletcher working as a barrister in London in the early seventies...' Alice knew it was too much to hope for.

Suzie sighed deeply as Alice wished her research was wrong.

'Peter Henry Fletcher. No, there was certainly only one.'

'Oh.' Despite everything, Alice was still shocked. 'Peter Henry?'

'He was christened Peter, called Fletch at school and he changed to his middle name when he started university. He never liked Peter.' Suzie put her pint glass down and gripped the work surface, momentarily giddy. She turned to Alice. 'Cup of tea?'

'Dad had a child with another woman and you want a cup of tea?'

'How can you be sure?'

'Zoe and I have made some calls and it seems to be pretty definite. All roads lead to Dad. I wish they didn't but...'

Suzie wasn't really listening. 'It's just, I mean, it does all seem rather convenient.'

'Convenient for who?'

'Maybe there's been a misunderstanding.' Suzie was talking to herself. 'Another child.' She addressed the ceiling. 'You assured me you'd been careful. Damn you, Henry. Why aren't you here?' Her heart was racing but there were no tears in waiting.

'Mum, are you sure you're okay? Can I get you a whisky or something?'

Suzie sat down again. 'Poor Zoë. How is she? To be honest, I've sort of been waiting for one of his love children to turn up for the last thirty years.'

'Now you're being ridiculous. No one could have predicted this and you absolutely don't have to be able to handle it. You have permission to fall apart. I can help.'

Suzie stared out of Alice's kitchen window. 'He was forty when we met. He'd had sex with a lot of women. Contraception wasn't what it is today. Things go wrong. I'm definitely not naive about that.'

'But this wasn't just sex, this was an affair.'

'Thanks. I'm acutely aware of that.'

'Well, allegedly.' Alice blushed. 'I just wanted to make sure you were listening.'

'But if it was before we were married…' Suzie was miles and years away. '…Zoë's how old?'

'Nearly thirty-one.'

'He definitely can't have known about her or he would have insisted on sending some maintenance money, at the very least. He might have been reckless in his youth but he was a kind man and a doting father. Not to mention responsible— it's where you get that incredible sense of duty from…'

Alice was unconvinced by Suzie's performance. 'Don't you want to hit something, don't you want to cry? Doesn't this change everything?'

Suzie stared over Alice's shoulder. 'And Zoë's certainly a strong enough character. Give her some time and she'll be fine. How long is she staying up in York? Maybe she—'

Alice interrupted. 'She got back this afternoon.'

'Well, don't you think we should get her over here?'

'I'm not sure that she—'

Suzie picked up her handbag. 'Sod it, let's go over to her.'

Suzie drove her Mini Cooper like a rally-car driver as Alice started to wish she hadn't nervously drunk quite so much white wine with her dinner and could have driven herself.

As Suzie took a corner at forty in a thirty-mile-an-hour zone, Alice did her best not to grip the edge of her seat too obviously. Suzie's mind was clearly racing as fast as her engine.

'Well, I guess this certainly puts our dating challenge into perspective.' Suzie braked suddenly as the traffic lights twenty feet away suddenly turned to red.

Alice couldn't help but smile. Maybe some good was going to come out of all of this.

Momentarily stationary, Suzie turned to address Alice. 'It just shows, you can never know everything. You just have to live in the present and make the most—' She interrupted herself, starting in a new direction. 'I meant to remind you, you have booked a restaurant for Thursday evening, haven't you?'

'Of course.'

'Where are we going?'

'It's a new place in South Ken. The Oasis.'

'That's not a new place.'

'Well, it's under new management or something. I read a review somewhere,' Alice fibbed. 'And they had room.'

'As long as you think that's a good sign.'

'Well, to be fair, it was all a bit last minute.'

'Shock horror, these men have lives and other commitments. I think we've done pretty well to get it organised. I only came up with the idea a week ago and Thursday nights take some coordinating.'

Suzie slipped into gear as she waited for the lights to change.

Alice braced herself for the acceleration. 'Presumably you're still not going to tell me who you've picked for me?'

Suzie sighed. 'It's a surprise.'

Having reverse parked around the corner from Zoë's flat, Suzie took Alice's hand as they stood at the entry phone.

Suzie pushed the buzzer and waited for an answer. Zoë clearly wasn't expecting anyone. Suzie buzzed again.

Eventually a weary but familiar voice answered. 'Hello?'

Suzie stepped up to the mouthpiece. 'Zoë? It's your stepmother and your half sister. I'm afraid we're about thirty years late. Terrible traffic.'

Alice followed her mother inside with a swell of pride. Anyone could be a mother but not everyone could be Suzie.

Chapter Twenty-Five

Zoë scanned the crowds on Oxford Street. 'So where is he?'

Alice checked her watch. 'He's still got ten minutes.'

'I thought we were meeting him at two?'

'I told him two-fifteen.'

'Allie…'

'Old people are often early.'

'Your mother isn't.'

'Trust me, Geoffrey is.'

'Well then, maybe they're not as compatible as you seem to think.'

'Zo, whose side are you on?'

'Today? Suzie's.'

The crowds were three deep and even nestled outside the HMV opposite the entrance to Bond Street tube station, Zoë was being buffeted by an assortment of shopping bags and pushchairs as mothers used their three-wheeled buggies as weapons to clear pavements and take rival shoppers out at midcalf level. According to the papers, the introduction of the Congestion Charge had had a negative impact on shoppers in the West End, but Zoë couldn't see room for any more. She sidestepped a gang of teenage girls who were determined to mow her down with their attitude. 'Shouldn't they be at school?'

Alice rolled her eyes at her best friend. 'In August?'

'Well, there should be summer school or something. Are you sure you couldn't have picked somewhere a little busier for us to meet?'

Alice gave Zoë a friendly shove. 'Look, Geoffrey will be here in a minute. And even if we are related, you still have to be nice to me.'

'Says who? What happened to unconditional love?'

'That's mothers and daughters.'

'Not half sisters?'

'I don't think so.'

Zoë fidgeted impatiently. 'I haven't given someone a makeover for ages.'

'Maybe it would just be easier to give Mum a makeunder. Think sensible shoes. Think khakis.'

Zoë ignored her. 'And I've never made over an older man.'

'Well, you can't shop for men but you can help them shop. And at least we've got our outfits sorted.'

Zoë rubbed her hands together gleefully. 'I can't believe you've agreed to wear a dress.'

'It's not too late for me to change my mind.'

'You're going to look stunning. And the shoes we bought are so cute.'

'Puppies are cute, Zo. Shoes are shoes.'

'You'll see.'

Alice couldn't decide if she was nervous about Saturday

evening or not. The threat of Dermot's presence was certainly adding to the pressure on her to look fantastic rather than just okay, hence the new dress hanging in her wardrobe.

'We still haven't decided what we are going to do with your hair.'

Just at the point Alice was considering posting herself somewhere a long, long way away for the weekend, Alice spotted a familiar figure crossing the road. 'Here he is…'

Zoë watched as a silver-haired man extricated himself from the crowd and pecked Alice on the cheek. His hair was far too long and fluffy but, she mused, at least he had plenty of it.

As Alice watched Zoë practically licking her lips with gleeful anticipation, she fleetingly wondered if she was doing the right thing.

'Geoffrey, Zoë. Zoë, Geoffrey.' Handshakes were traded as Zoë started giving him the once-over.

Carefully, Geoffrey rolled up the sleeves of his checked shirt before turning to Zoë for instructions. 'Where do we start?'

'Selfridges, definitely Selfridges, then Fenwick. You've got a facial booked there at four-thirty…'

Geoffrey frowned. 'I'm sure I don't need one of those.'

'It's not about need. In fact, I'd like to ban that word for the rest of today.' Zoë started carving a path through the crowds. 'Follow me.'

Geoffrey took Alice's arm for support. 'She's quite bossy this friend of yours, isn't she?'

Alice nodded. 'That's why I like her.'

'Reminds you of your mother, does she?' Geoffrey's smile was mischievous.

Alice smiled. 'Not in the slightest. But by comparison I appear very easygoing.'

Geoffrey laughed as they fell a few steps behind. Zoë turned to check on them.

'Come on, you two, we need to get cracking. Geoffo, you've got a haircut booked at six so we need to have done most of the purchasing before then.'

'I'm all yours. Just as long as I'm ready for tomorrow evening.'

'You'll be readier than you can imagine.' Zoë increased her pace as they neared the entrance.

Conspiratorially, Alice addressed Geoffrey in a stage whisper. 'Thanks for saying yes. I thought you might think I was being very cheeky when I called.'

'Hey, it's not every day a man gets the opportunity to go on a date with someone he really likes, and as for the offer of two women to restyle him—well, I haven't been shopping in ages, unless you count supermarkets and the garden centre.'

Alice shook her head, normal volume returned. 'They definitely don't count.'

'Zo, you are a genius.'

Alice stood proudly alongside her best half sister as Geoffrey admired his new rejuvenated self in the mirror behind the small bar at the Wolseley. They'd done Selfridges, Fenwick, Liberty. His slacks had been replaced with fitted cords, he owned new jeans, a leather jacket, a few T-shirts, a couple of polo shirts, new jumpers, new shoes, a facial moisturiser, fake tan and aftershave. Without any surgery (haircut aside), Geoffrey had been reinvented.

Alice had always taken pride in her ability to pick great birthday presents, but this time she couldn't help feeling she might just have surpassed herself. She could barely wait for tomorrow evening. 'So, what can I get you to drink?'

Geoffrey shifted his weight from one foot to the other. He looked uncomfortable. 'Why don't you girls let me treat you.'

'No way.' Alice's expression was non-negotiable. 'Get used to letting women pay. Well, let us buy the odd drink and don't worry, we'll always let you buy dinner.'

Zoë laughed at Alice's double standard. 'I think you, young lady, should concentrate on practising what you preach.'

Geoffrey put his impressive array of shopping bags down at his feet. 'Fine, I'll have a pint of bitter then.'

'Oh no you won't.' Alice was adamant.

Geoffrey's brow furrowed apologetically. 'I'm afraid I don't really drink lager. Too cold, too tasteless and, well, too gassy.'

Zoë intervened. 'Too much information. How about a cocktail?' She could see exactly what Alice was up to and she approved.

Alice nodded encouragingly as Geoffrey looked from one girl to the other, wondering how men had allowed women to become so overtly bossy over the years.

He smiled. 'I believe this is what is known as peer pressure. Okay I'll have a Campari soda.'

Alice paused. 'I was thinking more along the lines of a martini.'

'That's very strong, isn't it?'

'I'd prefer to say powerful.'

Fleetingly, Geoffrey lifted his arms in surrender. 'Okay, whatever you say. I didn't think I liked sushi, either, and I was wrong. A martini it is, shaken and not stirred.'

'Of course, Mr. Bond.'

'Excellent. Jolly good.'

Alice made a mental note. If Zoë could work her magic on his appearance in a few hours, she was sure it wouldn't take long for her to brush up his colloquialisms.

Taking a seat as they waited for the drinks, Zoë produced

a few magazines from her bag for Geoffrey's perusal. Alice was impressed. When it came to his rejuvenation, she really had thought of everything.

Trimmed eyebrows slightly raised and climbing ever closer towards his newly shorn hairline, Geoffrey leafed through *Heat, Zoo, Maxim* and *New Woman* magazines and as the waiter approached, he surreptitiously slipped them into his bag as guiltily as if they were porn.

'Mind if I take them home and have a flick through later—for research purposes, of course?'

Zoë smiled. 'That's exactly what they're here for. As for volunteering for extra homework, you get extra points for dedication to your cause.'

'I aim to please.' Geoffrey held his martini glass aloft for a toast. 'So, my little style gurus, do you think this is going to work? I'm still the same man beneath the new shirt.'

'Geoffrey.' Zoë's tone was formidable as she admonished him. 'What did I tell you earlier? No apologising, no self-deprecation. You're one hell of a catch.'

Bemused, Geoffrey forgot his drinks order and took a large sip from his glass. Smarting momentarily at its alcohol content, the vodka began to work its uplifting magic and he drank a little bit more. His invincibility was only a few more sips away.

Alice joined his fan club. 'For all her talk, she's just as lonely as the rest of us and the beauty of tomorrow's blind date is that it isn't blind at all. You can skip the small talk and get right down to business.'

Geoffrey blanched and Zoë giggled.

Alice intervened, determined to redeem herself. 'That's not what I meant. And there's no need to panic. You're meeting at a bar, not a brothel. Just have fun, be positive, be assertive and be forward looking—I mean look to next week, not to the rest of your lives. There's no rush. Think of it as a fresh look at an old favourite.'

Geoffrey smiled wryly. 'I thought she wanted to meet the right guy by the time she was sixty.'

Alice nodded. 'Ah, but what she's forgotten is that she's going to be sixty for a whole year.'

Zoë added her endorsement. 'Don't worry, Geoff, she's going to love you.'

'I've never been a Geoff.'

Zoë looked surprised. 'Well, I think it suits you.'

Geoffrey tilted his head slightly to one side as he tried it out, his lips forming a half smile. 'Actually, it doesn't bother me at all.'

'Right, that's settled then. Tomorrow you're Geoff, and can I suggest the powder blue Smedley jumper, jeans…'

'Jeans? For dinner?'

'Absolutely.'

'Not the cords?'

Zoë smiled. 'Anything we bought today is fine but go on, I dare you to wear the jeans.'

'We'll see. I just hope she goes for all this.'

'Well, if she doesn't, there are plenty of others who will.'

'That's not what I meant. You've taken ten years off me.'

'No one gets old these days, they just get a new look.'

Geoffrey touched the nape of his neck. 'I do seem to be missing quite a bit of hair.' He sighed. 'I was lucky enough to still have some.'

'You've still got plenty. You've just gone from mad professor to George Clooney.'

'I fear I'm probably closer to Clint Eastwood these days.' Geoffrey smiled. 'So, now I've had a drink, can I ask why you two are doing all this for me? Sure, Suzie's told me all about her mission to find the right man. But I've never even been on her radar. And I did get the impression she was looking for a younger model this time around.'

Alice held her hand up to silence him before Zoë took umbrage.

'We all take the people closest to us for granted. And you've been there for her for, what, a year?'

'I fear it's more like three. Off and on.'

Alice was contemplative. 'Well, I want you to promise me something.'

Geoffrey shook his head. 'Old solicitors never promise anything in the abstract.'

'Okay, so let's make it more of a gentleman's agreement, but say tomorrow doesn't go well, for whatever reason, will you please promise me you'll look elsewhere?'

Geoffrey nodded confidently. 'Let's just see what happens, shall we? Don't write me off yet.'

Zoë clapped her approval. 'Excellent fighting talk.'

'And let's just say I've got a few things up my sleeve.'

Alice looked at him quizzically. 'Like what?'

'You've done your bit, now let me do mine. I've been dating longer than you've been breathing.'

Geoffrey drained his martini glass with a flourish.

'Right, I'd better get home and unpack and I guess I'll be seeing you two at the restaurant tomorrow evening.'

'Actually, Geoffrey, it'll just be me. Zoë has managed to sidestep this whole barmy idea of Mum's.'

Geoffrey smiled. 'She might be on the eccentric side, but you do have to admire Suzie's energy.'

Alice winked. 'Hopefully by the end of tomorrow evening, she'll be admiring yours.'

Geoffrey gave Alice a hug. 'Thank you both so much. I'm really looking forward to my last chance.'

'Think of it as her last chance.'

Laden with yellow, green and purple paper carrier bags, Geoffrey headed to the exit. He paused inside the revolving door and started rummaging around for his free tube pass.

Alice dashed after him. 'Just one last tip, when it comes to going home tomorrow and it's all going well, get a cab. Mum doesn't do the tube.'

'Got it.'

Alice and Zoë watched him walk down Piccadilly, new-look head held high.

Zoë took Alice's arm. 'Right, fairy godmother, let's have another drink.'

'I just hope the evil stepmother appreciates what you've done.'

Zoë smiled. 'There's nothing evil about my stepmother.'

'Just wait until she starts writing articles about you, then you'll love her a little bit less.'

Zoë focused on her partner in crime. 'So who do you think she's picked for you?'

'I don't know and I don't care.'

'As usual, you're lying.'

'Okay, I'm curious but—' Alice rubbed her hands to-gether conspiratorially '—I can't believe he'll be as perfect as Geoffrey is for her. Besides, it looks like I've got Dermot as my walker for Saturday, so as far as first appearances and unfounded gossip goes, I'm sorted.'

Chapter Twenty-Six

2 days to go
Suzie 12, Alice 3

A mere eight o'clock at the Oasis and Suzie was already singing her camel to bed, or at least that's what Alice thought she was warbling on about. As she led her to the bar, she wondered whether insisting on pouring them both a large G&T had perhaps been more of an error than a masterstroke.

Suzie's hot-pink kitten heels clicked on the newly sanded and varnished floorboards underfoot. 'So come on, darling, surely you can tell me who I'm meeting now.'

'Patience, Mum.'

Alice felt more nervous about Suzie's date than she did about her own. This was one scheme that she didn't want to backfire.

Impressed, Suzie looked around her. 'Well, you get ten out of ten for venue. They've done wonders with this place.'

Alice was doing her utmost to take its makeover in her stride. The formerly dingy bar area was now awash with fairy lights and Moroccan lanterns and the ceiling had been painted the dark blue of a clear sky just after sunset. The walls had been whitewashed inside and out and, as they approached the doors to the garden, Alice was delighted to see that they were flung wide open, revealing rows of low-slung lanterns, flaming torches embedded in newly landscaped flower beds and a smattering of small tables nestled amongst new bushes and potted trees. A large sail, suspended horizontally from barely visible poles, sheltered a few tables by the wall, the sound of running water radiating from a small fountain in the midst of a sandstone-lined pond in the location of the formerly green, algae-ridden puddle. The unmistakable scent of jasmine wafted in, mixing harmoniously with the faint aroma of sandalwood in the bar area. Someone had been listening very carefully. She should have booked somewhere else. She was supposed to be moving on, not revisiting the past.

Suzie licked her lips. 'The food smells delicious. At least if you've picked me a dud bloke, I'll get to have a great supper.'

'What happened to your innate stamina and optimism?'

Suzie sighed wearily. 'I should have listened to you ages ago. I can't wait until all this formal dating and party business is out of the way. I'm exhausted.'

Alice was thrown by her mother's mood swing. 'Hang on just one moment, Saturday is going to be fabulous. And you certainly deserve the celebration.'

'I deserve a soul mate. Look at me, I've got a brand-new kitchen and I haven't eaten at home for ages. What a state I'm in. I want my slippers not my slingbacks and a cuppa not a cocktail.'

Alice knew she should have poured them vodka instead of gin. This was no time for Suzie to start acting her age. Alice was determined to jump-start her mother's excitement before all her preparations fell flat on their face. 'So, where are you hiding my mystery man?'

Suzie assessed every man they passed for potential. 'Where are you hiding mine?'

'He should be at the bar any minute now.'

Suzie looked around the place, confused. 'So should yours.'

As both women scanned the crowd with a combination of hope and trepidation, Suzie grabbed Alice's arm firmly and pointed. 'What are those two doing here?'

Alice followed Suzie's finger to a familiar couple hunched over a bottle of white wine at a nearby table.

Richard and Zoë had clearly thought they were disguised as a couple on a date, but their failure to look at each other, even once in a while, was giving them away. Accidentally catching Alice's eye on one of her three-hundred-and-sixty-degree surveys of the bar, Zoë blushed, returning her gaze to her faux partner.

Alice was indignant. 'I had no idea they were coming.' She was going to have to talk to them about the fine line between friendship and stalking.

Typically, Suzie was less fazed than Alice. 'Well, let's make sure we give them something to stare at.'

Alice took her mother's arm. To her amusement she'd just spotted Geoffrey nursing a martini. 'Okay, show time. Come and meet your date.'

Alice managed to get Suzie all the way to the back of Geoffrey without her realising who it was. 'Mum, meet Geoff.'

As the man formerly known as Geoffrey got to his feet and turned to greet his date, Alice wished she'd had a camera. Suzie was mute with surprise. Alice was sure she could hear Zoë whooping from across the bar.

Geoff pretended not to notice as Suzie looked him up and

down. Instead, he proffered her a martini he'd ordered for her earlier. Judging by the condensation on the glass, it was still ice cold. 'I thought you might need one of these, but I'm sure I could organise a cup of hot sweet tea if you'd rather, you know, for the shock.'

'Look at you.' Suzie's incredulity couldn't have been any warmer as she took her drink.

'Oh, you know.' Geoffrey casually fingered his brand-new Sea Island cotton jumper. 'I just thought it was time to buy a couple of new things.'

'Fuck, you're even wearing jeans.'

'Not just any jeans.' Geoffrey gave her a slow twirl. 'Bloody cool Paul Smith jeans…'

To Alice's relief Geoffrey wasn't wearing an old-man belt, nor had he hoisted the waistband to his armpits. He was doing incredibly well.

'…I've been rebranded.'

Suzie turned to Alice. 'He wasn't on the list I gave you.'

Alice beamed, relishing the sweet smell of success. 'I decided to go à la carte. Or should I say à la phone. He was in your contacts.'

Suzie was still staring at Geoffrey.

Smiling, he took control. 'Our table's ready when you are. I've managed to get us one outside.'

Suddenly Alice wished he was hers for the evening. She was still on her own.

As Suzie took Geoffrey's arm and prepared to lead him astray, Alice coughed politely. 'Um, sorry to interrupt, but where's my date?'

Suzie regained her focus and panned the room slowly. She checked her watch.

Alice felt her stomach knotting. She wasn't sure her ego could handle being stood up by a stranger. Better to have a bad date than no date at all or at least it was when you had an audience.

Peering into the main restaurant area, Suzie registered a moment of triumph. She indicated a table for two currently being occupied by a single man reading a book. 'Over there.'

Alice clocked the familiar figure at once.

'Andy?' Her incredulity and disappointment were captured in two syllables.

Okay, so she hadn't had a list, short or otherwise, and therefore Suzie had been forced to use her initiative, but she clearly hadn't looked very hard or very far. In fact, she'd only got as far as *A* in her own directory of possibilities.

'You were only telling me the other week how much you liked him.'

Not wanting to ruin the atmosphere, Alice put on a brave face. After all, a girl had to eat. Turning to wish Suzie well, Alice discovered she was already on her own, and engrossed in his book, Andy had no idea she'd arrived. For a split second, Alice contemplated cutting and running, but her momentary hesitation proved to be her downfall as Andy looked up and waved hello. Resisting the urge to wave a white flag back, she walked over.

Alice and Zoë washed and dried their hands simultaneously.

'So how's it going? He looks chatty enough.'

Zoë was determined to be encouraging even though it was clear from her body language that so far, Alice had been far more interested in her meal than her date.

'This is so typical of Mum.'

'To have a better evening than you?' Zoë wasn't sure what Alice was driving at.

Alice shook her head. 'To bring someone along who fancies her.'

Zoë's expression was sympathetic. 'Oh no.'

'Oh yes. And if I have to endure many more anecdotes illustrating how fabulous, witty, talented, attractive and ballsy my mother is, I think I may have to fake a migraine and leave. At least if she and Geoffrey don't hit it off, she's still got enough time to get Andy on her arm before Saturday. Heads she wins, tails I lose.'

'What a shame. I have to say that from afar, he seemed okay.'

'What—two arms, two legs?'

'Quite animated, quite jolly…'

'Jolly well in lust with my mother. Just what you need on a last-minute date.'

Zoë frowned. 'But when I last spoke to her she was really excited that she'd found the perfect guy for you.'

'Well, at least this way, if I'd picked her a nightmare, her evening wouldn't have been ruined.'

'You really think she's that devious?'

Alice checked her hair in the mirror. 'I know she is.'

Zoë was contemplative. 'I think she genuinely thought you liked him.'

'Look, she might be your brand-new stepmother but if you start jumping to her defence all the time, I might have to divorce you.'

'I'm not.'

Alice berated herself for her barbed tone.

'Sorry, Zo. I'm just…I could be at home having a lovely evening for one, or we could be out together instead of gossiping next to the hand driers.'

'It doesn't make sense. If she and Andy have a thing going, why haven't they been on a date before?'

Alice paused. 'Maybe she doesn't like him enough. Maybe he's just a reserve, a last resort. You know, break heart in case of emergency.'

'But if he's so smitten with her, why would he agree to go on a date with you?'

'Probably because he wants to ingratiate himself with her by doing her a favour. Either way he certainly likes her more than enough for the two of them.'

'But surely he's going to be at the party anyway?'

'You'd have thought so.' Alice sighed. 'Anyway, only coffee to endure and then I'll be joining you at the bar. It could have been worse. At least I'm not having to fob off unwelcome advances, even if it does feel like I'm having dinner with the chairman of the Suzie Fletcher fan club.'

Tiring of being serious, Zoë giggled. 'Well done for seeing the funny side. So how are you going to let him down?'

'Don't worry. I think he's probably wondering the same thing.'

'Go gently.'

'So, more importantly, anything to report from the garden party?'

Zoë shook her head. 'Irritatingly they seem to have managed to get a table in the wilderness and neither have reappeared yet.'

'Damn.'

'Well, I guess you should count yourself lucky that you're not at adjacent tables.'

'Well, well, well, if it isn't the witches of Hammersmith and Fulham.' Suzie had timed her trip to the ladies' perfectly. 'Fancy finding you both in here at the same time.'

'So?' Alice didn't have time to be subtle. 'How's it going?'

She had to get back to her table before Andy thought she'd done a runner or had a bowel condition—neither of which were ideal in the circumstances.

Suzie checked her still-perfect makeup in the mirror and

failed to hide a smile. 'I may have to concede that for once, darling, you may have had a point. He really is a lovely man.'

Alice and Zoë resisted the urge to high-five there and then.

'I almost can't believe he's the same guy. He does scrub up well.'

'Well, Mum, it looks like this is your night. I think Andy likes you, too.'

'Likes *me*? What about you?'

'I'm merely your daughter and, I'm sure as far as he is concerned, hopefully the fast track to your heart.'

'What nonsense.'

'Mum, please don't pretend you hadn't noticed.'

'Well, he might have said the odd nice thing to me.'

'What, like, "You're the most exceptional person I've ever known"?'

Suzie shrugged. 'Look, he's really not my type.'

'A cast-off. Gee, thanks.'

'No, I'm sure I remember you mentioning him a few weeks ago.'

Alice sighed. 'Maybe you need a hearing aid to reduce distortion. I did mention him…'

Suzie's reaction was one of victory. 'See.'

'…As someone who had a crush on you.'

'You did? Damn. My memory isn't what it used to be. I must be getting old.'

'You're not old, you're just not concentrating.'

'So you don't like him at all?'

'He's a nice guy, nice enough personality.'

Suzie grimaced. 'I feel a big "but" coming on…'

'But he's not my type. Not really. Not at all. Nor am I his.'

Suzie tutted. 'Silly me. Oh well, I haven't given up yet.'

'Oh yes you have. I'm retiring. We agreed this would be it and even you admitted earlier you'd had enough.'

'It might be enough in terms of my aims for the party, but not for the rest of your life. Now, if you'll excuse me, I must get back. I think I'm going to invite Geoffrey back home for coffee.' Suzie's innuendo was worthy of a *Carry On* film.

Alice couldn't have been more delighted at the outcome, especially now that Suzie was back in her own house. 'That's great, Mum.'

'The man is a revelation.'

Alice ran her fingers through her hair. It was time to reenter the arena. 'We just helped him choose a few new clothes and suggested a haircut.'

'We?' Suzie looked to Zoë for the explanation she knew she wasn't going to get from her daughter.

Alice pushed her way past Suzie, to the door. 'Time to suggest Andy and I adjourn to the bar for coffee where we are going to "oh-my-goodness-what-a-coincidence" stumble across Richard and Zoë.'

Zoë beamed. 'Rest assured we'll be very surprised to see you.'

'I love a bit of spontaneity, don't you?' Alice grinned at them both as she left the ladies'.

Alice was very drunk. Andy safely dispatched in a taxi nearly two hours earlier, Richard had plied her with both consolatory and celebratory drinks. Her ordeal was over.

The Dark Horse of the Night award had gone to Geoffrey who had whisked Suzie off to the St. Martin's Lane Hotel. Alice was impressed. She would have put money on him being a Savoy man. But that was the old Geoffrey. This new model had caused quite a stir, especially when he'd gone outside to hail a taxi and then not batted an eyelid when, meter running, Suzie had taken a good five minutes to leave the bar.

Alice rested her lolling head on Zoë's shoulder. 'What a summer.'

'It's not quite over yet. You still have to survive Saturday.' Richard leaned in. 'We *all* have to survive the party.'

Alice righted herself. 'Hang on, I'm not sure, I mean…' Embarrassingly, she was sure Suzie hadn't sent him an invitation.

'Stop panicking. She called me this week, grovelled about leaving it so late and everything, hoped there were no hard feelings and then biked me an invite.'

'Wow.' Alice was both impressed and relieved. 'So we can go together after all?'

Richard hesitated. 'I don't think Rob would like that.'

'She invited Rob, too?'

Richard nodded proudly. 'By name. Says she wants to get to know him better.'

Alice ran a calming hand through her hair. 'You want to watch out there.' Becoming a mother again had definitely had an effect on Suzie.

Richard laughed. 'Believe me, Rob will be only too happy to spend some time with Suzie. He thinks she's gorgeous.'

'And funny, too, I'll bet.'

'How did you know that?'

'Oh, I just had a hunch.'

'Well, that leaves us then, Zo. The perfect party partners in crime. Some things never change, eh?'

Zoë raised her glass in a toast. 'Thank bloody goodness for that. Hang on, what about Dermot?'

Alice forced herself to sit up without leaning on anyone or anything. It was taking a surprising amount of effort. 'He can come along, too, but you know my rules…' She slurred her words through a combination of alcohol and exhaustion. 'Never mix business with pleasure.'

'Right.' Richard and Zoë exchanged disbelieving glances.

'Right.' Alice drained her final glass of the evening. The only hot date she wanted from now on was with her duvet.

Chapter Twenty-Seven

1 day to go
Suzie 13, Alice 4

Excited by the prospect of a long weekend of overspending in London and still buzzing after her black taxi ride from the station, Helen let herself into Tom's flat, humming to herself.

As she pushed against the front door, reluctantly it gave way, sweeping a large pile of envelopes and Dial-a-Pizza leaflets back in a semicircle. Unless Tom received more mail in a day than most people got in a week, it didn't look as if the cleaner had been for a while.

Scooping the post into her arms, Helen wheeled her suitcase into the middle of the sitting room. As always, she was momentarily silenced by the view of Tower Bridge and the Tower of London from the floor-to-ceiling windows. Her brother had the perfect flat. And she had three child-free days ahead of her. Making herself comfortable on his sofa, she started sifting through the letters. She knew she probably shouldn't be but she also knew he had headed off into the sunset expecting life to look after itself in his absence. He was lucky to have an older sister like her.

Tutting at the volume of bills and mesmerised by the sheer variety of food she could have delivered within half an hour, by far the most intriguing item was a hand-written cream envelope. Leaving it to one side, she set about restoring life to Tom's gasping houseplants and, having forced three-quarters of a pint of semi-skimmed milk-now-yoghurt down the sink, made herself a cup of black tea.

Returning to the sofa, she tidied the mail into a neat pile in the centre of the coffee table. As she placed the hand-written envelope tantalisingly on the top, she noticed that it wasn't very firmly sealed. Resting it on her mug of tea for a couple of minutes, the envelope flapped open without much encouragement. Carefully, she edged the contents out, absorbing every detail so she could return it to its exact former state and hoped that state-of-the-art loft apartments didn't come fitted with CCTV as standard. However, should justification be required at a later date, Helen reminded herself that Tom had asked her to look in—albeit to the flat in general and not envelopes in particular.

'*Bonjour ma soeur.* Thought you'd call me at my own expense, did you?'

Helen paced the length of his picture window wondering what would happen to the traffic jam if Tower Bridge had to open suddenly. 'Do I take it from your linguistic skills that you're in France now?'

'*Oui, oui.*'

'Good.'

Tom detected a note of urgency from his sister and stopped mucking about. 'What is it? Is everything okay at the flat?'

'Everything's fine.' Helen decided not to mention the fact that his cleaner was missing in action.

'So why the sudden interest in my location? I haven't heard from you in nearly three weeks.'

'Look, either you want to get away from it all and us all or you don't. You can't have it both ways. So, are you having a great time?'

'Not bad…'

Tom looked over to the topless girl sunbathing on the adjacent lounger. Thanks to her MP3 player she was oblivious to his conversation.

'…Quite good actually. I needed to get away.'

The international language of love and fast motorbikes were doing him very well and he was enjoying his full-blown midlife-crisis moment. Stefanie was a sophisticated twenty-three years old with all the confidence of youth. Her breasts were mesmerising and yet, at times he'd never felt older or more uncomfortable. When she'd turned up for a day trip on the bike dressed in a bikini top, high heels and an unfeasibly short dress, all he'd been worried about was making sure he got her home safely in case she had an older brother who might take a dislike to him. He probably would have taken a dislike to himself at this point if he let himself think about it.

'So, not planning on being home tomorrow then?'

'No.' Despite her bizarre line of questioning, Tom felt nothing but affection for his sister. No one else had called him. 'Why, are you planning on having a party at the flat?'

'Absolutely.' Helen paused just long enough to wind Tom up. 'The sort of party that just involves me, a takeaway and a DVD. You on the other hand have a far more interesting offer.'

'Have you been reading my mail?'

Helen blushed. 'The envelope was flapping open.'

'Flapping? Really? So you haven't been steaming letters open again?'

Helen blushed. 'Again?'

'Valentine's Day 1976.' Tom loved the fact that they had a shared past. In the absence of any living parents it was very comforting.

'I can't believe you remember things like that. And I was just copying something I had read in an Enid Blyton book.'

'People don't change, Hel. It worked then and I'll bet it—'

Guilty as charged, she interrupted him.

'As if I have time for those sorts of capers these days. Anyway, I just thought you might like to know you've been invited to a party.'

'I know I have a reputation for working hard, but that's hardly a once-in-a-lifetime occurrence.'

'But I thought you might want to go to this one.'

'*Je pense pas.* I don't miss London at all.'

'Well, I'm sure Alice will be disappointed.'

Tom sat up, his apathy and cool forgotten. 'Alice?' Getting to his feet, he walked across the sand and sat at the sea's edge. He frowned. 'She's invited me to a party?'

'She wrote you a letter and, before you say another word, I think you should let me read it to you.'

As Helen finished, Tom let his feet sink into the soft sand that the receding waves only just reached. 'When's it dated?'

Helen re-examined the hand-written page. 'It just says Thursday. Hang on…' Reaching for the envelope on the table, she studied the postmark. 'She posted it two weeks ago.'

Tom sighed. 'Why didn't she just call me?'

'I doubt she was expecting you to leave immediately.'

'Who writes letters anymore?'

'People who want to be taken seriously?'

'Is this some sort of girl thing I just don't understand?'

Helen lay on the sofa and sighed as she stared up at the double-height ceiling.

'Letters are very romantic, you know. I can't think when I last received anything hand-written from James, unless you count cheques of course.'

Tom laughed.

'Mind you, he barely sends me e-mails these days unless it's to remind me to book the car in for a service.'

'You make marriage sound so appealing.'

'You can't beat having a soul mate and a family.'

Tom kicked his leg out and flicking wet sand off his instep, splashed the shallow water. 'Shit.'

Leaning back on his elbow, he felt something dig into him. Righting himself, he combed the area and as he brought the offending item around to inspect it, he was surprised to find a small dark pebble, incongruous on the golden sand. He rolled it through his fingers.

'So, I guess you haven't read any papers over there?'

'Not for a week or so. I trust the world is running perfectly well without me.'

'No tabloids or gossip magazines?'

'I don't even read those at home.'

'Well, maybe you should start. Alice has announced that she's retiring from life coaching…'

Tom was taken aback. His shock transmogrified to humour. 'Blimey, I didn't think I was that difficult a client.'

'Ha bloody ha.'

'She was in the paper? I didn't realise she was that well known.'

'Well, it wasn't the *Times* or the *Guardian*. Where in France are you, anyway?' Helen's voice was humour-free.

'Surely you're not suggesting I race back for some girl?'

'Not just some girl.'

'You haven't even met her.'

'You seemed pretty smitten three weeks ago.'

'Well, that was then.'

'Fine. Well, whenever you decide to come back, you're in for a treat.'

'I am?' From Helen's tone, it didn't sound like his favourite sort of surprise.

'Alice is everywhere. Magazines, billboards, buses…'

'How come?'

'She's going to be the woman that most of Britain wakes up to in two weeks' time.'

Tom was rapidly becoming frustrated by the riddles being generated by his sister. He was on holiday and an overdose of sun had clearly impaired his ability to decipher anything more complicated than menus. 'What are you talking about now?'

'She's going to be the new co-presenter on the breakfast show on Channel 6 with Dermot Douglas.'

'That bald twit?'

'For someone who allegedly never has time to watch TV, you do a—'

Tom interrupted. 'I have occasionally been known to flick over from the financial and hard-news channels while I'm having my coffee.'

'Well, I, like many women, happen to think that Dermot is a good-looking, very sexy Irish bloke, albeit with less hair than most. And the gossip columns are already speculating about their off-camera relationship.'

'Do you think…?'

'Absolutely not, but it's all part of the publicity machine. And well, give it time, maybe…'

'I'm not just going to drop everything for her.'

'Of course not.'

'Why should I? She wouldn't drop everything to come away with me.'

'Forgive me for saying so, but you gave her about ten minutes to decide and nothing promising to go on.'

'I'll call her when I get back.'

'Fine. I mean, you haven't replied so I doubt she's still waiting to hear from you anyway. Two weeks is a long silence if you've put your feelings on the line.'

'She's only invited me to a party.'

'Actually, she's said you're the only person she would consider taking as her date.'

Tom stared out to sea. 'There's no guarantee I could even get home in time.'

'I just wanted you to know, that's all.'

'Thanks.'

'That's more like it.'

'And I will call her.'

Helen brightened. 'When?'

'When I'm home. Stop interfering. I'm supposed to be having time away from everything, from everyone.'

'Well then, I'm sorry to have disturbed you.' Tom could hear her irritation.

'I didn't mean that, Helen. You're not everyone. I'll be back in a week or so. We'll talk more about this then.'

'Fine.'

'Please stop saying fine when you don't mean it.'

'Fine.' Helen paused. 'I'm sorry if I've ruined your day. I was rather hoping I was going to make it. Guess it serves me right for meddling.'

'No, I appreciate the call. I didn't mean to snap.'

'It's okay. Now let's stop trading apologies. You've got the sun to worship and, prepare for the British economy to strengthen further—I have shopping to do.'

Chapter Twenty-Eight

0 days
Suzie 13, Alice 4
Party time

Zoë found Alice lurking near the entrance to the bar, anxiously shifting her weight from one foot to the other.

'Surely you're not thinking of doing a runner already?'

Alice pushed up on to her tiptoes before relaxing as far as her shoes would let her. 'Don't tempt me. Where the hell is everybody?'

'No one ever gets to a party before nine.'

'Well, then why are we here?'

'Because Suzie can hardly be left to celebrate her birthday on her own.'

'She hasn't been on her own since Thursday. I was planning to lose myself in the crowd. Instead, I feel like a standalone exhibit. I can't believe you talked me into this bloody outfit. First it's a dress, second it's pink and third it's pastel. If there's one fabric that had its heyday in the last sixty years, it's denim. Much more my style. Plus, my feet are killing me already and I haven't even brought a pair of trainers for the dancing later.'

Zoë folded her arms. 'Right, that's it, stop whining. You look fabulous, your shoes will stop hurting as soon as you focus on something else and there are enough canapés in this room to stop you from falling over even if you drink lots of champagne.'

Alice brightened. 'Maybe that's it. I'm just not drunk enough.'

'Spoken like a true alcoholic. Come on, let's get another one.'

An hour later, to Zoë's relief, both the party and Alice were in full swing. The private bar at Soho House was buzzing, and as a constant stream of new arrivals fought their way through the crowds of other guests to speak to the birthday girl, Alice found she was having a lovely time in her mother's wake. She banished the memory of the first hour to her emotional archive.

As Alice had predicted, most guests had erred on the cautious side of the sartorial theme, merely marrying a single item of slightly dated clothing with their normal party uniforms. Suzie's dress, on the other hand, was both showstopping and party enhancing and she was enjoying her role as the vintage designer belle of the ball. Alice had also won several compliments thanks to Zoë's decision to dress her in the style of Audrey Hepburn. Her dark hair swept up, off the back of her neck, she just hoped she was looking as glamorous as she felt overdressed.

Every fancy-dress party unearths a couple of extroverts and this one was to be no exception. A wave of silence, somewhere between shock and admiration, rippled through the bar as two guests arrived, resplendent as Starsky and Hutch.

Alice grabbed Zoë from a nearby conversation as she recognised the fanciest dressers by far. Her party had started. 'That's my boys.'

Richard Starsky and Robert Hutch, down to their no doubt painfully glued sideburns, swaggered straight over to their hostess and Suzie kissed them both, delighted at the amusement they were generating. 'I guess every court needs a jester or two.'

Richard raised his shades. 'Hey, lady, just think of us as the cabaret.'

Suzie took his arm. 'At least now I can enjoy the rest of the night safe in the knowledge that I have two detectives watching out for me.'

'I don't know. I'd say it looks like your personal security is all taken care of.' Richard Starsky nodded in Geoffrey James Bond's direction. The man with the newly trimmed silver hair was exuding class in a freshly pressed dinner jacket, a yellow water-pistol-golden-gun protruding from his waistband.

Suzie laughed. 'What is it with boys and dressing up?'

Richard shrugged. 'It's only fair. Women get to dress up every day.'

'Some of them do.' Alice swept over as glamorously as she could in her heels and gave Richard and Robert a kiss. She wondered if you could do enough damage to your feet to get bunions in one evening.

Richard took a step back and whistled. 'Look at you.'

Rob was animated with delight. 'Don't tell me, *Breakfast at Tiffany's*. Holly Golightly.'

Alice blushed. 'I'm not in character, I'm just in a dress.'

'Oh, no,' Rob was quick to intervene. 'Not just a dress. A fabulous dress as, Suzie, is yours.'

'Brown nose in the ring...tra la la la la.' Richard was half singing, half laughing.

Alice fidgeted self-consciously. 'Not too over the top?'

Richard beamed at her. 'You look gorgeous. Although I have to say you weren't even this dolled up on our wedding day.'

Alice hit him with her pastel clutch bag. It was infuriatingly inadequate for the job. 'We only decided it was our wedding day that morning. This has been in the diary for months.'

Wisely Richard decided to change the subject. 'So where's Dermot?'

'Fashionably late.'

'If he's stood you up, I *will* find a way to sack him.'

Alice shook her head. 'I told him to meet me here. He's not my date. Just a friend.'

'The gossip columns will love that even more. There's nothing like a bit of denial to get them really interested. Always best to leave a venue five to ten minutes after each other for maximum speculation.'

'It's all quite innocent, I assure you. Dermot hasn't got to where he is today by being the first to arrive at parties. Plus, this is the one night of the week he gets to stay out late.'

'Alice Fletcher, are you taking the side of your co-host over your ex-husband?'

'Well, thing is—' Alice grinned mischievously '—we're a team now.'

'I thought *we* were a team?'

'I'm afraid you no longer have exclusivity. Anyway, who said I could only be part of one team?'

Richard sighed. 'So what does a cop need to do to get a beer around here?'

'Sure you don't want a coffee and a doughnut?'

Rob laughed a little too loudly.

Alice pointed to the far side of the room. 'Sounds like you two need the bar. Also, you couldn't do me a favour, could you?'

Richard put his Ray Ban Aviators back on and shot Alice a winning smile. 'Sure thing, pretty lady, is kitty stuck in a tree?'

'Just hold this for a minute.' Alice handed over her clutch bag. 'The canapés look amazing but I can't hold a glass, mingle and eat one-handed.'

Richard smiled. 'Always the lady.'

Relieved at her temporary liberation, Alice grinned. 'Always. See you at the bar in a minute when I've refuelled.'

In the absence of enough time for a sit-down and a snooze, Tom had gone for the shower option. He'd been riding all day. His eyes were tired, his shoulders were sore but at least now he was clean and in the right city.

Pulling in to the kerb on the Embankment, Tom extracted the letter from the inside pocket of his leather jacket and scanning it realised that he was on a road to nowhere. Somewhere along the line he hadn't noticed that Alice had failed to provide him with his final destination, only a date and a time. So at the moment he was three hours late for a party that was happening somewhere in London, with a girl who wasn't expecting him. He was beginning to see the error of his ways.

Richard stood at the bar and wondered how long he had to keep his wig and leather jacket on. Holding his ice-cold beer bottle on the pulse points at his wrists, he willed the slightly cooler blood to make it to his head before he passed out. He could feel sweat starting to drip down his neck. This was why glamour and fancy-dress parties didn't go hand in hand.

As his jacket started to vibrate, he patted down the pockets in search of his phone before discovering that the culprit was Alice's. He bet himself another beer that it was Dermot, smooth talking his way out of his late arrival, and grateful for the distraction, answered it without a second thought.

'Alice's phone, BlackBerry, gooseberry, whatever…' Tucking his big hair behind his ear, Richard strained to be able to hear anything.

Standing next to the river at Battersea, Tom hesitated, grateful that the phone had been answered, somewhat relieved that it wasn't Alice herself but surprised to hear a male voice.

Richard persevered. 'Dermot, is that you? Hello? Can you hear me?'

Shyly, Tom ended his call and then castigating himself, dialled again. This time it barely rang before the same man answered.

'Hello. Alice's phone.' Putting his beer on the bar, Richard stuck a finger in his other ear to try and make out the caller over the ambient noise. He hadn't identified the incoming number.

'Hi. I don't know if you can help me. I'm on my way to Suzie Fletcher's sixtieth birthday drinks, only I don't know where I'm going. I don't suppose you could tell me where you all are?'

Richard frowned. The guy sounded pretty awkward. Did Suzie have a stalker?

'I don't suppose I could.'

'Oh, right.'

'Or at least not unless I know who's calling.' Richard didn't want to be the one responsible for letting an uninvited member of the press in.

'Sure, sorry, it's Tom. Tom Taylor. I don't suppose I could speak to Alice, could I?'

'Tom?' Richard's voice crescendoed with nascent excitement. 'Where are you?'

'Chelsea Bridge.'

'She thought you were away.' Richard silenced himself a sentence too late.

Tom was even more confused than he had been a minute ago. And he hadn't thought that had been possible. 'Sorry, who am I speaking to?'

'Richard. Her ex. We met briefly at the Whole Body Centre a couple of months back. You really need to get your arse to Soho House. The entrance is on Greek Street and we're in Bar 19/21.'

Encouraged and energised by Richard's enthusiasm, Tom was back on his mission. 'Great. Thanks. Will you tell her I'm on my way?'

'Of course,' Richard lied with ease.

Call over, he returned Alice's BlackBerry to her bag and reacquainted himself with his beer. It was none of his business, although he might just sportingly add Tom to the guest list in a minute.

Richard jumped as Alice grabbed him from behind and he felt the only remaining dry areas of his T-shirt stick to his back under his jacket. Gently he removed her arms and led her around. 'Feeling better?'

'Much. Thanks. A girl can't do endless champagne without carbs. Everything okay?'

Richard grinned as a sweat droplet skated down his temple.

'What's with your mood improvement?'

'You know how much I love a party.' Richard was grateful that Starsky wore shades as he turned to face her. 'Everything's perfect.'

'Good crowd, don't you think?'

Richard surveyed the scene. 'And it's still early…' He caught sight of a familiar head at the entrance. 'Hey, Al, I think your date has arrived.'

As if she needed confirmation, breathless, Zoë appeared at her side, Rob hot on her heels.

'Dermot's here. And I don't care what you say, he's bloody gorgeous.'

'Tone it down, Zo, the man has excellent hearing and if you want me to introduce you, please don't behave like a groupie.' To Alice's bemusement, Zoë was uncharacteristically all over the place.

Dermot arrived at the bar and kissed Alice on both cheeks. Zoë's eyes were wide but her mouth was firmly closed.

'You look fabulous.' He acknowledged Starsky and Hutch with a nod. 'Glad to see you're being looked after. Good effort, guys.'

Alice smiled. 'I think you'll find Detective Starsky here is someone you know only too well.'

Richard whipped off his unfeasibly large sunglasses much to Dermot's amusement. 'Wow, chief, that's quite a look.'

Alice surveyed Dermot's simple Diesel jeans and black shirt. 'And you would be?'

'Someone who didn't read the invitation properly until I was in the cab.'

A foot to her left, Zoë's laugh was almost a cackle. Alice ignored it.

'Swap those jeans for a white suit and you could be 1970s disco.'

'Or indecently dressed. I'm no John Travolta on the dance floor… I'm going for present day. That's my story and I'm sticking to it.'

That was the trouble with fancy-dress parties. Unless you

were under ten, the people who arrived dressed as themselves always looked the coolest.

'…But look at you and just check out Suzie. Wow. I can't believe she's sixty.'

'Save all that gushing for her. I'm just hoping I got her anti-ageing genes as opposed to my father's.'

Dermot scanned the crowd, returning a few nods and waves of acknowledgement. 'Is he here?'

Alice smiled. 'Unfortunately not. He died nearly twenty years ago.'

'Oh, shit. Sorry. Well, I guess at least he never had to worry about going grey like the rest of us then.'

'No…' Alice paused, slightly surprised at Dermot's absence of tact. 'But I think he'd rather have acquired a few grey hairs than a bed six feet under.'

Now he was looking over her shoulder. Alice knew she shouldn't have been surprised or offended.

Sprinting away from the subject, Dermot was determined to move on. 'So, it looks like a great party.'

'It's getting better all the time.' Alice's tone was laced with sarcasm as yet again Dermot looked around him for reassurance. He only had to look as far as Zoë.

'Hi, I'm Dermot Douglas.' He proffered his hand for shaking.

'Zoë…Hudson.' Zoë congratulated herself for two simple but perfectly pronounced words and no sweaty palms, grateful she'd gone for a stylish monochrome Mary Quant-inspired outfit.

'Well, Zoë…Hudson, I hope we get a chance to chat later. But first of all, Alice, I don't suppose you could do me a favour and come with me for a second, do you?'

Alice cocked an eyebrow. 'It's not that sort of party.'

Dermot laughed. 'I just want us to have a photo taken together at the entrance.'

'You're shameless.'

'I know. And so are the media.'

'But I've been here for hours and they've just seen you arrive on your own.'

'Come on, just one hurried snap of us walking towards the entrance together and no one will know the difference. They don't give a toss about the facts. Just remember every picture tells a story.'

'Okay, one photo. In exchange for a dance.'

'I told you, I'm no…'

Alice wasn't budging. 'One good turn deserves another.'

'Fine. Come on.'

Taking his hand, Alice followed Dermot down the stairs and out through a side door to the venue, only to arrive at Soho House for the second time that evening.

Tom parked his motorbike in a bay a few streets away and wove his way through a gaggle of paparazzi at the entrance of Soho House. There was a definite buzz. Clearly he had just missed someone big.

Walking through the front door, he was greeted by a super-cool, super-slim, super-firm receptionist. His stomach knotted. Her smile was far too saccharine to be genuine. And he was sure that nobody was expecting him.

The skinny blonde stepped up to her counter. 'Can I help you?'

Tom rested his motorbike helmet on his knee and did his best to look as if this was a place he came to all the time.

'I'm here for Suzie Fletcher's 60th.'

'And you are?'

'Tom Taylor.'

'Are you a member here?'

Tom shook his head.

'Okay, let me just check the guest list.'

Tom felt his hopes melt away as he looked around, wondering how he could possibly crash this party. Maybe he could ask Richard to come down and let him in. He'd seemed friendly enough on the phone.

'Okay, Tom, if you could just sign in here. And if you'd like to check your helmet in at the cloakroom, someone will show you where to go.'

Still reeling from the ease of his entry and wondering if there was another Tom Taylor with a higher media profile than his own, Tom was ushered up to the bar. He hesitated for a second at the top of the stairs before entering the fray.

The room was packed, and instantly too hot in his leather jacket, he took it off and slung it over his shoulder. They'd tried to persuade him to leave it in the cloakroom, but full of keys, his phone and an important letter, it was in fact less of a jacket and more of a handbag—a manbag.

And then he saw her. Alice. Dressed to impress. Tendrils of hair teasing her neck. Helen was right as usual. She wasn't just some girl.

Zooming in on his first impression, as she moved slightly Tom could see that she had a man's arm around her shoulder. His throat suddenly dry, the words of her letter appeared before his eyes. He was a fool for believing there was only one person she would have brought to this party and he was an even bigger fool for not calling first and for giving up so easily in the first place.

Spotting Suzie holding court near the bar, Tom wondered at what crazy point he had decided this was a good idea. Daring himself to make the most of the adrenaline that had got him this far, he walked straight over before he had time for second or even third thoughts.

Alice listened to Dermot flirting with Zoë. It turned out they had more in common than a love and admiration for fashion designers. Feeling her concentration falter, she scanned the room for an escape route.

Either she was hallucinating or Tom Taylor was making his way across the room towards her looking a little James Dean. Black jeans, white T-shirt, a seriously bad case of helmet hair and what she could only imagine was a helmet tan. He was brown from the nose down and far too individual to be a mirage. Ducking down, she slipped out from under Dermot's arm. Barely noticing, he repositioned himself, leaning on the bar, alongside Zoë.

Shimmying between guests, Alice found her mother and managed to pull her to one side without seeming as rude as she could have been.

Suzie was far from impressed. 'This had better be worth it.' She analysed Alice's expression. 'Are you not having a great time?'

'Did you invite him?'

'Him? Oh, damn. I know I should have said something. I completely meant to and then it slipped my mind.'

'Slipped your mind.' Alice felt her chest tighten.

'Andy had always been on the guest list. I had no idea that Thursday was going to turn out the way it did, but there are plenty of other people here you can hide behind.'

'I don't give a toss about Andy. I'm talking about Tom.'

'Tom?'

To Alice's relief, Suzie looked genuinely surprised.

'Don't be ridiculous, darling. Why on earth would I do a thing like that? I've organised a party, not my own funeral.'

'I thought it might have been some sort of charitable gesture for me, you know after Thursday night turned out to be such a disaster.'

Suzie laughed. 'You do come up with some funny ideas sometimes.'

Alice snorted indignantly. *She* had funny ideas.

'But just for the record and to put your mind at rest, I don't think I'll be speaking to him again anytime soon.'

'You might want to revise that statement. He's here.'

'He's what? Are you sure?'

'Look over my right shoulder now. Do you see him?'

Suzie surveyed the throng. 'Well, I never.'

'Mum, this isn't time for you to go for an Oscar.'

'I promise I didn't know he was coming. Now turn round and look surprised before he realises we're talking about him.'

Alice wheeled and feigned surprise. As Tom looked past her to Suzie, she nearly burst into tears.

'Happy Birthday, Suzie.' Tom leaned forward and kissed her on the cheek. 'This looks like a great party.'

'I'm so glad you could come.' Suzie's sarcasm was all too obvious. And the last thing Alice wanted was for Suzie to scare him off again.

Geoffrey arrived with a fresh glass of champagne for his date and to his delight was rewarded with a kiss as she slipped an arm around him proprietarily.

'Me, too, although it really was touch-and-go whether I'd make it. Anyway, I hope you'll forgive me but…'

'What again?'

Tom hesitated. He wasn't sure Suzie was joking and he didn't really have time to find out.

'Um, actually, I came to have a quick word with Alice.'

Alice sighed internally. A quick word didn't sound like he was about to declare his undying love.

Suzie nodded impishly. 'Go ahead. Be my guest.'

Tom turned to face Alice, his eyes searching hers as Suzie looked on feeling surprisingly unflustered. She wished Tom would just go ahead and kiss Alice and put them both out of their misery.

Tom took Alice's hand. 'Wow, basically. You look amazing.'

Alice stared at him, still not quite believing he was there. Maybe it was a mirage. Maybe it was just a dream. In which case Brad Pitt would definitely have been somewhere in the room, she'd have been six inches taller, a size smaller with perfectly straight hair and Tom would have been wearing nothing except a pair of jeans. As it happened she could see her ex-husband over her ex-date's shoulder and her feet hurt. This was definitely the real world.

'Nice suntan.' It wasn't quite what she had been planning on saying had she ever got a chance to see Tom again, but it would have to do for now. Hopefully she was still warming up.

'Is that the only compliment I get after driving all day and all night to be here?'

'I'm trying.' Alice looked him in the eyes. She could feel herself losing her balance and for once it had nothing to do with her shoes. 'It's good to see you.'

Tom took her hand. 'Any chance we could go somewhere private?'

'That might be pushing it, although—' Alice took a firm step away from her mother and led Tom to a corner of the room '—it would be optimal to at least be out of earshot and eyeshot of a certain sixty-year-old.'

Alice noted Suzie was now being ushered in the other direction by the wonderful Geoffrey.

Now on the periphery of the party, Alice took her hand back.

'So what are you doing here?'

If her mother was innocent, maybe there was an interfering half sister or ex-husband to blame.

Tom was thrown. 'You invited me.' He shook his head. 'This never happens in the movies. Men don't ride non-stop across countries to be asked what they are doing here.'

'I invited you?' It all started to fall into place. And now she could only blame her hungover and forgetful self. 'I'm sorry. I didn't mean to doubt you.'

'Hey, I can't blame you for that. I've let you down pretty badly once already. And yet you sent me an amazing letter. I'm only sorry it has taken me so long to reply. You see, I actually only received it yesterday.'

Alice placed her hand on her forehead in disbelief. 'Serves me right, I guess, for trusting the bog standard post.'

Tom shook his head. 'No, I mean I was already away when it arrived.'

'And you're back already?' Alice smiled as her world fell back into place. 'So it didn't take you long to find yourself then?'

Tom laughed. 'I think everything I needed was at home in the first place. But I only got back to London about two hours ago. France is much bigger than you think.'

Alice tried to put one and one together, but so far she was only getting 11. 'I'm afraid I don't understand.'

'Helen found your letter. She was staying at my flat.'

'She reads your post?'

'Don't even go there. Just be grateful you don't have an interfering older sister, although if I'm not too late I think I might have to thank her for sticking her oar in, just this once. You should have called me.'

Probably not the right moment to confess to calling, hanging up without leaving a message and then opting for the less interactive pen to paper option. 'You might not have answered your phone.'

Tom paused, considering his response. 'You're right, I might not have. But if you'd left me a message, I'd probably have called you back. I don't think I could have resisted.'

'"Probably" wasn't good enough odds. I really wanted you to listen to what I had to say and I knew I'd only have one chance.'

'Well, I'm here now. And I'm all ears…'

Alice observed a concerned Zoë looking over and shook her head as imperceptibly as she could. She didn't want any interruptions.

Tom felt Alice's attention shift elsewhere. He paused. 'What's the matter?'

Alice berated herself for taking her eye off the ball. 'Nothing.'

'You're here with someone else, aren't you? When I arrived you were with a guy at the bar.'

Alice smiled at his misapprehension. She loved the fact he'd been watching.

'I'm glad you think it's funny. My entire body is still vibrating from the Autoroute.'

'Just let me explain. Yes, I'm here with someone else.'

Tom punched his thigh in frustration. 'I knew it.'

'You see that guy standing at the bar. The tall one in the black shirt, talking to the girl in the black-and-white dress…'

Tom nodded dejectedly. 'That's Dermot, isn't it?'

'Yes, and the girl he's talking to who keeps looking over here and distracting me is my best friend, Zoë. I'm here with her.'

The start of a smile crept across Tom's features. 'Just with her?'

'Just with her.' Alice couldn't help but be delighted at Tom's obvious relief. 'So you see, you're not too late at all. I mean, ideally I like my dates to collect me on the way to the event rather than just turn up a few hours later…'

Tom smiled. 'I can change.'

Alice folded her arms in front of her and raised an eyebrow. 'That's what they all say.'

Tom's eyes searched Alice's. 'I really want to kiss you.'

'Okay, so here's another thing, ideally I like my dates not to ask permission first.'

Tom was grinning as their lips met and Alice kissed him back hungrily before remembering where she was and regaining her composure.

'I don't think kissing in the corner at my mother's party is actually the best idea.'

Tom smiled cheekily. 'Want to go somewhere else?'

'Tom Taylor.' Alice pretended to be shocked and offended. 'Who do you take me for?'

'I don't know. But I'd really like to whisk you away somewhere.'

'Haven't you done enough travelling recently?'

'I was thinking more along the lines of my place, or I know a great little Oasis in South Kensington if you're hungry.'

'How about being a little less presumptive?'

'You sent me a love letter and now you're playing hard to get?'

'That's twenty-first-century women for you.'

'You're the one who told me to focus on what I wanted personally and go after it.'

'Well, you know…' Alice nodded. 'I can't fault that, it's pretty good advice. Although I think you'll find I said make time for it rather than go after it.'

'And here I am, and with all the time in the world. Why wouldn't you come away with me?'

'Life is all about timing. And yours was lousy. I had to be here for this. Plus I had a few things in the pipeline careerwise.'

Tom smiled esoterically. 'I nearly came off my bike at Marble Arch when you pulled up alongside me on the side of a bus. Congratulations. That's a huge career move.'

'It's a huge poster. And it is an exciting time, although not without repercussions.'

'Nothing ever is.'

Alice spotted a couple of incoming detectives. 'Do you remember Richard?'

Tom nodded. 'Very well.'

Richard propelled Rob towards Tom as they arrived in Alice's personal space.

'Tom, good to see you again, this is Rob.' Alice marvelled at Richard's memory for people.

Tom grinned as he shook Rob's hand. 'Surely you mean Hutch?'

'So,' Richard addressed Tom. 'Glad to see you found us okay.'

Alice looked from one man to the other.

Tom doffed an invisible cap. 'Thanks for the directions.'

She prodded Richard. 'What have you been up to?'

'Nothing.' Richard knew his denial had been a little too high-pitched to be genuine. 'I know better than to interfere in your personal life these days.'

Alice's hands found their way to her hips.

Tom intervened. 'It's not his fault. Your invitation omitted one key detail, the venue. So I called him. Well, I called you actually. He answered and talked me in.'

Alice eyeballed Richard. 'It is absolutely not okay for you to answer my phone.'

'I thought it was going to be Dermot…' Richard raised his hands in surrender.

'I wouldn't be here if he hadn't.' Tom slapped Richard on the back gratefully.

Richard was buoyed by the praise. 'If we're going for a total confessional, you might as well know that I also added him to the guest list but watching you a few moments ago, I doubt you're going to hold any of this against me.'

Alice was incredulous. 'You spoke to Tom earlier this evening and you didn't tell me?'

'It wasn't that long ago.' Richard turned to Rob and shrugged. 'It doesn't sound good, Officer, does it?'

But Alice was finding it difficult to sustain her irritation. A smile broke out. 'All right, that's it, I'm divorcing you.'

'Again?' Richard's shoulders slumped in mock despair.

'This time it's worse.'

'But you've already got the house.' Richard feigned panic. 'No. No. Not the *West Wing* box sets. You can't. You gave them to me.'

Alice hugged Richard just a little too tightly. 'No more secrets, okay?'

Richard wrestled himself free. 'Got it. Now, will you stop being such a lousy hostess and please go and get Tom a drink while I ask him Twenty Questions…'

'Yeah, like I'm going to leave you two on your own to talk about me.'

'Good evening. Ladies, gentlemen…'

Alice shuddered as her mother interrupted them from

across the room. Some misguided individual had given her a wireless microphone.

'…Detectives, Mr. Bond…'

Suzie winked at Geoffrey.

'…And my partner in all crimes, the beautiful and extraordinary Alice. I'm afraid it's that time of night when the hostess, having invited you here to enjoy yourselves, has drunk enough herself, to think that making a speech is a good idea. I do hope you'll all forgive me in due course.'

Alice smiled warmly, Suzie was in her element. She felt a surge of pride.

'As some of you will know and others of you will have read, I haven't exactly been looking forward to my sixtieth birthday.

'Some milestones are better than others—first bra, first kiss, first marriage, first divorce, but being a pensioner was never on my to-do list and as most of you will know, I was determined to find myself a man to help me over the threshold into my seventh decade.

'However, despite a very concerted effort, I almost failed. It's down to one person, and one person only, that I arrived here this evening with Geoff, and so I must move on the part of my reluctant accomplice, Alice.'

Alice wished she could leave as nearly a hundred people tried to pick her out of the crowd.

'In some ways Alice has been my reluctant accomplice for years. When my first husband died, she was eight and I was thirty-eight, and we both thought we had been abandoned, but thanks to her I never once felt alone.

'I am lucky enough to have a daughter who is a friend, who is comfortable criticising me and who is honest enough and cares enough about me to make me a better person. I'm not the best mother in the world, but I do, by some fluke, seem to have the best daughter.

'By the way, she'll be hating this speech. She'll think this public declaration of my affection is tacky, but rest assured, darling, this is it. I promise none of this will make it to a future column, comedy drama…'

Somewhere in the room Andy cheered and, to her relief, Alice realised that she hadn't spotted him all night.

'…screenplay, novel, Internet blog, chat room, etc.'

Suzie paused for a sip of her drink.

'I would also like to take this opportunity to publicly welcome a new member of the family.'

Tom reached down for Alice's hand and took it gently. To his delight, she didn't resist. He leaned down to whisper in her ear, 'This isn't going to be about me, is it?'

Leaning against him, she slipped her arm around his waist. 'No offence, but I bloody hope not.'

'Just under two weeks ago I discovered that I have a step-daughter. Zoë, I just want to say, welcome to the madhouse.'

Zoë, misty-eyed with champagne-fuelled emotion, was apparently taking it all in her stride no doubt helped by, Alice noted, the fact that Dermot was still at her side. Alice raised her glass.

'Cheers, Zo.'

Similar sentiments echoed around the room. As they died down, Suzie continued.

'So all that remains for me to do is to toast my friends and family, most of whom are interchangeable, and to thank you all for coming to help me celebrate this evening.

'It occurs to me that these days, women are no longer aspiring to be like their mothers but like their daughters. I, for one, am staring youth in the face and I like what I see.

'It's far more fun dancing to the same tune than tottering

alone towards wrinkles and infirmity. So for those who are that way inclined, the disco will start in a few minutes. Kick off your shoes if you need to, but please help me dance the years, and the canapés, away. The music will span the last six decades. You have been warned. So, here's to life and all its twists and turns. Alice, thank you. See you on the dance floor.'

Suzie lowered the microphone. Then, smiling at Alice across the room, she raised it again.

'And by the way, you two look good together.'

As Tom squeezed her hand, the room erupted into applause and a series of impromptu toasts were called out as everyone drained their glasses in Suzie's name.

Alice emptied hers with a combination of relief and celebration. She had survived the party.

Or had she? Alice prickled. Dermot now had the microphone. Dermot, who had met Suzie once for five minutes about an hour ago…

His stance was confident.

'Excuse me—ladies and gents, I'll be keeping this brief but I just wanted, on behalf of everyone here, to say thanks to Suzie for being an incredible hostess. I'm sure you'll all agree this is a fabulous party. And I know there is someone else here who should say a few words and without whom this party would not be happening. Let me introduce you to my new breakfast buddy and to the woman who has kept Suzie as young as she is…Alice.'

Alice couldn't believe Dermot had managed to trail the breakfast show, yet she had no time to admonish him as a moment later she had the microphone in her hand. Everyone turned to watch her as Tom wisely took a couple of steps back, out of the spotlight. Alice wished she'd interspersed her alcohol intake with the occasional glass of water.

'Erm, hi.' Alice cleared her throat and started again. 'I

wasn't expecting to have to make a speech this evening—hell, I wasn't even expecting to be wearing a dress.'

As everyone chuckled heartily, Alice relaxed. The crowd was full to the brim with alcohol and good feeling.

'Anyway, most of you here know Suzie incredibly well and I, for one, can't believe she is sixty. First of all, because she still shops at Top Shop, second of all because it means that I am nearly thirty (which for the record, Mum, means I am no longer a child) and thirdly because she has more energy and stamina than most and is one of the most determined people I know. She is possibly the most intimidating but inspiring mother a girl could hope to have and I think I can speak for everyone here when I say that once you have met Suzie Fletcher, your life will never be quite the same again.

'So, raise your glasses, tilt your heads back and get ready to be outdanced by the birthday girl. I love her and I know you do, too. To Suzie.'

The crowd erupted. 'To Suzie.'

Shaking, Alice turned the microphone off and handed it to a passing waitress, eager to put the moment she had told the room she loved her mother behind her. It was, of course, a statement of fact, but public declarations of love were not something that came easily to her. Luckily no one seemed to have spotted anything out of the ordinary.

As the DJ started his set with "Saturday Night Fever", the lights changed as the room twitched as one to the beat. Alice watched as her not-so-shy and retiring mother started dancing and a sea of guests closed in around her. Richard and Robert looked on, heads bobbing and toes tapping but to Alice's slight irritation, they were still standing next to her and Tom wasn't.

Forcing herself between them, she put an arm around

each of their waists and exerted a slight forward pressure. 'Go on, you two. Surely this is your era this evening.'

They didn't need any encouragement, simultaneously striking a John Travolta pose and pointing at the ceiling before shaking themselves out and obediently strutting over to the 70s in their hired Cuban heels.

Richard shouted back over his shoulder, 'Don't make me drag you over here.'

'I'll be there in a minute.'

'I'll bet you won't.' Robert's retort was lost in music.

Almost immediately, Dermot shimmied over, already dancing from the waist down.

'I owe you a dance.'

Alice folded her arms. 'Good news. You're off the hook.'

His expression was one of stunned disbelief. 'You're turning me down?'

Alice nodded. 'I'm afraid so.'

'But your mother said we looked good together.'

'Um, don't take it personally, but she didn't mean you. In fact, I don't suppose you could do me a favour?'

'Well…' Dermot sucked air in between his teeth. 'I do owe you one. Will I like it?'

'I think so. It's just that something's come up…'

'Don't you mean someone?' Dermot's smile was a cheeky one.

'…And I don't want my original date for the evening…'

Dermot interrupted again. 'Me?'

'…Zoë, to be left without a dance partner.'

'Zoë was your date?' Dermot cocked an eyebrow. 'Kinky.'

'No, best-friendy.'

'Some might say sisterly.'

'Hey, she was my best friend long before any of this came

to light. And, far more importantly, she'll never forgive me if I leave her to dance around her handbag alone, so if you could look after her, I'd be very grateful. She's very nice when you get to know her.' This time it was Alice who got to give Dermot a mischievous eye.

'That's the favour?'

Alice nodded. 'Yup. So...' She feigned concern. 'Do you think you might be able to help?'

Dermot grinned and leaning in, gave her a kiss on the cheek. 'Can I just say I am going to *love* working with you.'

Saluting her, he turned on his dancing heel and made a beeline for Zoë. Alice gave her a double thumbs-up from over his shoulder as she looked over as suspiciously as a girl could, whilst flirting.

To Alice's relief she was finally alone. Miraculously, Tom had found a recently deserted table in a darkish corner away from the DJ and, desperate to escape the attention, she meandered over. She couldn't wait to sit down.

'Table for two, madam?'

'Fantastic.' Alice sighed with relief as she slipped her shoes off and stretched her feet out under the table.

'So, Alice...' Tom leaned in earnestly to escape the Bee Gees, his hands clasped together as eagerly as a talk-show host.

'Yes, Tom.' She mirrored him.

'Say I was to call you next week and ask you out...'

Alice did her best to look circumspect. 'Forgive me if I don't get too excited but, as you know, I've heard all this before.'

Tom shook his head. 'Probably the worst morning of my life.'

'I'm not sure my kitchen will ever feel the same again.'

'Do you think we can put it behind us?'

Alice tilted her head thoughtfully. 'Only if you're not dat-

ing anyone else I might know. And when I said dating anyone else I know, I meant dating anyone in the whole world.'

Tom nodded solemnly. 'I'm all yours.'

'I do just have a couple more questions.'

'Fire away.'

'Have you ever fancied guys?'

'Absolutely not.'

'Ever thought Rob Lowe was even vaguely attractive?'

Tom laughed. 'Nope. Not even that handsome. Too
pretty.'

'Do you own every Kylie album?'

'No again.'

'Do you own a Kylie album?'

Tom paused. Could it matter?

'…From before 2000?'

Relieved he could be honest, Tom shook his head. 'No.'

'And you do realise that I'm a younger woman and therefore you might be having a midlife crisis after all?'

'I didn't think you believed it even existed as a concept.'

'I still maintain it's basically an excuse for men to behave
as idiotically as they like for a few years.'

'Well, thank goodness I've got that out of my system already.' He grinned. 'So if my midlife-crisis fantasy is over,
does that mean I am mature, responsible and extremely eligible?'

'Don't push it. I, on the other hand, am an incredible
catch.' Alice was only half joking.

Tom's expression was suddenly serious. 'Do you think fate
and timing are the same thing?'

Alice paused. 'It sounds like you had way too much time
to think on your travels.'

'I did some thinking, yes. And some other stuff, too.'

'I don't want to know about the other stuff.'

'You don't?'

'Not unless you want to hear about all my dates.'

'How many are we talking here?'

Alice remained enigmatic. 'My mother is a difficult woman to please. But you'll be relieved to know our dating challenge officially ended yesterday.'

'Now that's what I call timing.'

'Some might say fate.'

'Don't play with me.'

Alice took his hand in hers as their eyes searched each other's for clues as to what happens next. 'I don't play games.'

Tom was silent for a second, the music barely registering. 'So, coach, say I've met a woman and I think she might be the one, what do you suggest I do about it?'

'I'd say if you're sure, give it your best shot. You've got nothing to lose.'

'Except her.'

'You can't lose…'

'…what you haven't got,' Tom finished off for her. 'I get it.'

'You need to be true to yourself.'

'Just like that film with Bridget Jones and the kid with glasses.'

'Jerry Maguire?'

'You complete me.'

'You complete my sentences.' Alice, as ever, was erring on the side of the defensive. 'I'd just be yourself, if I were you.'

'Okay, you win.' Tom nodded. 'I'll ask her out.'

'I'd be tempted to do it sooner rather than later.' Alice concealed her rush of nerves and excitement.

'But I want to get it right this time. You know what they sing?'

Alice strained to pick up a relevant lyric from "Saturday Night Fever". Nothing was making sense so far.

Tom watched her. 'Not these guys, I was thinking of Diana Ross and the Supremes…You know, "You Can't Hurry Love".'

'At least you didn't say Phil Collins, but in my youth it was much more along the lines of "A Good Heart" being "Hard to Find".'

Tom smiled. 'So, do you think this DJ does requests?'

'This is Soho House not a school disco. If I were you, I'd just ask the woman in question out now, you know, just in case and to be sure…' Alice congratulated herself on her directness and, leaning forward a little farther, prepared to say yes.

Tom got up and extended his arm. 'Do you want to dance?'

Alice was thrown. 'Now, this minute?'

'I've ridden a long way for this party and the night is still young, even if your mother isn't.'

She took his hand firmly. 'Well, I guess it's about time you showed me your moves.'

As he pulled her towards him, Alice felt her inner disco queen rising. Shoes abandoned, she shimmied her way into the midst of the flashing lights and flailing limbs. A few steps ahead, she turned to face him, shouting above the music.

'You know, I'd be careful, things happen on dance floors.'

He caught up with her and held her close. 'Do they?'

Her heart pounding with a cocktail of adrenaline and aerobic activity, Alice continued to dance. 'I think it's the beat, the rhythms and the hormones.'

Tom raised an eyebrow. 'Funny, I always thought it was the dark, the sweat and the alcohol.' Ignoring the disco vibe, he took her hand and twirled her.

'Men are just so romantic.' Alice let Tom's hand go and disappeared deeper into the disco inferno, her arms in the air.

Catching up with her, Tom slid his hand onto the small of her back and turned her to face him in a surprisingly slick move. As he kissed her tenderly and publicly, the high-pitched energy of Cyndi Lauper replaced the Bee Gees and Alice was transported back to her teens, only this time around she was a girl who was ready to have a lot more fun. They did look good together. And it felt even better.

What do you do when the other woman is you?

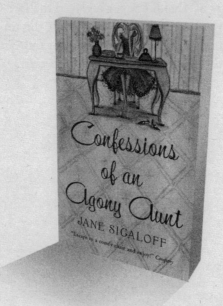

Lizzie Ford is London's most popular agony aunt who's been sitting on the bench for three years waiting to get back in the game. So Lizzie can't believe her good luck when she meets Matt Baker, only there's one problem – Matt's wife may not be happy with this new arrangement.

The strange thing is that even while she's hoping that Matt will get a divorce, she's actively helping a writer to her column save her crumbling marriage – a marriage that bears more than a passing resemblance to Matt's…

Available from 16th March 2007